LIVING NIGHTMARE

As soon as I stepped through the door of the auditorium I was struck by the unnatural stillness. I stood by the door, listening to the faint hiss from the amplified videotape. Then I heard the woman's horrified voice and I understood the hushed room.

"It's the worst experience of my life. I want to scream, but I can't open my mouth. Every muscle is held tight, like a vise. I keep trying to take a breath and speak. I hear the voices of two men— one on my left, one on my right. I'm trying to let my surgeon know the anesthetic didn't work, that I'm still conscious, but I can't speak or move. They're putting cold stuff on my stomach. They say something about towels, someone touches my belly. Someone touches my eyelid, maybe opens it for a second. I hear more bits of conversation. I keep thinking that the only thing worse might be being buried alive. Then I know I'm wrong . . . I hear a man say, 'I'm ready *to make the incision now.' "*

It was a month since I'd seen her, but I had no trouble recognizing Kitty Evanston's distinctive voice as she broke into sobs. I remembered what she'd told me. *"I have nightmares where I'm hearing these voices . . . and I see people who mean to hurt me . . ."*

Other Dr. Haley McAlister Mysteries by
Janice Kiecolt-Glaser
from Avon Books

DETECTING LIES

JANICE KIECOLT-GLASER

UNCONSCIOUS TRUTHS

A DR. HALEY McALISTER MYSTERY

AVON BOOKS ◆ NEW YORK

AVON BOOKS
A division of
The Hearst Corporation
1350 Avenue of the Americas
New York, New York 10019

Copyright © 1998 by Janice Kiecolt-Glaser
Published by arrangement with the author
Visit our website at **http://www.AvonBooks.com**
Library of Congress Catalog Card Number: 97–94311
ISBN: 0–380–78992–2

First Avon Books Printing: March 1998

AVON TRADEMARK REG. U.S. PAT. OFF. AND IN OTHER COUNTRIES, MARCA REGISTRADA, HECHO EN U.S.A.

Printed in the U.S.A.

WCD   10 9 8 7 6 5 4 3 2 1

For my father, with love.

In memory of my mother; for her,
the book she never wrote.

Chapter 1

"I can't go through with this—"

Kitty Evanston stood by the open window in my office, her hands pressed against the screen, gulping air. Beads of sweat dripped down her face, leaving white tracks on her rouged cheeks.

Watching her, I felt as if someone had dribbled ice water down my spine.

Kitty had been late for her appointment for psychological testing. She'd called from a phone booth across the street, asking if I had a window in my office that I could open. And could I come to the entrance and escort her up?

When I'd found her outside, she was pacing and wringing her hands. "I know I'm late," she said. "I've been standing out here for ten minutes, trying to make myself go inside, but I couldn't get through the door. I'll be okay if you can just walk me to your office."

"What's bothering—"

"I can't talk out here. Walk me inside. *Now.* Before I lose my nerve."

She'd grabbed my shoulder as we started inside, squeezing it like a drowning woman clutching a life preserver. I was sorry I'd snipped out the oversize shoulder pads in my yellow silk dress; Kitty clutched so tightly that I wondered if she'd leave bruises. As soon as we'd reached my office she'd gone straight to the open window.

Hardly the normal behavior I'd expected from a research subject for what was supposed to be a simple, straightforward study of memory and concentration.

Now her ragged voice sounded close to tears. "I thought if I came here first, got used to being inside the hospital, maybe it wouldn't be so bad."

Kitty was thirty, but she looked ten years younger. Tendrils of short curly brown hair framed her small, round face. Pink lipstick outlined bow lips. She had the face of a cherub, complete with dimples she flashed in an unconvincing attempt at a smile. "You must think I'm crazy, Dr. McAlister."

As a psychologist, I'd heard that line from a lot of patients.

"You're pretty scared, that's obvious." I didn't know enough to make any other judgments yet, only that something felt very wrong. "Do you think you're crazy?"

She gave me a sharp, reproving look, probably meant to let me know she wasn't pleased I hadn't reassured her. "I assumed you'd be a man."

Haley, my first name, sometimes leaves people unsure about whether to expect a woman or a man. But Kitty's acidic tone made me think she meant something more, as if something stronger and tougher lurked beneath her Alice-in-Wonderland air. Something equipped with sharp claws.

I wondered what else Kitty had expected, whether it had anything to do with the care she'd taken in dressing: her short form-fitting navy dress with its white sailor collar showed off her body to advantage. Under the dress she wore white hosiery and black patent pumps with a bow at the toe. At forty-one I was only eleven years older than Kitty, but it felt like several decades.

Someone whose first name was Katherine might be called Katherine, or Kathy, or Kate, or Katrina, or Kat— or even Catherine the Great. I wondered how she'd come to be called Kitty.

If she'd been a psychotherapy patient, I'd have asked if seeing a woman made a difference. But she was a research subject who'd come for a battery of memory tests prior to surgery next week. "What's frightening you?"

"I don't know. I mean, I'm scared to death of coming into the hospital and having surgery—but I don't know why." I was standing next to Kitty by the window, but she didn't turn to look at me as she spoke. "Only, well, the last time—nothing went wrong, but I've been scared ever since."

"Last time?"

"I had my gall bladder out on Valentine's Day. Nothing's been the same since then."

For a second, I thought she was joking. "What happened?"

"I feel dumb telling you this, but . . . sometimes, in strange places, or whenever I'm feeling nervous or stressed . . . I have to have windows open." Her lower lip was trembling.

"Anything else?" There had to be more.

"I've had terrible problems falling asleep. I have nightmares where I'm hearing these voices—and I see people floating over me—people who mean to hurt me. Waking up, I'm not sure whether I'm dead or alive for a few minutes."

Outside the temperature was in the low seventies, a

lovely May morning that promised another unseasonably hot day in Houston. I'd cranked up my air conditioner to try to make Kitty more comfortable; drops of sweat still dotted her forehead while I had goose bumps on my arms—and a tense feeling in my stomach.

"I keep telling myself that one really good thing came out of my surgery," Kitty said. "I lost weight, finally."

She intercepted my skeptical look at her body.

"I used to weigh more. A lot more. I've got a picture that was taken just before my surgery."

She rooted around in the black patent purse that matched her shoes, unearthing a dog-eared picture. I had to look twice to be sure it was the same person—a stout woman wearing a blue-striped tent dress that made her look like a walking advertisement for an awning company, caught in a candid shot as she held a single-dip ice-cream cone in front of a double-dip chin.

"I used to eat like a horse and never gained weight." Kitty was wearing a pendant around her neck, a red enamel apple the size of a pecan, a green vine wrapped around the apple. As she talked she toyed with the apple. "Then my doctor discovered I was hyperthyroid and began treating me for it; my metabolism slowed, my eating didn't. I got fat."

A door slammed nearby. Kitty jumped at the sound, then flashed me a truculent look that warned me not to comment. "My husband complains that I've gotten real nervous. But he's pleased about all the weight I lost after my surgery. At first I didn't have much appetite, but then"—she shrugged—"I just kept going. Like I was driven, somehow." Her breathy voice sounded closer to a teenager than a woman of thirty.

She looked at me, clearly waiting for me to applaud her weight loss. My stomach tensed again. Something was very wrong with Kitty that I didn't understand.

"Have you told your surgeon how you're feeling?" I asked.

Frowning, Kitty shoved the picture back in her purse, snapping the clasp like another woman might have slammed the door in a temper.

"I'm supposed to see him tomorrow. I don't see how I'll get myself through the surgery . . ." She started fumbling with her necklace again; as she turned it in her fingers I saw that what I'd thought was a vine wrapped around the apple was a green worm with rhinestone eyes.

"What's this surgery for?"

"Endometriosis."

"Must be very painful," I said gently. Uterine tissue growing in the wrong places could be agonizing.

Making a show of looking around, she avoided my eyes. In the same office for almost thirteen years, I'd painted three of the walls a pale turquoise; around the windows I'd used a darker shade, with stronger notes of blue. The rug, swirled in blues and greens, concealed institutional beige linoleum. Watching Kitty, I had the feeling she wasn't really seeing anything. I waited for the something more she wasn't saying.

"My gynecologist made it clear that surgery's my only good option . . . he's tried everything else." Kitty had a way of casting her eyes heavenward that accentuated her cherubic look. Her breathing quickened. "I'll feel better if I go to another hospital for my operation, I'm sure—just bad associations here . . ."

Looking at Kitty with her face next to the screen, the sweat beading her forehead, I didn't share her faith in a quick fix.

"I don't have to stay for the tests today if I'm not getting surgery here, right?" Kitty asked.

"The testing's purely voluntary in either case," I said.

"But if you're not sure you'll have surgery here, there's certainly no reason for it." My evaluation was designed to assess the effects of different anesthetics on memory and concentration; patients were supposed to be tested before surgery, then retested two, four, and six days after surgery. Other researchers on the project were examining the effects of the anesthetics on immune function and wound healing.

"Besides your gall bladder, have you had any other surgeries?" I asked.

"Oh, yes." Looking away, she swallowed heavily. "Hardly my favorite activity. I had surgery for endometriosis two years ago. It obviously didn't take care of the problem."

I looked at Kitty's face. Vulnerable. Scared. "Anything else happening around the time you had your recent surgery?" I was wondering if some other stress in her life might have triggered her nightmares and weight loss, or if the timing had simply been coincidental. I was also trying to figure out how I could get close enough to circle her roadblocks.

Turning away, Kitty stared out the window. I was about to repeat the question when she finally said, "Not really," her voice wavering.

"Sounds like 'yes.' "

"*No.* Nothing, nothing at all."

"Is there anything I can do to make it easier for you?"

"*No.*"

I waited a long moment before I said, "I'll give you the names of several psychologists you could call—if you still feel as frightened after you schedule surgery somewhere else." I couldn't imagine she'd magically feel better; I didn't think she'd want to come back to see me. "Other people have offices that aren't in hospitals, a couple have home offices. I could refer you—''

''I certainly don't think I'm in need of a shrink.'' Looking offended, Kitty paused, as if waiting for me to apologize. When I didn't say anything, she said, ''I had rheumatic fever when I was young, and this kind of stress can aggravate my heart problems. I'd appreciate it if you'd walk me back downstairs. *Now*.''

As we walked along the corridor she grabbed my shoulder again without asking, gripping so tightly that her nails dug into my skin through my dress. Outside, I held out my hand as we said good-bye. Hers was clammy and cold.

After she'd turned and walked away, I stood still, staring after her, visualizing the hand I'd just shaken. Her fingernails were so short that for me to have felt their bite through my dress she must've gripped my shoulder at an odd, awkward angle as we'd walked down the corridor.

Like a tarantula riding atop my shoulder.

A month later, on June 11, I went to Grand Rounds, our department's weekly clinical lecture. This week's speaker was Murray Snelling, a psychiatrist who had his office in the fashionable River Oaks section of Houston. His talk, ''Recovering Memories through Hypnosis,'' gave him another avenue for parading his supposed expertise on the topic, like the gaudy brochures for his annual workshops he mass-mailed to the professional community—and the media.

His brochures always included his picture. His hair was black with gray streaks, thick and curly, a mop that would have looked more at home on a poodle's head, and his smile was oily.

I remembered the first time I'd met Murray, thirteen

years earlier. I'd been a new assistant professor in the medical school, all too conscious of the fact that I looked younger than my age. He'd been in the last year of his residency in the Department of Psychiatry. Older than his fellow trainees, he'd gone to medical school after completing his Ph.D. in biochemistry—which meant he was older than I, a fact he'd gone out of his way to emphasize as often as possible, usually mentioning his dual training in the same breath.

As a resident, Murray would parrot newspaper accounts of medical research, pretending to have read the original journal article. He could talk as if he knew a subject well, speaking convincingly enough to mislead someone who didn't know the material and couldn't spot his flagrant errors.

Two years after he'd finished his residency, I'd read a newspaper story about his testimony as an expert witness. Murray had concluded that the defendant was acutely schizophrenic when he robbed a bank, then holed up in the desert. Fully consistent with this patient's behavior during previous acute schizophrenic episodes, he'd explained at length. Clearly not a man who could be held responsible for his actions, he testified, describing the patient's bizarre behavior when he'd interviewed him. Then the prosecutor had asked Murray to explain the fact that the patient had spent the loot playing the horses before heading to his desert hideout.

Murray had sent me a sympathy card right after my husband Ian had been killed in a car accident a year and a half ago, then invited me to dinner precisely two months later. Offended when I'd declined, he'd suggested I was too young to mourn for long, advising me in the next breath that a woman of my age couldn't afford to let "good opportunities" pass by.

I found Murray Snelling as sexy as head lice.

I attended Grand Rounds most Wednesdays, but I'd considered not coming today because he'd left a message for me: "I wanted to make sure you knew about my presentation," he'd said. "There's a case you'll find of interest."

I suspected he'd left similar messages for half the faculty, a self-promotional maneuver designed to ensure a decent-sized audience for his talk.

I walked into Grand Rounds twenty minutes late because a committee meeting had run overtime. As soon as I stepped through the side door of the auditorium, something felt wrong. Medical students are required to attend Grand Rounds during their psychiatry rotation; more often than not their boredom communicates itself through fidgeting and whispering, an irritating undercurrent to the lectures. Today I was struck by the unnatural stillness, the hushed silence. The door's groan as I pulled it shut was the only sound in the room. Two people seated nearby gave me irritated looks before they looked back toward the video monitors up front.

I stood by the door, listening to the faint hiss from the amplified videotape, waiting for my eyes to adjust to the dimness. Then I heard the woman's horrified voice and I understood the hushed room.

"It's the worst experience of my life. I'm completely paralyzed. I want to scream, but I can't open my mouth. I can't lift a finger or blink my eyes. Every muscle is held tight, like in a vise. I keep trying to take a breath and speak—I can't even control the rhythm of my breathing. I feel like I'm suffocating. It's the most terrifying feeling of absolute helplessness . . ."

I realized I was still standing by the door, my hand clutching the doorframe. A month since I'd seen her, but I had no trouble recognizing Kitty Evanston's distinctive voice as she broke into sobs. My knees felt wobbly as I tiptoed to an empty seat on the aisle.

Now I could see Kitty on the video monitor. Wearing a short green dress over navy blue hosiery, she was sitting in a black Naugahyde lounger. Her face was half-turned away from the camera, her eyes closed. Her expression was anguished.

"I hear the voices of two men—one on my left, one on my right. I'm trying to let my surgeon know the anesthetic didn't work, that I'm still conscious, but I can't speak or move."

The horrifying images made me feel weak and tremulous.

"My eyes are closed, but there's a big light right over me, I can sense the glare, I feel the warmth from it. I hear the metallic click of instruments. I hear this damned barbershop quartet singing in the background, someone in the room humming the bass part, off-key: 'You're nobody 'til somebody loves you.'

"They're putting cold stuff on my stomach. They say something about towels, someone touches my belly. I hear someone, a man, say it's going to be like operating on the Goodyear blimp." Kitty's voice sounded desolate.

"Someone touches my eyelid, maybe opens it for a second. I hear more bits of conversation, but voices are distorted, like people in a tunnel.

"For a while I keep thinking that the only thing worse might be being buried alive. Then I know I'm wrong . . . I hear a man say, 'I'm ready to make the incision now,' and he starts to cut me. All I feel is pain. Terrible pain. Overwhelming pain." Kitty broke into harsh, racking sobs. "I hurt so bad I want to die. I black out a couple of times."

I remembered what she'd told me: *I have nightmares*

where I'm hearing these voices—and I see people float-ing over me—people who mean to hurt me. I wanted to put my hands over my ears and run from the room so I wouldn't hear any more.

"I'm conscious again. I feel them stitching me up." She was sobbing. "Searing pain every time the needle goes through me."

"Do you remember anything else?" Murray Snell-ing's nasal voice on the videotape.

"The man who called me a blimp—they're stitching me up, he's calling me a beached whale."

A living nightmare. I realized I'd been gripping the arms of the chair so hard that my hands had cramped.

"When we end this procedure, you'll remember what you need to remember, and you'll forget what you need to forget," Murray said. "In a moment, I'll count from one to three. When I reach three, you'll be fully wide-awake and alert, remembering only what you want to remember."

Opening her eyes at the count of three, she looked around, blinking and yawning.

"How do you feel?" Murray asked her.

"Relaxed. Sleepy."

"What do you remember?"

She blinked rapidly as she bit her lower lip, staring away from him. Someone's pager buzzed nearby in the audience, and I saw a woman grab her pocket and slap the button to turn it off. I looked back at Kitty Evanston on the video monitor, her forehead wrinkled in concen-tration.

"What do you remember?" he asked again.

"I'm sorry, I must have dozed off. I don't remember anything specific." Her voice sounded labored, stilted.

Murray stopped the tape and the room erupted in whispers. A medical student in front of me turned to her neighbor, her voice incredulous: "She doesn't *remember* what she said?"

Not surprising—patients could "forget" traumatic memories after hypnosis if they weren't ready to deal with them.

Murray started to lecture, explaining the hypnotic procedure he'd used. "Some members of the audience aren't medically trained, so I'll try to simplify things as much as possible." He looked over at me, pointedly, as he spoke in a patronizing tone. He'd always seized any opportunity in conversations with me to point out the advantages of an M.D. over a Ph.D.

"Typically, a muscle relaxant or paralyzing drug is used in tandem with an anesthetic. Even with adequate anesthesia, the evidence suggests that hearing remains intact: It's possible for patients to hear and understand conversation during surgery without any conscious memory of the message. I've read a number of cases where patients remember details from operating-room conversations."

So Kitty's hearing could have been intact, accounting for memory of the derogative comments about her weight, and the barbershop songs?

"Clearly, in this case there's something more," he continued. "We're seeing the fallout from inadequate anesthesia."

Remembering his propensity for instant "expertise," I wondered how much I should trust Murray's statements about anesthesia.

As if he'd heard my doubts, he said, "There are some well-known case histories of similar problems. One from a cardiologist who talked about his experiences in *Lancet* in 1975—"

Old data, I told myself, as I made a mental note to

look up the article. Surely there couldn't be similar problems nowadays.

When Murray asked if there were any questions, a medical student raised his hand. "I've already rotated through surgery and anesthesiology. Some of the drugs used before surgery can induce bad dreams. Some patients confuse drug-induced dreams with the actual surgery; that's what must have happened to this patient."

"I don't think so," Murray said in the condescending tone I remembered so well. "This is my third session with this patient. I worked hard to get her this far."

I wondered if the student could be right—I hoped so, fervently. I wanted to believe that the memories I'd heard weren't real.

Could Murray's zeal to unearth repressed memories have led him to search in a way that assured he'd discover something—whether or not it was based in fact? Could his repeated suggestions have helped Kitty create her "memories"?

After Grand Rounds I went up to him. "You recognized the patient?" he asked.

I nodded.

"Kitty's new surgeon told her he wouldn't operate until she got herself calmed down. She called me after she saw a newspaper story about my work." He fondled his tie as he spoke. "I gather *you* weren't able to persuade her to start therapy with you?"

Before I could answer he said, "Probably just as well, since I've had so much experience with repressed memories." He gave me a smug, officious smile.

"There's something more I didn't want to mention here, for . . . obvious reasons. Kitty called me on Monday to tell me she'd remembered what she'd said during hypnosis—and what had happened during her surgery.

She's considering a malpractice suit; she wants me to provide expert testimony.''

Two medical students came up to ask questions, and I stepped away. I needed to know more, but I had to catch a flight to Washington for a professional meeting.

Three days later, back in Houston, I learned about Kitty Evanston's death.

Chapter 2

As part of my research on lie detection, I'd gotten interested in speech patterns, in analyzing how people chose words. If someone was describing a street scene and said, "I saw my neighbor's car," or "her car," they were more apt to be telling the truth. People who were lying tended to be less precise—more distant: "I saw the woman's car." Driving home from the airport early Saturday morning, I was pleased that the new studies I'd just presented at an American Psychological Society meeting had been well received.

I'd studied the language of research volunteers in artificial situations, but I didn't doubt that my findings translated into real life. I thought of a couple I'd seen for marital therapy recently. The wife told how she'd come home from work early one afternoon; surprised to find the front door locked, she was rummaging in her purse for her key when her husband finally opened the door. He was wearing bermuda shorts—but no shirt or shoes—and he'd smelled of beer. Then her husband's second cousin emerged from the bathroom, her lipstick smudged, a button unfastened on her blouse.

Her husband told the story differently. Not feeling

well, he'd fallen asleep when he came home from work.
He'd been awakened when the girl, stopping by to return
something he'd loaned her husband, had rung the doorbell. He'd offered the girl a beer as a gesture of hospitality.

The husband's story didn't address the locked door or
the delay in answering, but I was struck by the compelling detail in the wife's account compared to her husband's lack of precision—and the distant, detached way
he'd referred to his visitor: "the girl."

I thought of Kitty Evanston, the vivid details she'd
"remembered" from her surgery. What had really happened? Lost in thought as I stood on my front porch,
mining my purse for my front-door key, I jumped when
the man bellowed at me.

"You don't live there!" At least six feet tall and over
two hundred pounds, he slurred his words, heading toward me with the slow shuffle and sideways sway of
someone uncertain about his balance. "A man lives
there, a skinny man." Brown hair gone mostly gray, he
wore jeans and a black T-shirt that said ENDANGERED in
red letters over the picture of a giant panda. His heavily
muscled arms and chest strained against the thin cotton
of his T-shirt.

As he got closer I could see the scar tissue that coars-
ened what had once been a handsome face. Thickest
around his nose and eyes, the well-battered face of a
man in his late thirties who'd fought hard and often. His
hands, clenched in fists, were raised high in front of his
chest.

"I'm Haley McAlister," I said, trying to speak without a quiver in my voice as I held out my hand, keeping
my eyes on his. "The skinny man moved out last month.
I live here now."

I thought he lived next door, but I wasn't sure; I

hadn't met many neighbors yet. It was the kind of funky street in the Montrose area where Spanish stucco kept company with old frame Victorians, where I'd seen neighbors wearing everything from navy blue suits to rainbow caftans. I hoped I wasn't being foolish by trying to hold my ground rather than running.

The man studied me, staring at my face, not moving. He didn't smell of alcohol, I noticed, my relief short-lived as he continued to stand and stare, ignoring my hand. He pantomimed punching, one-two, one-two, a ferocious smile on his face, watching me closely. Hoping for something, I realized. Waiting for me to respond.

After an eternity he spoke again: "Do you follow boxing?" Then, not waiting for the answer, he said, "I'm Derek Zellitti. Maybe you remember my fights?" He stared at me, a pleading look on his face as he fingered a religious medal on the gold chain around his neck.

"Of course," I said, smiling; remembering the name but nothing else, not wanting to disappoint.

His face glowed with relief and pride. "I knew you'd remember," he said. "I'll show you my pictures, if you like—"

Footsteps sounded on the concrete walk and Derek turned at the sound quickly, eagerly, as if anticipating the arrival of another fan.

The short blond man hurrying up the walk looked angry. "I'm sorry he's bothering you," he said in an exasperated voice. Then he turned to the man beside me: "Derek, come home now," speaking in a peevish tone.

"But she remembers me, and she wants to see my pictures—"

"I'm *sure* she doesn't want to see your pictures. Come along now." A head shorter than Derek, his body plump and out of shape, I could still see the family resemblance between the two—and important differences;

despite his scars, Derek's battered face somehow conveyed a feeling of good-natured warmth, while the blond man's most memorable features were his pursed lips and resentful eyes.

When I glimpsed Derek's stricken face, I said, "If it's not a problem, I'd like to see his pictures—just let me set my things inside." As I pointed at the briefcase and overnight bag at my feet I wondered at my impulse, remembering all the chores I'd planned for today.

The plump man introduced himself as Tony Zellitti, Derek's brother. His older brother, he added, looking at Derek sternly. He asked me again if I was sure I wanted to see Derek's pictures, looking at me in a way that made it clear he had his doubts about me. Then, as we started next door, he said, "Derek's punch-drunk," his querulous voice loud enough that I was sure Derek, walking on my other side, could hear. "Brain damage from getting hit in the head thousands of times. Probably remembers every fight he ever had, but half the time he can't remember what he just did. Last night the waitress at Denny's brings the meal he'd ordered, he tries to send it back—says he never ordered it."

I'd read about boxing injuries. "Dementia pugilistica" was the medical term for brain damage caused by repeated blows to the head that ruptured blood vessels and left brain cells dying. All too common among boxers because damaging the opponent's brain—a knockout—was the surest road to victory.

On my other side Derek whacked his belly with his fist. "Still like granite," he said, pride lighting up his face. I wasn't sure if I imagined the look he shot at his brother's plump body.

Tony muttered something under his breath, but I only caught two words: "This neighborhood—" Following his gaze I saw a thirtyish woman in a purple tank top

and skintight pink pedal pushers coming toward us on a
bicycle. Her dark hair was cropped close to her head,
and she had one silver ring clipped to her nostril, three
large hoops snaking up each ear.

When she spotted me, she waved, and yelled, "Doing
fine!"

Beaming, I gave her a thumbs-up sign as she passed.

"Who's that?" Tony asked, giving me a skeptical
look that was layered with suspicion.

Claudia Wilson was a patient I'd seen in therapy for
a year, a poet whose verse could make a color-blind
person see the world in Technicolor. When we'd discussed her mother, stigmata sometimes appeared on her
face, large red welts that puffed up spontaneously—
places where she'd been struck repeatedly as a child.
"Someone I met along the way," I said, deliberately
vague.

"What kind of work do you do?" Tony asked suddenly.

If I hadn't just seen Claudia, I might have given him
a straight answer—in spite of his demanding tone. But
not now. "This and that; I like variety. And you?"

Driving home from the airport, I'd pulled my red hair
back in a rough ponytail before putting the top down on
my vintage Corvette. The wind had tugged at my hair,
freeing chunks of it. Tony eyed me as I brushed hair
back from my face, making no attempt to hide his obvious distrust.

"I'm an attorney," he said. "A lawyer."

Maybe he thought I wouldn't know what an attorney
was. Perhaps he just wanted to underscore his trade.
"What kind of practice?"

"Personal injury cases." He smoothed the front of his
plaid sport shirt as he spoke, the complacent gesture of
a man used to stroking his tie.

Derek's house, red brick with white shutters, was the smallest on the block. Inside, the wall of photos and newspaper articles was the focal point for his living room. The framed memories from his glory days showed a much younger Derek, trim in satin shorts. The biggest picture showed him standing with his arms raised in victory, blood oozing from a cut over a swollen eye.

As Derek pointed at the pictures he named the place, his opponent, and his strategies for each fight. He seemed to stand taller as he talked, his commentary articulate and smooth.

I looked from the dense wall of memorabilia to the neat, sparsely furnished room; Derek's past glories dominated his home, just as they dominated his life. But I didn't have any leeway for quibbling about such things. For a full year after his death I'd kept the box with my husband's ashes beside my sofa, graphic testimony to my difficulty letting go. My friend Glee had looked at the box once, and said, "Kind of crowds out any other man."

I realized Derek had paused, waiting for a response. Looking from the battered fighter beside me to the young man in the pictures, I forced a smile as I made admiring noises. "How'd you get started?"

As Derek answered, I thought back to when I was twelve, the time when my mother had died after giving birth to my brother. I'd spent the next year doing dangerous things. Exploring deserted places, sneaking out at night to walk darkened streets, climbing trees to see just how high I could go. I'd asked my father, a former college boxer who still worked out on a speed bag in the attic, for boxing lessons; he was clearly horrified by the notion.

A year later, I was diagnosed with leukemia. Thirteen, in the eighth grade, I spent the next two years in and out of hospitals. During my illness my father read history and nature books to me, his favorite topics. When I was told I was "cured"—but would still need annual checkups for the foreseeable future—I repeated my request for boxing lessons. I buttressed my argument with a line from a story he'd read me about James J. Corbett, a legendary boxer from the 1890s: "You can't be beat if you can't be hit." My father applauded my memory and firmly refused.

"You live by yourself?" Derek asked abruptly ten minutes later, cutting short the story of his last big fight, his worst loss.

On my own again after eight years with Ian, I'd rattled around in the house we'd shared. After I'd finally scattered his ashes last October, I'd had a dream where I was standing at a busy intersection, fearful about crossing the street. Ian had appeared at my side in the same red polo shirt he'd been wearing when I'd last seen him. Telling me it was OK to walk to the other side, he'd smiled as he touched my arm. I'd put the house up for sale the following week.

In May I'd gotten a full-price offer for my house with the contingency that I move within two weeks. As a stopgap, planning to find another place before the end of August, I'd taken over the last few months on a lease.

"Not exactly alone," I said. "I have a dog, a Great Dane. His name's Pavlov."

His brother had been sitting on the sofa during Derek's monologue, staring at the pink-and-green-striped leggings I was wearing underneath a green cotton T-shirt. Now he came to stand beside us. "Derek's been married twice," Tony said, giving me a wary look. "Wives spent all his winnings, left him with nothing—"

"I know your dog, I've played with him," Derek said to me. "I mean, through the fence . . ."

I left Pavlov in the backyard during the day. I'd come home a few times to find him tired and sweaty, once seen scuffed footprints in a damp spot. I'd assumed it was a neighborhood kid. "Of course," I said, nodding and smiling in recognition. Derek's eyes widened in response, and he shot a look at his brother.

I'd been about to say that Derek was welcome to play with Pavlov, that I'd often felt guilty about not exercising him more, but his furtive response made me pause. "Thanks for showing me your pictures," I said to Derek. "I've got to go pick up Pavlov at the kennel."

"I can take care of your dog when you're out of town," Derek said. "I'd be happy to water and feed him. You don't need to put him in a kennel."

Shooting his brother a repressive look as he stepped in front of him, Tony said, "I'll walk you back to your house." Outside, he pointed to my 1960 Corvette, sitting in the driveway where I'd left it. "That your car?" When I nodded, he said, "How's it run?"

"Just fine." An understatement—I worked hard to keep it in pristine condition.

"Old cars break down pretty often. Newer cars, you don't have so many problems. Tell you what, let me take it for a spin. If I like it, I could give you as much as ten thousand for it—enough so you could get yourself a newer model without all the problems."

A remarkably generous offer—he'd take it off my hands for a third of its value.

"That's . . . *kind* of you," I said, hoping he heard the irony, "but we've been together for a long time. I'm not interested in selling."

"Let me know if you change your mind—but I can't promise I'll still be willing to pay quite so handsomely in the future," he said, giving me a meaningful look.

As I started to say good-bye, Tony jerked his head

toward his brother's house: "Derek's had problems getting lost when he's walked too far—I worry how much longer he'll be able to live here alone . . ."

I didn't like the way Tony so readily cataloged Derek's defects for a stranger. Maybe he was just displaying the understandable concern of an older brother—but it felt like he was trying to warn me off.

I could see all the obvious reasons. I just wasn't sure they were his real motivation.

Chapter 3

Thumbing through the *Houston Chronicle* after picking up Pavlov, the sight of Kitty Evanston's picture in the obituary section stopped me cold. Not believing, not wanting to believe, I read the paragraph beneath her photograph three times, trying to make sense of her "sudden death on Wednesday." No mention of the cause of death. No clues about where she'd died.

Wednesday, the day I'd watched her on videotape.

Last September I'd discovered the body of one of my patients in her car in Rugton's parking lot, an apparent suicide that proved to be a well-planned murder. I kept remembering Kitty's fearfulness in my office, her terrified voice on Murray's tape. *Did Kitty kill herself?*

A car accident, that's how a woman of thirty would die suddenly. *Don't jump to conclusions*, I told myself.

My hand was shaking when I called the funeral home. "We don't give out . . . that kind of information on the deceased. You can talk with a family member if it's . . . essential for you to know." The funeral director's prim voice insinuated he was accustomed to callers who took a ghoulish pleasure in the details of strangers' deaths.

Only her husband and parents were listed as survivors;

not a good time for a stranger to intrude, asking how she'd died.

Who else? Murray Snelling. I scowled as I looked up his office number, unable to think of a reasonable alternative.

I'd expected to reach his answering service on a Saturday afternoon, but he picked up the phone after the first ring. I'd heard his practice wasn't exactly flourishing; maybe he'd adjusted his hours to accommodate as many patients as possible.

I told him how shocked I'd been to see Kitty's obituary in the paper. "How'd she die?"

A long pause. "I'm not free to talk now. Why don't you stop by my office this afternoon, around five?" A chord of self-satisfaction in his voice.

About to take a sip of coffee, I stopped, my cup in midair. I wondered if Murray actually knew anything— or if he was hearing the news of Kitty's death for the first time from me. And if he thought I'd seized on her death as an opportunity to call him.

Either way, I still needed to grill him about her "recovered" memories, and I wanted to ask him to loan me her videotape. "See you then," I said, suppressing a sigh.

When I was a new assistant professor in the department, I'd directed the residents' psychotherapy seminar, and Murray had presented one of his cases. His patient, a weasel-faced man of twenty-five, boasted how he'd worked in military intelligence while in the army, emphasizing the injuries he'd sustained when he'd been captured, his dramatic escape. The story was as convincing as those strip joints that advertise "sophisticated adult entertainment," but Murray had brushed aside other residents' comments about the incongruous details, the patient's vague answers when pressed for particulars about his military career. I'd watched his fellow trainees shift restlessly in their seats during his pompous monologue, remembered one muttering, "If brains were leather, he couldn't saddle a flea."

I didn't think he'd heard until I saw his face go blank, the smugness disappear, and then I felt bad for Murray. For a second, he'd had all the animation of an actor playing a corpse, and I'd found myself wincing in sympathy as I changed the topic.

The patient's story was pure fantasy, his injuries sustained in drug-related brawls—facts Murray learned only after his patient was arrested for selling narcotics on hospital grounds. Facts he'd tried hard to conceal from the members of his seminar and me.

"How nice to see you," Murray greeted me at five, putting his hand on my shoulder, standing so close that I could see the gray threads in his curly black hair, the veins coursing down his swollen nose, the tufts of black hair in his ears.

"I don't want to keep you." I stepped back. "I just wanted to find out how Kitty Evanston died—and to ask a few questions about her memories of her surgery."

"Of course." He gave me a look of smug disbelief, fingering his tie; it featured the double helix of a DNA molecule spiraling down its length in multicolored splendor, a not-so-subtle reminder of his dual training. "But since you've driven all the way here, I'm sure you'd enjoy a tour of my suite."

Meaning he had his own agenda, and I'd have to go along with it if I wanted any information. But I'd already learned one thing: He wouldn't be acting so self-satisfied if Kitty had killed herself. I took a deep breath and followed him.

I've noticed that men have a compulsion to show off their workplaces; maybe it's an ingrained behavior, some kind of programmed step in their mating rituals. I remember my first and only date with an entomologist who studied ticks. He'd given me a painstakingly detailed tour of his laboratory, at the end proudly exhibiting four tick-infested rabbits as he made jokes about how he "never brought work home."

Murray opened a side door and I saw the black Naugahyde lounger where Kitty had been sitting during her hypnotic session. I stopped short, remembering her harsh sobbing: *For a while I keep thinking that the only thing worse might be being buried alive. Then I know I'm wrong . . . I hear a man say, "I'm ready to make the incision now," and he starts to cut me.*

I told myself that I couldn't be sure it had really happened—repeated it, trying to make myself believe it. Hypnosis can help recover real memories—but it also makes it easier to plant and nurture fine imitations. People feel more confident about their "enhanced" memories after hypnosis—whether or not they're accurate. Kitty had been truly terrified by something, but I wasn't convinced it was her surgery. Not yet.

I could hardly ask Murray whether he might have accidentally seeded false memories in his sessions with Kitty. "Do you videotape many of your patients?" I asked, trying to find a back door to my concerns.

"Only a handful, where it looks like the tapes would be useful for my workshops," he said. "Makes it come alive for people when they see parts of a real session—one of the reasons my workshops are so popular."

I tried not to grimace. "What made you decide to tape Kitty?"

"During my first session with her, something she said reminded me of the case I mentioned in my talk, the cardiologist who wasn't adequately anesthetized for his own abdominal surgery. I wondered if the same thing might have happened to Kitty.''

Which meant that Murray could have started early— asking leading questions that planted bogus memories. Or he might have simply guessed the truth.

Smiling, he paused as if waiting for me to congratulate him on his clinical acumen. When I didn't fill in the silence, he said, "I was surprised to hear that you were testing patients yourself these days. Must be pretty tight in your department."

Kitty Evanston had been one of the first half dozen patients scheduled for the anesthesiology research project. As head of the Psychometric Laboratory, I supervise the three psychometrists who administer psychological tests. When I'd arrived at the office and found two of the psychometrists out sick, the third still on vacation, I'd canceled appointments wherever possible, seen Kitty myself when I couldn't reach her to reschedule. A fortunate accident.

Looking at Murray's self-satisfied smirk, I realized just how much he was enjoying the feeling of knowing things I didn't know, being one up on me. "How many times had you seen her before the tape you played in Grand Rounds?"

"Twice, including her initial evaluation."

As he closed the door to the treatment room, and we stepped back into the reception area, he said, "More colorful than those drab faculty offices you're assigned in Rugton, right? And I designed it—how do you like it?"

Reflecting an obvious obsession with royal purple, he'd chosen a darker shade for the upholstery, lighter for the carpet. The remarkably ugly wallpaper featured purple flowers and gold bows against a pale mauve background. So unlike a hospital, maybe it wouldn't have evoked the same terror for Kitty as Rugton Hall.

"Innovative—very imaginative. Do you have a tape from Kitty's second visit?"

"Of course. You'd like to see it?"

"Very much."

"Since she gave me permission to discuss her case and show her tapes for teaching purposes, I'd be happy to watch it with you." He smoothed his tie. "Perhaps we could go out for dinner tonight, and I could show you the tape afterward, at my house?"

A novel way of inviting me to view his etchings. "I'm afraid I already have plans. Could I borrow the tape?"

"I couldn't lend my only copy." His expression chilled, his affability sounded forced. "Another night, perhaps?"

"I'm seeing someone." Not true, but a kinder way out. "Was anything else important happening in Kitty's life around the time of the first surgery?"

"Probably nothing . . . I mean, I'm sure nothing relevant to her surgical problems."

Really? I thought about the things Murray hadn't asked patients in the past. Not something I could pursue now. "If she mentioned any other specific details like the barbershop song she heard, I'd like to see if I can check them out—"

"You're not suggesting she made it up, are you? Kitty told me you thought she was crazy, but I assured her you were wrong. Not the kind of thing you should be saying to a patient, even if you think it's true." Obviously pleased to be able to put me in my place, he spoke in the righteous tone of a television evangelist exhorting a sinner to repent.

I tried to keep my voice level. "Could you tell me any other details she remembered from her surgery, so I could check them out?"

"You're the lie-detection expert, right? So you should have been able to see that Kitty was telling the truth. You can always register for my next workshop if you want additional information."

"How'd she die?"

"She had an ectopic pregnancy—she died in the emergency room Wednesday night. She postponed going to the hospital in spite of the pain, traumatized by what happened in February. Not a drinker, but she'd been trying to guzzle enough beer to pass out. Her husband was out of town, unfortunately; when her suffering finally became unbearable, she called 911."

"No," I said, my mouth open. "She died because of her fear?"

"Actually, it's quite a bit worse than that. When I was taking her medical history, she told me how a childhood episode of rheumatic fever had damaged her heart. As a consequence, she had a cardiac arrhythmia—an irregular heartbeat—severe enough that her physician had warned her not to drink caffeine, to avoid any strenuous exercise, and to be very careful about stress."

"Yes, she mentioned it. But you're saying she died from an ectopic pregnancy—"

"No, she had a cardiac arrest in the ER when they tried to prepare her for surgery."

Imagining her terror, I leaned against the wall for support.

Looking closely at me, he added, "A particularly unfortunate accident for a former medical-center employee."

"What do you mean?"

"Surely you knew that she used to work in the Department of Anesthesiology . . . ?"

"No. No, I didn't."

"Really, you do need to learn to get a more thorough

history from patients. You didn't know about the way she was harassed before she quit?''

''No—''

''Someone kept leaving Kitty packages of condoms when she was working in the department.''

''And?''

''She said she'd made no secret of her heart condition, she was sure the harassment was designed to stress her.''

''But she didn't die at work—''

''There's one part of her tape I didn't play for my talk. After her surgery, she remembered a man's voice saying one more thing: 'You were lucky. But remember, what goes around, comes around.' A gloating voice, close. Like he was whispering in her ear.''

Looking all too pleased with himself, he opened the door for me. ''So we have to assume that someone knew about Kitty's rheumatic heart—and he planned the problems with her anesthesia accordingly. And, in the end, he killed her.''

Chapter 4

When I was young and ill, one of the historical books my father read to me had an odd anecdote about a battalion in South Korea: *Whenever they moved into a new area, they'd capture one of the enemy, carve their insignia on his back—then release him. A message that they'd arrived.*

Maybe Austin Danziger had heard the same tale. He was the chairperson (he'd have said chairman) of the Department of Anesthesiology, the kind of man who saw himself as supplying the glue that holds the universe together. Back when Austin was in his first year as a department head, one of his senior professors complained about how few departmental decisions were brought to the faculty for a vote. He'd ended his impassioned speech in the medical staff meeting by shouting, "Who do you think you are anyway, God?" This was late on a Friday afternoon. The professor arrived for work on Monday to find his books and papers stuffed in boxes outside his office door, his key a mismatch for the new lock. When he went to protest, he was told that Austin had left orders about "reallocation of space" before leaving on a two-week vacation.

Austin was the principal investigator (the director) for a multimillion-dollar Anesthesiology Center grant from the National Institutes of Health, one he'd held for four years, now up for renewal. I'd been coerced into working on the project by my boss, Kurt von Reichenau, the chair of the Department of Psychiatry.

Kurt had summoned me to his office to give me the news in late April: "Austin Danziger has asked me to find someone who can handle the memory-assessment component for his Center grant. I tried to think of someone else who could work with him, but you're the only one who fits the bill."

Roughly translated, Kurt meant that I'd accumulated enough relevant scholarly publications so a grant-review panel wouldn't question my competence on the topic, the only person among the six psychologists and twenty-four psychiatrists in our department who had the necessary expertise.

I didn't object to the work itself, but the spin Kurt put on it: "Austin's the leading candidate for Dean when Verbrugge retires—important to be helpful to him. *Very* important."

Psychiatry, a perpetual stepchild to the big, wealthy departments like Surgery and Internal Medicine, had little muscle in our medical school. Kurt was obviously hoping to curry favor with Austin, eager to please his future boss.

"I assured Austin you'd be fully cooperative," Kurt had said.

I'd been at odds with Austin Danziger from the beginning.

On Monday morning, two days after learning about Kitty Evanston's death, I'd convinced Austin's secretary that it was urgent that I see him early in the day.

Now I sat in Austin's office and told him about Kitty's

fearfulness when she'd come for testing, her obvious terror in the tape I'd seen at Grand Rounds. When he finally spoke, his tone was caustic: "*This* was your emergency?"

A handsome man in his midfifties, his hair and beard were silver, his eyebrows still black. Underneath his white coat he wore a claret-and-black-striped shirt and a claret tie with black diamonds. Standing in excess of six-foot-three, he carried himself in a way that suggested he was all too aware that he looked down on most everyone.

"Obviously you don't know much about anesthesia," he said, "but surely you're aware that most of the memories supposedly 'recalled' after surgery are false?"

"But some are real—"

"I see several possibilities. The most likely: Anesthetics can produce all kinds of peculiar dreams. The patient confused bad dreams from the anesthetic with the actual surgery. When patients are frightened about having surgery, their dreams can be unpleasant."

"But she had such vivid recall—"

"Of *course*. Patients who are prone to worrying tend to have vivid nightmares. Just how much alcohol did this woman drink?"

"I never got far enough into the evaluation to ask her—"

"You never got 'far enough' to ask her? *Really.*"

Austin was sitting behind an L-shaped desk with a black lacquer finish. In the matching display cabinet behind him, discreet lights illuminated a collection of crystal and glass; the central piece was a hawk, swooping down, talons extended.

"It's extremely important to get a patient's alcohol and drug history," he said. "Aside from the fact that you need that information to make sense of memory problems, hallucinations aren't uncommon among alcoholic patients after surgery. Some patients don't tell us they drink like sponges, so they go into withdrawal when they start to dry out in the hospital.''

"But—"

"A third *obvious* possibility—the patient is malingering. She figures she'll make money with a malpractice suit."

I remembered Murray Snelling's pride in his role as an expert witness. If Kitty's case had gone to trial, his testimony would have netted him plenty of attention— a splendid tonic for his lagging practice. I could easily imagine Murray assuming he knew what was troubling Kitty, then implanting false memories by clumsy, inept questions. And Kitty, a woman who'd sought him out because of a newspaper story, would be all too susceptible to his efforts.

As I was leaving his office on Saturday, I'd asked Murray Snelling if I could use Kitty's name to try to track down what had gone wrong.

"No problem," he'd said. "Kitty signed a release giving me permission to use her tapes for educational purposes, up to and including national television—if it would help someone else, of course. And I'm sure you'll want to credit me as the expert who uncovered her traumatic memories whenever you discuss her case with anyone."

I winced as I remembered that conversation now, particularly because one piece of Kitty's surgery story raised the specter of Murray's influence. Judging by the picture Kitty had shown me, she'd lost thirty pounds. She'd been heavy for her height, but not remarkably so—which made it hard for me to believe that anyone would have made such scathing comments about her weight. It gave me another reason to worry about how many details Murray might have helped Kitty "remember."

If Murray had helped Kitty create bogus memories, then he shared responsibility for her death—a circumstance that would make him unusually keen to find villains in the woodwork.

Austin gave me a triumphant glance when I didn't respond immediately. "I don't suppose you know the name of the patient's anesthesiologist?"

I shook my head no. Not knowing what he'd thought of Kitty—or if he'd known about her harassment—I deliberately hadn't mentioned her name.

"No, of course not," he said, his tone implying negligence. "When did this *alleged* problem surgery take place?"

"February 14."

His eyes widened, and he stared off in the distance. *Austin knew something*—or he had his suspicions.

"Based on your limited information, I'm certainly not convinced there was ever any problem." He shrugged dismissively, but I noticed his posture had stiffened and his eyes were still looking past me.

Almost convinced by Austin's litany of "explanations," his off-key response set off alarms in my head. "She died on Wednesday, last week." I heard the change in pitch as I spoke, my voice tightening. I took a deep breath as I watched Austin closely. "A cardiac arrest in the ER—"

"So there's no easy way for either of us to check out the possibilities I've suggested. If you can show me there's really a problem, I'll work on it. So far you haven't given me anything concrete. Now, if there's nothing else, I've got a lot of work waiting—" He started to stand to signal the interview's end.

I deliberately hadn't mentioned that I had a way to

check out Kitty's memory. If I could verify her memories about barbershop music and the conversations during her surgery, then I'd have to believe the gloating whisper wasn't an accident—and all that it implied.

But I wasn't going to show my hand to a man who played his own cards so closely—especially when he might have reasons to overlook problems.

In late March questionable financial dealings had come to light between the hospital and a private medical corporation owned by the current head of our medical school, Dean Verbrugge. Following a month-long investigation, the Board of Trustees had advised him to take early retirement in the summer while they searched for a pristine successor.

Austin's closest competitor for the job, the chair of the Department of Pharmacology, was a very distant second following a well-publicized FDA investigation of drug-trial improprieties in the fall; even though the problems didn't involve him directly, his lax monitoring of his departmental faculty had tainted him.

"We've had problems with two other patients recently," I said, not moving. "One thought she'd been referred because her anesthesiologist questioned her sanity, another suspected his anesthesiologist believed he was senile. Neither was willing to be tested."

"And just what do you expect me to do about *your* problems managing patients?"

"I want to meet with each of your faculty who refer patients for the study—we'll discuss how to describe the tests so we don't get so much unnecessary resistance. And I want you to explain to your faculty that it's important for the grant—*your* grant." I didn't tell him I had another agenda altogether for those meetings.

Back in late April, when I'd first met with Austin to discuss my participation on the project, he'd made it clear that I was part of a duress package: "The memory-testing piece is a colossal waste of time, but they're making it a contingency for our Center grant renewal."

"If the tests aren't necessary, why are they required?" I'd asked.

"No good reason."

I raised my eyebrows.

"A handful of patients always claim they have memory problems a couple of weeks after surgery. It takes some patients longer to recover than others"—he picked up a pen on his desk, then set it down again—"but that's only a matter of a day or two, at most—nothing close to a week."

I'd gathered that being the principal investigator for one of the five Anesthesiology Center grants gave Austin high scientific visibility among his peers, elevating him from a competent chair to a distinguished scientist. Not the only jewel in his crown, but one he obviously cherished.

Now Austin looked like he wished he could tell me that he didn't require my services on the project any longer—but he needed my credentials for the reviewers. And he needed the data I was trying to collect.

Picking up the phone, he made a call: "Jerome, you need to see Haley McAlister this afternoon, the psychologist who's doing the memory assessments. You'll serve as her liaison with our faculty."

As he spoke on the phone, I thought about Kitty. According to Murray, the problems with her anesthesia were deliberate—which, if accurate, meant that the person responsible had killed her.

The logic seemed straightforward to me. If I'd deliberately shot someone who survived the attack, the charge would be attempted murder. Should my victim die two weeks later because of wound-related complications, the charge would be upgraded to homicide. If Kitty's anesthetic problems were both genuine and deliberate, her death was no less a murder because it occurred well after the fact—except that the absence of any physical evidence made it virtually impossible to demonstrate intent or prove culpability.

And I couldn't help thinking that I'd had a chance to help her, and I'd blown it. I'd let her down, and she'd died. Not perfectly rational—but that's how I felt.

Hanging up, he said, "Two o'clock. Jerome Pettit will work with you to make sure there's no difficulty on our end. Now you need to take a closer look at the way you do business on your side of the tracks. You obviously need to learn how to explain your procedures to patients—"

I remembered another story I'd heard. One of Austin's Anesthesiology division chiefs, incensed about cutbacks, had sent his boss a group picture in which he'd crossed out all the faces of people who'd left and not been replaced. The picture was returned to him within the hour, a red "X" over his own face.

"We'll make a deal," I said. "I won't tell you how to anesthetize people. You won't tell me how to handle my evaluations."

"You really think you know more than I do?" A warning tone in his voice.

"About psychological testing—absolutely." But I had the feeling we were talking about something much more fundamental.

I was opening my appointment book to see if I was free at two o'clock when I heard a muted buzzing. Austin pulled a cellular phone out of the pocket of his white coat, turning away from me as he opened the case.

Even from eight feet away I could hear the woman's shrill, frightened voice over the phone: "Something's happened, there's blood everywhere, blood on everything, no one around—''

"Where?" Austin asked, his voice tight.

"The core lab—"

"You're there now?"

"Across the hall—"

"I'll be right there," Austin said. "Don't talk to *anyone* about it before I get there."

Chapter 5

"Dearie, I'm his *wife*," the woman who answered the phone told me, when I called Gary Jenkins late Monday morning. "You're another of his conquests?"

"This is Dr. McAlister, I'm trying to reach him to schedule an appointment regarding his insurance claim—"

"He's out fishing."

"I beg your pardon?"

"You heard me. He doesn't live here anymore, no way I'd let him stay after catching him in bed with his bimbo. I'm not covering for him any longer, not after he cheated on me."

Last November the *Phoenix*, a commercial fishing boat, had capsized in the Gulf of Mexico. Responding to flares sent from the life raft, another vessel had rescued five of the six men aboard, Gary Jenkins among them.

Eight months later, the five survivors were all pursuing personal injury claims. Each had sought consultation with a psychiatrist, and all five had received a diagnosis of PTSD, post-traumatic stress disorder. The fact that none of the five had returned to work was an obvious red flag for the insurance company that had underwritten the *Phoenix*. Retained by the defense counsel, I had agreed to conduct independent exams on the five crewmen.

"He's been fishing a lot since the accident," Mrs. Jenkins continued, "not at all like his story about being afraid of the water."

The seamen unquestionably met the first criterion for PTSD—the sinking boat posed a clear threat to their lives. However, PTSD symptoms include terrifying nightmares, flashbacks, and insomnia—all subjective, nonspecific, well publicized, and easy to fabricate—so malingering was one viable alternative diagnosis.

"Is there another number I should call—"

"And another thing," she said. "He'll tell you he can't sleep, but that's a big, fat lie—I know, because he snores like a bear. And I helped him make up nightmares to tell the shrink."

Responding to the insurance company's sense of urgency, I'd agreed to finish the assessments as quickly as possible. When I'd reviewed the packet of materials left by a courier early Monday morning, I found several unpleasant surprises. The lawyer who represented four of the five seamen was none other than my neighbor's pompous brother, Tony Zellitti. He'd contacted each of the crewmen on their return from the disaster—and he'd referred three of his clients to Murray Snelling.

A key section of Murray's report on Gary had said, "The symptoms are clear and unequivocal, a textbook case. No psychological testing was requested because the facts of the disaster are incontrovertible, and the patient's symptoms so very consistent with a traumatic response."

Another reason to doubt Murray's diagnostic acumen—and to worry about his work with Kitty Evanston.

I left word for the insurance company's lawyer to let me know if she still wanted me to evaluate Gary Jenkins, once she'd spoken with his wife.

Just before two o'clock I grabbed a tall latté from the cappuccino stand in the hospital lobby and went in search of Jerome Pettit's office. As I knocked, I wondered if Austin Danziger's secretary had given me the correct room number; this door had a biohazard label, a black emblem on an orange background. Startled when Austin stormed past her, she'd tried to ask him something, but he'd ignored her. I'd taken advantage of the turmoil to inquire whether Austin took a turn in the surgery schedule; only for certain high-level VIP patients, she'd assured me, he was far too busy with administrative duties and his work directing his Center grant. Which meant that Austin hadn't been Kitty's anesthesiologist.

No answer to my knock, so I tried the knob.

I stopped short as I was about to step inside, my mouth open. A row of freezers and other equipment ran down the center of the lab, blocking one section from view. The part I could see was lined with cabinets, equipment, and sinks, a laboratory no different from others in the medical center—except that everything had been sprayed with blood.

Blood was splattered over the cabinets, bloody rivulets ran down the walls, puddles of blood dotted the floor.

At the side of the room I saw a plump young woman seated in a chair, her head tilted back, her eyes closed. Absolutely motionless, deathly still, she was wearing a low-cut peasant dress; while her cotton frock was a pristine ivory, the unbuttoned white coat she wore over it was smeared with blood. Her hands, encased in rubber gloves and neatly folded in her lap, were stained crimson. But what held my attention was the bloody line across the pale skin of her neck.

I remembered the shrill voice over the phone in Austin's office: *Something's happened, there's blood everywhere, blood on everything—*

I could feel my stomach muscles knotting, my breath coming fast. I wanted to throw up, to scream.

As I was about to turn to run, I recognized the odor: a tomato smell. As I looked closer at the red liquid oozing over everything, the woman in the chair moved. A grin appeared on her face and she opened one eye, then jumped up, giving me a look that mixed embarrassment with disappointment. "But I thought—you're not Nick—"

In her twenties, the wavy blond hair that cascaded past her shoulders bounced as she coughed hoarsely. Looking away from me, her pale cheeks flushed, she began buttoning up her lab coat.

The tomato smell of ketchup, not blood. *A live woman, not a body.* I laughed with a relief that came out as a strangled giggle, my knees weak.

"Who are you? What do you want?" The man's angry voice came from behind me. "Coming back to check your handiwork?"

The woman's eyes widened as she looked beyond me. She shot me a quick pleading look before she grabbed a sponge from the counter and attacked a puddle, wiping the streak from her neck on her sleeve.

Turning, I saw a white-coated man in his early forties, short and thin. His black hair, combed straight back from his face, was so thick I might have mistaken it for a badly cut toupee if it weren't for his heavy black eyebrows, his dense dark brush of a moustache.

"I'm looking for Jerome Pettit—"

"You found him. Who are you?"

My hospital ID was clipped to the lapel of my navy suit. I watched Jerome read my name and check my face against the picture on my badge. He didn't say anything, even though I was sure he'd figured out the who and why.

"I'm Haley McAlister—"

"Surely you know you don't eat or drink inside a biohazard lab," he said, pointing at my coffee cup. "My office is down the hall, and I was on my way to meet you there. Why'd you come here?"

"Austin's secretary gave me this room number. What's going on?"

"Sydney, get the place cleaned up as fast as possible," he said, speaking to the woman whose face was now studiously averted as she busied herself wiping down a counter. "Keep this door locked whether you're here or not—do make more of an effort to control who gets in. And don't talk to anyone." Motioning for me to follow him, he slammed the door and started down the hallway.

Struggling to keep up with him, trying to hold my coffee level so it didn't slosh, I repeated my question: "What's going on?"

He waited long enough to make me think he wasn't going to answer before he said, "Someone made a bogus call to clear out the lab by telling the technician to pick up a big order of supplies at the loading dock. We were lucky it wasn't worse. The imbeciles who vandalized the place pulled a plug on one of the freezers, and the alarm scared them away."

"The alarm?"

"Lab freezers have alarms that go off when the power's interrupted." He looked back at me like he thought I was an idiot and could barely keep from saying it out loud. ''You can't afford to lose frozen samples because they thaw at the wrong time.''

''Who'd want to trash the lab?''

''Probably animal-rights fanatics—they do a lot of damage.'' He stopped in the middle of the hallway, deserted except for the two of us, and spoke in a low voice: ''It's important to keep it quiet. You can't mention what you've seen to anyone. No one, no matter who. Those people thrive on hearing they've done damage.''

''Have you had problems before—''

''Don't you remember what happened at Rockefeller a few years back? They had a prankster in one of the labs, someone with a grudge against another faculty member; the joker wrote a couple of nasty notes and set a small fire in a closet before he got caught. No big deal, but some newspaper got hold of the tale and it hit the wire services. The tabloids had these lurid headlines: 'Who's trying to kill the Rockefeller gene-splitters?' Spreading this story would play right into their hands— and turn this place into a circus.'' He started walking rapidly again, not looking back.

A clever way to dodge my question.

''*This* is where you were supposed to meet me,'' he said, unlocking a door with his name plate beside it— and speaking in a tone that told me he was still expecting apologies.

''Where shall I sit?'' Stacks of files, books, and journals covered the extra chair and a sagging plaid couch. Boxes overflowing with computer printouts hugged the wall.

He made a show of moving a pile of patient charts from the chair to the floor. ''One of the studies I'm conducting with Dr. Danziger,'' he said, patting the top of the stack. Speaking with something uncomfortably close to reverence, he conveyed the message that I was usurping a chair that had been serving a more vital purpose.

When we were seated facing each other, I said, "Austin said you'd help me with problems I've been having with—"

"*Dr. Danziger,*" Jerome looked at me, making sure I'd registered his correction, "*Dr. Danziger* relies on me for many things. He's a very busy man. A very important man." He checked his watch. "I'm not going to have much time today, myself. I've been out of town for two weeks, and I already had a full schedule when he called me at the last minute."

He gestured toward the blackboard mounted on the wall behind his desk, a lengthy TO DO list filling most of it.

"That's fine." I gave him an insincere smile. "If you're not free, I'll ask Austin to suggest someone else."

Speaking like a teacher reprimanding a troublesome student, he said, "Tell me about the memory assessments. I need the necessary background—if you want my help."

As I outlined my piece of the project, I kept picturing the crimson-splattered lab. Remembering how I'd felt when I opened the door and confronted the appearance of slaughter, I took a deep breath. Designed to shock and offend—and frighten. Who had been the intended audience, the target?

"Was that your lab?" I asked when I'd finished.

"The room you saw is part of a shared core lab . . . Dr. Danziger's in charge of it. Faculty like myself who work with him use the core lab and the rooms that branch off from it."

So the target could have been Austin—but not necessarily. "Is the core lab used for studies for the Center grant?"

"The core lab, and the smaller labs," he said, his voice grim. "We can't afford any downtime right now, obviously."

"Why would animal-rights activists go after this particular lab?"

"One of our protocols involves comparisons of various anesthetics; putting it simplistically, we measure production of stress hormones during surgery in mice. Less pain means lower levels of stress hormones, maybe faster wound healing. The research has direct applicability to humans—but animal-rights extremists prefer to ignore human suffering: better to worry about rodents."

I grimaced. I don't have a lot of sympathy for animal-rights fanatics; if it weren't for the contributions that animal research made to the development of effective treatments for childhood leukemia, I wouldn't be alive today.

"Despite the mess you saw, we were lucky," he was saying. "It could have been much worse. They'll wreck a project by sneaking into a laboratory and letting all the animals out of their cages . . . they don't care that most of the animals they 'liberate' will have to be destroyed. I've always wanted to let a few rats loose in their homes, see just how long it takes them to set out poison to get rid of the vermin."

Checking his watch, he said, "We don't have much time before my next appointment. Tell me about the problems you're having with your memory assessments."

When I finished telling him about patients' misunderstandings, he said, "My colleagues probably never bothered to read the information about the study. I've found a surprising number of faculty who act like they're above the rules." He gave me a glance that suggested he had his doubts about me.

"Professionals who should know better can make the most incredibly stupid mistakes," he added, his expression self-satisfied. "I'll talk with my colleagues about they way they prepare patients for you."

"I appreciate your help," I said, not at all sure it was true. "But it's important that I meet with each of them myself." I read him the list of names I'd gotten from Austin's secretary, three besides himself: Fred Verlin, Eva Aarastadt, and Nick Treece. I didn't know if Kitty's anesthesiologist was among the group, but at least it was a place to start asking questions.

"I better tell you a few things to make sure you don't get blindsided by a few of my esteemed colleagues," he said. "Some of them like to make things difficult for women." He straightened a pile of papers on his desk. "Have you ever seen Fred Verlin?"

"I don't think so—"

"If you'd met him, you wouldn't have forgotten. Fred's *quite* memorable: He's totally hairless. Bald head, no eyelashes, no eyebrows, no beard. No hair, anywhere." He patted his own thick hair complacently.

"Recent cancer treatment?"

"No, alopecia totalis. Maybe you've heard of it—an autoimmune disease where the immune system attacks the hair follicles. He lost all his hair back when he was fourteen. I've heard that stress can be a trigger for the disease, and that makes sense: I'm sure he's always had problems, always been a misfit. You're a psychologist, you can imagine the kind of . . . warped personality an experience like that can produce."

I took a sip of my coffee to avoid a response. Watching me, he asked, "That's regular coffee, not decaf?"

I nodded, and he shook his head disapprovingly.

"Fred's last name is Verlin, but female students and technicians call him Vermin behind his back," he continued.

Not a common word, vermin. Used twice in the space of a few minutes.

When I didn't respond, he said, "Caffeine's not good for you. Did you know that people under stress show bigger blood pressure increases when they drink caffeine?"

"I'm not prone to hypertension." I didn't say what I was thinking: Jerome's company was undeniably stressful.

"Personally, I never touch the stuff. You really ought to consider switching to decaf . . . if you can't live without it." Before I could say anything, he continued: "When Fred was finishing medical school, he married a girl about to graduate from high school—probably the only girl who'd have him. A few years ago he got caught in a sweep of prostitutes and their customers when he was away at a meeting in New Orleans. His wife left him when she found out about it.

"His wife—his ex-wife—said he dealt best with women when they were unconscious—that's why he went into anesthesiology."

Struggling to keep up with Jerome in the hallway, I'd entertained fantasies of tripping him, jarring his self-righteousness. Now, listening to him, I found myself looking around his office, feeling apprehensive, as if I had reason to be vigilant—a vague fear, no less real because I couldn't see any obvious reason for it. More than just the lingering creepiness of the simulated massacre.

"Before Fred separated from his wife, the secretary who sorted the mail told me he got catalogs and packages from Frederick's of Hollywood. Must've had an affair going, didn't want to send things home where his wife might see the stuff. No other explanation, right?''

I gave him a noncommittal shrug. Fred might have had packages delivered at work so he wouldn't have to pick them up at the post office if no one was home when mail came. Or he might have been buying gifts for his wife and wanted them to be surprises. Or he could have been ordering lingerie for himself, for cross-dressing. Maybe Jerome had a limited imagination; perhaps he was fascinated by certain vices.

''And then there's Eva Aarastadt, she's one of the newer additions to the Anesthesiology faculty—she started trouble right after she arrived in January. She's supposed to oversee the animal studies for the Center grant, and that's all she wants to do. Makes a stink about taking her share of the routine anesthesiology schedule.''

Dropping his voice, he leaned forward: ''Came here because of problems in her old job—or so it's rumored. She had the animal-rights types after her back in New York—and it looks like she brought the trouble with her.''

The phone rang, interrupting his tally of Eva's sins. From what I'd heard so far, I guessed that Jerome was the departmental bully, and Eva and Fred were among the small cadre who'd stood up to him. As he argued with his caller about the best time for a committee meeting, I read his TO DO list: Credentials Committee folders. Review May charts—QA violations. Draft QA report—faculty meeting. An interesting list of assignments, based on what I'd learned about his department.

After meeting with Austin this morning, I'd looked up Anesthesiology in the on-line directory and counted slots: twenty-two full-time faculty, three-quarters at the assistant or associate levels. Jerome and Fred were associate professors, Eva Aarastadt and Nick Treece were among the few full professors. Most departments rotated membership on the hospital's Quality Assurance—QA— committee like a hot potato, the assignment dropped into the lap of the newest assistant professor. The departmental QA representative had the distasteful task of scolding faculty colleagues about never-ending problems like timely completion of patient discharge summaries or inadequate documentation in patients' charts.

Just the kind of work Jerome Pettit would enjoy.

When he hung up the phone, I stood. "Thanks for your time. I appreciate your help." Then, treating it like an afterthought, I told him about Kitty Evanston, not mentioning her name or the date or the whispered voice at the end, framing it for him as a possible QA problem. I didn't tell him I'd already talked with Austin about the incident.

After I finished, he sat doodling on his pad. I waited, expecting the same litany I'd heard from Austin when I'd mentioned problems with anesthesia.

Finally he said, "Get me the patient's full name, her hospital ID number, and the surgery date. I'll find out which anesthesiologist was scheduled."

Watching him, I had the feeling he wasn't at all surprised. As if this wasn't the first time he'd heard about a patient with similar problems.

His voice low, his eyes locked on mine, he said, "Don't mention this to *anyone* until I've had a chance to check it out."

Chapter 6

I'm about to grill hamburgers—join me?'' Derek Zellitti called over the fence Monday evening, as I was
greeting Pavlov after work. Before I could answer, he
added, ''There's a catch—you have to bring your dog.''

Half an hour later, Pavlov and I were standing in Derek's backyard. Dressed in jeans and a red polo shirt,
his battered face creased in a smile, he looked far less
fearsome than the day we'd met. Away from his brother,
he was more relaxed and articulate. He told me that he'd
recently started working at the Y where his favorite jobs
involved coaching kids. If his rapport with Pavlov was
any guide, he was good—gentle but firm.

''I just asked a woman for a date,'' he said, during a
lull in the conversation. ''I need some advice.''

I looked up and saw that he was blushing, his anxiety
making him look younger and oddly vulnerable as he
poked at the patties on the grill. I'd been about to tell
him it wasn't exactly my expertise, but I said, ''Sure.''

''The thing is—well, you know her—Claudia Wilson.''

My former patient, the poet we'd seen on her bike—
the short-haired woman who had prompted Derek's

brother Tony to make the disparaging comment: *This neighborhood.*

"How'd you meet?" I asked.

"I'd seen her around the Y a few times before we ran into her on the street on Saturday. Yesterday I used the excuse that we knew someone in common to introduce myself."

Claudia had been twenty-four when I'd seen her, so she must be thirty-two now, maybe five years younger than Derek. Every year or two, she'd send me a letter updating me on her life; I'd been touched by her notes, honored by her regard. The last I'd heard she was working in a bookstore for her day job, lamenting the fact that she wasn't seeing anyone regularly.

"She tells me you're a psychologist," he said, grinning. "My brother will really be surprised."

Indeed—especially when we meet over the Phoenix *survivors.* "I'd appreciate it if you wouldn't mention my occupation to your brother."

"Sure—but why?"

"I'd rather tell him myself."

"Claudia said she'd been a patient of yours," he said, then added quickly, "and I'm not asking you to tell me anything personal about her. But I'm trying to figure out where to take her."

"Where were you thinking?"

"There's a concert in the park—folksingers—but would she think that was too corny?"

"Ask her," I said, guessing she'd be pleased. "Why does your brother try to warn off women?"

Making a face, he said, "Partly he's just protective, in a weird way. I was married twice, and neither choice was real smart. And he's convinced that he knows what's best for me, better than I know myself, because he's a lawyer."

Maybe Tony just liked keeping Derek under his thumb—perhaps he relished the fact that Derek was no longer the golden boy. With the kind of ambulance-chasing mentality he'd demonstrated with the *Phoenix* survivors, I didn't have any trouble believing the worst of him.

Trial lawyers have a clear vested interest in presenting themselves as likable, credible, and trustworthy. From what I'd seen thus far, I wondered how Tony managed to pull it off.

Seated in the reception area near my office, the burly middle-aged seaman from the *Phoenix* was hunched forward, a yellow legal pad clutched in his hand, a hopeless look on his well-weathered face.

"Lou Ramsey?"

The carpet had muffled my steps, and he jumped perceptibly when I approached him on Tuesday afternoon.

"Would you like coffee or a glass of water?" I asked, after shaking his hand.

"Coffee . . . I guess," he said, eyeing me warily. With his thick white hair and bushy ivory beard he could have been transformed into a credible Santa Claus, but his faded green sweatshirt and wrinkled khaki pants made him look more like a street person.

Seated in my office, I said, "Mr. Ramsey, I'll be asking you many of the same questions you answered for Dr. Turkin." Lou had seen a psychiatrist I knew slightly, and I'd been impressed by his report—but I wasn't prepared to take anything on faith.

"I only saw him because the lawyer told me I should be evaluated by a shrink, and he knew someone good . . . I mean, I wasn't acting weird or anything, it was just one of the things he said to me."

His hands told a different story—his nails were bitten

to the quick, his well-chewed cuticles peppered by scabs.

I knew from his file that he was a high-school graduate in his early fifties, married for thirty years; he'd been working as a seaman for the same company for the last ten years. He'd rarely missed a day of work prior to the accident. "How are things between you and your wife?"

"Just fine," he said, gesturing with his arms as if shoving something away.

I raised my eyebrows and let the silence stretch out.

"She's threatening to leave me," he said, slumping back in his chair. "She says it's like there's a glass wall between me and her."

"That sounds rough," I said, feeling distinctly sympathetic with his wife. "Were things different before the accident?"

"It's worse now . . . but only because money's so tight, what with me not working." He stroked his ivory beard nervously; his Adam's apple bobbed up and down as he swallowed convulsively.

"How have you been sleeping?"

"Not great."

"How bad is it?" Maladaptive arousal needed to be found in at least two guises for a PTSD diagnosis: insomnia, irritability or temper outbursts, difficulty concentrating, hypervigilance, or an exaggerated startle response. I'd already given him a point for his jumpiness in the waiting room, and the dark circles under his eyes gave their own testimony.

"Hard to sleep, sometimes. I have trouble falling asleep, then bad dreams . . ."

This morning I'd awakened in a tearful panic from a nightmare where I'd smashed into a woman with my car, killing her; one of those unusually vivid dreams, so lifelike that I'd lain in bed afterward, breathing hard, telling myself that it hadn't really happened. And then, as my mind replayed the moment where she'd stared at me in horror just before I hit her, I realized the woman had been Kitty Evanston.

"Bad dreams?" I asked, feeling my throat tighten with compassion as I imagined what it was like for him, night after night.

"Sometimes."

For someone who stood to gain by reporting symptoms, he was his own worst enemy. "Tell me the story of how the *Phoenix* sank."

Picking up the legal pad he'd set down beside him, clutching it like a talisman, he said, "I've written some notes about the accident. I'll read them to you."

"I'd rather have you tell me your story yourself."

"I have trouble keeping things in order. I've got it all written down here—"

"I'm sorry, I need to hear it from you." I could smell his fear, a thick coating on the air.

Grasping his pad tightly enough to wrinkle the pages, his expression pleading, he said, "But don't you want to read them?"

"If you'd like, you can leave the notes for me to read later, and I'll make sure to send them back to you. Or I can make a copy before you leave."

"But I hate to talk about it."

"I'm sorry for the necessity," I said, meaning it—all too aware of exactly what I was pushing him to do.

Avoidance, another PTSD hallmark, requires at least three of seven possible symptoms: efforts to avoid thoughts, feelings, or conversations related to the trauma, an inability to remember an important aspect of the event, clearly diminished interest in significant activities, feelings of detachment from others, a restricted range of emotion, avoidance of situations that provoke memories of the event, or a sense of a foreshortened future.

Either Lou was a truly remarkable (and devious) actor—or I was doing the equivalent of asking him to thrust his hand in the fire.

Finally, like a soldier surrendering his weapon to the enemy, he bowed his head as he handed me his notepad.

"How did the trip start out?" I asked.

"We were short-handed because the twins got sick— lucky for them, as it turned out. I hadn't felt all that swift myself, but we get paid a percentage of the catch, and I needed the money."

Wringing his hands, he said, "The weather was getting rough because a storm was moving in. I was just coming up from belowdecks when the boat felt like a giant hand was shaking it. I don't get seasick, I've been lucky, but all of a sudden I started feeling weird. It was pitching like crazy, then it began to roll over. I was screaming . . . I thought—I thought I was gonna die. Water was pouring in on me. Somehow, I don't know how, I didn't lose my grip on the ladder—I managed to climb out." Biting his lip, he looked away.

"We were lucky," he said. "The other guys snagged a life raft from the *Phoenix* before they jumped in the water, and it had flares. We'd passed close to another fishing boat a few minutes earlier, the *Vantage*, so we got picked up pretty fast . . . they say."

Turning away again, he started blinking rapidly. "Just something in my eye," he muttered, a pained look on his face.

I busied myself writing notes, giving him a chance to recover and take up the story at his own pace. When he started speaking again, his voice was strained: "After they picked us up, they managed to tie the *Phoenix* alongside. There must've been an air pocket inside, we could hear the captain inside the hull, pounding on the metal. And—and shouting . . . I couldn't—I couldn't make out the words—''

He started sobbing, great loud whoops of pain, his arms wrapped around himself. ''Coffee?'' he mouthed, some minutes later.

I took his coffee cup out for a refill, my throat aching in sympathy.

''I'm sorry,'' he said. ''I have so much trouble talking about it . . .''

We'd already gone well past the allotted time. When I'd stepped out I'd seen my next patient waiting, a woman who was wearing a scarf over her hair, two blouses and a cardigan, a skirt over a pair of pants, and a tight-lipped glare when anyone ventured near her.

''That's fine,'' I said. ''Take your time.'' If Lou stopped now, I wasn't sure that he'd give me—or himself—another chance.

''He—the captain—kept pounding and shouting . . . I wanted to do something, it felt so awful just listening. I wanted to swim down and try to bring him out, but they held me back . . . there wasn't any diving gear on the *Vantage*, they kept saying it was too dangerous and we had to wait for the Coast Guard helicopter. But just before it got there, the *Phoenix* shifted position, and—and this big air bubble came up. Then the pounding stopped.''

In the silence, my eyes were moist as I watched him weeping.

''I've had this terrible guilt since then, like, why him and not me? Why'd he drown, and I came home without a scratch?''

''You said you were climbing up from belowdecks when the boat started to capsize, and then you talked about being rescued by the *Vantage*. What happened between those times?''

His eyes widened and he took a deep breath. ''I was in the water, and then they picked me up . . . that's all.''

''How long?''

''Not . . . not too long.''

''Think back. After you got out from belowdecks, what happened?''

He burst into tears again, sobbing fiercely, his head in his hands.

Once he'd gotten down to an occasional hiccup, I said, ''There's a gap in your memory?''

He nodded, not meeting my eyes. ''Next thing I knew, I was paddling in the ocean—and then I was on board the *Vantage*.''

''Do you remember anything at all from that time?''

''Just the taste of seawater. And blood in my mouth, my own blood. And a feeling that I was going to be left alone to drown. Nothing else.''

I believed him. And I wondered about Lou's missing piece.

My phone rang, and I told the receptionist to reassure the waiting woman that I'd be with her soon, that I was sorry to be running late.

After I hung up, I asked Lou, ''Do you have any thoughts that keep coming back over and over, things you can't push out of your mind?''

''Bert's wife . . . the captain's wife . . . at his funeral she told me how his hands and arms were all cut up . . . from banging on the hull, trying to let us know he was still there. All the time, I keep picturing his hands, thinking about how terrible it was for him.''

I tried not to flinch as I pictured the scene.

''I can't shut it out.'' He was clasping his hands together so tightly that his knuckles were white. ''I dream of being in his place, trapped . . . or trying to get him out. Or being lost at sea, knowing I'm about to drown. There are times when I'll be doing something else, and then it'll be like I'm right there, and it's happening all over. Sometimes I wake up and I'm sweating and shaking and I throw up because I'm so upset.''

''Have you tried to go back to fishing?'' Looking at Lou's anguished expression, feeling the tightness in my own chest in response, it seemed like a remarkably foolish question—but one I had to ask.

A shamed look on his face, he shook his head, his white hair bouncing with the movement. ''I won't even drive anywhere close to the ocean. I used to work as a stonemason, I—I thought I'd try it again. But there was all this loud pounding the first day I walked on the job site. I tried to tell myself it wasn't the same thing, nothing like being at sea, but the noise made me feel so shaky and scared. I started breaking out in a cold sweat, and—and then I couldn't get away fast enough and I . . . I almost fainted.''

Like Kitty's response to the hospital. I felt my breath catch as I remembered her wide-eyed look of fear.

The last of the criteria for diagnosing PTSD requires that patients report at least one symptom related to reexperiencing the trauma: recurrent intrusive thoughts, flashbacks, repetitive nightmares, intense psychological distress on exposure to situations that resemble the traumatic event, or physiological reactivity to reminders of the trauma. Lou had textbook features across the board.

After he left, as I was walking out to greet my next patient, I pictured Kitty standing at my office window, her hands pressed against the screen, gulping air, beads of sweat dripping down her face. I remembered how she'd jumped at the sound of the door slamming in the hallway, her stories about her nightmares, her fearful avoidance of the hospital.

And I wondered about the gap in Kitty's memory—if there might be more missing than I'd heard so far.

Chapter 7

"Haley McAlister, let me introduce you to Fred Verlin,'' Jerome Pettit said when I walked into the Department of Anesthesiology's conference room late Tuesday afternoon.

No hair, anywhere. Jerome's description of Fred and alopecia totalis hadn't prepared me for the reality: Absolutely bald, not a shadow of a beard, no eyebrows or eyelashes, no hair on the backs of his pale, fleshy hands.

Sitting across the table, his thick black hair and bristly moustache a striking foil to the hairless man, Jerome said to Fred: "I told her about you." As Fred reddened, Jerome gave him a sardonic smile. "About your research, I mean—of course.''

Fred stood and held out his hand, scrutinizing me, his posture stiff, his face wary.

Waiting for my response to him, to his odd appearance, I realized. I tried hard to focus only on his eyes as I shook his hand, but it was difficult. Remarkably difficult.

"Austin said we had a lot to cover tonight, so I ordered a pizza,'' Fred said, gesturing toward an open box on the table. "You're welcome to have some.''

"That's very thoughtful—"

"Personally, I'm trying to watch my cholesterol." Jerome spoke loud enough to override my response.

"The oat bran and high fiber world of morality," Fred muttered, taking an enormous bite. Five-foot-eight, overweight by at least fifty pounds, he had a matronly feel about him even though he couldn't have been more than thirty-five.

The ham-and-pineapple pizza was as appealing to me as burnt toast, but I didn't want to reject his courtesy. "Thanks," I said, taking a piece, smiling at Fred, ignoring Jerome.

"I'm sorry to be late, I had a phone call," Austin Danziger said as he walked in, shutting the door behind him. "Nick had to see a patient, so he won't be joining us tonight, and Eva's out of town." Then, turning, "Fred, let's start with your talk for the site visit."

"I'm not entirely ready," Fred said as he thumbed through the pile of typed pages beside him. "I couldn't get the data together because of the lab mess—"

"Let's hear what you have," Austin said. "Stand at the end of the table. Pretend we're the site-visit team here to review the grant."

Pretend you're wounded, and you're swimming with sharks.

"I'll time you," Jerome said, taking off his watch, setting it in front of him. Pushing buttons on the keypad below the time display, he gave Fred a malicious smile: "I'll use the stopwatch function—to make sure it's accurate."

Fred gave him a venomous look, and I felt another burst of sympathy.

The entomologist I'd dated had worn a similar timepiece. After seeing his tick-infested rabbits, I was less than thrilled when he demonstrated how he'd added my phone number to its memory bank.

"I'll begin by describing the endocrine studies," Fred said. "On the morning of surgery, each patient will have an indwelling catheter placed in his arm for collection of serial blood samples . . ."

Like Clark Kent ducking into an alley, Fred was transformed as he talked about his research—standing straighter, his voice became more forceful, his gestures strong and confident. Obviously bright and knowledgeable, now he took on a remarkably dignified air for his age, becoming someone you'd trust if you were his patient, a researcher whose expertise would be respected by his colleagues.

A door slammed nearby, and I heard the sound of footsteps in the hallway and a man singing, "Oh, What a Beautiful Morning." Hardly sentiments I shared; I'd been feeling distinctly out of sorts lately—lonely, if the truth be known. With Glee Dennison absent because of a three-month Australian sabbatical and Quinton Gibbs away in Toronto on family business, I'd lost my major friends and confidants.

I'd gone out with several men in the last few months, but no one that I wanted to see more than a couple of times. I wasn't good at the casual affair—I couldn't make a connection that left me feeling vulnerable and then discover a man didn't see it as meaningful. Better to sleep alone than to feel that I'd been painting a portrait when a man only meant to snap a Polaroid and drive away.

"I thought I'd talk next about the preliminary data from my newest studies," Fred was saying. Austin had been sitting with his arms across his chest, listening attentively, and he nodded his approval. A second later Jerome yawned widely, theatrically; like a compass pointing north, Fred began casting anxious looks at Austin, seeking reassurance.

On the wall beside me, a silver-framed pen-and-ink drawing titled "Before Anesthesia" showed a patient tied to a table, straining against the ropes that bound him, his expression terrified, a man holding a knife poised over him.

Jerome must have followed the direction of my gaze. Leaning over, he whispered, "But we've come so far. Before we had decent anesthetics, patients shrieked through their surgery." A long look. "Just imagine how it was."

The image of Kitty lying paralyzed and conscious during surgery jerked me to attention, my heart beating fast. My mouth was hanging open, and Jerome was wearing his most sanctimonious expression when Austin turned to glare in our direction.

Coldly calculated savagery, if Murray was right. Could Jerome have been responsible?

I realized Fred had finished, and Jerome was speaking: "When you review a paper for a journal, you think about whether it should be rejected, accepted, or accepted with revisions. I think Fred's newer studies *probably* merit publication," he paused long enough to make his skepticism obvious, "but they could certainly benefit from *substantial* changes—"

"I didn't realize you were an expert in this area," Fred said. "Perhaps I missed something you've published?"

"You needn't be so defensive—"

"Surely you must have published *something* relevant—"

"Fred's presentation sounded very good to me—" Austin was saying when I heard a buzzing sound. Pulling his cellular phone out of the pocket of his white coat, he hurried out of the room, closing the door firmly behind him.

The last call I'd seen Austin take on his cellular phone had been the message about lab sabotage. Now Fred and Jerome sat frozen, staring at the door as if straining to listen.

In the silence I heard a door slam nearby, then the same baritone we'd heard earlier was singing "Mack the Knife" softly, the tune growing fainter as the sound of his steps receded.

"My wife," Austin said, walking back in the room, "reminding me that I'd promised to be home in time for company tonight—I'd forgotten. I'm sorry, but we'll have to reschedule."

"Of course. Anytime that's convenient for you," Jerome said. "Maybe I could talk with you as you're walking out. Some QA problems I've discovered . . ."

As Jerome scurried out in Austin's wake, Fred said to me, "You know how Jerome was criticizing my data? He's jealous. Austin made some complimentary remarks about my research in a faculty meeting not long after I'd joined the department. Afterward, Jerome asked me for copies of my articles, but not because he cared about my findings—he just wanted to count the number of pages in each paper. Then he wrote me a memo with a copy to Austin saying I should think about writing longer papers if I 'ever expected to be promoted.' "

"But you obviously made it—"

"Then, get this, I found out that Jerome had big problems when it came time for his own promotion and tenure. Great with minutiae, terrific with details—but zero creativity."

As I stood up, he said, "Jerome thinks of himself as doing all the important work, but the reality is that Austin gives him the junk jobs: overseeing the paperwork for appointments to the medical staff, chairing the department's Medical Records Committee, serving on the hospital QA Committee. A master of administrivia.''

"Thanks for the pizza—that was thoughtful of you.''

Ignoring the hint, he began digging around in the papers piled in front of him, pulling out a memo with pages stapled to it. ''This is his latest—and it's typical.'' He handed me a memo Jerome had written in his role as chair of the Anesthesiology Medical Records Committee.

re: DOCUMENTATION IN THE MEDICAL RECORD

Problems have continued because of INADEQUATE and UNTIMELY medical record completion. Below is a list of some of the issues that require your IMMEDIATE ATTENTION:

1. Sign and date all telephone and verbal orders.
2. Medical students or residents must write a final progress note.
3. Corrections in the record are to be done as a single line through the error, dated, and initialed.

PLEASE NOTE THESE ISSUES. IT IS MUCH EASIER TO COMPLETE THE RECORD CORRECTLY THE FIRST TIME.

Interesting that Fred found the memo so offensive—despite its tone, the content was eminently reasonable.

"Any time Jerome finds problems in a chart, he makes two copies: one for the faculty member, one for Austin,'' he said. ''Jerome doesn't want anyone else to look good in front of Austin. He's afraid someone else's glory might dim his own light by comparison—a realistic concern since he's operating with such low wattage.

"Something's happened—Jerome's always been a guilt-slinger, but he's gotten much worse lately. And now he's crowing that Austin will make him his second-in-command when he becomes Dean." For an instant, Fred's expression was despondent and forlorn—like someone talking about an unrequited love.

"I've got to—"

"Look . . . I know Jerome tells stories about me," he said. "Every chance, especially someone new, he wants to pollute the water."

Remembering the tale of how Fred had gotten caught in a sweep of prostitutes' customers, I shrugged noncommittally.

"A while back I had a . . . misunderstanding when I was away at a meeting—just the wrong place at the wrong time . . . No big deal, but he spread the story around, putting the worst possible spin on it, making sure that everyone drew the wrong conclusion." He looked at me closely, as if gauging my reaction.

"Sure," I said, taking a step toward the door.

"It's not just me," Fred said hurriedly. "Eva Aarastadt's also very good, so Jerome's been as unhelpful as possible to her. Have you met her yet?"

"No, and—"

"A very fine scientist. And a remarkable woman." His voice was earnest, and his cheeks had turned pink. "Talk to almost anyone, and you'll find that Jerome isn't a popular guy in the department. People learn fast that you don't walk by him and say something like, 'Nice day.' He'll make some crack about how he was too busy working to notice—something designed to make you feel guilty.

"He likes to police his colleagues' work habits. He'll wait until just before five o'clock to call to ask a question or schedule a meeting. And if you're not there, he'll make sure he leaves a message saying he was 'so sorry' to have missed you."

I could see how easily Fred would have become a prime target for a bully like Jerome.

"Another example: I got a note from Jerome, chastising me because I'd tossed one of those reusable campus envelopes in the trash where he'd spotted it. Two empty address slots left at the bottom, he pointed out. He's got the time to spend on that sort of thing." His tongue darted out, moistening his thick lips. "He wants to dictate exactly how everyone else does their work— or lives their life, when it comes down to it."

Snapping my fingers as if I'd just had a thought, I said, "Someone told me something recently that surprised me." I put on my most innocent expression. "Is music ever played in operating rooms?"

If he thought the question was strange, he didn't show it. "Some surgeons bring CD or tape players."

"One of the patients I was supposed to test for this project told me she remembered music playing during an earlier surgery. Is that possible?"

"Sure. I mean—at least some patients can hear even when they're well anesthetized."

"She had a really clear memory—she said it was barbershop music . . . and someone was humming the bass part, off-key."

"Means the surgeon had to be Redman," Fred said, clearing his throat. "He used to sing barbershop."

" 'Used to sing . . . '?"

"Dead, now. Had a stroke, back in April—and he was only fifty-two." He rolled his eyes. "*Exceptionally* arrogant, even for a surgeon, so he's not exactly an object of mourning.''

My shoulders drooped with the news. I'd been hoping to trace him to see if he remembered any details about Kitty's surgery. ''A stroke in a fifty-two-year-old man—were they certain about the cause of death?''

''They did an autopsy.'' Then his eyes widened, and he said, ''You should know what Jerome's already saying about you. He heard the story of how you found out that your patient's suicide was really a murder, so at the lab meeting this morning he was making jokes about how you wanted to know all about the lab sabotage, calling you 'Nancy Drew.' ''

Peachy. I thought about asking Fred about Kitty more directly, but decided against it. Not so soon after Jerome had been at work, polluting the well.

I didn't fancy Fred for Kitty's anesthesiologist for one simple reason: It was hard for me to believe that a man who was overweight himself would denigrate a plump woman quite so openly as Kitty's memories of her surgery suggested—or that her surgeon would have made such comments when Fred was the obvious comparison. Not exactly hard evidence; some men could be remarkably oblivious to their own flaws while focusing on every woman's shortcomings.

''Has the ketchup in the core lab been cleaned up yet?'' I asked.

For a minute, he looked like a frightened adolescent caught in mischief. ''How did you hear about that mess?''

''I walked in on it after Austin's secretary told me to meet Jerome there.''

Fred hesitated, then said, ''Austin's trying to keep the accidents quiet, but it's obviously not working.''

Accidents, he'd said. More than one. *Trying to keep them quiet.* Related to Kitty?

Trying to sound disinterested, I said, "Jerome told me it was an animal-rights activist."

"Right, that's just the kind of thing he'd say. I think he's behind it—at least part of it."

"Jerome?"

"Look at the facts." Fred was speaking with more animation than he'd shown during his talk. "Absolutely everyone in the lab but Jerome used to drink coffee when we had lab meetings. So, big surprise, he was the only person who didn't spend his day vomiting and having diarrhea after sodium fluoride landed in the coffeepot."

Jerome's voice echoed in my mind: *Set out poison to get rid of the vermin.* I could see him fouling the coffeepot, acting smug when everyone else got sick.

But maybe Jerome was the real target. Perhaps someone like Fred was trying to make Jerome look like the prankster.

"Why are you so sure it was deliberate?" I gave Fred my best skeptical look.

"There was a typed note beside the coffeepot the next morning: 'Coffee flavored by sodium fluoride.' A warning that it could've been much, much worse—that stuff can be deadly in larger doses."

Making sure the sabotage wasn't mistaken for simple bad luck.

When we'd first met to discuss his Center grant, Austin had referred to his group as his research "team," the word implying comradery and shared purpose. Not what I'd seen thus far.

But maybe that was the goal of the joker. If the tricks meant that you began to doubt who could be trusted, that you suspected each of your colleagues in turn, that you worried who might be trying to sabotage you—then the pranks that were poisoning the atmosphere of Austin's research group were indeed remarkably malicious—and effective.

"I don't think it's any coincidence that Eva and I got hit hardest by this latest disaster," Fred said. "I'm between grants, so I don't have anyone who works exclusively for me—I really need some technical support, and the girl who was scheduled to run experiments for us had to mop up the ketchup instead . . . another reason I think Jerome's behind it."

"Did you call hospital security?"

Watching Fred's face go blank, I knew immediately I'd said the wrong thing. "Not much they could have done, under the circumstances," he said, looking away. "Water under the bridge."

Of course. I was missing the obvious: Austin wouldn't have wanted the gossip that could follow a visit by hospital security. With his eye on the Dean's position, he needed to maintain the air of being in control, of managing a well-run ship.

Accidents, Fred had said: *plural.*

The anesthesiology laboratories were a dangerous playground for a prankster on the prowl.

Chapter 8

"I got the patient information you need to check out the problem," I said to Jerome Pettit on Wednesday afternoon. We were standing in the hallway outside the core lab; stopping by without warning, I'd run into him here. "Her name was—"

"Not here," he said, looking over his shoulder as he smoothed his black bottle-brush moustache. "We're not far from my office, and I'll need to write down the information."

Seated across from him, I said, "The patient's name was Katherine Evanston." I paused, watching Jerome closely as I spoke: "Kitty Evanston. Her surgery was on February 14."

Blinking rapidly, Jerome looked away; after a brief hesitation, he pulled a green note card out of the pocket of his white coat and started writing on it. "Hospital number?"

Not a word about knowing Kitty when she'd worked in his department.

"I schedule anesthesiologists for hundreds of surgeries a month—" he was saying, when someone knocked on his door, and he jumped. He paused long enough to make me wonder if he was going to answer before calling out, "It's open." As I looked toward the door, I saw him turn the green note card facedown.

The man standing in the doorway wore a black-and-white houndstooth-checked jacket over a white shirt and gray slacks. Tall and trim, midforties, his face still had a boyish look. As he brushed back the shock of silky blond hair falling down his forehead, our eyes met and held. Blue eyes. A bright, vibrant blue. Attractive. Very attractive.

"You missed Fred's presentation last night," Jerome said to him.

"I missed the session because I'd just found out we had a possible research subject for today and I had to see her right away." The blond man looked from Jerome to me, his tone mild. "I need to talk to Eva about this patient, and I can't find her anywhere; have you seen her?"

"She's out of town—she missed the session as well."

The blond man looked at me again, a glance that spoke of his exasperation with Jerome at first, then faded into something else. His face was square, his Roman nose slightly crooked, his eyebrows thick and golden brown.

"Austin cut the practice session short," I said. "You didn't miss much."

"Maybe, but I am sorry . . ." Rocking back and forth on his heels, jingling coins in his pocket, he smiled at me. "I'm Nick Treece—"

"We *are* busy, if you don't mind," Jerome said.

As soon as the door had closed, Jerome said, "Nick came here for a sabbatical while he's working out his divorce . . . a messy parting, so I've heard."

I schooled my face into what I hoped was polite inquiry with only mild interest. "About Kitty Evanston—"

"I'll look into it as soon as I can. With the site visit coming up, I've got plenty on my plate. Frankly, I'm very worried about keeping our Center grant. We've got to get data, we're behind schedule . . . and I've gotten word that the animal-rights fanatics have targeted Dr. Danziger's lab."

"Really?" Fred Verlin thought Jerome was the culprit—if he was right, was Jerome setting the stage for more "accidents"?

"I worry that they've got inside information," he said. "The saboteurs knew exactly how to get the technician out of the lab long enough to do their dirty work."

"Who do you think—"

"I'm not prepared to make accusations without proof," he said, picking up two paper clips from his desk and linking them together, "but . . . Fred's been having big problems getting his experiments to work. Now he's got an excuse for not having data. *Very* convenient."

His tone caught me short. Off-key, not right?

"I've got a plan to get irrefutable evidence," Jerome added, after a long pause.

Looking at his drawn face, I knew what hadn't sounded right—the note of fear in his voice.

In that moment, I saw Jerome in a different light. I didn't know if he was lashing out as a way of coping, if he was pointing out his colleagues' misdeeds as a way of protecting himself—but he was clearly frightened about something.

A handsome man in his midtwenties with broad shoulders, curly black hair, blue eyes magnified by tortoiseshell glasses, even a perfect cleft in his chin,

Perry Urbay had the look of a man who would have pledged the "best" fraternity in college, the type who would remember the brotherhood's secret handshake and use it often, the kind who'd been elected fraternity president and would eventually be a CEO.

As with many things in life, his appearance was deceptive.

"I have those dreams where I'm about to take an exam when I realize I haven't attended the class, I haven't even opened the textbook," Perry said, as we were walking to my office late Wednesday afternoon to review his work for the week. "Those are bad enough— I wake up in a cold sweat and can't get back to sleep half the time—but last night I had a new version."

A second-year graduate student, Perry was working toward his goal of becoming a psychologist in the face of strong opposition from his father, a high-powered lawyer. Over the nine months we'd been working together, I'd developed a lot of affection for him—and respect.

"Last night I dreamed that I'd somehow forgotten to see a patient assigned to me—I'd never even scheduled her intake interview."

Perry was responsible for administering psychological tests for the anesthesiology project. After considering the three psychometrists who worked under my supervision, I'd selected him for the job.

As we passed Rugton's lecture hall, Perry stopped short. The Eichon drug representative had left literature on their latest antidepressant spaced strategically around a tray of bagels and cream cheese on a table beside the door.

"No lunch today," he said apologetically.

Using his thumb and forefinger to pick up the bread

knife sitting beside the slab of cream cheese, he grimaced as he cleaned the remnants of cream cheese from the blade with a napkin. He wadded up the napkin and threw it away, then got a second and polished the blade, then the handle, then his fingers. He used the knife as a shovel to move several bagels from the top of the pile, picking up one that had been buried at the very bottom.

"Wish I could wash it first," he said, eyeing it cautiously before lifting it to his mouth. And then, grinning at me just before he took a bite, he added, "That's a joke."

I raised my eyebrows.

"Well, it would be nice—"

I'd asked Perry to handle the testing personally because he'd be careful and thorough, crossing every "t" at least twice. And I needed someone who'd be absolutely meticulous—particularly in recording answers to the questions I'd added, the ones that weren't part of the standard anesthesiology protocol, the inquires for each patient's first postsurgical assessment: *What was your last memory before going to sleep for your surgery? What was your first memory when you awakened after your operation? Do you remember anything that happened between?* And the key one: *Do you remember any dreams or fragments of dreams during the time you were anesthetized?*

"It's such a *relief* to get back to sanity," Quinton Gibbs informed me as we were walking out to the parking lot after work on Wednesday. A psychiatrist in his midfifties, he'd been a mentor and good friend since I joined the department thirteen years ago. "One of my mother-in-law's friends kept bragging about how she'd never told her physician she smokes like a chimney—even though she has allergic asthma."

Brilliant and more than a little eccentric, Quinton was the kind of man who remembered every patient he'd ever seen and every professional article he'd ever read—despite the fact that he had enormous difficulty recalling where he'd last laid his glasses, or if he'd eaten lunch. Describing him as "high-maintenance," Sue, his wife, made a habit of calling him midday to remind him to get some food. Reluctantly leaving Sue behind in Toronto, where his mother-in-law was recuperating from surgery, he'd returned to Houston last night after six days away.

"One of Sue's aunts hasn't spoken to anyone in the family for ten years because she was relegated to the fifth car in a funeral possession, not the first or second," he said, rolling his eyes. "On Saturday she showed up at the hospital to tell us that she's cut everyone out of her will."

Even if he hadn't told me, I'd have known his wife was out of town by the way he was dressed: an ancient tweed sport coat with leather patches, a wrinkled white shirt, a flowered cotton tie narrower than the current fashion—and faded green golf slacks. A truly lovely man with a genuine fondness for people, he never knew what to wear when his wife didn't lay out his clothes.

At a tiny family-run restaurant in Bellaire that serves authentic, down-home Tex-Mex, the meat smoked out back over mesquite, we both ordered the chicken and rib combo. It came with potato salad and pinto beans, soft white bread, sour pickles, onion slices, and hot sauce on the side.

"Something's bothering you," he said, once we'd been served.

Quinton had seen Kitty's videotape during Murray's Grand Rounds lecture, so he already knew something about her. As he attacked his food with an intensity that made me wonder if he'd missed lunch again, I told him the rest of the story, ending with her death in the ER.

"That's really ugly, if it's true." Then, looking closely at me, he said, "I get the impression that you feel responsible, somehow."

When I nodded, he said, "If I had to guess, I'd say Murray's probably right—it fits with the way she looked on the tape—but either way, I don't know what more you could have done." Punctuating his point, he waved a rib, one he'd just slathered with extra sauce; a glop flew off and landed on the front of his white shirt.

Looking at his pleasant, open face as he tried to sponge off the splotch, I felt a rush of affection for him; I could understand why patients and staff alike sought him out. I'd heard the story of a teenage karate expert who'd been hospitalized recently on Quinton's inpatient unit after destroying the interior of his parents' house with his bare hands; the boy had been looking for the microphones he knew were hidden there, the ones that picked up his thoughts and broadcast them to the world. When he started attacking the hospital walls, male attendants converged on him, each holding a foam mattress as a shield until the patient was surrounded by a ring of mattresses so he could be subdued. Arriving in the middle of the scene, Quinton waded in, saying, "Boys, let's not play so rough." The patient, responding to Quinton's mild voice and calm authority, had quieted down and taken his medication without protest.

Now I told him about the core-lab pranks, the rancor in Austin's research group, and my concern that they were somehow related to Kitty's death. "It feels like I've stumbled into a nest of vipers. Do you know any of the players?"

"I met Austin when I subbed for Kurt on the executive committee. He's pretty authoritarian as a chair, but his faculty generally speak highly of him. When he took over, his department was in shambles; he created order out of chaos.''

And made his share of enemies along the way.

''Last fall Jerome and I were on the animal-investigations committee,'' he said, referring to the university panel that had to approve all research activity involving animals. ''He'd stand up for experiments he thought had promise, even if half the members were hot to disapprove them—and even when, in a couple of cases, he obviously loathed the investigator in charge of the project. Once he had his teeth in an issue, he wouldn't let go. In the end, he generally convinced the majority to vote along with him.'' Taking a sip of iced tea, he stared at his plate as if amazed to find it nearly empty. ''Jerome's behavior didn't endear him to the animal-rights types who monitored the committee's activity.''

''So Jerome could be the real target for the lab pranks?''

''Maybe . . . but the mischief doesn't have the activists' signature—they're not big on subtleties.''

I nodded, remembering stories of malicious raids that had destroyed years of careful work—file cabinets jimmied open, their contents doused with paint, computers demolished, lab notebooks shredded—labs trashed beyond redemption.

''There's another possibility, although it may be a bit far-fetched,'' he said. ''Because anesthesiologists have easy access to so many interesting drugs, a number get hooked—among medical specialties, it's at the top of the list for drug abuse.''

A teenager wearing a purple blouse and black satin shorts shuffled past us to the take-out counter, her attention focused on the bubble she was blowing with her gum; it was half as large as her head when it burst and smeared across her mouth.

"Some of the drugs would be hard to detect because they wouldn't alter behavior dramatically," he continued. "I saw one fellow after he got caught and was forced to seek treatment. He claimed he could be as high as a kite when he was using fentanyl—it's a narcotic, the drug of choice for addicts in anesthesiology—and yet still be totally functional. Maybe Kitty's anesthesiologist was taking something that seriously impaired his judgment."

Hardly a reassuring prospect. "If the drugs don't alter behavior dramatically, how do drug abusers get caught?"

"Usually they're cadging drugs from normal supplies, and colleagues or nurses notice things like high drug wastage or heavy use of adjuvant drugs. Or they'll notice that someone always wears long sleeves—covering up so no one will see where they've been injecting. If things look suspicious, they can pull the doc's anesthesia records and look for a pattern."

His words triggered the memory of Jerome's office, his couch piled high with patients' charts: *I've found a surprising number of faculty who act like they're above the rules*, he'd said.

As we talked, Quinton had been stacking packets of sugar like miniature bricks, building a wall. He'd once described himself as hyperactive as a child, a label that wasn't inconsistent with his fidgety style, his inability to sit still for any length of time. Now, as he set the last of the packets on top, the structure collapsed. Smiling at his comic expression of dismay, I said, "Fred Verlin intimated that Jerome was behind the tricks."

"I don't know Jerome well, but I'd guess that he's too much of a stickler for pranks like polluting the coffee. He takes his responsibilities very seriously—he's a fanatic about making sure the minutes for any meeting are exactly correct—and I gathered that he spends hours working on his lectures and tutoring any student who asks for help. Not warm and fuzzy, but he gets the job done.''

I was about to ask if he thought Jerome might act differently if he were frightened and fighting back when Quinton's beeper went off. Returning from the phone, he apologized for needing to return to Rugton right away; the teenage karate expert was refusing his medication and tapping on the walls again in a way that was making the on-call resident very nervous.

As I drove home, Quinton's farewell stayed in my mind: ''The accidents in the lab have a bad smell about them. But with Kitty, it's something altogether different—to rig an anesthetic would be monstrous.'' Touching my arm, he'd said, ''I'm concerned that you're getting too close to something that could be dangerous.''

Chapter 9

"**I** don't understand why I have to talk to *you*," Davy Crockett Bayless informed me as he stood in my office doorway on Thursday afternoon. "I've already been through all this with a shrink who knows his stuff: I got PTSD after the *Phoenix* sank—terrible flashbacks and nightmares. It's really stressed me out. What else do you need to know?" Twenty-eight years old, no taller than five-six, he had a buzz cut like a new army recruit. His black muscle shirt and tiny blue shorts strained against muscles so overdeveloped that they verged on grotesque.

"Mr. Bayless, I can't interview you effectively if you're bellowing at me," I said. "Please sit in that chair, and we'll talk about how you're feeling."

Glowering, he hesitated a long moment before he took a seat.

"I'd like to tape the interview—"

"Yeah, OK. Look, let me start out by telling you the story of how the *Phoenix* went down—then maybe you'll understand why I've got PTSD."

"That's fine." From his file I'd learned that he'd enlisted in the army after high school because he thought it would be like the movies and he'd be a hero, like his namesake—but his personal history had been something less than heroic thus far. Booted out of the service with a dishonorable discharge, his erratic work record included assorted construction jobs before he'd joined the crew of the *Phoenix*. He'd managed to marry and divorce twice between the ages of twenty-two and twenty-five; he had one child by his first wife, another with a woman he hadn't married.

"It was a *terrible* time—stormy, waves crashing on the deck, thunder and lightning all over the place," he said. "We were short-handed; the captain should never have gone out when we didn't have enough men, not in that kind of weather. That's part of the reason it's the company's fault, you know—" His tone monotonous, he stared at the wall as if reading off it.

"It was stormy when you first set out?"

"Stormy, waves crashing on the deck, thunder and lightning all over the place. And we were short-handed." As he spoke he ran his fingers along a six-inch scar on his left forearm.

"The nets were full, and we were trying to haul them in," he said. "Then something happened, I'm not sure what, maybe a really huge wave just when the nets were so full—and the boat started to roll over. One of the guys yelled that we should grab hold of the life raft, and then we were in the water, trying to climb inside it. The *Vantage* picked us up a while later—and I've had PTSD ever since."

Similar to the story I'd heard from Lou Ramsey, but Davy told the tale with all the emotion of a dead minnow. "Who was in the raft?"

"All of us—everyone except the captain, of course. We were all rescued." He gave me a condescending smile. "I would've thought they'd have told you that much, at least."

"Who got in the raft first?"

"Vince—or maybe Willie, I didn't see which one. That's Vince Gambier and Willie O'Rourke, you haven't met them yet. And then me and Gary Jenkins." Crossing his arms over his chest, he said, "Gary is really a flake—I'm surprised he actually made it back OK. His elevator doesn't reach the top floor, if you know what I mean. He's got big-time problems with booze and pills— half the time he's so pickled he doesn't know what's happening.

"And then there's Lou Ramsey. Lou's always been suspicious, a paranoid kind of guy. Something about him's just a little bit off—probably why he never got along well with anyone. Maybe he got hit in the head or something when the *Phoenix* went down, but he wasn't in his right mind—we were trying to pick him up and he just kept swimming away from the raft, acting like he didn't see us."

Leaning forward, he said, "Both of them are real losers—know what I mean?"

"Would you go back over what happened when the ship started to roll?"

"Why does that matter?"

"There are some things I didn't quite follow. I want to make sure I get the details straight."

He sat cracking his knuckles, watching me, taking his time before he finally started speaking: "Like I said, we had this really big wave when the nets were full, maybe we could've handled it if we weren't so short-handed— and the boat just started to roll over. One guy yelled that we should take hold of the life raft . . . then we were in the water, trying to climb inside the raft."

Bingo. Exactly the response I'd expected.

"I don't want to talk about it anymore," he said. "Talking about it makes my nightmares worse."

"That's fine. Tell me about your nightmares."

His expression smug, he said, "I keep dreaming of the ship sinking, over and over. Every night, the exact same scene—sometimes more than once."

Interesting. "What happens—"

"And then I wake up and can't get back to sleep. It's terrible, not ever getting enough sleep, no way I can go back to work when I feel like this."

So distraught after the *Phoenix* sank that he hadn't been able to work—but not so incapacitated that he couldn't spend hours lifting weights each week? "Earlier you mentioned you had flashbacks. What kinds of—?"

"Lots of flashbacks. It was lightning and thundering like crazy. Now, I hear a noise on the street, anything loud like thunder, it's like I'm right there again, feeling the boat tilting under my feet."

"And then what happens to you?"

He sat up straighter, his expression wary. "What do you mean?"

"You said, 'It's like I'm right there again, feeling the boat tilting under my feet.' What happens when you feel like that?"

"I can't go back to work," he said, his voice rising. "I'm just too traumatized. And I'm not feeling well, your questions are really upsetting me."

"I'm sorry, but it is necessary. If you prefer, we can schedule another time—"

"No, let's get the damn thing out of the way!"

A while later I asked, "Have you ever been in trouble with the law?"

"Not really . . ."

I picked up a folder beside me and started leafing through it as if looking for something, mostly thinking about the fact that the hamburger I'd gotten for lunch was sitting heavy in my stomach.

"Look," he said, biting his lip, "this was back a couple years ago, and it wasn't my fault."

Of course. Setting aside the file, I asked, "What happened?"

"I was in a car accident, and my girlfriend got hurt, that's all."

"How'd she get hurt?"

"We were driving home from a party. This jerk pulled out in front of me and I couldn't stop in time. When I rear-ended him, I had my gun on the front seat and it went off, somehow—my girlfriend took a bullet in her arm."

"You had a gun on the front seat?"

"The party was in a bad part of town." He shrugged. "I didn't want any problems."

"I guess I just don't quite understand. Your girlfriend was in the front seat and the gun went off. What kind of trouble did you have with the law?"

"My girlfriend—ex-girlfriend, now—was pretty drunk. She told the cops I'd shot her because I was jealous." Looking away, he touched the scar on his arm. "Like I said, it wasn't my fault, but I ended up in jail for a couple of months anyway."

"Do you take any medication regularly?"

His head came up and he ran his fingers across the pimples that peppered his chest about his muscle shirt. "Not really . . ."

"If we looked into your medicine cabinet at home, what would we find?" Steroids, I was betting. Consistent with his muscles and his temper.

"I'm healthy—except for my PTSD." The tendons were standing out on his thick neck and his fists were clenched. "Why are you asking me all these questions?

The first shrink didn't have to ask so many things—I guess he knew a lot more than you—''

"Maybe he did," I said, nodding. "Let's go back to your time in the army—''

"What does that have to do with my PTSD problems?''

"Your life didn't start with the *Phoenix*.'' Symptoms like insomnia or nightmares might be lifelong patterns, rather than a consequence of the trauma. Or they might be the echoes of other stressors in his life.

And then I remembered Kitty's evasiveness when I'd asked if anything else had been happening around the time of her surgery.

A half hour later he swaggered out of my office, and I began drafting my report.

Lots of things didn't ring true. He'd been so proud of his repetitive dream—but genuine PTSD nightmares usually show variations on the theme of the traumatic event, not just continual reenactment. When I'd asked Davy to go back over parts of his story, he'd repeated the same stock phrases—which left me wondering why he'd rehearsed—and what he'd needed to guard.

Feigning illness wasn't a new problem; I remembered stories of how Roman conscripts would cut off fingers to make themselves unfit for military service. Hardly a strategy that would have appealed to Davy, a man so charmed by his own body.

I wondered if he'd heard the stories about how steroids shrivel testicles.

Chapter 10

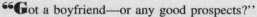

"Got a boyfriend—or any good prospects?"

Friday afternoon, unprepared for Thelma Lou's direct frontal attack, I made a serious strategic error: as a diversion, I picked up one of the homemade cookies from the plate on her desk.

"Thanks for the treat," I said, studying the cookie with trepidation. Lumpy, or were those raisins?

Our clinic receptionist's episodic memory problems, a legacy from a close encounter with lightning some years ago, meant that she often left vital ingredients out, like sugar—or forgot and added twice the salt. Diabetic, she never tasted the final product herself.

Thelma Lou was the kind of woman who always had a cache of seasonally appropriate cocktail napkins: turkeys and Pilgrims near Thanksgiving, Santas in December. Independence Day was still two weeks away, but the napkin she handed me was covered with pictures of exploding fireworks.

"Got plans for the July Fourth weekend?" She peered up at me over the top of her reading glasses.

I tried not to wince as I made a show of sampling the

cookie. Today the lumps were baking soda. "Delicious, as usual."

Feeling a surge of affection mixed with guilt as she beamed at the compliment, I pointed at the frame on her desk that held the latest Polaroid snapshot of Greta, the cement goose who sat beside Thelma Lou's front door. "What a cute outfit." Today Greta was wearing a miniature red top hat perched on her head and an apron with blue stars tied around her waist. And then, before she could return to her original line of questioning: "Know anyone in the Department of Anesthesiology?"

"I could manage," she said, her tone complacent. With the kind of natural warmth that inspired confidences, she'd built up a formidable intelligence network during her twenty years in the medical center.

"A woman named Kitty Evanston used to work in Anesthesiology," I said. "She died recently, heart problems, she'd come to the clinic once—"

"The woman who came for the research project who wanted you to meet her outside?" In her fifties, short and wide, Thelma Lou's taste in clothes veered heavily toward pastels and ruffles. Her latest efforts to arrange her hair in the early Farrah Fawcett–style achieved a resemblance near enough to be obvious, if not close.

"That's the one. I'd like to know how long she worked there and what she did there."

"I'll ask around. Why—"

Just then a woman walked up to the reception desk to check in for her appointment, giving me the opportunity to fade into the woodwork. I was hoping Thelma Lou's friends might add some color to the black-and-white data I'd requested.

On my way to the computers in the biomed library, I passed the glass case that held part of the library's history of medicine collection. From a collection of wax models used for teaching medical students in the early nineteenth century, the most recent display included a woman's head that was cut open just above her eyebrows to show her brain in cross section; her eyes were closed, her expression peaceful. Nothing like the image of Kitty's face, tear-stained and twisted in terror, that kept intruding on my thoughts.

I started out by looking for references to anesthesia and memory. Murray had claimed that hearing could remain intact even with adequate anesthesia. Austin had told me that most of the memories recalled after anesthesia were false—just bad dreams produced by the anesthetic. I wanted to read enough to make my own judgment.

The first two articles I found said that patients could be well anesthetized and still hear conversation. Depending on the type of anesthetic and kind of surgery, maybe 1 to 2 percent of patients had vague memories.

But even without any conscious memories of surgery, the brain can register important messages that affect behavior.

In an older study, one that would never have gotten approved by a human subjects review committee these days, a dental surgeon had deliberately made a false statement during surgery about serious problems to ten patients who were receiving an ether anesthetic. None of the patients had any conscious memory when questioned after the surgery, but four patients gave near-verbatim descriptions when hypnotized; instructions to remember the surgery during hypnosis had evoked marked discomfort in four more.

Which still meant that Kitty's hearing could have been intact—but the rest of her story might have been a ''bad dream'' like Austin had suggested, a product of her anesthetic.

I went to check the computerized listings to see if the library had some of the more obscure medical journals I needed. On the far wall above the row of computers was a sign: PLEASE DO NOT EAT, FEED, DEVOUR, GULP, DINE, NIBBLE, GNAW, DRINK, IMBIBE, QUAFF, SIP, SUP, TIPPLE, SMOKE, CHEW, OR SPIT IN THE LIBRARY.

Underneath the sign I saw a man eating a candy bar as he scowled at the computer screen in front of him. Nick Treece, the man with the corn-silk hair I'd seen in Jerome's office. I watched him for a minute, remembering the glance we'd shared when Jerome was scolding him. He didn't look up.

Half an hour later I'd found a series of articles that told about patients who'd not been adequately anesthetized, all because of technical failures—a pulmonary ventilator that delivered room air because it wasn't firmly attached to the machine, an empty nitrous-oxide tank, the simultaneous failure of nitrous oxide and cyclopropane when the cylinders ran out.

Because there's no definitive way to verify that a paralyzed patient is unconscious, the problems hadn't been discovered until after surgery.

But what about Kitty? Could she really have been paralyzed but not adequately anesthetized during her operation?

I read case studies of patients who hadn't been given enough anesthetic. Some became irritable and anxious, a number reported repetitive nightmares.

Some anesthetics induce postoperative amnesia, so patients don't remember any problems afterward, I learned. And more than one writer suggested that awakening while paralyzed produces such overwhelming stress that the patient may later be amnesic for surgical memories.

Kitty's nightmares had begun after her surgery. She'd

said her jumpiness started after her surgery.

I read about malpractice suits filed because of inadequate anesthesia; more common in Great Britain, far from unknown in this country. Much of the work I read was older, and several writers made the point that newer equipment had additional safeguards for mechanical problems—but nothing was fail-safe.

Had the problems during Kitty's surgery resulted from a simple equipment failure? It would have been a credible possibility if it weren't for Kitty's prior harassment—and the gloating whisper afterward.

I stopped, unable to shake the feeling that I was missing something obvious in what I'd read. As I sat trying to capture the wisp of an idea, I had an odd feeling of someone watching me, a creepiness around my shoulders. Someone standing close behind me, looking over my shoulder at the books and articles fanned around me on the table.

I turned suddenly and looked up into the blue eyes I remembered from Jerome's office, the same apologetic expression he'd worn when talking to Jerome. Nick Treece.

"You're Haley McAlister, right? I saw you in Jerome's office. When I ran into him later he told me you're part of the Center grant team—we'll be working together."

Nick's handshake was strong, his eyes holding mine as he introduced himself. "May I join you for a minute?"

I nodded as I stacked up the articles I'd copied, putting my notepad facedown over the top of the pile. Not much I could do with the books except push them to the side, turning them so their titles weren't in full view. I felt my face flush as I looked down and saw the seam gaping in the side of my dress. Running late because I'd overslept this morning, I'd thrown on a navy silk dress, only noticing the problem when I got to my office. I'd tried to close the split with a couple of safety pins. Now I pressed my arm against my side, hoping it covered the gap.

"Jerome always manages to make me feel like I'm in second grade," Nick said. "I'd sent word that I'd be missing the meeting because a patient had just been admitted that I needed to see. Jerome made it sound like I'd been negligent, that I'd missed something important—so I wanted to thank you for telling me that Dr. Danziger had cut the meeting short."

"Jerome plays the same number with me." I was finding it hard to meet his eyes.

"When I moved here at the beginning of March, I dropped by the department a week before my formal start date to say hello and leave my local address and phone. Jerome came in the office when I was talking to Dr. Danziger's secretary. First thing he said after we were introduced was that they were short-handed, so he'd add my name to the call schedule right away; I told him I'd come early to set up my apartment and get together with old friends. In a real nasty voice, he said, 'Did you come here to socialize or to work?' "

So Nick wouldn't have known Kitty—or had any connection with her surgery. "Vintage Jerome," I said.

He shook his head and his hair flopped down on his forehead. "I didn't want to get off on the wrong foot with new colleagues . . . Finally I said, 'As long as you put it that way, I guess I'll start sooner.' " He had a wonderful voice, deep and resonant. And sexy.

Looking at the journals piled on the table, he asked, "Reading about anesthesia?"

"Just finishing up a lit search for my part of the grant."

"Anything I can answer for you?"

Watching his lips, I'd been wondering how he would kiss. "You—uh, you mentioned you'd missed the practice session because you were seeing one of the study patients. Would an anesthesiologist normally meet a patient before surgery?"

"Usually, if it's not an emergency. Some anesthetics wipe out memories of things that happened just before the operation. As a demonstration for med students, I'll sometimes ask patients to remember a color and a shape—like green and a star—when I meet with them prior to their surgery; afterward, maybe half won't have a clue when I ask if they have any recollection. That's why I need to see research participants far enough in advance of their surgery to explain the study and get them to sign the consent form."

"I've been doing all the talking," Nick said. "What kind of research were you doing before you got caught up with anesthesiology?"

"I study lies," I said.

His mouth half-open, Nick gave me a searching look, as if checking to see if I was making a joke. Then he looked down, speaking to his hands: "How interesting."

As I walked into Rugton the next morning, I was thinking about what I'd read in the library. Kitty's story was certainly plausible, but—

Pausing in the stairwell, I saw another possibility clearly for the first time: *What if her anesthesiologist was the primary target, not Kitty herself?* Someone with no responsibility for her surgery could have made an educated guess about probable anesthetic choices and rigged the equipment accordingly. If I was right, the trickster was the winner whether or not Kitty survived her operation—in either case, her surgical problems were designed to impeach her anesthesiologist's competence. The saboteur's whisper at the end, a scene probably staged in the recovery room, was meant to be the last nail in the coffin, a way to ensure that Kitty's difficulties wouldn't be attributed to a simple accident.

And the plan only failed when the unexpected happened: Kitty survived her surgery with no conscious memory of any problems.

If someone had already gone so far as to rig Kitty's anesthetic, what would he try next?

Digging in my purse for my office keys, I didn't look up until I was only a few feet away from my office.

Stopping short, I stared at my door—and then began backing away, my hand covering my mouth.

Someone had posted a black human silhouette printed on a white background, a standard target like the ones you might see at a shooting range.

This one had a hypodermic needle stabbed in the vicinity of the heart.

Holding my breath, the only sound I heard was the distant whirring of an elevator. Eight o'clock on a Saturday morning and the hallway was empty except for me.

Put up sometime late last night or very early this morning, the logical part of my mind was saying. Only a moment's work for someone to unfold the target, stick a couple of pieces of clear tape at the top to attach it to the door . . . and then remove the protective sheath from a hypodermic secreted in the pocket of a white coat.

I tried to tell my heart to slow down to normal, but it wasn't listening.

Forcing myself to approach slowly, I kept looking around to assure myself that I was truly alone in the empty corridor.

I felt a chill down my neck as I read the words printed in block letters across the top of the target.

In retrospect, everything up to that point had been the prologue, the warm-up act, the calm before the storm.

The message was short and direct: DANGEROUS TO PLAY NANCY DREW.

Chapter 11

"**L**et me tell you my latest managed-care horror story," the man was saying to his companion. "This morning I saw a guy in the ER who had just tried to hang himself, he was already unconscious by the time his wife found him—he's got rope burns around his neck from the noose, and that's the least of his problems. So I'm on the phone trying to get authorization for a measly two-day psychiatric admission, and his insurance rep's asking me, 'What's his white cell count?' "

The Saturday night party at the university's Faculty Club honored the people who'd made big donations to the medical school. The invitations for Western Night, hosted by the Office of Development, the fund-raisers, featured a coiled rattlesnake on the cover—an all-too-apt image for the evening, as it turned out. Waiting to order a drink at the bar, I was eavesdropping on the conversation of a couple dressed in matching black-satin rodeo shirts.

"Verbrugge doesn't look so good; I heard he's finally scheduled his bypass surgery for July." The man in front of me pointed toward the Dean, who was standing with a group near the entrance.

"Who's the lucky surgeon?" the woman asked, laughing. "Lots of folks would like the chance to take a piece out of his hide—and are they going to let him stay overnight, or kick him out as soon as he's been carved?"

As they moved away, the bartender greeted me heartily, recommending the margaritas. "Texas-size," he announced in a booming voice, tipping his Stetson as he passed me one in a tall green glass shaped like a cactus.

Nodding hello, Jerome Pettit sidled up beside me, his thick black eyebrows raised superciliously at my oversize drink. To the bartender, he said, "Mineral water, no ice. And, *please*, make sure the glass is clean."

My stomach muscles tensed as he turned to me. DANGEROUS TO PLAY NANCY DREW, the message had warned. Left by Jerome himself, assuming I wouldn't have heard what he'd been saying? Or had someone else adopted his nickname for me?

"That's Eva Aarastadt," he said, pointing toward a blond woman among the dancing couples on the nearby patio. "You haven't met her yet because she's been out of town again, the third time in a month—so other people have ended up covering her load, as usual." His tone was scornful, but his eyes followed her.

Moving with an energy that commanded attention, an intensity that hinted at strong emotions, she stared past her partner, flicking her long straight hair back with her hand, her high cheekbones complementing her air of aristocratic hauteur. Her straight back spoke of a woman used to being noticed, to taking charge. Wearing a red cotton shirt, a red-and-blue gauze skirt, and dainty red high-heeled cowboy boots, she looked like a fair-haired gypsy queen, regal and exotic. Even though the way she danced wasn't provocative, there was something uncommonly sensual about her—a mermaid disguised for traveling on land but still smelling so strongly of the sea that no man would ever mistake her for a mortal.

"A me-me-me, mine-mine-mine kind of woman," Jerome said. Half-turned from the dancers, his eyes darted over the moving couples with the air of someone observing odd foreign customs—but his gaze kept returning to Eva.

The invitation had said "Western dress." Garbed in a rumpled white shirt, a red tie, and brown polyester slacks, Jerome was one of the few people who had made no effort to add a Western touch to his clothes. I was wearing jeans tucked into black cowboy boots, a blue-and-purple plaid Western shirt adorned with pearl-headed snaps, and a bolo tie with a silver slide. Still jittery after my discovery this morning, I would have felt more comfortable in a chain-mail suit.

I'd called hospital security after finding the target, only to be told that they were short-handed and occupied with more pressing problems; optimistically, someone might be able to come over around noon—but unless something had been stolen or damaged, there was little they could do.

Afraid that patients or visitors might stumble across the display, I'd donned rubber gloves before taking it down and stashing it in a drawer—and then packed my briefcase and headed home, where I could work without jumping at every little noise.

"Anything you mention, she knows something about it," Jerome said, waving his hand dismissively as he stared at Eva. "As preposterous as those eight-page menus you find in hole-in-the-wall Chinese restaurants—you know there's no way she could really do everything she claims."

She looked over as Jerome gestured in her direction,

her animosity obvious as she looked from Jerome to me. *Guilt by association.*

The sky had been darkening in the west as clouds moved in. Now, lines of lightning blazed a warning. "Looks like a storm coming up," I said.

Glancing over, I caught sight of Fred Verlin standing nearby, his eyes fixed on Eva. He was so engrossed by her, he appeared oblivious to the attention he was drawing from a nearby couple, unconscious of their apparent fascination with his hairlessness. As he stared at her, longing was written across his face—with something darker writhing underneath, like the belly of the storm cloud—outrage?

"I remember when she got a box of roses," Jerome was saying. "After she read the card, she hurled the box against the wall in the department office. And that's not the only time she's shown an explosive temper." Pausing, he stroked his thick moustache with his index finger. "Maybe associated with her . . . problem, according to what I've heard—something you might know about as a psychologist."

And then, as if he'd accomplished his goal, he raised his eyebrows, his expression sardonic before he turned his back on me.

Staring after him, I tried to tell myself that the surge of apprehension I felt in his wake was only my response to the plunging barometric pressure, a primitive reaction to the approaching storm.

Surely something to eat would ease the hollow feeling in my stomach . . .

In line at the buffet, I spotted Kurt von Reichenau farther up, on the opposite side of the table. Looking remarkably uncomfortable, he was wearing a Western shirt and jeans, both obviously brand-new, and a holster complete with plastic guns; the overhang of his belly hid the front of his belt. "More salad, perhaps?" his wife was saying, as he shoveled an oversize slab of ribs on his plate.

"I didn't get to the top of the food chain to eat vegetables," he said, his tone petulant.

As I was looking away and biting my lip to keep from laughing, I caught the eye of the man just behind me in the line. In his early seventies, portly, bald except for wisps of white hair above his ears, he wore a plaid sport jacket, a blue-rayon shirt, and a red clip-on bow tie.

"Know him?" he asked.

Warmed by his wry smile, I liked the stranger immediately. "My boss."

"Then I won't make a joke about how snakes are carnivorous—no herbivores among them."

As I burst out laughing, out of the corner of my eye I saw Kurt turning my way; his face now absolutely straight, the man beside me pointed at the table and nodded solemnly at me as if we were talking about the food, his pantomime so smooth that it might have been choreographed.

Once Kurt had looked away, he said, "I'm Burgess Coppersmith."

As I introduced myself and we shook hands, I noticed he wasn't wearing a name tag. Unless he was one of the medical school's more eccentric benefactors, he'd crashed the party.

After we finished filling our plates, we moved together to one of the nearby tables. Pointing at the beige porcelain salt-and-pepper shakers fashioned in the shape of cowboy boots and the vinyl tablecloth stippled in black and white like the hide of Holstein cattle, he said, "Doesn't really look like the Old West, does it? But then I grew up on a ranch in south Texas, where everything was poisonous, or had thorns, or both—including the people.''

Something happened as we were talking, something passed between us, back and forth, a sense of connection, an unexpected camaraderie. He told stories about his days as a college student: ''I made a game of getting into football games without a ticket—using a different story each time, dressing to fit whatever tale I'd concocted for the week. I'd tell them I was the governor's son, or a priest, or a reporter—in the end, I always managed to talk my way into the stadium.'' Winking, he said, ''I had a season ticket, but I liked the challenge of bluffing.''

Then I told him about the gifts I'd shipped today to my friend Glee in Australia after she'd written that she was homesick: a bottle of Tabasco sauce, a bucket of salsa, two jars of jalapeño jelly, and a battery-powered Elvis doll that swiveled at the hips as its tinny voice crooned ''Love Me Tender.'' Glee loved Mexican food and loathed Elvis.

Half an hour later, we were looking over the dessert table when I spotted Nick Treece standing close to a short blond woman in a Navajo-print blazer, his head bent toward hers. Dressed in a black cowboy shirt and black jeans that accentuated his blond hair and lean body, he looked like the bad guy in a Western. As I watched, he brought his hands up from his hips like a cowboy pulling guns out of holsters, pointing his index fingers at her; the woman slapped him playfully on the arm and smiled widely up at him.

Feeling my shoulders droop, I was surprised at my disappointment—but I should have guessed that a man like Nick Treece wouldn't come to the party without a date.

''You have such lovely blue eyes,'' Burgess said, following my gaze. "Now, how many of the desserts are we going to sample?"

As we were checking out the pastry tray, a heavy-jowled, potbellied man wearing blue ostrich-skin boots and a matching band on his Stetson stepped between us: Chester Moats, the director for Development. Glancing toward my name tag just long enough to make sure I wasn't worth his time, he took Burgess by the arm, and said, "I need a word with this man, if you'll excuse us."

"We're busy now," Burgess said, surprising me by speaking with the calm authority of a man accustomed to having and using power. "Come back in ten minutes."

Mumbling apologies, his face flushed, Chester backed away.

"Marilou had blue eyes like yours," Burgess said, after we were seated with our desserts. "We were married for fifty years."

In conversation with a member of the Board of Trustees, Austin Danziger waved at Burgess as they passed us. Pointing toward him, Burgess said, "When she was dying of cancer, she was in pain, a lot of pain. Her oncologist wouldn't give her anything strong enough to really help, he kept telling me 'too much chance of addiction.' Know-nothing, peabrained dingleberry really honked me off.

"I checked around and found that Dr. Danziger knew something about pain control for cancer, so I arranged for him to see Marilou. Nothing he could do for her cancer, but he helped her live her last few months without so much suffering. I made a donation in her name through the Anesthesiology Research Foundation so he could hire a couple of faculty." He swallowed heavily as he stared off in the distance, his eyes shiny. "A good doctor. A very good doctor."

As I felt my throat tighten in sympathy, I heard the distant rumble of thunder.

Chester had been hovering nearby, keeping a respectful distance. When Burgess finally looked over, he hurried to his side.

"Burgess, how are you? And the little lady who was monopolizing you?"

Leaving them to their business, I joined the crowd near the patio. As I was dancing a Texas two-step with a bearded cardiologist I knew slightly from our time together on the curriculum committee, I saw Nick Treece watching, but he turned away as soon as I looked in his direction.

"I understand you do research on lie detection," Jerome said to me, speaking loudly enough to draw attention, his tone making it sound like a less-than-respectable obsession. Intent on snagging a diet soda while the band was taking a break, I hadn't seen him standing nearby with Austin and Fred until it was too late.

"Must make people kind of jumpy around you," Fred said. "I mean, certain people, at least. How can you tell if someone's lying?"

Eva Aarastadt had just walked up beside Austin, and she gave me a startled look as she was putting her hand on his arm.

"Yes—what pearls of wisdom do you have for us?" Jerome chimed in.

If he hadn't goaded me, if the oversize margarita hadn't fueled my anger from the morning, maybe I'd have kept quiet—and perhaps things would have turned out differently. I sipped my soda and looked around the circle. "People who are lying often choose their words carefully, one good clue. It's a lot easier to control your words than your face, your voice, and your hands. It's difficult for liars to monitor everything they're doing, to guard against any slip—so the effort makes them more anxious, compounding the problem.''

Looking toward Austin and Eva as I spoke, I saw her left hand twitch, her eyes widen. And then her eyes caught mine, and her expression switched from pained to fierce.

''Strong emotions make it harder to camouflage lies,'' I said. ''A good liar needs a good memory, especially when they lie to more than one person.''

Putting her hands behind her back, she stared at me, a glaring, angry look. I felt her antagonism, a coldness, a sense of challenge. As if I'd wounded her, and now she hoped to see me bleed.

Standing beside Eva at the edge of the circle, looking at the ground, Austin gave the appearance of disinterest—at odds with the tension in his posture.

''Lies improve with each telling—and the liar comes closer to believing the lie,'' I said. ''But not all liars prepare their story well or carefully enough, and sometimes the emotions behind the lies are too strong.''

Pausing, I saw lightning flash across the sky. At the same moment the party had gone quiet, as if everyone had paused to draw breath. In the stillness that followed, Eva stepped forward. Looking squarely at me, a pressured note in her voice, she said, ''We haven't met.''

We exchanged names, but I was certain mine wasn't new to her. I wondered why she'd been so bothered by what I'd been saying—why had she needed to interrupt?

As I shook her hand, we sized each other up. The fine lines in her face whispered that she'd passed forty several years ago. But even without seeing her up close, I would have known she wasn't a kid—not the way she radiated authority and self-assurance.

"I understand you came to Houston in January," I said. "What brought you here?"

Eva stood still, a look of cold disbelief on her face, as if I'd just slapped her—and something behind it that might have been fear. "Business," she said, after I'd decided she wasn't going to answer, "purely business."

I saw Nick standing in the shadows. Remembering the odd look he'd given me when I'd mentioned my research in the library, I felt my face redden.

Stepping forward, Fred said, "Eva, may I get you a drink?" And then, two beats later, he added, "Or a refill for you, Haley?"

"I don't drink," Eva said flatly. "Why wipe out brain cells for brief pleasures?"

As I turned away from her, I spotted the short blond woman who I'd thought was Nick's date. She was holding hands with a man almost as short as herself; when she reached over and patted his cheek with her left hand, I saw the sparkle of a diamond.

So much for my fine-tuned observational skills.

The shadows were growing darker as the clouds moved in. I was looking for Nick in the gloom when Jerome appeared at my elbow again. Flourishing his drink, he said, "It's a Virgin Mary—no alcohol."

"How nice," I said, my voice deliberately flat.

"That woman you mentioned, Kitty Evanston? She worked as a secretary in Anesthesiology before she left for another job. She wasn't married when she first started working for us; I knew her by Jones, her maiden name, so I didn't make the connection."

I studied Jerome, trying to decide if I should credit his alleged ignorance: Kitty wasn't a common nickname.

"Funny thing—Kitty looked so young and angelic, right? A prime example of how looks can deceive," he said. "Round heels—seductive with anything in pants.

She even slept with Fred Verlin, which shows you how badly her judgment was impaired before she got proper medical attention—and how Fred took advantage of her.''

Fred? "Her judgment was impaired?"

"She was hyperthyroid: distractable, irritable, anxious, couldn't tolerate heat, and hyperactive. Hardly a clinical mystery. Undoubtedly started the affair with him because of it.

"Kitty liked to be provocative. She used to get Popsicles from the cafeteria and walk around the hallways eating them slowly, deliberately lingering over them, just nibbling at the top. Had every man who walked past her crossing his legs.

"One department Christmas party, Fred and Kitty were over in a dark corner, slow dancing—she must've thought no one could see them. Sure looked like she was dancing with her hand down the front of his pants.''

Jerome's white shirt seemed dingy and soiled. Maybe a trick of the light—maybe a reflection of his mind.

"When she finally got treated for her hyperthyroidism, she gained weight and lost interest in Fred.'' A small murmur of satisfaction crept into his voice.

His comments about Kitty showed as much compassion as a swarm of hornets toward someone violating their hive.

"Her story about her surgery—"

"I tried to check the schedule for that problem surgery. Not as straightforward as I thought—"

Thunder cracked loudly, drowning out the last part of his sentence. The crowd, anxiously looking upward, began moving toward the Faculty Club door.

Problem surgery, he'd called it. Nothing like Austin's elaborate denial. "What do you mean?"

Jerome took a bite of the celery stalk from his drink,

chewing it vigorously as he watched me. Deliberately delaying, stretching out his revelation, making the most of an opportunity to make someone wait.

"Something else I remembered about Kitty . . . just after she moved here, Eva had Kitty working on a grant. I walked in on a major scene between the two of them, Eva screaming at Kitty about some trivial mistake, probably the reason Kitty left so abruptly—" He sipped his drink.

"I don't know the identity of her anesthesiologist yet, because the person scheduled wasn't the person responsible—I'm sure of that much." The background clamor had dwindled to a dull hum, but Jerome hadn't dropped his voice.

To my right, the string of lights fashioned in the shape of jalapeño peppers that dangled above the bartender's table looked like red warning lights, signaling danger. "What do you mean?"

"Dr. Danziger was scheduled as her anesthesiologist, but he got called into an emergency meeting in the Dean's office at the last moment—"

Austin? "That's a little hard to believe, since his secretary told me he didn't share the mundane clinical work—"

"That's quite true—and certainly appropriate—but he's willing to help if necessary. Naturally, since I'm in charge of scheduling, that's only in the most dire of circumstances. And someone else was able to cover the case, after all. I'll need to get Kitty's chart to confirm, but . . ."

Predictably, he took another bite and began chewing again, making me wait him out. "I'll check it out before I say anything, wouldn't want to accuse someone without proof . . . but I think that either Fred or Eva took over for Dr. Danziger. That'd make things interesting, wouldn't it?''

As we stared at each other, I said, ''I understand that drug abuse is a problem among anesthesiologists.''

Blinking rapidly, he gave the drink in his hand his full attention. I'd decided he wasn't going to respond when he finally broke the silence: ''Maybe you've heard stories you want to share?''

Lightning lit the sky, close, thunder following almost immediately. Glancing past Jerome, I saw movement, a shadow slipping away, the gloom too dense to see more than the flash of a light-colored head. *Someone eavesdropping in the darkness?*

As I remembered the message on my door, the hair on the back of my neck prickled, seemed to stand up.

Chapter 12

"Yes?" Responding to my knock on her office door on Monday morning, Eva Aarastadt greeted me with her hands on her hips, a scowl on her face.

I hadn't called in advance; after the odd way she'd acted at the party, I wanted to catch her unprepared, so I could watch her reaction.

"I wanted to talk with you about how to introduce the memory assessments to your patients," I said. "It's really a simple procedure—"

"I've read the protocol. Frankly, it seems like wasted effort. So what if patients experience a week or two of memory problems after surgery—that's remarkably trivial. I see no reason to spend time studying it."

She was wearing a short straight red-and-black-checked skirt, a sleeveless black turtleneck, black hose, and black heels. A simple outfit, she looked terrific—and more than a little intimidating.

"You've certainly communicated your views to your patients—directly or indirectly. We've had problems with the last three patients—and it turns out that all of them were yours."

We locked eyes. Her face was sculpted into hard lines,

112

classically beautiful, the face of a goddess, as white as alabaster—and as cold.

"We'll go outside to talk," Eva said, turning her back on me as she walked to her desk. Picking up a pack of cigarettes, shaking one out, she said, "If I have to waste the time, I'll make it a smoking break."

The floor-to-ceiling bookcases that filled one entire wall of her office drew my eye, the shelves crammed with medical journals: *New England Journal of Medicine, British Journal of Anaesthesia, Lancet, Archives of Neurology, Anesthesia and Analgesia, Neurology, Archives of Internal Medicine*, and *Anesthesiology* were among the two dozen titles. If she paid a hundred a year for each journal subscription, a conservative estimate, she must spend in excess of two thousand each year to maintain her personal collection.

As she was pulling her office door closed behind her, I caught sight of a vase of red roses sitting on the floor in the corner. Past their prime, their necks drooping, the petals that had fallen on the linoleum looked like drops of blood.

Jiggling the knob to make sure it was locked, she said, "Equipment and supplies grow legs around here."

Drugs? "What's gone missing?" I asked, as we started walking toward the entrance.

"You name it. A power supply unit for gel electrophoresis. Some P-32. A Precision Balance."

"Nothing else?"

"That's not enough?"

Not an answer to my question. "What's a Precision Balance?"

"That's a brand name."

How helpful. "It's used for—?"

"Just what the name implies—measuring small quantities."

I had the impression she was trying to walk fast enough to make me work to keep up with her, but her tight skirt and high heels conspired to hobble her, keeping her steps short.

I thought of how the feet of Chinese women used to be bound, leaving them to walk on tiny, deformed stilts, never running free. An incongruous association to such a strong, dominant woman.

"Is P-32 a chemical?"

Eva snorted. "It's a radioactive phosphorus isotope."

"Someone stole a radioactive isotope from your lab?"

"Not the kind for making bombs. It's used for labeling DNA, for gel electrophoresis."

Once she'd explained the jargon in her condescending way, I sorted out the story. P-32 was stored in lead "pigs" the size of water glasses. Until the monthly inventory came up short, she hadn't known that one of the half dozen she kept in a cabinet just outside her lab had disappeared.

"But they found my P-32 eventually, at least some of it . . . it turned up in two women's urine." Her voice was low-pitched and husky, her tone biting.

Stopping short in the hallway, I took a deep breath. The sodium fluoride in the coffeepot was trivial by comparison—and now I had a strong personal interest in the tricks. "How—?"

Two medical students were walking toward us, arguing loudly about whether immunology or biochemistry had been more difficult. She waited until they'd passed before she looked back at me.

"They'd drunk from the watercooler where it'd been dumped." She resumed walking, and I followed. "The university's Radiation Safety Office discovered the problem during a routine lab inspection when a woman set off a Geiger counter. She'd been exposed to two hundred to three hundred microcuries of radiation.''

"That's serious—"

"Not that bad, really. Federal safety guidelines allow six hundred microcuries annually. But they almost shut down my lab.''

As much empathy as a Bengal tiger. "Who got exposed?''

"Just lab technicians," she shrugged. "Call it an occupational hazard. The cooler was just outside the core lab.''

The core lab again. "Something I don't understand," I said. "It's a biohazard lab, so you can't drink coffee there. Where's the lab coffeepot?''

"Next door. It used to be a broom closet, so it's just big enough for the coffeepot and a small refrigerator. In answer to your next question, we go into one of the empty classrooms down the hallway for lab meetings— same thing if someone wants to take a coffee break. I take it you've heard the sodium fluoride story.''

"Fred told me about it—"

"Fred moaned a lot about how it messed him up, but I got hurt worse. Two weeks of work down the drain when I lost data from a key experiment because I was too sick to run the final step on time.''

"Any particular reason for someone to go after you?''

We'd reached the front door of Denton Hall, the building that housed the Department of Anesthesiology. Through the glass I could see raindrops splattering the pavement. "We'll be fine on the porch under the eaves," she said, pushing past me as I stood hesitating.

Outside, she took her time lighting a cigarette, a strange vice for a woman who'd spoken so forcefully about the dangers of alcohol. Finally she said, "When I joined the department, I was given a lab that Jerome Pettit wanted.''

The second person to tell me that Jerome was the prankster. I thought of what Jerome had said about Eva: *Had the animal-rights types after her back in New York. Looks like she brought the trouble with her.* ''Jerome told me he thought the lab accidents were the work of animal-rights activists. He hinted that they were getting inside information.''

Her arm jerked and a pained, frightened look flashed across her face. A second later her expression was carefully blank. ''Bad back . . . goes into spasms.'' She didn't look at me as she massaged the small of her back with her free hand.

I stared at her high heels—hardly the obvious footwear choice for a woman with back problems. Looking up, I saw her watching me, her expression guarded.

''I could see Jerome inventing stories about the mistreatment of lab animals,'' she said, ''setting up someone else to do his dirty work. Letting someone else take the fall.''

Did she really believe that her explanation sounded credible? ''Jerome's hardly Mr. Congeniality . . . but would he really go to so much trouble just because you'd gotten a lab he wanted?''

Taking a drag of her cigarette, she stared off into the rain. ''I only came for a one-year appointment, they'll hold my line in New York for a year if I want to go back—but there's already plenty to make me think I shouldn't stay. I got a letter when Austin was trying to recruit me, an anonymous letter—sent to my home, not my office.'' She flicked her long blond hair back with her hand, exposing hoop earrings: thick silver wires, twisted at the top like a hangman's noose.

''It was typed on department stationery. The writer

warned me that Austin couldn't be trusted to keep promises made during recruitment interviews. It said I
shouldn't count on getting the resources or lab space I'd
need for my research. I came anyway and Austin kept
his promises . . . so when nasty things started happening,
I didn't assume it was just coincidence.''

"That's ugly . . . You're convinced it was Jerome?"

"He tells all kinds of wild tales about me, even
claimed he'd seen a gun in my lab—as if I'd ever let
him inside. I've had no problems, aside from him.''

"What about Fred?" His expression as he'd watched
Eva at the party hadn't been entirely benign.

Looking at me sharply, she said, "Fred's lending me
equipment until I get replacements for the things that
were stolen.''

So Fred had offered to help? Because the cost was
prohibitive, the medical center didn't carry insurance for
thefts—money for replacements had to come out of her
grants, or out of departmental funds. Could Fred have
engineered some of the thievery as a way to curry favor
with her?

The rain was coming down harder now. I stepped
back farther under the porch.

She stood perfectly still, watching me. Studying me.
Waiting to see what I'd do with her story, I guessed.

I was sure she was leaving out something important—
a key piece. *Started causing problems after she arrived
in January*, Jerome had said. And he'd talked about
Eva's "problem": *Something you might know about as
a psychologist.*

"I saw the core lab when it was covered with
ketchup," I said. "Jerome seemed upset that I'd stumbled onto it. He emphasized Austin's interest in keeping
the accidents quiet.''

Without missing a beat, she said, "So you want to

know why I'm talking about these things with a stranger—particularly you.''

Perceptive. "And?"

"Things keep happening to me . . . sometimes it's big, sometimes it's small, but it hasn't stopped since I came in January. Take the ketchup episode, for example: Sydney, the technician who was supposed to be starting a study for me that day—she had to spend the next day and a half scrubbing down the lab instead. Keeping quiet hasn't helped.''

Keeping quiet hasn't helped. Biting my lip, I tried to suppress the thought that kept popping into my mind: *What had the prankster planned next for me?*

"It's not just paranoia," Eva said. "Fred's told me that Jerome's been spreading stories about how I mistreat people who work for me. It started when I got here. A secretary scratched the wrong computer file, which meant missing a grant deadline—so I got pretty upset. Jerome walked in just after I discovered what she'd done." She flicked back her long hair with an air of disdain. "Naturally, he started stories about my terrible temper, how I'm a rotten boss. Now we've lost one of the two core-lab techs because of the isotope incident, and it's impossible to find a competent replacement—so he tries to blame me.''

Did Jerome's comment about Eva's "explosive temper" reflect his inevitable conflict with any strong woman—or something more?

Eva was all too familiar with Jerome's propensity for dishing dirt—maybe this was her version of damage control. Or perhaps she'd been the eavesdropper I'd glimpsed in the shadows when Jerome was talking about Kitty.

I had my own agenda. "I hear there's a surgeon who plays barbershop music during surgery—''

"They play all kinds of music." She turned to stab out her cigarette in the sand-filled urn beside the door, looking away from me in the direction of a tall man who was hurrying toward the porch where we were standing. His face screened by a black umbrella, he took the steps two at a time, moving with the fluid stride of an athlete. Stopping beside us, he lowered his umbrella: Nick Treece.

"Flowers blooming in the rain," he said, looking from Eva to me, smiling at me.

"Hello, Nick," she said, her voice flat and unwelcoming.

"I didn't mean to interrupt," he spoke quickly, looking at me. "You'll be in your office later?"

I nodded. On Saturday night, the party had ended abruptly when the storm finally broke. I hadn't run across Nick after I'd glimpsed him watching me.

"I'll call you," he said, heading toward the door.

"You wanted to talk with me about referring patients for your memory assessments," Eva said, looking pointedly at her watch.

As I gave her my spiel about how to describe the study to patients, it took an effort not to grin like a fool. I wanted to forget business with her and go skipping down the hallway after Nick.

"That's a remarkable amount of work to detect minor memory deficits," she said, when I'd finished. Then, not waiting for an answer, she headed toward the door, not looking to see if I was following.

Her comment brought me back, abruptly. Something about her voice and the strained look on her face made me remember Marsha, a patient I'd seen a few years ago. With Marsha I'd needed all my wits. I needed to concentrate so I could hear the nuances, the pauses, the changes in pitch. Sick once, coming down with a cold, preoccupied with finding a tissue for my running nose, I'd missed a moment. I'd awakened that night and thought about the dream she'd been describing, heard her tight, high voice, the words she'd used: "Hanging rabbits, freshly killed." *Child abuse*, I thought, *she's worried about losing control and hurting her kids*. I'd called Marsha early the next morning, heard her relief when she recognized my voice, a confession of how close she'd come.

Now I wondered about something I'd heard in Eva's voice before we'd been interrupted—something she'd said that I couldn't recapture.

"Memory problems aren't trivial for the people who have them," I said, as we walked into the foyer. "Or for their families."

Eva flinched and raised her hands up, palms outward, as if warding off a blow.

Chapter 13

"My friend Nancy in Radiology sings in the church choir with one of the secretaries in Anesthesiology," Thelma Lou told me after waving me down on my way back to my office. "I asked her to see if she could find out anything about Kitty Evanston."

I thanked her as I looked down at the frame holding the latest Polaroid of Greta; it showed the cement goose wearing a miniature baseball cap and an apron with the logo of the Houston Astros.

"Kitty was one of three secretaries who worked in the departmental office in Anesthesiology," she said, leaning forward and lowering her voice. "Her main assignment was working for Austin's research group. Dr. Danziger was furious when she quit to take a job in Dean Verbrugge's office."

Interesting that Jerome hadn't mentioned those facts.

"A few days after she left, Dr. Danziger ran into Nancy's friend having lunch with Kitty on a bench in front of Denton; that afternoon he called her into his office and told her she shouldn't be hanging around with Kitty, not after the way she left the department."

" 'The way she left'?"

"Kitty didn't say a word to anyone about looking for another job. She stayed way late finishing work on her last day before she was due to go on vacation and take a medical leave after that—and then she left a note on top of her empty desk saying she wouldn't be back."

"What was going on?"

"She said that Dr. Danziger expects people to ask how high when he tells them to jump, but there was something else . . ."

Tapping the Lucite frame with Greta's picture, she shook her head apologetically as she looked at me. The lightning bolt etched into the corner of the frame had become Thelma Lou's logo after she was struck five years ago. Messages signed "LL," her shorthand for "Lightning Lady," meant she was having a bad time with her memory that day.

"She got married just before she left the department . . . I'm sorry, I can't remember the rest . . ."

Patting her hand, warmed by her efforts, I thanked her again for checking for me. As I walked to my office I wondered about the rest of the story: *What had driven Kitty away?*

If Austin regarded Kitty's abrupt departure as a defection, then Jerome might well feel the same—if he hadn't been the one who chased her away in the first place.

After staring at the phone for five minutes I reluctantly called Murray Snelling, figuring he'd be the quickest source of information—if he'd tell me what I wanted to know. And if he hadn't yet learned that I was assessing the *Phoenix* survivors and wasn't reaching the same conclusions as he.

"I understand that Kitty left the Department of Anesthesiology before her surgery in February," I said, leaving it open to see how he'd respond.

"I can certainly understand your concerns about Kitty—especially in view of your . . . involvement with the Department of Anesthesiology." Murray's tone made it sound somewhere between depraved and dishonest. "But she was unable to go to work in Dean Verbrugge's office after her surgery as she'd planned— because she couldn't bring herself to work in an administrative office that would have required her to run occasional errands in the hospital."

Of course. "Did Kitty mention a name when she talked about her anesthesiologist? Since she might have known the person."

"You'd have expected Kitty to meet her anesthesiologist before her surgery—that's the usual procedure. But her only memory was during the surgery itself, when everyone was wearing surgical masks and caps—effective disguises, you must admit."

According to what Nick Treece had told me in the library, Kitty's anesthetic could have wiped out memories before her surgery—but it still felt wrong.

"She didn't mention recognizing the voice?"

"Not really—but she couldn't talk about her surgery easily, as you saw. So much raw emotion clouding her memory . . . not surprising, not when you think about it."

"Do you know if the whispered voice after Kitty's surgery was one of the voices from her surgery?" *What goes around, comes around.*

"I . . . I'm not absolutely sure, but I believe so . . ."

"Was Kitty sure it was a man?"

A longer hesitation, then, "I believe so . . ."

He obviously hadn't considered the possibility of a woman in the role. Which meant that his work with Kitty had probably fostered the assumption that it had been a man—whether or not it was true.

Murray's voice came back now, stronger, triumphant: "I do believe she knew him, of course, and that it was a factor in her death."

"What do you mean?"

"The obvious: Kitty was planning to check on the identity of her anesthesiologist on the day she died. I assume the answer must have been a severe shock."

Two hours later, I got a call from George Breckley. After we'd gossiped for a minute he said, "So psychologists have recently been honored by appointments to the medical staff at your hospital," his Southern accent still strong despite two decades in New York. George had been the director of Clinical Training when I was a graduate student at Rochester; we'd kept in touch after I got my degree.

"Not an 'honor' I'd have chosen," I said.

After psychologists became members of the medical staff as mandated by the hospital accreditation board, the Credentials Committee made us jump through hoops that had little to do with the practice of psychology: I had to produce proof of vaccination or immunity for rubella, rubeola, and hepatitis B. I had to get annual skin tests to show I wasn't infected with tuberculosis. I had to pass a blood-borne pathogens exam, answering questions about procedures like needle disposal—despite the fact I never used needles. I had to get letters from three people who said I was fit to practice. George had to write a lettering confirming that my graduate program had really and truly awarded my Ph.D. All this to continue doing exactly the same work in the very hospital where I'd been practicing for thirteen years.

"I just got off the phone with a doc in your shop— he was asking if you'd had any problems back when you were a student."

"Problems as a *student*?"

"The guy wanted to know if there was any reason they should look more closely at your application. Asked if you'd ever had any troubles that might not have been mentioned, any difficulties that might have been over-looked at the time—or if I'd heard rumors of anything since you'd finished. When I told him I thought highly of you and knew of no problems either past or present, he suggested that it was important to be open, not to try to cover up."

Someone hunting dirt on me. "Who was the man?"

I wasn't surprised by his answer. I'd already seen how much pleasure Jerome Pettit derived from unearthing his colleagues' sins.

As I went storming past Thelma Lou's reception desk on my way to confront Jerome, she flagged me down, waving a message slip—a summons to see my boss, Kurt von Reichenau, in person: "URGENT."

"I just got off the phone with Austin Danziger," Kurt said as he sat glaring at me from behind his desk five minutes later. "He's asked me to find someone else to take your place on his Center grant."

For a minute I just stared at him, not knowing what to say. The grandfather clock in the corner struck the quarter hour, the tone loud in the silence.

"Why's Austin asking for a replacement?" I thought of Jerome's search, wondering if he could have found something—though I couldn't imagine anything that would have prompted my dismissal.

"Austin said you'd had trouble getting patients to par-ticipate—and you'd also had problems getting along with members of his research team." His thick lips were folded in anger. "He wants a letter from you that he'll forward to the administrator in charge of Center grant reviews. You should write that you're no longer able to be personally involved because of other commitments, but you'd be pleased to act as a consultant for your replacement.''

Austin wanted me out. I'd designed the memory component, so he'd be able to cite my record. On paper I'd be a consultant, a ploy to maintain the illusion that he had the necessary expertise for his grant review.

Part of me, hearing Kurt, was livid, red-hot, wanting badly to run out, find Austin, punch him—wanting to draw blood, somehow. Furious that he'd not even bothered to speak directly to me.

Another part was absolutely incredulous, trying to work out the timetable, the likely precipitant.

Problems getting along with members of his team. Something so troublesome that Austin didn't want to wait until after his grant had been reviewed.

Three scenes replayed themselves: the ''message'' on my office door. The silence when I'd talked about studying lies. The eavesdropper in the shadows at the party.

Maybe I was jumping to conclusions, and the answer was much simpler. If drugs had been stolen along with equipment and supplies, Austin would have a strong incentive for keeping the lab troubles quiet—and Jerome had made sure everyone knew I was asking questions about the sabotage. Or perhaps Eva, in her imperious way, had spoken to Austin after our conversation and argued that I was more trouble that I was worth.

''So I can call Austin and tell him you'll write the letter?'' Kurt asked.

''Under no circumstances will I resign voluntarily. Austin can replace me if he chooses, that's his prerogative. But if I'm off the project, I'm not going to front for someone else. Either I'm a full player or I'm out. And that means I won't hand over data I've collected thus far to my replacement.''

"Surely," he stopped and coughed, clearing his throat loudly, "surely, that's not what you expect me to tell Austin." He fondled the suspenders he'd favored at work since his belt had snapped during a heated discussion in a faculty meeting.

I felt an odd burst of sympathy for Kurt. He'd aged perceptibly over the last year—I'd heard rumors of trouble with his children, his disappointment when he wasn't tapped for a position he'd coveted on Dean Verbrugge's staff. I could chart the stress in his life by the growth of his belly.

We'd had an empty line in Psychiatry for a year, ever since the university slapped a freeze on faculty hiring. Austin Danziger had managed to put both Eva Aarastadt and Nick Treece on the payroll, despite the embargo— but that was the difference between Anesthesiology and Psychiatry—and between Austin Danziger and Kurt von Reichenau.

"There's no need for you to get back to Austin," I said. "I'll talk to him myself. Especially since there really isn't anyone else who's got the time . . ." I didn't belabor the obvious: Even if someone else had the expertise, they wouldn't be able to collect sufficient data, not with the site visit looming in August.

"I don't think—" His phone rang, and he gave me a peeved look as he picked it up. I looked around his office while he talked with someone about scheduling a meeting.

Diplomas decorated a section of one wall; next to them he'd hung framed pictures of himself in the company of the university president, members of the Board of Trustees, and several minor television celebrities. He displayed the same forced smile across the montage that he wore now as he hung up the phone and turned back to me. "Something just occurred to me . . . I saw you talking with Burgess Coppersmith at the party on Saturday. Did you put in a word for the department?''

'' 'A word for the department'?''

"He's a major-league moneyman. Surely you knew that?'' Kurt had bulbous eyes and an oversize nose that he rubbed when he was anxious. He was rubbing it now.

"Not really—''

"Coppersmith's given plenty to the medical school in the past. And you know our department could use a little help . . .''

A major understatement. Struggling to maintain appearances in the face of ugly facts, Kurt's imaginative narrative in our department's recent annual report had glossed over a multitude of problems.

"Tell you what,'' he said. "Why don't you call Coppersmith and invite him to visit us?'' As he glanced toward the wall with the photographs, I remembered a story I'd heard: the "von'' part of von Reichenau signified a kind of nobility in Germany—an addition Kurt had made to his name after visiting that country as a medical student.

I finally got the message: *quid pro quo*. Kurt couldn't force me to write the letter that Austin wanted—but he could punish me by assigning aversive duties. And he wouldn't hesitate if I didn't invite Burgess for a visit.

When Kurt had become department chair seven years ago, he'd had aspirations and dreams that many considered grandiose: He'd transform the Psychiatry Department into the leading light in the medical school, he'd be the next Dean.

Now I guessed he was dreaming of a big gift for our department, maybe big enough to parlay favors with the next Dean.

"I'll call Burgess and ask him to visit,'' I said.

Standing up to signal that the meeting was over, he

said, "I don't want to hear any more from Austin about problems with your work. If he complains again, we'll have to make other arrangements."

I was in a foul mood by the time I finally cornered Jerome in his office late in the afternoon. "I just heard you've been calling around, asking about me." I moved folders from a chair and sat down without waiting for an invitation.

"Of course. Part of my work on the Credentials Committee." Jerome busied himself straightening the overflow from the wooden correspondence trays on his desk as if highlighting how much work awaited him. When he'd finished with the last of the piles, he gave me a particularly grating smile: superior, condescending, haughty. "Was there something else?"

"Why?" I tried to keep my voice calm, but I wasn't completely successful. Jerome had gone hunting for ammunition to tarnish me. On his own initiative, or at Austin's behest? "Why were you calling about me?"

"As a member of the hospital's Credentials Committee, I think it's important to check on our medical-staff applicants. A year ago I found that a man's claim of a medical degree from France was bogus. A little more digging and it became clear that this wasn't his only lie, not by a lot."

Looking at his expression, placid and self-satisfied, I felt cold—there's nothing so dangerous as a man convinced of his moral superiority.

"I've been on the faculty for thirteen years," I said. "I got word last month that my appointment to the medical staff had been approved. It doesn't make sense that you'd be calling my graduate school to ask about my behavior as a student, not now."

"Perhaps there's some reason you're worried about

having your credentials verified?'' He sat watching me, not moving—as still as stagnant water.

''Hardly.''

''Then I can't understand why you're so obviously upset. If you'd read the bylaws for the medical staff, you know that your signature on the application authorizes the hospital to consult with anyone who may have information bearing on your competence, character, or ethical qualifications.'' He folded his hands and leaned forward. ''I did a bit more checking, quite frankly, because I wondered about your odd preoccupation . . . with lies.''

Perhaps Jerome knew that Austin wanted me off the project and this was his way of being ''helpful'' to Austin.

Maybe Jerome had other reasons for going after me. The thought made my breath come faster.

Chapter 14

"But I kept *my* word," the woman was saying, her tone strident.

Still seething after my talks with Kurt and Jerome, I'd headed for Austin's office, running into the man and a woman at an intersection near the core lab.

Facing away from me, all I could see of the woman was a blond ponytail above her white lab coat, but her long-haired companion had an angry look on his thin face. His T-shirt showed a can of Budweiser above the legend: MORE THAN JUST A BREAKFAST DRINK. He gestured widely as I was marching past, and I sniffed something that flashed me back to my days as a graduate student: the scent of marijuana on his clothing. And then he was stepping toward the woman, shaking his fist, and she was backing away, covering her face.

"Is there a problem?" I said loudly, turning toward them, stopping in the middle of the empty corridor. "Do you need help, miss?"

"Mind your own business," the man said, but he dropped his fist.

"No, no, everything's cool, I'm fine," she muttered as she took off down the hallway to her right, her hand still shielding her face. The man shot me a vicious look before he grimaced and headed off in the direction I'd come. I stood watching until she was out of sight.

When I got to Austin's office, his secretary told me he'd just left for the airport.

Back in Rugton, Thelma Lou handed me a message from Nick Treece. Returning his call, I was told he was in a meeting.

After work, all too aware of how tense I was, I drove to my athletic club. Ten minutes after I'd begun working out on one of the stair climbers, my machine flashed a bulletin across the screen: NO GUTS, NO GLORY. And then, a minute later, DON'T STOP NOW.

Resisting the impulse to stick out my tongue, tired of being told what to do, I climbed off.

Outside, the sun in my eyes, intent on digging in my purse for my keys, I almost collided with Nick Treece when I rounded a turn on the path to the parking lot.

"Haley! I didn't know you came here," he said, smiling broadly. Carrying a gym bag, he was still dressed in his shirt and tie. "Got time for a drink?"

I felt a warm glow in my chest; for a second, I found it hard to answer. "Sounds good."

"We'll get something inside, if that's OK," he said, jerking his head toward the club. "Much as I'd like to go somewhere else, I've only got an hour before I have to go back to the hospital, and I'm scheduled tomorrow morning, early. All courtesy of Jerome—he's made it clear that the new kids on the block need to pay their dues."

"I tried to return your call—"

"I know. And you were gone when I was free—"

As we were turning to go inside, a woman called, "Nick!"

A plump young woman, her wavy blond hair cascading down her shoulders, was waving at him, smiling broadly: Sydney, the technician who'd been pretending to be a corpse in the ketchup-splattered anesthesiology lab. I remembered her disappointment when she'd been expecting Nick, and I'd "discovered" her instead. And, unless I was mistaken, she was the same woman I'd seen earlier today.

Nick looked back at me after he raised a hand in acknowledgment, missing what I saw—her smile shift to a scowl.

Climbing the stairs to the café, he told me he'd just joined the club on Sydney's recommendation. I'd never seen her here before, but the club's location made it popular with the medical-center crowd.

We were sipping iced teas and trading stories about our exercise routines when Sydney came up to our table.

"I'm *so* glad you're still here, Nick," she said, smiling at him. Wearing a pink T-shirt and denim cutoffs so tight they could have been painted on her, she looked even younger up close—twenty-two at most. "I need to go back to the lab tonight to finish up the work for you, but my car won't start. Could you take a look?"

"Sure," Nick said to her. And then, to me, his tone apologetic, "It'll only take a minute for me to figure out if it's something I can diagnose. Haley, have you met Sydney, the mainstay of Dr. Danziger's lab?"

"We've met," she said. "In the core lab, just after it was sprayed with ketchup. Dr. Pettit asked her if she was coming back to check her handiwork."

"I'll tell you the story when you get back," I said. "I'm not in any rush."

She gave me a look that could have drawn blood.

"A loose battery connection," Nick told me as he sat down five minutes later. "I tightened it, and she's on her way."

The very kind of "trouble" that would have been easy to rig?

"Sydney explained how you stumbled onto the lab after it'd been trashed, and Jerome gave you a hard time," he said. "She said to be sure to tell you that she hoped you wouldn't mind her little joke."

"Little joke," indeed. She'd given him a sanitized version before I had a chance.

I told Nick about the argument I'd witnessed near the core lab this afternoon between the man in the Budweiser T-shirt and the woman with the ponytail.

"If it was Sydney, the guy was probably her old boyfriend," he said. "They were living together, and he's given her a hard time ever since she told him to move out. I feel bad for her—she's a good kid and she's been having a tough time—and she tries so hard to be helpful in spite of everything. We're short-handed, and she's been terrific about working overtime for me."

No doubt.

"She's very good, very careful, but Jerome's given her a hard time about lab safety. Last week she mentioned she'd felt a tingle when she touched one of the exhaust hoods, like it might have a short in it. When she told him she was worried about using it, he acted like she was just a whiny kid trying to get out of work."

I remembered Eva's story: Two technicians had drunk radioisotope-laden water from a cooler outside the core lab. Sydney must have been one of the victims. And now, despite the isotope incident, despite Jerome's hostility, she hadn't quit.

"A week later Jerome sent her this creepy memo that she showed me: 'Please be sure to follow ALL biosafety regulations. Remember that laboratory policy forbids smoking, eating, drinking, and applying cosmetics. You may not wear open-toed shoes or clogs in the laboratory.

You should also be reminded that you are never to unplug equipment by jerking out the power cord. Eternal vigilance must be *your* motto!' ''

Was Jerome deliberately creating a climate where potential safety problems wouldn't get reported? Or was he laying the groundwork to indict Sydney for carelessness, establishing a paper trail so she'd be blamed for future problems?

Or could she have really been a safety hazard, her behavior overlooked by Nick because she worked so hard for him?

"Sydney wasn't anywhere near the lab during the ketchup episode, but Jerome tried to blame her for it. She's getting pretty fed up with him. She says he's got it in for her, she doesn't know why."

"Any reason Jerome might have wanted to get rid of her?" He had hinted that an animal-rights activists might be getting inside information.

"Only one that I could see. He doesn't want any competition for Dr. Danziger's attention—and he certainly didn't welcome me or Eva Aarastadt. Maybe he figures that if we have enough trouble getting work done, we'll look elsewhere."

Nick glanced at his watch and grimaced. Clearing his throat and wetting his lips, he said, "Uh, I've got to go in a minute. Look, there's a party at Dr. Danziger's house Wednesday night, a good-bye affair for the residents who are finishing up. I know this is short notice, but would—would you come with me?"

"I'd love to," I said. I felt my stomach lurch with excitement and anticipation. And nervousness.

Driving home, replaying the conversation with Nick, I realized that Sydney reminded me of a patient I'd seen for a consultation recently.

It had just begun raining when I was walking past a

window that overlooked the entrance to Rugton. A pretty dark-haired woman in a tight red dress caught my eye as she climbed out of a yellow Miata in the parking lot. As I watched, she unfurled her umbrella and started toward the door. Halfway there, she stopped in mid-stride. Returning to her car, she tossed her umbrella into the front seat. The rain soaked her as she strolled, unprotected, back to the building. Upstairs at the reception desk, she told Thelma Lou that she had to see me right away, it couldn't wait; late for her appointment, she didn't have an umbrella in her car, but she'd been so desperate to talk to me that she hadn't even bothered to wait for the rain to let up.

Interesting that Sydney reminded me of a woman whose husband was trying to force her to seek treatment because of compulsive lying.

Chapter 15

"You're in for a treat tonight," Nick told me as we walked up to Austin's house on Kirby Drive. The massive white columns gave the mansion an antebellum flavor. "You'll get to see Dr. Danziger's collection."

Hardly my idea of a treat. When I'd gone hunting for Austin after talking with Kurt on Monday, I'd left word with his secretary that I looked forward to reviewing my data with him on his return—a pointed message to let him know that I wasn't prepared to bow out gracefully. Now I was wondering if he'd gotten the news yet—and how he would react when he saw me.

"Collection? Like the glass and crystal in his office?"

"Not a bit," Nick said, laughing. "What would be your wildest guess?"

Guns. Knives. Antique armor. But I didn't think I should say these things aloud—not when Austin was our host.

As we turned the corner, I realized that even my most outlandish guess wouldn't have come close.

Canvas sideshow banners, fun-house mirrors, and carousel beasts lined the walls of the large room. In the center I saw what looked to be a penny-arcade collection from traveling fairs and amusement parks in the days before everything went video. In the corner, a player piano was clanging out ragtime.

"Wow—it's wonderful," I blurted, after realizing I'd been standing in silence, my mouth open.

"Once we get drinks, I'll give you a guided tour, if you like—I know most of the stories," he said, his smile warming me. "For example, the banners were remarkable pieces of false advertising." He gestured toward one that shouted PENGUIN BOY in blue-green letters above a picture of a short black-haired boy who had flappers instead of arms. Dressed in a white T-shirt and black-and-white shorts, he was standing on an iceberg, surrounded by a flock of penguins. "Once the customers got inside they'd find a short man with stubby little arms smoking a cigarette."

A bartender was pouring wine for us and we were laughing when Austin appeared beside us. "Dr. Danziger," Nick said, coming to attention.

I felt myself tensing as well. I'd chosen my clothes carefully for our date: a heavy gold-silk blouse over a short black skirt, sheer black hosiery with a seam down the back, and black patent heels. Suddenly I felt unsteady, as if walking on tiptoe. I didn't think it was just because I'd worn higher heels than usual.

"Welcome," Austin said, shaking hands with each of us in turn before he gestured toward a banner that screamed ALLIGATOR BOY in red letters across the top, "Haley, do you know anything about ichthyosis?"

The canvas painting showed a figure lounging on the shore of a river, a tangled jungle thicket behind him. The crudely drawn man had a muscular torso above his waist, the scaly tail of an alligator below.

"Not a thing," I said.

"It's a dermatologic disorder; patients have very

rough, leathery skin that's so dry it cracks in patterns like a reptile's hide. For a cheap, authentic-looking alligator boy when the real thing wasn't available, sideshow operators would paint diluted Casco glue all over someone. Once it dried and they moved around a little, the cracking effect looked almost exactly like ichthyosis.''

"Your collection is wonderful," I said, meaning it. And thinking that I could hardly confront Austin when he was my host.

"I'm glad you like it. Some of the carousel animals date back to the turn of the century; the mechanical pieces were manufactured in the thirties and forties.''

"And they still work?''

"Mostly,'' Austin said, his smile rueful. "I spend all too much time keeping them running.''

Pointing toward the next banner, BOBBY, THE BOY WITH THE REVOLVING HEAD, he said, "Another interesting one from a medical standpoint. They had a man who could turn his head around backwards by dislocating various vertebrae.'' Motioning at the right corner, where the word "alive" was printed in pink, he said, "That was a key word for a lot of banners because the public had gotten wise to the dead fakes created by show operators—they'd get a taxidermist to sew a fish's tail on a monkey's body and call it a mermaid, or they'd sew a couple of extra legs on a dog's body and claim it was an 'absolutely genuine' freak of nature.''

When Austin excused himself to greet some new arrivals, I asked Nick how he'd met him.

"After my first year of medical school, I was thinking seriously of dropping out. I'd gotten a summer job in Dr. Danziger's lab, just fetch-and-carry stuff, but I was thrilled to have the opportunity to work for him. One day I asked if there was any chance for a permanent position if I didn't go back to school in the fall. He sat me down and told me I'd spend my life regretting it if I quit.'' Wearing a navy blazer, a navy bow tie with small golden horseshoes, and gray slacks, he'd obviously dressed carefully for his boss's party.

"He was absolutely right," he said. "I owe him, bigtime, for his advice. If it weren't for him, I wouldn't be where I am today."

As I turned my head to the right, I winced. This morning, following a warm erotic dream starring Nick Treece, I'd awakened with a crick in my neck. "You don't call him Austin?" I asked, rubbing the sore spot.

He looked sheepish. "I've tried—but it doesn't feel right. I mean, I've looked up to this guy since I was a raw medical student—I went into anesthesiology because of him."

As we were looking at Austin's collection, one of the residents approached Nick. "I've got to go back and see a patient tonight, and I'm not sure—" he was saying. Excusing myself, I strolled away to give them some privacy.

Over the babble of conversation, I heard Eva Aarastadt's distinctive husky voice. Laughing at something, she was standing beside Austin, her head high, her back straight, her hands on her hips—so unlike his other faculty, who automatically adopted submissive postures when they came into his orbit. Dressed in a black-velour top over skinny black tights, her blond hair a bright waterfall against the dark fabric, she stood out in the crowded room like a bright star in a dark sky.

Turning away, I saw myself reflected in a fun-house mirror that made me look twice as wide and half as tall.

"No traveling fair was complete without a fat person or a midget." Jerome Pettit had appeared at my side, smiling sardonically at my distorted reflection. I'd seen him in the room earlier—had he waited until Nick was away to corner me? "Of course, we don't call them midgets anymore, now we call them 'vertically challenged.'

"Fat women were a better draw than fat men," he continued, pointing at a banner beside the mirror. A WHALE OF A WOMAN showed an enormous black-haired woman in the tiniest of yellow bikinis holding the hand of a short, skinny man, the scene captioned at the bottom in purple: OH MY! BUT *SHE* IS FAT!

"I wasn't entirely honest with you when we talked about Kitty Evanston and the anesthesia problem." Jerome's watch beeped, signaling the hour, and he fondled it absently. "I didn't want to tell you the rest of the story until I'd confirmed a rather important detail about her past."

Indeed. And I didn't believe he'd be "entirely honest" with me now, either. He was trying to set me up, that was the clear message I was getting through his "confidences." At a minimum he wanted me to fight with other members of Austin's lab on his behalf—but I thought he had a bigger agenda in mind. And if he could find out something disreputable to use against me, all the better. " 'The rest of the story'?"

"I do wonder if you weren't meant to be her dupe," he said.

Walking over to a glass case holding a mechanical belly dancer, he made a show of digging in his pocket and sorting through his change.

"Exactly the kind of toy that Fred Verlin would like," Jerome said, "his personal dancing girl—only he'd prefer less clothing."

A transparent veil covered the manikin's nose and mouth. Her oversize plaster breasts strained against a tiny red-and-white-striped top. A belt of silver coins, positioned just below her navel, held up her crimson floor-length skirt.

Dropping a dime in the slot, he watched the belly dancer shimmy as she rolled her glass eyes.

"So what's your hot new information about Kitty?" I asked.

"Her malpractice suit—after her first surgery."

"Malpractice suit?"

With the first and middle fingers of his right hand he stroked his thick black moustache in a one-two (pause) one-two (pause) rhythm as he stood watching the mechanical dancer. Waiting me out. So clearly enjoying himself. "Her initial surgery for endometriosis didn't fix everything perfectly—hardly a reasonable expectation for that kind of medical problem, of course, and a risk she was surely told from the outset—but she sued anyway." As he turned his head, I saw fingerprints on the lenses of his glasses.

"Remember, Kitty worked in Anesthesiology for several years," he said. "So she'd have known how to concoct a story that sounded quite realistic."

Murray Snelling had told me that Kitty came to see him after reading about him in a newspaper article—undoubtedly a story about recovered memories. Could Kitty have led Murray down the garden path? "You told me you were looking for her chart to check the identity of her anesthesiologist."

"She was a disgruntled employee trying to set up some kind of half-cocked revenge and make herself money in the process. Surely you can see there's no reason to bother checking any further."

I'd been so sure Kitty's story was true.

Now I pictured Kitty standing by my office window, clutching the enamel apple on the chain around her neck, the green worm's rhinestone eyes winking at me. Was this the news that Thelma Lou hadn't been able to remember?

"You don't *really* think—" I said.

"Unless you have some clear corroborative evidence, you need to assume Kitty's so-called memory was just her vivid imagination—suitably embellished by the prospect of easy money."

Nick joined us, handing me a fresh glass of wine, a twin to the one he'd gotten for himself. After they'd exchanged unenthusiastic greetings, Jerome turned to me, and said, "By the way, Nick has a number of . . . colorful stories—"

"I don't think—"

Ignoring Nick's interruption, Jerome said, "You should be sure to ask him for the details. *All* the details. Don't worry—they're clean, the kind of thing he could even tell his mother. You'll find it a most . . . informative experience, I'm sure."

"Jerome—" Nick's voice was low, his irritation obvious.

"I wasn't finished," Jerome said. "There's a saying about our profession: 'Like a man walking in a blizzard, an anesthesiologist's footprints are erased as soon as he passes.' But that doesn't apply to the anesthesiologist's memory—at least one hopes it doesn't." Smiling broadly, he walked away.

I saw, in that moment, the rigidity of Nick's posture, as if he wore a brace holding his back unnaturally straight. I wondered at its origin; fear seemed unlikely, judging by his face—but anger was a strong possibility.

Nick laughed, and the emotion was cloaked. "Jerome likes to engineer quarrels among his colleagues—then he sits back and watches. It looks like we're his newest target." He reached down and gently squeezed my hand.

"There's nothing of interest, no lurid tales—unfortunately."

Looking over, I caught Eva staring at us, her arms crossed over her chest. She was standing beside a wooden carousel "sea horse" that sported the head and forequarters of a horse and the swirling tail of a fish, its saddle carved in the shape of a water lily. Painted in shades of blue and green, it was hardly a cuddly Puff-the-Magic-Dragon; looking as if poised to spring on terrified prey, its forelegs ended not in hooves but in unsheathed claws, and fangs jutted from its snarling mouth. Eva's expression was no warmer or friendlier than that of the sea horse beside her.

"Come over here—I want to show off for you," Nick said. His hand on my elbow, we walked over to a life-size Uncle Sam doll with a meter in the middle of his chest. Setting his wine on a nearby table, he pulled a dime from his pocket, dropping it into the slot. As he squeezed the manikin's iron hand, the meter swung all the way to the far right.

" 'Stronger than a moose,' " I said, reading the legend on the meter. "I'm suitably impressed."

"To tell you the truth . . . I tried it out before I came to show you—just to be sure I could do it."

He picked up his glass from the table as he looked across the room where Jerome now stood talking with Austin; still watching them a moment later, he set it down. He didn't seem to realize he hadn't drunk from it.

As I was looking across the room, I saw Austin's wife, Doris, a handsome silver-haired woman, step quickly over to her husband and whisper in his ear. Dressed in a peach-colored linen sheath, a necklace of black pearls at her throat, she exuded a polished, sophisticated aura—but she had a worried crease in her forehead.

Then Austin was walking rapidly toward the door as he pulled his cellular phone out of his jacket pocket.

"I liked Austin's collection so much that I've bought a few things myself," Nick was saying. "Nothing like this, of course"—he gestured around the room—"but I'd really like to show it to you—"

When Austin reappeared, his expression was grim as he went around, tapping members of his research team on the shoulder and crooking his finger like a Pied Piper: Jerome, Eva, Nick. And then, his eyes lighting on me, he said, "Haley, you'll have to come as well." He herded us down the hall into a formal living room furnished with antique English rosewood tables and heavily carved chairs upholstered in white-and-raspberry-striped silk. Shutting the door, he said, "I've just had a call from hospital security people. They found the core-lab door open, Fred out cold on the floor inside; he'd stopped to check on an experiment on his way here, and someone jumped him."

Beside me, Jerome made a noise in his throat.

Austin's hands were balled into fists, his tone was strained. "Fred says he thinks he's OK, but he needs to head over to the ER to get himself evaluated. I assume you'll each want to check your own labs to make sure nothing's damaged, and you'll need to look over the core space as well. The security man will stay until you arrive. I can't walk out on my own party, or I'd go with you." His eyebrows were drawn down, his eyes squeezed half-closed: a worried man.

"This is clearly consistent with the message I passed on to you," Jerome said to Austin. "The anonymous caller who told me that an animal-rights demonstrator was planning another incident for the lab. Maybe related to . . . past trouble?'' He looked at Eva.

Her lips folded in a thin line of disgust, Eva rolled her eyes at Jerome.

''Fred didn't see any sense in getting the police involved, at least not at this stage,'' Austin said, frowning at Jerome, ''because he couldn't tell them anything useful about his assailant. But the final decision will need to be made once you've had the opportunity to check out the labs.

''In the meantime, I would hope you'd keep quiet about the trouble.'' Austin looked pointedly from me to Nick, making it obvious that even though my presence was problematic, he could hardly tell Nick that I needed to find my own way home—at least not directly. ''The fewer people who know the details, the better.''

In the car, I said, ''I hope Fred is OK. I'd have thought he should be heading over to the ER, not waiting around.''

''I agree—but that's Fred's choice here.''

In theory—but I imagined that Fred had tried to guess what Austin would want, and acted accordingly. ''Jerome told me that Eva had problems with animal-rights activists in her old job.''

''I heard something about that,'' Nick said, ''but not the details.''

So that particular tale of Jerome's had probably been accurate. And others?

''I can't believe it's really an animal-rights type,'' he said. ''Dr. Danziger is a control freak. I think someone's using the lab accidents as a way to harass him, someone who knows the best way to get to him is to undermine his sense of being in charge.''

Remembering Austin's obvious strain as we were leaving, I nodded. ''Who's your guess?''

"When he became chairman, the department was in bad shape; he was brought in as a paladin to clean up Dodge City. Along the way he's offended plenty of people—take your pick."

If Austin was the target for the pranks, then the search for Dean Verbrugge's replacement might be accelerating the mischief. But I could see other possibilities as well. "Eva told me that when she was considering this job, she got an anonymous letter that warned her not to come here."

"Really? I hadn't heard that. I could see why someone might want to warn her off, aside from any wish to get to Dr. Danziger—she has more ambition than any three people I know, put together. She's absolutely driven. Woe to anyone who gets in her way.

"She can't stand anyone trespassing on her territory," he said. "Jerome, Fred, Eva, and I each have our own labs, smaller rooms that branch off from the core lab; the doors have combination locks with push-button numbers instead of keys, just like the main door. She won't give anyone else her combination, and it's a real nuisance because she has a habit of taking equipment from the core lab, and then 'forgetting' and locking it up.

"Just after he got back from his vacation, Jerome changed his lock, and he's been very secretive about the combination—kind of a joke, really—in response to the fact that Eva wouldn't share with him."

We'd stopped at a light, and Nick looked over at me. I felt my breath catch as we gazed at each other for a long moment. Reaching over, he put his hand on mine. His Adam's apple bobbed up and down as he swallowed. Then the driver behind us leaned on his horn and Nick accelerated through the intersection, both hands back on the steering wheel.

When we got to the core lab we found a white-faced

Fred Verlin slumped in a chair, a bloody knot on the back of his bald head. Brushing aside our concerned comments, he assured us he'd go to the ER as soon as everyone had looked over the labs. Eva and Jerome were already here checking their rooms, he told us, and Nick should do the same—as soon as possible.

At the door to his lab, Nick dropped his voice, and said, "Would you keep an eye on Fred while I look around? He doesn't look good. Keep him talking, if you can."

Pulling a chair over beside Fred, I said, "Mind a little company?"

"Fine—but I'd rather wait to tell the story until everyone's done . . . so I won't have to keep repeating it." The last part of his sentence came out faster than the first.

"Sure. This is Austin's lab?" I asked, looking around.

Like a commercial kitchen designed to maximize both counter and storage space, avocado-colored steel cabinets lined the room. Note cards taped to the cupboard doors below the counter declared their contents: glassware, gloves, pipettes, petri dishes, Vortex mixer.

"The core lab is Austin's, technically," Fred said, "but we all use it." He sat up straighter as he spoke, and some color began to return to his cheeks.

The glass-fronted cabinets mounted on the wall near us held assorted chemicals in brown glass bottles or white plastic jars. On the counter below, a white plastic bucket was labeled in bright red: CHEMICAL SPILL KIT. TREATMENTS FOR CAUSTIC, ACID, AND FORMALDEHYDE SPILLS. Stacked next to the bucket were boxes of hypodermics, tagged with pictures of needles and sizes: 3cc, 5cc, 10cc.

Picturing the target on my office door, fear tightened my throat.

Fred's voice brought me back: "There are two large rooms in the core lab; the smaller labs are like miniature satellites around the core, but the only entrance is through the main door."

Like paths in a labyrinth—with only one exit.

"Does Austin ever work down here?"

"He's far too busy," Fred said, looking at me as if wondering about my judgment.

A bright blue cabinet nearby caught my eye, white letters six inches tall across the front spelling out the warning: CAUTION CORROSIVES. Underneath the white banner, a red label informed me that the corrosive acid storage cabinet met with OSHA requirements.

I shivered—a dangerous place for a prankster.

Hearing a door close, I was pleased to see Nick walking toward us. "Everything looks fine," he said.

"No problem in my lab," Jerome said, coming behind him.

Eva joined the circle. Standing in front of Fred, her hands on her hips, she said, "Tell us what happened. In detail."

"On my way to the party I stopped here because I needed to finish an experiment I'd started earlier in the day," Fred said. Underneath a dark blue suit that looked too heavy for the warm evening, he was wearing a white shirt and a navy tie dotted with crimson. "I thought I heard a noise inside when I was unlocking the door, but when I turned on the light I didn't see anything, so I decided I'd been mistaken." He pulled out a handkerchief and wiped beads of perspiration from his forehead.

"I was just taking off my jacket, so I could put on my lab coat, and then—wham! I find myself lying on the floor with a splitting headache, trying not to throw up all over myself." Looking sideways at Eva, he winced theatrically as he touched the bloody knot on his bald head.

A metal rack, mounted on the wall near the door, had half a dozen white lab coats dangling from its hooks. Fred would have been standing with his back to the door as he took off his coat, so his assailant might have come from the hallway—or the intruder could have been inside the lab when Fred unlocked the door, maybe hiding behind the row of freezers and other equipment that ran down the center of the lab, blocking one section from view.

As if she'd been pursuing the same train of thought, Eva asked, "You'd left the door to the hallway open behind you?"

"Only for a minute, because I had my hands full . . ."

Eva peered at the bloody spot on Fred's head. "Doesn't look that bad to me, unless you have an eggshell skull."

"I was wearing a hat, fortunately, and it cushioned the blow—"

"Had you been inside my lab for some reason?" she asked.

"No, I never went back—"

"Just how long were you unconscious?"

"A while, I'm not sure how long . . ."

"Guess." A harshness in her voice.

"Maybe . . . maybe ten, fifteen minutes, somewhere in that neighborhood—"

"Interesting. *Very* interesting." Her hands on her hips, Eva stared at Fred, her expression mixing contempt with disbelief. "Because someone was searching my lab, maybe during the time you were 'unconscious.' "

"You can't mean you think I—"

I saw genuine pain in Fred Verlin's face. And I watched Eva look at him, register it—and then turn away without a word. A sentence, a few words, she just needed to say something to make it easier for him. But Eva couldn't be bothered—as if normal human emotions and concerns didn't touch her, as if any plea for mercy would be as futile as shouting for help in the middle of a desert.

Chapter 16

"I'm sorry about screwing up the appointment time," Vince Gambier said to me, his expression not at all remorseful, "but my memory's shot—just more evidence for my problems since the *Phoenix*."

Tall with the unhealthy thinness of a heavy smoker, the seaman was wearing sunglasses with mirrored lenses, a short-sleeved denim shirt, and jeans. His brown hair, shot through with dirty gray, was tied in a rough ponytail—a style that highlighted his receding hairline and made him look older than his age, thirty-five. His red nose made me wonder if he had a drinking problem—as did the fact that he showed up for his Wednesday afternoon appointment on Thursday morning, smelling of cigarette smoke and beer.

"I can't work, so I need help while I get back on my feet," he said, continuing his litany as we walked from the reception area to my office. Taking off his sunglasses with a flourish, he exposed unappealing protuberant eyes, the lines around them drawn tight—and not, I guessed, from laughter.

He was carrying a manila accordion folder, the kind that closes with a flap like an envelope; he set it on the end table, a few inches from my tape recorder, as I was closing the door behind us. Then, without waiting for an invitation, he plunked himself down in a chair and leaned back, his hands clasped behind his neck.

As I reminded him about the purpose of the evaluation and got his permission to tape the session, I felt myself tensing, feeling a need for vigilance—as if I'd picked up the scent of a predator.

"The way I understand it, you're working to keep me from getting the money I'm due," he said, his tone flat, his look challenging.

"I was asked to conduct an independent evaluation. It's quite possible that I'll concur with Dr. Snelling's findings—however, I could come to a different conclusion."

"As long as you'll keep an open mind . . . let's get on with it." And then he smiled—a look with no warmth behind it.

I thought about what I knew about him from his records. The middle of three children, his mother died when he was four; Vince left home at seventeen when his father brought home a new wife. After spending twelve years in the navy, he'd worked in casinos in Las Vegas before moving to Houston a year ago "on a whim." Never married, no children, his father now dead, he hadn't kept contact with his brother or sister. No obvious reason for my sense of unease.

"I understand this has been a difficult time for you."

"You said it—and the insurance company just keeps stalling. They owe me, and they're gonna pay—"

Once he'd finished his monologue, I said, "Tell me about the day the *Phoenix* sank."

Haltingly, he told the same basic story I'd already heard, his shoulders hunched, his voice low and strained, the very picture of a man still distraught after a terrifying experience. Midway through, he got up and started pacing back and forth along the length of my office, walking from the door to the window, relating how Willie had snagged the raft and climbed inside first, he got in next, then Gary and Davy. Waving a hand stained yellow with nicotine, he told how Lou, apparently confused, kept swimming away as they were calling to him—the same vignette I'd heard from Davy.

On the top of my desk I had two journals, the departmental Grand Rounds schedule for July, computer printouts for a research project, and a picture of Pavlov sitting in my Corvette. Not particularly fascinating material, but Vince looked them over well—just as he tried to sneak a peek at my notepad.

He sat down again to answer my questions about flashbacks and nightmares, giving me chapter and verse with diagnosable symptoms. He did a fine job of describing himself as a troubled man, but every so often I caught a glimpse of something else—a coldness, a sense of calculation.

"Let's back up a bit," I said. "Why did you enlist in the navy?"

"To see the world and get money for college, that was my original plan. You probably read in my records about how I was part of Desert Storm—a real shame we didn't get to do all the mopping up we should have done once we were there and had the chance—"

"Why did you leave the service?"

"A couple of officers had it in for me. If it hadn't been for their bad attitude, I'd have stayed, no problem." But I noticed his hands had stilled.

"And after the navy you moved—"

As I turned my head to the right, I winced. Last night, as we were walking to my front door after leaving the core lab, Nick had said, "Your neck is sore, isn't it?"

"How'd you know?"

"At the party"—he smiled down at me—"a couple of times you turned your head and your expression got kind of pained—and then you'd start kneading the spot."

He'd been watching me more closely than I realized. Digging in my purse for my key, remembering my dream about him, I was glad for a reason to avoid his eyes for a minute.

"If it would help," he cleared his throat, "I'd be glad to massage the spot—purely for therapeutic purposes, of course." He wiggled his eyebrows at me.

"I had a wonderful evening, at least until we got the call about Fred," I said, "but it's late, and tomorrow's a workday. How about if I take two aspirin and call you in the morning?"

"This wasn't exactly the evening I'd planned for us—and I have to work this weekend because I'm away the next couple of weeks. If there's any chance you could take off Friday, we could rent a boat in Galveston and go sailing—"

Early this morning I'd arranged to take Friday as a vacation day, rearranging a couple of supervisory appointments to make it possible.

Now Vince said, "I headed to Las Vegas because I'd never been there before, just planned to visit, but I stayed on. When I decided I was spending too much money gambling, I moved here."

"How did you get along with the rest of the crew of the *Phoenix*?"

"OK, I guess . . . so we're back to the disaster again, huh?" He checked his watch, then pulled a pack of unfiltered Camels from his breast pocket with the air of a poker player displaying a royal flush. "Bet you're going to tell me I can't smoke these here, right?"

"Right. The hospital's all nonsmoking."

"I just gotta have one. I can't sit still and talk about this shit without a smoke." He stood up. "I'll come back once I've smoked outside." Picking up his accordion folder from the table but not his sunglasses, he said, "My personal notes on my case—I don't like having them out of my sight."

"I'll go outside with you. We can keep talking while you smoke."

The wary look appeared and vanished from his face in a blink.

"Some kinda nuthouse you work in, all right," he said, as we walked down the corridor. "Sitting out here, waiting all that time for you, I couldn't believe the things I heard."

"Really? Like what?" Outside, in the wake of a recent cloudburst, the air was heavy and moist, pressing closely, like a hothouse. Steam was rising from the rain-splattered asphalt like ghostly shadows.

"These two guys, doctors I guess, they look awful young but they're wearing white coats—one says, 'I have a new patient, you ask him to write something, he just makes zeros; if you ask him what it says, he tells you he's God, and that's a sentence.' "

A maintenance man in blue coveralls was slinging trash into a Dumpster behind the building. Picking up an old metal stool, he lifted it over his head and tossed it up high, as if aiming a basketball for the net. It clanged and echoed as it bounced against the metal walls of the Dumpster.

Vince, still talking as he stopped to light a cigarette, his folder tucked under his arm, seemed untouched by the noise. "Then the other guy says, 'I've got a therapy patient who wears a bulletproof vest when she comes to our sessions.' "

He took a long pull on his cigarette, tossing the match on the sidewalk behind him. "When they saw I was listening, they hushed up—just when it was getting good."

"They shouldn't have been talking like that in a public place." Checking my watch, I asked, "Do you remember what they looked like?"

His descriptions were detailed enough for me to put names to the first-year residents who had been so indiscreet.

Standing beside a bus stop just up the street from Rugton, a well-endowed teenager with enough makeup to look eighteen going on twenty-five was wearing a yellow halter and low-riding yellow-and-blue-striped shorts that left her tanned midriff bare.

"Never saw babes dressed like that when I was in Kuwait." He'd thrown back his shoulders and stuck out his scrawny chest as we walked toward her.

"Did you have any problem parking, or finding your way to my office?" I asked.

"No, I got a good spot on the ground floor over there"—he gestured toward the visitors' garage, his eyes still fixed on the teenager—"and I went straight to the waiting area.

"Hey, hey—" he said, smiling, when we were within a few feet of her. A bored expression on her face, the girl looked once in our direction and then away. Vince hawked loudly and spat on the street as we passed her.

A few minutes later, as we were approaching Rugton, he said, "I need to use the men's room—I assume you won't want to follow me there." He was walking too close, crowding me. Deliberately, I assumed, from his sideways glance.

"I'll meet you upstairs . . . unless you'd prefer I wait for you?"

"I can find my way," he said, rolling his eyes.

Back in my office, Vince gently set his accordion folder next to my recorder before plopping down in the chair.

"How did you get along with the rest of the crew of the *Phoenix*?" I asked, picking up where we'd left off.

A fly was buzzing between us, looping back and forth. Following it with his eyes for a minute, Vince jumped up, clapping his hands together. Then, dropping it on my lap as if bestowing a gift, he smiled and said, "I never miss."

I had guessed that his bulky folder contained one of two things—booze or a recorder—which meant he'd used his trip to the men's room either to take a snort or to change the tape. His reaction time didn't fit with alcohol . . . but did mesh all too well with my growing sense of unease.

Flicking the dead fly off my skirt, I said, "How did you get along with—"

"Let's just say all of us weren't exactly good buddies. Davy's neck and thighs are as thick as his mind—his IQ must be somewhere below freezing."

"What about the others?"

"The twins weren't bad, just a little boring, always talking to each other and ignoring everyone else. Lou was always sucking up to the captain . . . Willie was the best of the bunch as far as I was concerned, at least he'd been around a little."

"And the captain?"

"I hate to speak ill of the dead . . . but Bert was the kind of guy who tells you it's his way or the highway. On the boat or off, he always wore his skipper's cap, if you know what I mean." Dark circles of sweat had appeared under the arms of his denim shirt.

With the other members of the *Phoenix* crew, I'd told

them we'd be doing formal psychological testing during a second session; I'd planned to interview everyone first. I hadn't fallen asleep until late last night, and I'd forgotten to pack a lunch because I was so drowsy this morning. Now it was already past noon and I had meetings and appointments scheduled straight for the rest of the day, beginning at one. All too aware of my rumbling stomach as I looked at the tension in Vince's posture, I made my decision. "Next we'll do some formal testing to evaluate your memory . . ."

He turned aside, stretching and yawning broadly. "I've got terrible problems—can't you see that without putting me through more tests?"

Once he'd left, I made two phone calls before dashing off to a departmental faculty meeting, where I was sorry to learn that Quinton Gibbs had headed back to Toronto when his mother-in-law took a turn for the worse. I'd hoped to set a time to talk with him about Vince—and I'd planned to ask him to get Kitty's chart for me now that Jerome seemed determined to assure me it was only a fool's errand.

As Kurt von Reichenau described his latest battles with hospital administration over the renovation of Rugton, I thought about Vince Gambier. Consistent with his reports of memory problems, he'd performed quite poorly on formal tests, particularly one where I read passages and asked him to tell me everything he could remember—but my chats with the two indiscreet first-year residents had confirmed that his recall of their conversation was entirely accurate—to their obvious chagrin. His clear and precise descriptions of their appearance half an hour after he'd seen them seemed at odds with his inability to remember simple designs long enough to reproduce them thirty seconds later. And while he'd insisted he couldn't remember practical information, he'd had no problem finding his way back to my office by himself, despite the deliberately circuitous route that I'd chosen through Rugton.

The memory discrepancies were not the only red flags. His fly-catching skills provided an interesting contrast to his abysmal performance on a reaction-time test just minutes later. His reports of jumpiness didn't square with his lack of response when we'd passed the maintenance man noisily slinging trash into the Dumpster. He had all the right words for his PTSD song—but he couldn't carry the tune.

Vince had lied fluently and often, but I was most troubled by what was missing when he talked about his life—deep friendships, love or family interests. His loyalties were as enduring as a chameleon's colors.

What stayed with me, when I thought about Vince later, was the memory of him as he was leaving my office, standing at the door, his hand on the knob, as I was telling him we'd need to schedule a second session—the way he looked down, then back up at me, his expression flat and emotionless, a muscle working in his cheek. It reminded me of a nature film where I'd watched the muscles tensing under a snake's skin—a rippling movement as it was preparing to strike.

Chapter 17

"Last night I was supposed to leave Sydney the protocol for a study she'll be starting for me today, but I forgot," Nick said as we were walking out to his car early Friday morning. "Mind if we stop at the lab before we head for Galveston? It'll only take a minute."

"Sure."

As he parked, he asked, "Would you rather come in with me, or wait in the car?" And then, before I could answer, he added, "I'll do my best Elmer Fudd imitation if you'll come along."

Our laughter was echoing in the empty hallway as he unlocked the core-lab door, and then I saw his face go blank. "The light's on," he said. "Maybe someone's here already?" Remembering Fred's recent attack, my heart sped up.

"Hello?" he called, his voice tense as he stepped inside in front of me.

I flashed back to the lab as I'd first seen it, covered in red. Now the sight of clean counters was a relief.

"Sydney's work area is just over here, behind the equipment . . ."

As we walked across the room I smelled something

odd, out of place, not the antiseptic smell I associated with laboratories. Something spoiled or burnt?

Wearing a blue-and-green plaid shirt with the sleeves rolled up, white jeans, and boat shoes without socks, I was shivering, I realized—but surely only because of the air-conditioning?

When we rounded the corner, I saw a man in a white lab coat sprawled on his back on the floor, his left leg twisted at an awkward angle. His eyes, half-open, were glazed.

I stood gaping, unable to make sense of what I was seeing—not wanting to take in the details: Jerome Pettit, staring sightlessly up at the ceiling, his skin a sickly white against the blackness of his hair and moustache.

"Jerome!" Hurrying over, we called out his name in unison, the fear in Nick's voice mirroring my own.

No response. No movement.

I kept watching Jerome's eyes, looking for a reaction. Waiting for him to blink.

"Call a Code Blue—" Nick said, waving his hand toward the phone mounted on the wall as he dropped down on his knees beside Jerome.

My hand was shaking as I picked up the receiver and dialed the emergency number. Like an echo, I saw Nick's hand trembling as he placed his fingers on Jerome's throat, feeling for a pulse.

Underneath his white lab coat Jerome was wearing a khaki shirt, jeans, and running shoes. His right hand lay open, palm upward, his arm at his side; his thumb and his index finger had yellow-brown circles at the tips. As I waited for the operator to answer I stared at his chest, willing it to rise and fall, trying to convince myself I saw movement. Trying not to think about the significance of his sightless stare.

"Cold," Nick muttered, so low I barely heard it. Then

his shoulders slumped, conveying the verdict all too clearly before he spoke: "He's gone. We're too late. Way too late."

"Emergency operator." An insistent woman's voice in my ear. "Is anyone there?"

"Code Blue?" I asked Nick—not believing. Wanting him to say there was still a chance.

He took the phone from me. "This is Dr. Nicholas Treece in the Department of Anesthesiology. Patch me through to the police." Wearing cutoffs and sneakers, his blond chest hair poking out of a pink polo shirt with an Izod emblem, he looked so out of place against the backdrop of the lab that for a crazy moment I wondered if it might just be a bad dream.

I listened as he identified himself again and said he was sure Jerome was dead, it looked like an accident, then recited the room number and directions. "He was electrocuted, I think," he said, looking at Jerome's body, swallowing heavily. "A freak accident. Laboratory equipment."

Another "accident"? I felt a sense of dread sidling in, insinuating itself, like fog.

On the counter above Jerome's body I saw a piece of equipment about half the size of a small microwave. Encased in gray metal, it had a handle on top, dials on the front. A small acrylic box, half-filled with a clear liquid, sat beside the unit; two thin cables, one red and one black, ran from the front of the instrument to sockets at the top of the acrylic box. Off to the side of the instrument, Jerome's watch.

Nothing else nearby. On the right side of the instrument panel, I saw the warning, printed in red: DANGER. TO BE OPERATED ONLY BY QUALIFIED TECHNICAL PERSONNEL. The dial for adjusting the current had been set at the upper limit.

"The police want us to wait here," he said, hanging up. "We're not to touch anything."

"This is terrible," I said. "It doesn't seem possible."

Nick put his arm around me, and I turned to lean against him, suddenly aware of how rubbery my legs felt. Neither of us moved for a long moment.

"Why do you think he . . . why electrical?" I asked, forcing the words past the lump in my throat.

"The marks on his fingers," he said, pointing at the yellow-brown circles at the tips. "Joule marks, they're called—characteristic of electrical burns. He must've gotten a bad shock from that power supply, bad enough to kill him."

I pictured the electric current as acid, flaming through Jerome's body, invading and corroding. Trying to shut out the image, I swallowed heavily and focused on Nick's face.

"Power supply? What was he doing?" I asked, making an effort to keep my voice level. Despite regular swallowing, my stomach was fighting its way up toward my throat.

"Looks like he was trying to run a gel. The clear plastic box is a gel box, and the equipment beside it must be the power supply. Got to be an old unit—I've never seen one that big."

Shaking his head, he said, "It doesn't make sense. Why would Jerome be running a gel in the first place? That's a long way from his expertise."

Checking his watch, he said, "I'm not thinking clearly. I've got to call Austin and let him know about Jerome. He'll be in his office soon, if he's not there already."

Frowning as he banged the phone down after dialing one number, he said, "His cell-phone recording says it's

not in service now. I'll try his regular number, his secretary gets in early . . .''

Half-listening as Nick told Austin's secretary about
Jerome's death and the likely cause, I remembered when
Eva had told me about the thefts from her lab: *A power
supply unit for gel electrophoresis.* Along with the P-32
isotope: *It's used for labeling DNA, for gel electrophoresis.* And she'd blamed Jerome.

Now I stared at Jerome's face, trying to read something there, some lingering emotion. Hostility, cunning—
maybe even regret. But it was slack and blank.

"She'll tell him as soon as he gets in," he said, hanging up the phone. "Let's wait around the corner." He
took my hand and we walked around to a point where
a bank of freezers shielded us from the sight of Jerome's
body. "Austin will be here soon to help us deal with
the police."

"I wasn't aware we needed his help in this instance,"
I said, regretting my curt tone as soon as I'd spoken.

Raising an eyebrow, he said, "Jerome was his right-
hand man. Surely you wouldn't propose to have him
learn about Jerome's death by running into a gaggle of
police in his own lab?"

Before I could respond, I heard the door open behind
us. "Austin?" he called out as he turned, dropping my
hand like a guilty schoolboy.

"Hardly," Eva Aarastadt said, looking us up and
down as she walked toward us. "Aren't we the casual
ones today?" Dressed in a white lab coat over a green-
cotton sweater and navy skirt, her blond hair gathered
in a twist, she looked wonderful—as usual.

"Jerome's dead," Nick told her. "We just found his
body. We're waiting for the police."

"I . . . don't understand. Jerome? Dead? How—"

"Jerome's dead?" Fred Verlin had appeared in the

doorway behind Eva. "Did I hear you say that Jerome's dead?" He laughed, a high-pitched, nervous snort that echoed in the silence.

"It's no joke," Nick said, his tone sharp. "He's on the floor, over there," he pointed. "Electrocuted, I think. It looks as if he was trying to run a gel."

Eva and Fred looked at each other for a long moment. Then, together, they walked just far enough so they could peer around the corner and see Jerome's body. "My God," Eva said, turning to put her arms around Fred, burying her face in his chest—missing the triumphant look that flashed across his face.

"It was supposed to be me," Eva said, her voice tremulous, when she finally stepped back from Fred. "Jerome knew I was going to start a new series of gels today. It's obvious what happened—he was trying to rig it for me and zapped himself instead."

"Did anyone else know you were planning to run gels besides Jerome?" I asked.

"Only everyone in the lab," she said, shrugging. "Last lab meeting, we'd talked about what we were planning when we discussed how to divide Sydney's time. But you're missing the obvious: Jerome didn't say anything about running any studies. He didn't have any reason to be using the power supply—he wouldn't have known how to run a gel if his life depended on it."

Her words hung in the air.

"Everyone knew Jerome had a serious grudge against Eva," Fred said. "She's a good scientist, and a woman—that's two strikes against her in his book. He must have been trying to rig the power supply to shock her, but he didn't know enough to pull it off. I doubt if he even knew how dangerous it could be."

Then how would he have known enough to try to rig it?

"That's your equipment Jerome was using?" I asked Eva.

"The power supply is the one that Fred was going to loan me—a temporary replacement for the one stolen from my lab," she said. "He'd left it there for me—"

"The newer models shut themselves off when there's a problem because they carry such high voltage," Fred chimed in. "The old kind didn't have an automatic cut-off."

"Normally, I wouldn't have run a gel myself," Eva said. "But I didn't have much choice after Belinda walked out—and Sydney wasn't going to get around to helping me until hell froze over."

"Belinda?" I asked.

"Belinda Luttrell," she said, her tone impatient. "The technician who quit after—"

The door opened and Austin walked in. He looked strained, his drawn face making it obvious he'd already heard the latest bad news. Wearing a short-sleeved blue shirt and tie without his usual white coat, he seemed underdressed. "Where's Jerome—his body?" he asked, and we all pointed in unison. Then, like plants following the sun, we trooped behind him as he went around the corner and knelt beside the corpse. In the silence I heard him exhale heavily. Then, gently resting his hand on Jerome's shoulder, he said, "Go in peace, old friend."

As Austin stood up, Eva said to him, "I'm not going to pretend I'm sorry about his death. That's not his equipment, and he had no reason for using it. He was obviously trying to set up an accident for me—"

"We don't know the cause of death yet," Austin said, turning to face Eva, his tone caustic, "though it does look like a lethal shock. But Jerome had a valid reason for borrowing the equipment. He didn't want to publicize it, but he'd gone away to Woods Hole for an intensive two-week workshop on molecular biology at the beginning of June—that's where he went when he said he was taking vacation. He wasn't going to say anything until he'd run at least one study successfully.''

In the silence that followed, Eva and Fred stared intently at the floor while Austin stood watching, his back rigid, his hands clenched in fists.

My stomach squeezed tight as I glanced over at Jerome's body, his empty gaze, the burns on his hand. I couldn't believe his death was only a freak accident—not after the attack on Fred, not after the isotope in the water cooler.

Not after Kitty Evanston's surgery.

The laboratory seemed menacing, a mine field of hazards. Looking around, I felt a wave of coldness.

When the police finally arrived after going to the wrong building, Austin tried to take charge; he was told politely but firmly to step aside, he'd be interviewed in his turn, leave word where he could be found. Clearly irritated, Austin paused on his way out of the lab and said, "Nick, I'll need your help this morning to reassign Jerome's work." Then, just before turning his back again, he looked at me: "Haley—we'll meet at noon in my office."

As the door closed behind him, I looked over at Nick. Shrugging helplessly, he said, "I'm really sorry—we'll have to go sailing another day. Look, if you want to take my car and go home, I can get a taxi to your place later—"

"No, I'll stay, at least until the afternoon; I have plenty to keep me busy in my office."

The officer who interviewed me a half hour later kept his face carefully neutral as I described my concerns about the laboratory "accidents" without mentioning

Kitty Evanston. When I'd finished, his pointed questions about how my job interfaced with Austin's lab suggested that he thought I didn't have much to contribute.

Halfway to Rugton, I turned around and went back to Denton Hall. Positioning myself at the far end of the corridor from the core lab, I stood between two doors that had numbered buttons beneath their knobs. Leaning against the wall, a campus newspaper in front of my face, I glimpsed Sydney heading toward the core lab; her face was averted, but it was clear she had an ugly black eye.

Five minutes later, a white-coated woman entered the lab on my left. Even standing eight feet away, I got the combination: 1-3-4-2-5-2. Eva might not have shared her combination with anyone, but it wouldn't have been hard to figure it out—or for someone to do the same for the main core-lab entrance.

Back in my office, I tried to draft my report on Vince Gambier, but I kept picturing Jerome's body, sprawled on the floor.

Jerome had claimed that an "anonymous caller" told him an animal-rights demonstrator was planning further mischief in the lab, hinting it was related to Eva—and then her lab had been searched during the party. Had Jerome really known something? Was Jerome's "accident" really meant for Eva?

I called Loretta, a friend at the medical school in New York where Eva had been a faculty member before coming to Houston; after we'd traded news for a few minutes, I asked if she knew anything about Eva's past problems with animal-rights activists. She didn't, but she promised to check for me.

As I was sorting through my morning mail, about to toss a memo to medical staff about "additions to the formulary of accepted drugs," I thought about Kitty and her surgery. *Idiot*, I told myself, for overlooking the obvious. Buttoning up the white lab coat that I wear when I lecture to medical students, clipping my ID to the pocket, I presented myself at the main hospital's medical records room.

Katherine Evanston's chart wasn't available, the silver-haired clerk told me regretfully. It wasn't that she had any problem with my request; unlike psychiatric charts, where access is strictly limited, consecrated members of the medical staff had full rights, as I'd finally realized—but it was already checked out to a Dr. Pettit, one of a dozen she'd pulled for his departmental QA Committee back on Monday, June 16.

Which meant that when Jerome had claimed he was checking the identity of Kitty's anesthesiologist, he'd known the answer all along. He'd requested her chart the first day that I'd mentioned the problem, a full two days before I gave him her name and hospital ID number.

At noon I found myself seated opposite Austin in his office, the expanse of his black-lacquer desk between us.

"The police are still talking with Fred and Eva, and Nick is checking Jerome's schedule to see what needs to be covered while we sort things out," he said. "In the meantime, I thought it might be helpful for the two of us to chat. You've already spoken to the police, I gather?" Leaning forward in his chair, his hands flat on his desk, his voice was mild.

"Yes."

Like varnished wood soaked in water, the pleasant edge began to peel off his demeanor. "They asked me about some of our recent problems in the lab and whether they might be related to Jerome's death," he said, looking pointedly at me, as if expecting me to deny I'd suggested as much.

"It seems too much of a coincidence that the very piece of equipment that probably proved lethal was an older model," I said, pleased that the police were following up on my comments, "especially after the new model with safeguards had been stolen."

For a second, he had a feral look. Then, speaking in a condescending, patronizing tone, he said, "There's no big mystery about the thefts. South America has an enormous black market for medical equipment. Houston's a gateway—every hospital in the medical center has gotten hit at one time or another. Two months ago someone lifted a new thermocycler from Pathology—twenty thousand dollars out the door."

"But the P-32 that was dumped in the watercooler wasn't stolen for the black market."

Austin gave me a measuring look. Maybe wondering where I'd heard the story? "Of course not. I'd guess our thief was upset because he couldn't lay his hands on anything from his shopping list that day—or maybe he just created a little chaos to draw our attention away from his other robberies."

In the black-lacquer cabinet behind Austin's desk, his collection of crystal and glass glittered in the light. "And those incidents had nothing to do with the attack on Fred," I said, "or Jerome's anonymous call about an animal-rights activist?"

A muscle in his cheek jumped. "Jerome was big on conspiracy theories—especially when he could tell stories where he cast himself in the role of the hero who would save us all." Raising his eyebrows, he looked pointedly at me.

So Austin was promoting Jerome's death as simply an unfortunate accident—not surprising when any whiff of scandal could quash his chances for becoming the next Dean of our medical school.

"The police said they'd heard that Jerome might have been behind the tricks," he said. "I agreed it was possible—even probable. But I also told them that I believed his death was simply a terrible accident: He died because he didn't know enough about the equipment he was using."

Had Jerome really been the prankster—or simply a convenient scapegoat? A choice target now that he had no way to defend himself?

"It's time to put the trouble behind us," he continued, speaking in the tone of someone who expects speedy compliance, who brooks no opposition.

Would Eva have voiced her suspicions to the police—and would she have told them that Jerome had been responsible for past problems? I hoped I wasn't the lone voice crying in the wind: Austin's measured responses had a way of sounding so terribly reasonable, and he was obviously motivated to provide an authorized text for the police to memorize and follow.

When I didn't answer, he said, "My grandmother had this theory about disability and professional choices—people destined to be musicians will get tinnitus, dancers will suffer from arthritis. Perhaps that means that psychologists get paranoid—at least the minority who weren't, already."

I knew that Austin routinely challenged anyone who came into his orbit; he worked hard to establish his dominance early—and he enforced it by humiliating anyone who didn't fall in line. The only answer he'd consider appropriate at this point was *mea culpa*.

Working hard to keep my voice level, I said, "I understand the Board of Trustees hasn't named Dean Verbrugge's successor yet.'' Then, looking pointedly behind him, at his collection of crystal, I added, ''Maybe men who live in glass houses can't afford to have stones thrown.''

Chapter 18

A section near the hospital gift shop's entrance displayed a mother lode of tacky Southwestern souvenirs: Texas-shaped ashtrays, Tabasco cookbooks, tequila suckers with embedded worms, stuffed armadillos atop billed caps, beer mugs fashioned as glass cowboy boots. It was hard for me to fathom the rationale behind the garish display; perhaps the manager had decided that out-of-towners, coming to visit an ailing friend or relative, would be charmed by bits of local color. The sign on the wall above the section warned that SHOPLIFTERS WILL BE MERRILY BEATEN TO A BLOODY PULP. Personally, I thought they should pay people to cart it away.

Behind the counter, talking on the phone, I spotted Belinda Luttrell, the technician who'd left Austin's lab after drinking the isotope-laced water. "I'm just feeling *too awful* to do much of anything today. My head aches, I've got a sore throat, I just feel *so rotten*."

She looked perfectly healthy to me. An attractive woman in her midthirties, she had shoulder-length auburn hair that curled at the ends, a fringe of bangs above her eyes. Her plump cheeks were tinted a delicate pink, her eyes were carefully outlined in black, and her tight, low-cut turquoise knit top showcased breasts the size of cantaloupes.

Hoping she might shed some light on the "accidents," I'd looked her up in the university's on-line directory. Her new job in the gift shop was a surprise; had she gotten spooked about working as a technician—or did she have trouble getting a good recommendation when she left?

After she'd hung up I handed her a pack of cherry Life Savers and a dollar bill. As she moved toward the cash register, I pointed at the hospital ID clipped to her breast pocket and said, "I recognize your name. I started working with Dr. Danziger's research group recently. I'm Haley McAlister." Still dressed in my white jeans and plaid shirt, my own ID stowed in my purse, I was hoping she'd assume I was a new lab tech.

As cover stories go, it wasn't terribly convincing— but I didn't want to try something more elaborate without knowing whether she'd kept in touch with anyone from the lab, or how she felt about the job she'd left. Or if word of Jerome's death had reached her yet.

Her eyes swept over me appraisingly, a calculated look that vanished in half a heartbeat, and then, her hand pressed over her ample cleavage, she said, "The news about Dr. Pettit's death really shook me up." Her eyes were wide, her tone appropriately somber—but she let go a private little smile of excitement, one she couldn't quite suppress.

As I'd hoped, tidings of Jerome's demise had primed her for talking. With minimal encouragement she told me how shocked she was when her cousin who worked in the ER called her with the story, how the news was so traumatic that she got the *worst* headache, how she found it so hard to believe that something so terrible could happen so suddenly—

"Perhaps you could interrupt your socializing for a moment?" The woman was in her sixties, her gray hair pulled back in a neat bun; she'd been standing by the register, two candy bars in hand, jangling her car keys and frowning while Belinda studiously avoided looking in her direction.

After ringing up the woman's purchase, Belinda said, "Sometimes I get the *worst* headaches—" Grabbing her purse from under the counter, she pulled out a box of Pepto-Bismol tablets, a wad of tissues, a package of Maalox, and a roll of cough drops before she came up with a small tin of aspirin.

She marched toward the door, her short, black, pleated skirt bouncing with her steps. Once she'd finished swallowing the pills with water from the fountain just outside the entrance, I asked, "How long did you work in the lab?"

"Just over a year. At first it was mainly for Dr. Verlin and Dr. Danziger, a few small projects for Dr. Pettit. Then, after Dr. Aarastadt and Nick—Dr. Treece—joined the group, I worked mostly for them until I left at the end of April."

"How was it for you?"

She looked down the corridor, her gaze lingering on two men in white coats who stood talking halfway down the hallway. "I get to meet a lot more men—people— in this job. In the lab, we'd get fellows or postdocs once in a while, but they were mostly foreign—lots of Chinese women"—she made a face—"and never any med students. Other things weren't great—Sydney's not the easiest person to work with. She always got snitty whenever Nick praised my work. Jealous." She turned back to the water fountain. "It's important to drink plenty of fluids," she said, gulping the equivalent of a couple of glasses.

Hearing her words, I felt my stomach twist. "You must've been pretty upset when you found out about the P-32 in the water."

The color drained from her face. Back inside, she took her time replacing the aspirin in her purse.

"I don't want to talk about it," she said, her tone firm. "Besides, I promised I wouldn't say anything. That was part of the deal when I left."

"You promised Dr. Pettit?"

Belinda nodded.

"Surely his death makes a difference now—"

"I told Dr. Pettit I wasn't going to work there anymore, and he didn't argue with me—well, he really couldn't, could he? I told him I wanted my salary paid until I found another job, and I wanted a good recommendation. He agreed that it was fair on both counts, as long as I'd keep quiet about the joker who dumped the isotope. I started here two weeks later."

Moving to the newspaper racks beside the counter, Belinda began straightening a stack of tabloids. "I'm surprised they actually found someone to take the job." She gave me a speculative look, as if trying to account for my flawed judgment. "I mean, I said *I* wouldn't talk about it, but word must have gotten around somehow—truthfully, I don't know how . . ."

A man wearing the short white coat of a medical student walked up to the counter with a pack of gum, and Belinda turned eagerly to him. Taking my cue, I strolled over to the greeting-card rack and started leafing through the nearest section, a series of get-well messages that seemed evenly divided between the unrelievedly saccharine and the deliberately and offensively gross. Belinda was smiling broadly and gazing into the future doctor's eyes as she quizzed him about what specialty he planned to enter.

After he walked away, I said, "I have to tell you that some of the stories I've been hearing about the lab have made me a little nervous. Did you get sick from the sodium fluoride in the coffeepot?"

"Did I get sick! I thought I would *die*, I had such horrible stomach cramps, I got this terrible watery diarrhea—"

Two minutes later, as I was starting to feel nauseated by her remarkably graphic descriptions, I asked, "Who else got sick?"

"Besides me?" A thoughtful pause. "Sydney. Dr. Aarastadt. Dr. Verlin. And Dr. Danziger."

Exactly as I'd guessed.

"But not Dr. Pettit, of course," I said, "since he makes—made—such a point about not drinking coffee." Waiting to see if she'd jump.

"I can't get Dr. Pettit's death off my mind," Belinda said. "I hope he didn't suffer." Her Southern accent made it come out as "suffah."

"Not at all, from what I've heard. They said it looked like he was electrocuted when he was trying to run a gel."

"He was trying to run a gel? His two-week course was barely enough time to learn the language."

It took a moment for her words to register. "But— how did you know that Dr. Pettit was trying to learn molecular biology? I heard he was trying to keep it secret."

"Some secret." Belinda rolled her eyes. "He left his application for the workshop lying on the counter in the lab."

I stared at her, hearing the echo of her words. "Who else would have known—"

"Belinda! How are you?"

Turning, I saw Nick Treece heading toward us, smiling.

I'd been standing behind a rack of greeting cards that would have screened me from his view as he approached. Catching sight of me, he looked startled. "Haley! I've just been to Rugton, looking for you."

And then, turning to Belinda, he said, "So you've met our psychologist?"

"*Psychologist?*" Belinda actually stepped backwards, away from me. "That's not what she told *me*—"

Chapter 19

The Szondi, a psychological test that dropped out of favor some years ago, used photographs of various types of psychiatric patients; people taking the test indicated which pictures they liked and disliked, and diagnoses were inferred from their choices. If I'd seen Nick Treece's photo among the rest, I wouldn't have picked him out—I've never been attracted to classically attractive men. Ian had a thin face, high cheekbones, and a strong jaw; despite green-blue eyes and wavy black hair, he wasn't handsome, but he'd certainly been arresting. So why did my heart accelerate whenever I caught sight of Nick unexpectedly?

"It's been a rotten day," Nick was saying. "I'm sorry I couldn't get back to you earlier, but Dr. Danziger asked me to cover for Jerome today—and to figure out how to redistribute his assignments over the next few weeks." He was wearing a white coat over green hospital scrubs, his blond hair was tousled, his expression strained—and I kept thinking how good he looked, how pleased I was that he'd come searching for me.

Once we'd gotten down the hallway from the gift shop, I repeated what I'd said to Belinda when I met her: I'd starting working with Austin's research group recently and I recognized her name.

"Belinda lives for drama," he'd said, waving away my explanation. "For her, audience appreciation is more important than accuracy. She's the kind of woman who'll give you a riveting story about how she almost died of pneumonia after she spent a few days in bed with the flu."

Now, biting his lip, he said, "I was really looking forward to the day with you—I'm sorry it all blew up. I was hunting for you to ask—is there any chance you'd feel like having dinner together tonight?" And then, before I could answer, he quickly added, "Our dates—attempted dates—have both ended badly . . . so I'd certainly understand if you thought maybe it wasn't such a hot idea, after all—"

"I'd love to."

Like kindling touched with a match, his face lit up. I found myself beaming in response.

"I'm still not sure when I'll be able to leave," he said, still smiling. "I've got to go over Jerome's schedule with Dr. Danziger and show him how I've set up coverage. I'll ring you as soon as I figure out what time I'll be able to see the light at the end of the tunnel."

Looking down at me, he squeezed my arm gently. "How are you doing? That was quite a shock this morning."

His concern warmed me. "Somehow it doesn't seem real, not yet."

"I feel the same. We'll have a good dinner, somewhere quiet." Staring at the ceiling, he asked, "How about L'Antibes?" When I told him I didn't know it, he said, "I'm glad—it'll be a pleasure to introduce you to it. Terrific food in a wonderful setting—small and intimate."

*   *   *

On my way back to my office in Rugton, I stopped by Perry Urbay's office to get an update on the memory assessments for the anesthesiology study. When he answered my knock, I asked him about the graph taped to his door.

His expression sheepish, he said, "I wasn't getting enough done, so I started keeping track of the actual time I worked on my research. At the end of each day, I plot the number of hours on the graph. Having it posted outside my door makes me work harder so I can avoid hearing things like, 'So what happened here on Tuesday, why this big drop?' "

"Of course," I said, smiling, trying to ease his obvious embarrassment.

Last fall I'd offered him a job as a psychometrist when he'd been about to drop out of school. He helped me out of a tight spot by taking the position, as I'd made clear to him—but he persisted in acting as if I'd single-handedly salvaged his dreams, and now his feelings for me seemed to be a mixture of hero worship, bafflement, and exasperation. While I suspected that Thelma Lou supplied him with stories that fueled his admiration, I'd never caught her in the act.

I noticed Perry glancing at my clothes, but I didn't feel like explaining why I'd dressed so casually. Prim and handsome, always wearing a coat and tie on weekdays, he had the overly fastidious look of a man who, punished as a child when he got his clothes dirty, had learned his lesson all too well. It wouldn't hurt him to believe I'd deliberately chosen an informal look for a change.

Seated in his small office, he told me that patients had been more cooperative with the testing lately—and the questions about awareness during surgery hadn't elicited any reports of dreams or memory fragments that sounded even vaguely problematic. After reviewing the latest cases for me, he said, "I'm not sure I understand the purpose of those questions."

"Just some concerns about side effects from the anesthesia." And then, to change the subject, I asked, "Any idea how many cases you'll be testing in the next couple of weeks?"

Turning to his computer, he began typing commands. Over his shoulder he said, "Wait a sec, and I'll call up the surgery schedules for the latest update." His small office was furnished with ancient castoffs, his wooden desk and chair well-worn relics from the fifties, his own state-of-the-art computer an anomaly.

He was counting aloud as he scrolled down the list— but I wasn't paying much attention because I was staring at the screen. For each patient it listed the surgical and anesthesiology nurses, any residents or other trainees scheduled as part of the operation—and the surgeon and anesthesiologist.

Once he'd finished, I tried to keep my voice casual as I asked, "Can you call up older schedules—say as far back as the beginning of the year?"

"I've never tried—but I'll see." He looked over at me. "You're not in a rush?"

I assured him I was fine.

Turning back to the keyboard, pointing to the last line on the schedule before he hit a key that erased it, he said, "A couple of times I've seen Dr. Danziger when he's been making rounds on patients who share a room with one I'm testing. He really impressed me."

Not another member of Austin's fan club. Perry, his back to me, couldn't see my sour grimace. "How so?"

"He's different from a lot of the other docs . . . He doesn't just walk in and out, he sits down and talks to patients when he rounds—and he asks if they have any questions. One time a med student was standing outside a patient's door, and he said, 'Did you hear that heart murmur? That's the clearest I've heard!'

"Dr. Danziger got real stern: 'Never assume that patients who aren't addressed don't hear.' "

Like Coppersmith's story about how Austin had taken such good care of his wife Marilou when she was in pain, dying of cancer. A side of Austin I hadn't seen—and didn't expect I'd ever see.

As he typed more commands, I realized I was holding my breath.

"I'm dating a nurse," Perry was saying. "She showed me how to check the schedule to figure out when we'd both be free . . . but I've never tried to get old information."

My meeting with Belinda Luttrell kept replaying in my mind, stirring up fresh worries each time. Her preoccupation with her health made her see everything as a risk; dumping the isotope into the cooler would have guaranteed her swift departure from the lab—and made it difficult to hire a replacement.

If I was right, it meant that the theft of the isotope wasn't just another incident in the series of pranks—someone had been setting the stage for death.

"I can't make it work," he told me, a few minutes later. "But I'll think about it . . . is there something in particular you'd like me to check—if I can figure out how to do it?"

"A patient on February 14 named Katherine Evanston."

"I have a morbid lifelong fear of bats." The voice on the phone sounded like Bugs Bunny. "Anything you can do about it?"

"I . . . beg your pardon?" Thelma Lou had just buzzed me to tell me I had a call from a "Dr. Watson."

"It's me, Nick," he said, his voice back to normal. "Mel Blanc was one of my heroes—the guy who did all the voices for the Looney Tunes cartoons. My alternative career if I hadn't gone into medicine, I've always told myself."

It was almost five o'clock, and I'd been gathering my things together, preparing to leave. Waiting for his call, starting to wonder when I'd hear from him, I'd been scowling as I plowed through paperwork. Now I found myself beaming as I assured him that yes, I already had a ride home, and yes, it would be fine if he picked me up at my house at seven.

When I hung up, I was still smiling. Ian had been the kind of guy who could name all the seven dwarfs and each of Santa's reindeer—a tough act to follow. I hadn't met another man who could match his playfulness.

After Thelma Lou dropped me off, I fed Pavlov and romped with him for a few minutes. I'd put a couple of Mary Chapin Carpenter's CDs on my stereo earlier; now, singing with her about how it had been too long since someone whispered, "Shut up and kiss me," I pulled on a short blue halter dress, white hose, and cream-colored sandals with high heels.

As I was applying blusher, I pictured Belinda Luttrell's pink cheeks—and then I flashed back to Jerome's body, lying crumpled on the floor.

I realized I'd been staring sightlessly at the mirror when the doorbell rang a few minutes later. Twenty before seven—surely Nick wasn't so early? Peering through the peephole, I saw Derek Zellitti on my doorstep. "Hello, neighbor," I said, opening the door. "What can I do for you?"

Brandishing a mangled corkscrew, he said, "Claudia's coming at seven, and I bought a good bottle of wine—'' Dressed in a white shirt and tie, his battered face reflected his anxiety.

"No problem. Come on in and I'll get you mine."

As I handed it to him, he thanked me and said, "One more thing . . . I'm pretty nervous about talking to her— I don't think she cares much about boxing, but I know she likes dogs. How would you feel about loaning me Pavlov for the night"—he glanced down at my dress and heels—"if you won't be needing him yourself?"

We grinned at each other. "No problem," I said. By the time we'd made the transfer, I had less than ten minutes left.

When I was a teenager, I couldn't pass a mirror without looking—without checking my hair, my makeup, never finding it right. Now, catching a glimpse of myself in the mirror after Derek left, I had the same feelings. I had just finished redoing my eyes when the doorbell rang.

"You look absolutely fantastic," Nick said. His navy suit, finely tailored, set off his blond good looks.

"Th-thanks." The word caught in my throat as I responded to the intensity of his look—and the feeling of something tightening in my chest in response. "Let me grab my purse—"

In my bedroom, I moved my wallet, keys, comb, and lipstick from the oversize black shoulder bag I normally carry and put them in a tiny straw clutch purse. And I took the time to dab perfume behind my ears, and at the bottom of the "V" in the front of my halter dress.

The continental restaurant he'd chosen was housed in an ornate Victorian mansion near downtown. A pair of prowling lions, cast in bronze, greeted us outside the entrance.

In the center of the room an alabaster chandelier,

edged with a bronze grapevine, cast a dim, milky glow, like moonlight. The fountain splashing softly beneath it was framed by a pair of iron cranes, stepping forward, wings spread as if about to fly.

"How lovely," I said, and Nick looked pleased.

Once we'd ordered drinks, he told me about the shock wave that Jerome's death had created in Anesthesiology, how he'd had to spend a good part of his day talking with colleagues who dropped by his office to hear the story firsthand. "I'm going to be extra busy once I finally get back, helping cover Jerome's responsibilities until we can shift them around.

"The timing isn't terrific"—he looked at me, then away—"but I was glad I was able to help Dr. Danziger, after all he's done for me."

The restaurant had a wonderful menu, and somewhere along the way we ordered our dinners, but my only recollection later was that I'd wanted to avoid any meat; the roasted smell from the morning still seemed to be stuck in my nostrils.

After the waiter delivered our appetizers, I asked the question that had been nagging at me: "Would you use equipment like Fred's power supply for any of your studies?"

"No." He gave me an appraising look. "I wouldn't have been using Fred's power supply, and I don't have anything like it in my lab that I could have loaned Eva— that's what you're asking, right?"

I nodded.

"Let me explain something that may help," he said. "For molecular work, you need a power supply. Even without knowing anything about what he was trying to do, without doing that kind of work myself, I can tell you that he'd need a power supply and a gel box. And you heard Dr. Danziger—Jerome was trying to retool, but he only had a two-week workshop.''

He hesitated, then said, ''When I was going over Jerome's schedule with Dr. Danziger, he told me about his talk with you. I hope you're not thinking there was something fishy about Jerome's death—that it was anything more than a terribly unfortunate accident.''

''I'm not entirely convinced,'' I said—a serious understatement. If Belinda had been driven away to set the stage for further mischief, then the stolen power supply was the next step in the fatal chain. It might have been Jerome's doing; perhaps he'd been trying to set Eva up for a bad shock without realizing the risk and had gotten snagged in his own net.

But if the accident wasn't Jerome's handiwork gone awry, who would know how to rig a lethal ''accident''? Eva and Fred were the obvious choices, but Sydney also had the technical expertise. And was Eva the real target all along?

Could Nick have anything to do with the troubles? He'd been indignant when Jerome was talking about his ''colorful stories''—but I'd been furious when I found out Jerome was checking on me, and I had nothing to hide. If Jerome's death was somehow tied to Kitty's surgery—and I remained convinced there was a link—then Nick's arrival in March ruled him out. And surely a card-carrying member of Austin's fan club wouldn't do anything that might hurt his idol.

As if he'd guessed the direction of my thoughts, he said, ''The police asked Fred and Eva to look over the power supply to see if they could spot any obvious defects.''

''Oh?''

''But I'd be very surprised if they came up with anything. Even though it's not kind of the equipment I'd use, I've certainly heard plenty about the risks. Jerome would have been trained with a newer power supply—he wouldn't have known the hazards of the older models—not like Fred or Eva.

"Jerome's fatal flaw was his own arrogance," Nick said, leaning into the portabella mushroom he was cutting with enough pressure to scrape the knife against the plate. "Once he'd learned a few facts, he'd have no trouble setting himself up as an expert on virtually anything."

He excused himself a few minutes later, and I watched as he walked to the men's room. He had a confident, graceful stride. I had visions of slow dancing with him, his arms around me, imagining the way his body would feel moving against mine . . .

A waiter walked past, breaking my reverie. I took a sip of wine and looked at an enormous mirror on the opposite wall, admiring the gilded serpents that slithered along the frame.

"How did you decide to move to Houston?" I asked Nick on his return.

"A year ago, Dr. Danziger called me in New Jersey; he'd read a couple of papers I'd just published, and he asked if I'd be a consultant for some similar studies for his Center grant. A bit after that, my wife told me she wanted a divorce." In the silence I heard the fountain splashing softly in the background. "I was really shaken up. I wanted to get out of town for a while—so this seemed like the ideal time and place for a sabbatical."

Touching a small cut on his chin, the gash still fresh and red, he said, "I know Jerome talked about my 'messy divorce' whenever he thought he could do some harm . . . did he say anything to you?"

"Nothing concrete." I was pleased that Nick had made the effort to shave before our date.

''That's worse, in a way . . . Let me tell you my version of reality—''

The waiter stepped forward to pour the last of the wine into our glasses. When we were alone again, Nick said, ''Zoe's a surgical nurse, a good woman, very bright. We've been together since I finished my residency. More and more over the years, she'd get upset for no reason I could see, but she wouldn't talk about whatever was bothering her—she'd just start throwing things. She threw expensive crystal champagne glasses, research files she pulled out of my briefcase, silverware from the table—whatever was handy. Usually she wouldn't aim at me, not directly at least, but once, near the end, she dumped a pot of stew in my lap. Only lukewarm—fortunately—but she hadn't bothered to check it first. I couldn't predict when she'd go into one of these moods. Her mother is manic-depressive, and Zoe has been hospitalized for depression a couple of times . . .

''She wanted children, but I wasn't sure—not with things between us like they were—and that was a major bone of contention.''

I blinked and looked away. Having my own kids had never been an option because the treatments for leukemia had left me sterile. Last Saturday, at a Bat Mitzvah for a friend's daughter, I'd been very moved at the point where the parents told their daughter about their pride in her; I could understand why children could be so important.

''Finally, she said that if I wasn't willing to be a father, she didn't want to be married to me . . . and she kicked me out.'' Biting his lip, he stared at his hands.

''I've told you everything I swore I wouldn't talk about tonight,'' he said. ''What is it about you that makes me feel so comfortable? Why do I drop my guard so easily?'' He reached over and put his hand over mine. I caught my breath as we looked at each other.

''Coffee, perhaps, with dessert?'' Beside us, the waiter was standing at attention. I hadn't even heard him approach. ''Let me tempt you with our selections this evening . . .''

''I've been doing all the talking,'' Nick said, when we were alone again. ''If it's not out of line, I'd like to hear about your former husband.''

At Austin's party, I'd mentioned that I was a widow when we were trading information about ourselves. Now, touched by his question and his obvious interest, I gave him a brief sketch, excusing myself when I felt my eyes getting moist. In the women's room, as I was emptying my clutch purse to get at my comb at the bottom, I stared at the keys I'd set on the counter beside the sink: keys for my office, not my house. I'd grabbed the wrong ones in my haste.

Back at the table, I told Nick about the problem—and asked him to detour to my office where I kept a spare house key in my desk.

''So I haff you in my power,'' he said, speaking with a thick German accent.

''You do, indeed.'' Throughout the evening my body had been humming, reminding me how long it had been. Now I felt myself blushing, as if I'd been broadcasting my thoughts.

Inpatient units occupy the upper two floors of Rugton, while clinical and research offices are spread across the first two floors. Busy during the workday, my hallway is largely deserted after five. Laughing at Nick's stories about his colleagues back in New Jersey as we walked down the corridor, I only caught a glimpse of a figure in dark clothes who vanished into the stairwell at the end of the hall.

Rugton didn't have fancy push-button locks like Denton. As I tried to turn my key in the knob, I realized my door was already unlocked. Could I have been that preoccupied when I left? Maybe the cleaning crew forgot to relock it after they emptied my trash?

"Something wrong?" Nick was asking, as I opened the door.

I stopped short and stood, staring.

The wall opposite my door is mostly glass; a large picture window starts about two feet above the floor and runs up to the ceiling. Divided into three large sections, one of the segments can be opened.

Now the light was on and the third section stood open, wide open, the sheer curtain pulled clear, the screen propped against my bookcase.

The top drawer of one of my two filing cabinets was open half an inch. A filing cabinet I always lock when I leave because it contains files for forensic patients.

"Someone's been here—" I could hear the quiver in my voice. Swallowing, I stalked to the open window, Nick close behind me.

The window is an old-fashioned kind that opens with an oversize crank. When fully open, as it was now, there was ample room for someone to step outside onto the five-foot-wide concrete ledge that ran the length of the building. And while my office was on the second floor, it wouldn't have been that difficult or dangerous to find a spot to dangle from the ledge and drop down to the manicured lawn below.

I thrust my head through the opening, looking right and left, trying to see if I could spot anyone, but I couldn't see past the point where light from my office pooled on the ledge. Nick leaned close behind me. "Can you see anything?" I asked.

"Nothing," he said. "I'll climb outside—"

"No, please don't. They're gone by now, almost certainly—and if they're not, it's probably not wise to try to corner them. I'll call hospital security." I didn't tell him that if I hadn't been wearing a dress and high heels, I'd have already been outside—a foolish move, obviously, now that I'd had time to think it over.

Once I'd dialed, he walked over and flipped off the light. As I waited for an answer, he stood leaning out the window, looking up and down.

"They'll be right over," I told him as I replaced the phone a minute later. "See anything?"

He turned the light on again. "Not a thing . . . any ideas about what's going on here?"

I pictured Vince Gambier—pacing back and forth from the door to the window as he told me about the sinking of the *Phoenix*—his silence as he'd stood looking out my window. But I couldn't tell Nick the story without violating confidentiality.

"Forensic evaluations don't usually endear you to your clients. I'm doing a series of PTSD evaluations for an insurance company . . . I'm guessing it's one of the men I've evaluated."

If only wishing could make it so. I wanted to believe it was Vince, because the alternative was distinctly nastier: another in the series of incidents related to Austin's research group, a follow-up to the hypodermic in my door.

"When we came into my wing, there was a man at the end of the corridor—did you see him?" I asked.

"No—quite frankly, I was too busy looking at you . . ." He smiled ruefully. "Recognize him?"

"He was too far away. He was a white man, dressed

in something dark, and he had some kind of cap on his head—or he had dark hair . . .''

Closing my eyes, I tried to reconstruct what I'd seen. "I heard something at the end of the hall, that's why I looked down there . . .'' I shrugged, not wanting to tell him the rest of my picture—with the "Nancy Drew" label Jerome had slapped on me, it would sound all too fanciful.

The man's hands had been dark—which probably meant he'd been wearing gloves—and he'd been holding something near his mouth—something that could have been a walkie-talkie. My door could only be locked with a key, so it would have been hard enough to unlock it the first time without trying to lock it again. Maybe they planned to lock up at the end, maybe they figured I'd just think it was the cleaning crew's error if nothing else was out of place. But they'd prepared the open window as an escape route just in case I came calling—and a lookout to signal danger, the man who went down the stairwell when we started down the hall.

And they knew how to open locked doors and files— or how to hire that kind of help. That really bothered me.

Looking over at my open file cabinet, I sighed. "The obvious question is whether we got here before they found what they wanted, but I don't want to touch anything until hospital security—''

"Dr. McAlister?" a uniformed man asked as he peered through the open door.

When we'd had a chance to look around my office, nothing appeared to have been taken, nothing damaged. The only thing with obvious resale value, my computer, hadn't been touched, at least as far as I could tell.

"Plenty of thefts around the medical center,'' the security men told us as they promised to keep a close eye on my office. "You were lucky," they added as they walked out.

Hardly sentiments I shared. My psychotherapy notes are part of my patients' clinic charts, and they're stored in a locked room behind Thelma Lou's desk—but I keep forensic files in my office. The *Phoenix* files had been in the top drawer—the open drawer—and there was no way to tell what they'd read. My notes about the accident, about the discrepancies in the three stories—that was what I hoped they hadn't found in time. And surely the fact that they'd been snooping there pointed the finger at the *Phoenix* crew—and not toward Austin's coterie.

An hour later Nick and I were each carrying a box of files from his car to my house.

Earlier, when I'd thought about the evening, I hadn't planned on inviting Nick inside after our date; much as I was attracted to him, I didn't want to move too fast—but once we'd stowed the boxes in a corner of my living room, I could hardly say good-night and show him to the door—at least that's what I told myself.

After we'd set down the boxes, Nick put his hands on my shoulders. Looking closely at me, he said, "While the security types were talking with you, I kept thinking that I really know how to show you a good time. On Wednesday we left the party early because of the attack on Fred, this morning we discovered Jerome's body—and now we stumble in on a break-in at your office . . . How are you doing?"

"Still shaken up," I said, walking over to my stereo and turning it on as a way to move out from under his touch, wanting to do something so I didn't have to meet his eyes.

Mary Chapin Carpenter started singing about how sometimes you're the windshield, sometimes you're the bug. Nick's hands on my bare shoulders had felt like a caress, a remarkably intimate touch. "How about you?"

"The same," he said, his voice husky, and for a crazy moment I thought he'd read my mind.

I felt as shaky and unsure as someone with a fear of heights trapped atop a broken Ferris wheel, desperately trying to hold still so I wouldn't sway my gondola.

"Something to drink?" I asked.

"What are you having?"

"Wine."

"I'll have some, also."

On my way to the kitchen, I stopped. "I loaned my neighbor my good corkscrew earlier. I just have the old kind that I can never make work. Could—"

"Of course."

As soon as I'd spoken, I regretted it. I needed time away from him, even if it was only for a few minutes. During my interview with the security men I'd looked over and found Nick staring at me, an intensity in his expression that made me stumble over my words.

In the kitchen I gave him a bottle of wine to open while I pulled out an apple and some cheese. As he was peeling off the foil seal, I watched him. He'd taken off his jacket while we were at my office, loosening his tie and the top button of his shirt on the way home in the car.

Maybe the shock was delayed, like the stories of soldiers who didn't notice they'd been hit by a bullet during the heat of battle—but when I closed my eyes for an instant, I pictured my open office window—and then I went back in time to this morning, when we'd found Jerome's body. My legs felt rubbery and weak.

"Ouch!" Distracted, the knife had slipped when I was slicing the cheese, and my finger was bleeding.

"Let me see," Nick said, taking my hand in both of his, turning it gently toward the light.

"It's nothing, really, just a small cut, no big deal—"

"I'm a doctor. I know how to treat wounds." Looking squarely at me, he raised the palm of my hand to his lips.

In the living room I could hear Mary Chapin Carpenter singing about how sometimes you're a fool in love.

As we stared at each other, my heart was beating a drumroll, and I was having trouble breathing. Then he had his arms around me and we were kissing and I felt as if I'd been standing beside a bonfire when someone threw gasoline on it.

Chapter 20

Four hundred fifty feet long and five feet wide, the suspension bridge over Capilano Canyon tilts and sways and quivers—as if threatening to drop its human cargo on the rocks and shallow rapids that lie more than two hundred feet below. A bit upstream there's a conventional bridge, solid and stable. In a classic psychological study, an attractive college student approached each young man after he'd crossed one of the two bridges. Explaining that she was doing a class project, she asked him to complete a questionnaire for her, and then, when he'd finished, she gave him her telephone number and said he was welcome to call if he wanted her to explain her project in greater detail "when I have more time."

Half of the men who crossed the precarious bridge called the woman, compared to less than 20 percent of those who crossed the stable one. Within the psychological literature, the study is widely cited as evidence that anxiety and fear can promote sexual attraction.

When Nick left my house early Saturday morning after a passionate night together, I told myself that I'd only behaved as I had because of all the horrors on Friday—adrenaline makes for arousal.

It was a lovely rationalization—one of my best.

On Monday morning, Thelma Lou buzzed me from the reception desk to tell me that an enormous vase of flowers had been delivered for me.

"A nice man?" she asked, looking at me hopefully.

Whenever I thought about Friday night with Nick, my heart went double time and my face would feel so warm that I imagined everyone could tell. I knew a boy in high school—"Randy, you're blushing," we'd say, and he'd turn red on command.

The note with Nick's flowers said, "Looking forward to our next Friday night," and I felt myself flushing as I read it. Scheduled to work through the weekend, Nick had rung me from the hospital Saturday afternoon just to say hello, and again on Sunday before leaving for almost two weeks: a five-day professional meeting in London, followed two days later by invited talks in Germany and France.

"A very nice man," I assured her, as I tried to tune out the small voice inside that was saying I really didn't know that much about him yet.

Willie O'Rourke, the last of the *Phoenix* crew members, was scheduled to see me at three o'clock on Monday. At twenty past the hour, when I called to see if he'd forgotten, I got his answering machine. Normally, I wouldn't reflexively phone forensic patients who didn't show for an appointment—I'd give them a chance to call me—but I was feeling uneasy about the *Phoenix* evaluations; surely that was only a logical response to my office break-in? After waiting another fifteen minutes, I told Thelma Lou that I was going to run some other errands and asked her to page me in Denton Hall if he appeared.

I found Fred Verlin in his office, his door open.

"How's your head?" I asked, looking at the spot where he'd been struck.

Exactly the right choice for an opening; inviting me to sit down, he turned to give me the full effect of his oversize bandage on his bald head, and I heard his litany about how he'd had such headaches since Wednesday night . . .

Once he'd wound down, I said, "Jerome's death was really a shocker."

"I have to tell you that I was taken aback to hear that Jerome was learning molecular research techniques—that's like a turtle pretending to be a greyhound."

I have to tell you—interesting word choice. "You had no idea?"

Fred blinked twice. "Of course not. And, obviously, he had no idea about what he was doing. If only he'd asked for help from Eva or me . . ."

But his one small response, the way he'd blinked after my question, told me I was right.

Fred had known. Just like Belinda, Fred had known about Jerome's "secret" efforts to develop skills in molecular biology. But when he'd learned of Jerome's death, he'd echoed Eva's concerns that Jerome had no business using the power supply.

"Nick told me that the police asked you and Eva to look over the equipment to see if you could spot any obvious problems," I said.

Fred looked odd for a moment. Maybe befuddled—maybe wary. "Yes . . ." He took off his stylish glasses, thin round tortoiseshell frames with "Giorgio Armani" on the side, setting them on his desk.

"What did you find?"

Under his white coat, Fred was wearing a blue shirt with French cuffs. Looking away, he fiddled with a cuff link, onyx mounted on sterling silver, his short fingers stroking its border. "Well, they wouldn't let us touch anything—"

"What did you see?"

"In the gel box, one of the wires had broken that led from the electrode into the bath—the solution—but you wouldn't notice the gap unless you went looking for problems."

How convenient. How very convenient. "What would that have done?"

"With the broken wire, he wouldn't have any current in the gel box. So he probably turned the power up high, trying to see if it was a faulty switch—that's why the knob was turned all the way to the right. Then, to make sure the electrodes were plugged in, he must have pushed down on them at the same time, one in each hand, checking for a loose connection—and when he did, he completed the circuit. That's how he got the lethal shock."

I swallowed heavily as I pictured the yellow-brown burns on Jerome's fingertips.

"There's probably a short in the power supply," he said, "it's an old unit, the police are still checking it out . . ."

His decor was utilitarian. A no-nonsense industrial grade of gray carpet, glass-and-chrome end tables, gray-and-black tweed chairs, a plain black desk: the office equivalent of a tract house. Avoiding my eyes, he was looking around as if fascinated by it all.

Had Fred set a trap for Jerome?

"When did you last use your old power supply?"

"The police were asking me that, too—it's been a few months. But it was back when we still had two technicians, and Sydney was using it for one of my studies—I wasn't using it myself, so I don't have any idea about when the problems developed. Overall, the police didn't seem terribly impressed that it was any big deal for them.''

Of course. It was the kind of case most prosecutors would have loathed—a man killed who was unfamiliar with the dangerous equipment he was using.

Clearing his throat, he said, "By the way, Austin scheduled a memorial service for Wednesday at two in the hospital chapel. Jerome's sister was his only close relative, and she's not planning anything except a grave-side prayer.''

I was pleased by Austin's decision. Jerome might not have been popular, but his colleagues needed a chance to say good-bye—and I wanted to make my peace as well. "Thanks for letting me know.''

I heard voices in the hallway as someone was passing, then laughter, loud for an instant. Fred flinched at the sound.

Jerome had claimed that Kitty had been dancing with her hand down Fred's pants at a department party. Watching his response just now, I couldn't imagine Fred leaving himself open to ridicule by behaving so indis-creetly in full view of his colleagues—particularly Aus-tin.

When I'd seen Kitty in my office, she'd felt much younger than her age—and naive. My impressions didn't square with Jerome's descriptions of her blatantly seductive behavior. Putting it all together, it suggested that I'd been hearing the way Jerome saw her in his fantasies.

Jerome had been like a visitor to a foreign country who imagined he understood what was happening even though he didn't speak the language, and he'd filled the gaps in his knowledge with his idiosyncratic notions about how people behaved.

The problem was that I couldn't be sure which of the

stories he'd told were his fill-ins—especially now.

Trying to sound casual, I said, "Do you suppose there could be any link between the assault on you and Jerome's accident?"

Rolling his eyes, he said, "No, there's no connection—it was just an old piece of equipment, and Jerome didn't know enough to use it properly."

Jerome's crowing that Austin will make him his second-in-command when he becomes Dean, Fred had told me. Was his obvious jealousy a motive for Jerome's murder? With Jerome out of the way, was he hoping that Austin might turn to him? Could he have banged himself on the head and made up the story about his attacker so he'd appear to be another victim?

"Jerome claimed that an anonymous caller had warned him that an animal-rights demonstrator was planning another incident for the lab," I said. "He mentioned it just after Austin told us about the attack on you."

"Right—he'd tell you *after* something happened, not before. His stories weren't very credible—he made them up because he wanted to blame his dirty tricks on someone else."

But Jerome had told Austin about the warning beforehand. "You think he was somehow responsible for the attack on you?"

"Realistically? No, I know he was at the party, and I don't think it was his style. But the other problems in the lab—the ketchup mess, the sodium fluoride in the coffee, the isotope in the cooler—they had his emotional fingerprints all over them."

"What about Eva's stolen power supply? And the problem in her lab after you were knocked out?"

"Simple thefts—someone looking to make money. And I was unfortunate enough to get in the way."

A tidy package, he was saying—too tidy for my taste. "When was Eva's power supply stolen?" April or May, I was guessing, around the time the P-32 made its way into the watercooler.

"A couple of weeks ago."

"*A couple of weeks ago?*" Sitting up straighter, I tried to modulate my tone. "When, exactly?"

"When they sprayed the lab with ketchup, most likely—but Eva didn't discover it was missing until the next day. They stole her Precision Balance at the same time."

That meant that Eva's power supply had been stolen around the time I'd first questioned Kitty's surgical problems. I felt the sweat trickling down between my shoulder blades.

Paranoia, I told myself.

But my fear wasn't unreasonable—not when I knew how much the trickster had already dared. And not when Fred had everything—means, motive, and opportunity—and I'd already caught him lying. "But I thought Eva kept her lab locked?"

"Mostly she does, but she'd left the door open that morning because Sydney was going to start a study for her and needed access. But—why does it matter?" Fred ran two fingers along the inside of his collar, as if loosening it. "If you're going to tell me it means that the ketchup wasn't Jerome's handiwork, then you're wrong. Jerome was always looking for ways to get at Eva and me, and stealing her power supply could have been another avenue for harassment—especially when he figured she probably wouldn't loan it to him if he asked her . . ."

Or Fred could have taken advantage of the situation and stolen Eva's power supply after the fact, making it look like part of the earlier chaos—and then made a point of being "helpful" by leaving the older unit out in the lab.

"But there were other tricks," I said. "Do you remember Kitty Evanston?" My tongue felt dry and furry, and I was wondering if I'd already gone much too far.

At the mention of Kitty's name, Fred's head came up. "Sure . . . you knew she died recently?"

Was it my imagination, or had there been a note of relief in his voice?

"Someone kept leaving Kitty packages of condoms when she was working in the department," I said.

"That had to be Jerome's handiwork. I dated Kitty for a couple of months. Once we'd stopped seeing each other, he asked her out and she turned him down. He couldn't tolerate the idea that she'd go out with me but not him, so he used to tell people that she'd only been seeing me because of poor judgment related to her 'medical problems.' And then he was absolutely livid when she left Anesthesiology to take the job in Dean Verbrugge's office." Drops of sweat appeared above his lip.

I thought about the whispered voice after Kitty's surgery: *What goes around, comes around.* An ugly message of revenge.

According to Jerome, Kitty had broken up with Fred. I wondered how he'd handled his anger when Kitty "deserted" him.

"Were you the anesthesiologist for Kitty's gallbladder surgery in February?"

Picking up his glasses from his desk, he made a show of polishing them before he put them back on. "No . . . I mean, I can't recall all my patients, there are just too many of them, but if I knew someone, I'd remember . . . why?"

Hardly a rousing denial. But even if he hadn't been her anesthesiologist, he could have sabotaged her surgery. "There may have been problems with inadequate anesthesia during her surgery."

"You can have real problems with anesthesia that you don't know about at the time. Why would you assume it was deliberate?" Obviously trying to feign poise, he looked wooden.

Looking squarely at him, I said, "I didn't say I thought it was deliberate—but that would be a reasonable concern, based on the ugly tricks in the department."

In the silence that followed, his phone rang. Seizing it, he turned away and began talking with far more animation about the on-call schedule than the topic would seem to have merited. When he hung up, I knew I'd lost him.

Clearing his throat as he made a show of checking his watch, he said, "I've got to be going—"

"Of course. But there was something else—wasn't there? Something about the power supply that you didn't get a chance to mention—because we got diverted . . ." Because he'd changed the subject.

He shot me a glance, and I tried to project confidence and assurance, as if I had no doubt he was about to tell me what he'd omitted. "If you need to go, I can check with Eva."

His expression was guarded, and he hesitated before he said, "The warning light may not have been working."

"Why not?"

"They called me later and asked if I'd remembered any other problems . . . when they unscrewed the cover for the light—it looked like maybe . . . like maybe the bulb was loose."

Chapter 21

If you put a new mouse in a cage with four mice who've already established a hierarchy, they'll attack the intruder. Vicious, the way they do it—they go for new guy's balls and try to rip them out. The visiting professor who delivered this morning's Grand Rounds lecture had been describing his research on the endocrinological consequences of social reorganization. Several men in the audience greeted his comment with barks of too-loud laughter, shifting nervously in their chairs. When they'd quieted down, the speaker said, *But that's just like real life—isn't it?*

As I was walking to Jerome's memorial service on Wednesday afternoon, I was thinking about the lecture—and wondering if Jerome had been the real target for the faulty power supply, or Eva. *Things keep happening to me . . . sometimes it's big, sometimes it's small, but it hasn't stopped since I came in January*, she'd said.

Late because I'd been talking with Perry Urbay, I arrived just as the ceremony was starting. The wooden pews in the small hospital chapel were filled with perhaps three dozen people. Wearing a gray twill suit two shades darker than his hair, his face drawn, Austin opened the service by recounting Jerome's academic history—where he'd trained, honors he'd won. Watching Austin, admiring the way he'd organized the service, I could appreciate how he inspired such loyalty from his faculty.

As he reviewed Jerome's service to the department, I was impressed by the lengthy tally; clearly a hard worker, he had carried far more than his share of the load. The next speaker, an assistant professor, described Jerome's helpfulness on difficult clinical cases, recounting instances when he'd been particularly supportive. Echoing what I'd heard from Quinton Gibbs, a medical student and a resident praised Jerome's teaching skills.

My mind wandered as the resident was finishing his comments. In my mail this morning, I'd gotten a Xerox of an article. Volume 51 of the *British Journal of Anaesthesia* had been missing from our library, so I'd requested a copy from interlibrary loan. Authored by a "medically qualified lady" who chose not to use her name, her 1979 editorial, "On being aware," told of her Caesarean section under a notably inadequate general anesthetic: "One pint of beer would have dulled my mind more . . ."

It was like having a tooth drilled without an anesthetic, when the drill hits a nerve, ". . . then pour a steady stream of molten lead into it—" only the pain during her surgery was much, much worse. As she lay paralyzed, she was fully aware of "every word, every sound."

My chest was tight when I'd finished reading.

Kitty had died, and now Jerome was dead—were they linked?

Then Perry Urbay had appeared at my door just as I was preparing to walk over to the chapel.

"It took some work, but I managed—!" Beaming

with pride, he'd handed me a piece of paper. It took a minute for the information on the page to register—dated February 14, the printout had Katherine Evanston's name at the top, other names below: *Kitty's surgery schedule.*

"That's impressive—quite impressive," I said, swallowing as I stared at the information he'd managed to retrieve from the hospital computer. Angelica Rudolph and Maria Tsai had served as the surgical and anesthesiology nurses, respectively. The late Harvey Redman was her surgeon. And Eva Aarastadt had been her anesthesiologist.

Eva.

Could Kitty have heard Eva's husky, low-pitched voice during surgery and thought it was a man speaking? Or had Murray's work with Kitty altered that detail in her memories, along with others?

Now I looked over at Eva, sitting in the back row with her arms crossed over her chest, her expression fierce. Beside her, Fred Verlin alternated between staring at the wall and casting quick, covetous looks at Eva.

Jerome had claimed that Austin had been scheduled as Kitty's anesthesiologist, but Eva or Fred had taken his place. Why had he lied?

After the short service ended with a period of silent meditation, I stood up, hoping to intercept Eva. As I turned, I almost collided with a tall woman who was poised by my elbow. "I'm Verna Ferguson. I understand you found Jerome's body." In her early forties, she was wearing a gray suit styled like a military uniform: stand-up collar, black piping, epaulets, and silver buttons marching down the front. Sunglasses concealed her eyes; her short black hair was swept back from a face as blank and welcoming as polished granite.

"I'm Haley McAlister—" Wondering if I was supposed to recognize her, holding out my hand, I saw Eva filing past, moving out of my reach.

"I know." Her fingers were cold as she gripped my hand too tightly. "I was watching you during the service." Her face was thin, the skin tight against the bones like the face of a mummy in a museum.

"Yes?" I tried to keep my face bland even as I felt myself tensing.

"You were listening to the service, but you were also checking out the people around you." Her voice wasn't loud, but it seemed to carry; I saw several of the remaining people turn our way, including Austin and Sydney, as they filed out. "Subtly, I'll grant you—but you were trying to gauge reactions."

She paused, as if waiting for me to apologize. As if she expected it.

"How did you know Jerome?" I asked.

"I'm his sister." She smiled at my obvious surprise, her expression tinged with malice.

"I'm sorry about your brother's death. Such an unexpected—"

"I'm not in the mood for platitudes," Verna twisted her mouth in an exaggerated expression of distaste, "and I can't imagine why you'd be sorry about Jerome's death—unless you were responsible."

She pulled off her sunglasses and I almost stepped back, so fierce was her look. I'd been expecting redrimmed eyes, a reason for hiding behind the dark lenses—but hers were dry and clear, her mascara and liner flawless—and the way she casually surveyed me made me think of a wolf, prowling for dinner.

"I beg your pardon?" I said, swallowing heavily.

"What had Jerome done to merit a violent death? Done recently, that is."

"What do you mean?"

"I know there has to be something—Jerome always managed to piss on everyone's shoes." She spoke with obvious relish, her voice coarse and loud.

Looking at her, I had no idea how to respond. And I guessed she knew it—and was enjoying my discomfort.

"Let me give you some examples," she said. "When he was a medical student, he'd deliberately start discussions with his fellow students about obscure trivia before exams, implying he knew it well—and hinting that they were in big trouble if they didn't."

Already standing too close, Verna leaned closer. I stepped back, wondering if she had the same one-beat-off interpersonal sense as Jerome, neither able to hear the rhythm behind the music.

"Another example," Verna continued. "When I was a senior in college, Jerome found out I was flying out for a hot weekend in Miami with one of my professors, this gorgeous married man. Three days before I was scheduled to go, Jerome gave me this video, *Final Approach*, and told me how much I'd enjoy it. It showed all kinds of airplane crashes—and I'd always been afraid of flying, as he well knew."

She looked down as if gathering her thoughts, but I noticed her studying my right ankle. I glanced down and saw a run in my hosiery that seemed to command her close attention.

"Last year Jerome told me how he sometimes carried an old aspirin bottle filled with dirt when he traveled," Verna said. "When he checked out of a hotel, he'd leave half the towels in his room just like he found them, looking untouched, folded in those fancy little rectangles—not a clue that whoever pulled one off the rack would get showered with dirt. He said the maids should always make sure every room had a complete change of linen whenever someone left, so he was just 'keeping the help on their toes.' ''

All too consistent with the man I'd known. But why was Verna telling me so much? Grief, or loneliness, or the simple pleasure of a listener—or some other reason? Her assumption of instant intimacy was distinctly disagreeable, like sitting in a chair warmed by a stranger.

"Perhaps it will help if I draw you a picture." Verna grabbed a pen from her purse. Turning over the program for Jerome's service to the blank side, using her purse as a desk, she sketched the stick figure of a man. She drew a circle around the figure, and then, after looking at me to make sure she had my attention, she drew a slash across the circle.

"I've given you three good examples of obnoxious behavior. Now, let me repeat my original question: What did Jerome do to his colleagues that might have gotten him killed? You don't need to spare my feelings . . . obviously."

"You're asking if your brother might have been murdered?"

"I thought I'd made that rather obvious."

No semblance of grief or remorse. No expression of regret, and she'd just lost her brother.

"I didn't know your brother well; I only met him in June—"

"I wasn't accusing *you* of killing him—I was asking if you thought it was a possibility—you are the psychologist who studies lies, aren't you?"

"How—"

"Jerome mentioned you once, of course. And because of your . . . skills, you seemed like the obvious person to answer my question. Was Jerome murdered?"

Her antagonism was like a sharp knife drawn ever-so-lightly against skin, leaving a trail of bloody drops to mark its passage. A process she clearly enjoyed.

Watching her closely, I said, "Your brother's death may well have been an accident—there's no way to know for sure. The equipment he was using probably had an electrical short, and the warning light wasn't working."

"And *motive*?"

"Some faculty . . . suspected Jerome was behind a series of ugly laboratory pranks. He might have been responsible—or someone else might have wanted him to look guilty."

Nodding matter-of-factly, she said, "I've wanted to kill him myself. Fortunately, I wouldn't have had access to his lab—or I'd certainly be a fine suspect."

"What are you trying to tell me?"

"Nothing. Nothing at all. Whatever gave you *that* idea?" You fool, she didn't have to add out loud.

"Only that," she paused, giving me a sly smile that made my skin crawl, "I am grateful to that . . . person."

Verna meant her brother's murderer.

Chapter 22

"**O**ne minute, I'm on the phone," I called out, covering the mouthpiece with my hand. It was five o'clock on Wednesday afternoon, two hours after Jerome's service had ended, and someone was banging on my door.

"When I asked around about Eva Aarastadt's problems with animal-rights activists, I heard an interesting story," Loretta, my friend in New York, was saying. "Her lab was next to one that bought dogs from an animal shelter for research. For several months, some joker had been switching the nameplates on doors up and down the hallway every so often. As it happened, they switched Eva's with her neighbor's just before an animal-rights raid—and Eva's lab got trashed. No other problems that I heard about, before or after."

So the mischief directed toward Eva wasn't likely to be the work of outsiders, plotting to do her in. And the incident probably wouldn't have been an impetus for her move to Houston, as Jerome had suggested.

"I'm coming," I said, my voice sharper in response to the second barrage, as I thanked Loretta for her efforts before I hung up. Irritated, I walked over and yanked my door open—and stepped back, involuntarily: Like a ghost invoked by calling its name, Eva Aarastadt stood there, regarding my surprise with haughty amusement.

"Fred told me you'd be looking for me soon," she said. "I thought I'd take the initiative."

Without waiting for an invitation, without asking if I was busy, she walked past me and seated herself in one of the chairs in my office, gesturing for me to take the chair opposite her—as if she were the hostess.

"So what did Fred tell you?" I asked, as I sat down. *What was so compelling that you sought me out?*

Dressed in a slim cranberry skirt and a pink sleeveless blouse with cranberry piping around the collar, her blond hair hanging loose around her shoulders, she looked calm and collected. "He said you wanted to know about the problems with the power supply."

If she was going to cut to the chase, I'd follow her lead. "When was your power supply stolen?"

"Probably when they trashed the core lab with ketchup—but, as Fred told you, I didn't discover it was missing until the next day—so I can't be absolutely sure."

"You said before that you thought Jerome stole it— do you still believe that?"

"Maybe I was wrong after all—at least about that." Rubbing her hands together briskly, she said. "I've been here six months and I still haven't gotten used to the way everyone cranks up the air-conditioning. My hands are always cold around here. I should have learned that I'm supposed to wear long sleeves, no matter what the temperature outside."

Whatever her secret was, one look at her bare arms made it obvious that she wasn't injecting drugs. "Do *you* think someone killed Jerome?" I asked.

Without missing a beat, she said, "Hard to say. Jerome suffered from delusions of adequacy." Raising her eyebrows, she gave me a mocking smile. "Despite his obvious limitations, he thought he could do anything—so he could have easily killed himself by accident.

"On the other hand, enough people had reason to kill him." She shrugged. "He was pretentious, petty, and vengeful."

Indeed. A man who spent his time piecing together fragments, snippets, and tidbits in order to discredit his colleagues had ample reason to be disliked. But it would have had to be someone who had ready access to the core lab—and they would have needed to know that Jerome was taking the workshop.

"Did you know that Jerome was going to Woods Hole?" I asked.

Aware that the day would include Jerome's service, I'd worn a tailored dark green suit with a cream-colored blouse; as she looked me up and down, she looked faintly amused.

"I thought I answered that one when we found his body," she said.

Jerome had known about Eva's secret, whatever it was. And I guessed that she had sought me out because she believed I knew something as well—and now she was fencing, trying to guess the limits of my knowledge.

"What about you?" I asked. "Did you have reason to murder him?"

I would have expected my question to give most people pause, but Eva responded immediately: "Anyone who worked closely with Jerome had reason." The calm way she looked at me as she rubbed her hands together reminded me of a cat, playing with its prey before the kill. *Dangerous to underestimate her.*

"I'm not sure what he said to you, but I'd talk to Fred if I thought someone had killed Jerome," she said. "Earlier this month, Jerome found Fred asleep in the conference room before a meeting—so he stapled Fred's tie to the table. And then, just as Fred was trying to tug it free, Austin walked in.'' Smiling, she added, ''Fred doesn't like to look foolish—especially not in front of Austin.''

''You came here to tell me that Fred's responsible?''

''I came here to find out why you're so interested in problems that don't concern you. Why so many questions? What's in it for you?''

''Do you remember Kitty Evanston?''

Perhaps she paused before responding, but it was short enough that I might have just imagined it. ''The name sounds familiar''—she looked off to the left—''but I can't place it.''

Had Fred told Eva that we'd talked about Kitty? Or would he have avoided the topic because it was linked to one of the derogatory stories that Jerome circulated about him? ''She was a secretary in Anesthesiology when you came to the department.''

''Of course—the woman who destroyed one of my computer files so I missed a grant deadline.'' Sitting with her hands clasped together, her back straight, her chin raised, her face was absolutely expressionless. But there was a wariness, an alertness about her that troubled me—as if her smooth facade was concealing strong emotions that might erupt when least expected.

''What about her?'' she asked.

Listening to her, I was thinking that it was unfair that someone so very attractive should have such a come-hither voice: sonorous and resonant and smoky. Not as high-pitched as most women's—but, hearing it now, not low enough to convince me that Kitty could have mistaken it for a man's voice. So how could I believe anything else Kitty had ''remembered'' with Murray's assistance?

"Could Jerome's accident have been intended for you?" I asked.

Staring at me, she exhaled heavily. "Rather an abrupt change of topic, isn't it? Certainly, Jerome was fully capable of planning my death—as I mentioned when we found his body. And he may have gotten caught in his own trap as he was setting up an accident for me." As if cold, she wound her arms around herself, and I flashed back to the outfit she'd worn when I tracked her down in her office last week—a sleeveless turtleneck with a short skirt. Odd—because her white coat would have been the ideal cover-up for someone overly sensitive to cooler temperatures—and now, staring at her arms, I couldn't see any trace of goose bumps.

Getting up from her chair, she walked past my desk and stood staring out the window, much as Vince had done. Then she turned and pointed at the flowers on my desk, gesturing toward them with an insolent grace. "How very . . . nice. An admirer?"

She must have guessed they were from Nick—a reasonable assumption since she'd seen us together. Watching her, I thought the sight of them bothered her. But she hadn't shown any interest in him, or he in her—so surely I was wrong.

Eva reminded me of my high-school gym-class nemesis, a girl who spiked volleyballs toward me with such force that I'd retreat and put up my hands to protect myself, rather than positioning myself to return the shot. And I always cursed myself for doing the wrong thing after the fact.

What would I regret later with Eva? There would be something, I was sure—because the conversation already felt like it was moving out of my control.

"Jerome said there was animal-rights harassment directed at the lab," I said. "He suggested it might be aimed at you. When I talked with a friend in New York, she told me the story of the switched nameplates.''

"Why are you checking on me?'' Eva's voice was loud and harsh, but underneath there was an barely perceptible undercurrent of fear, like a lone flutist in the midst of a brass ensemble. ''Why can't you just leave me alone?''

"Something happened on February 14—'' I started.

The energy and the light ebbed out of her face. Her hands, half-closed, looked like claws.

"You were scheduled as the anesthesiologist for Kitty Evanston's gall-bladder surgery.''

Turning to my desk, picking up the vase that held Nick's flowers, she held it in front of her with both hands as we locked eyes. For a minute, I thought she meant to drop it, to let it shatter. She watched me as she set it down, none too gently, before she stalked toward the door.

Her hand on the knob, she paused. ''When I first saw you talking with Jerome at the party, it seemed so natural—after all, vultures of a feather flock together.'' Slamming the door behind her, she left me sitting with clenched fists and my mouth open. *Predictable*, I told myself—but I had the feeling that I'd made a major misstep.

Jerome had said that Eva had problems with an explosive temper, ''something I might know about as a psychologist.'' What was behind his innuendo?

I remembered things Eva had said: *A week or two of memory problems—that's remarkably trivial*, when we'd talked about anesthetics. At the party: *I don't drink. Why wipe out brain cells for brief pleasures?*

The odd assortment of journals in her office that didn't have anything to do with anesthesiology or her research.

I remembered the patient that Eva had brought to mind—a woman worried about losing control.

I pictured the way her arm had jerked when I'd been talking about lie detection, her antagonism when she'd caught me watching.

I thought of how she'd worn sleeveless tops so she could pretend to be cold—an excuse for clasping her hands tightly together, for wrapping her arms around herself.

Recalling Jerome's broad hint about a psychiatric disorder, wondering what he'd found out, the image of a patient I'd seen years ago popped into my mind—a woman with a relentlessly progressive neuropsychiatric malady. I sat up straight, remembering a textbook list of diagnostic features, matching the symptoms with what little I knew of Eva. "No," I said, speaking out loud. But it fit together all too well. Believing I knew her secret, she must have thought I was taunting her.

I didn't know if it had anything to do with Kitty Evanston's surgery—but Eva's secret was truly terrible.

Chapter 23

"**I** have something to tell you." The woman's voice on the phone was angry, full of righteous indignation. "You'll find it very . . . interesting, I'm sure."

It was Thursday afternoon and Thelma Lou had buzzed to tell me that Jerome Pettit's sister was demanding to speak to me, saying it was "absolutely urgent" that we talk as soon as possible.

"Ms. Ferguson—"

"Haley, why be so formal? Just because Jerome wasn't the kind of man who'd ever be called Jerry, you shouldn't assume that I'm like my brother and I covet that kind of . . . propriety." She spat out the last word. "Call me Verna."

But she behaved so much like her brother—acting as if I should be flattered by her pretense of instant intimacy, never asking what she should call me. "You have something to tell me?"

"Only a key fact that puts a very different light on my brother's untimely death: a motive for his murder. A new motive—not the childish pranks that obviously bothered *you* so much."

"Can you tell—"

"I can't say any more now. You'll have to meet me at his apartment if you want to hear my story." Half-listening as she rattled off directions, I waited until she'd wound down to ask my key question: "You said Jerome told you I studied lies. How did he happen to mention it?"

"He said my stories were so intricate that even someone with your skills—your 'supposed skills,' that's what he actually said—couldn't untangle the truth from the rest. He thought you might be useful to him, if only he could find the right leverage with you. And I remembered your first name because it's like the comet, only you don't spell it correctly."

Meeting her at Jerome's apartment promised to be as much fun as wading knee deep in ice water—but she was right: I wanted to hear what she had to say enough to do as she asked. If Jerome had told her about me, maybe he'd spoken about others as well. We bickered a bit before we finally agreed on a time: tomorrow, July 4, at ten in the morning. "It shouldn't take long," she assured me, "so you'll have the rest of your holiday free." I should have known that Verna was no more reliable than her brother.

"Evidence of prehistoric life," Verna said by way of greeting, her expression contemptuous as she made a sweeping gesture toward Jerome's living room the next morning. Her black hair was ruffled, as if she'd been running a hand through it, her expression as coldly off-putting as I remembered.

Stepping inside, I was already sorry that I'd come. "You said you had something to tell me," I prompted her, "something urgent."

"Walk through with me, and then we'll talk," she said, her tone peremptory. "I want you to get a sense of how my brother lived.'' Her gray-velour tracksuit, obviously expensive, was clearly ill suited for any athletic activity; her only jewelry was a pin on her shoulder, a spider with a black-onyx body and rhinestone-studded legs.

Jerome had furnished his living room with an orange-and-brown plaid couch, two brown-vinyl chairs, and a Formica-topped coffee table and end tables—all sturdy, impersonal, cheap, and remarkably ugly. Aside from one picture on the wall, the only other decorative touch in the room was a trio of model airplanes made of balsa that sat on a dusty end table. Cardboard boxes were stacked up against one wall.

''Well, what do you think?''

Remembering his mineral water at the party, I pointed at a wine rack beside the sofa that held a dozen bottles. ''I thought Jerome didn't drink alcohol.''

''He always liked good red wine. Not in public, of course—that way he could maintain his air of moral superiority when everyone else was drinking. He tried to tell me he only drank it for medicinal purposes. Not credible when I knew he downed a bottle at a sitting.''

''Did you ever think Jerome might have a drug problem?''

Her smile showed teeth, but no warmth. ''You obviously mean prescription drugs, not street drugs, but that's still so far out of character for him that I can't imagine it.''

''Did he mention anyone else having a problem?''

Shaking her head no, she picked up one of the model planes from the end table. ''He saved these because he built them with Dad. Our mother died in a car accident when I was seven and Jerome was eight—eight going on eighty, even back then. Jerome tried to take her place, hoping Dad would pay more attention to him if he was the good little helper. Whenever I did anything wrong, Jerome always tattled to Dad.''

No different from the grown man I'd known with his slavish devotion to Austin. But I wasn't going to say anything to fuel Verna's air of righteous indignation.

Still carrying the model plane, she stalked into the kitchen, slapping the light switch with her free hand. ''I stayed here for a couple of days at the beginning of June when Jerome was away and my house was being painted. I want you to read the notes he put up, 'little reminders.' ''

One of the ceiling lights had burned out and the remaining bulb cast so little light that I had to lean close to read the note on his refrigerator: SLAM IT, DAMN IT, and, on the counter: NO HOT PANS.

Waving her hand at a scraggly poinsettia sitting in a corner on the counter, a drooping red bow tied around the basket, she said, ''He'd always send me one for Christmas, even though I'd told him repeatedly how much I hated them—in fact, he probably kept it up just because I told him to stop. Last year I left it back on his doorstep. Now, thanks to his . . . untimely death, I get it back.''

''Did he mention—''

''The tour first, and then we'll talk.''

In his bedroom, the curtains were drawn. A small television sat on an old wooden desk in the corner of the room. Stacks of books encircled the bed like islands, a path just wide enough to permit passage to the doorway meandering among them.

''As a high-school student, Jerome worked summers in the library; he had a habit of 'losing' books he didn't find 'suitable.' '' She sketched quotation marks in the air with her fingers. ''You can guess how often he disapproved. I've always wondered how many found their way home with him. Should be a real treat to go through his stacks, item by item.''

In the bathroom, an old wooden end table beside the toilet held three stacks of magazines, each a foot high. ''His ass was so tight he couldn't pass a BB,'' she said. ''He obviously didn't want to run out of reading material. And now it's mine—all mine. Aren't I the lucky one?'' Gripping one wing of the balsa-wood plane, she twisted it in her hand, deliberately breaking it off. As she stared at the mutilated toy, her expression was venomous.

''You're probably wondering why I'm so angry with him,'' Verna said, turning abruptly toward me.

I nodded.

''Just before Dad died, Jerome told him something about me . . . he never spoke to me after that. I never got to make my peace. I never got to say good-bye.''

I blinked at the naked pain in her face. ''I'm sorry—''

''Jerome was told from birth that he'd be a doctor, but girls didn't count in our family—Dad made it clear that I only needed something to keep myself busy until I found a husband. So my brother got an all-expense-paid ride through college and medical school in the Ivy League, and I got just enough to train as a medical technologist at a state college. And then—in spite of the fact that he'd gotten the best of everything—Jerome couldn't tolerate it when Dad paid any attention to me . . . so my *dear* brother cataloged my sins for Dad as he was dying.''

''That's dreadful. Why'd he do it?''

''The obvious . . . I'd told Dad something about him— nothing all that terrible, but Jerome had to get even. He could be ruthless when it came to revenge.''

And you? Imagining Verna and Jerome playing tit for

tat at the bedside of their dying father, I tried not to shudder visibly.

"Now that I've given you the grand tour, let's make ourselves comfortable in the living room for our little chat." She spoke in a way that suggested I was supposed to feel indebted to her for her kindness.

I sat down on one end of the plaid couch, and she seated herself in an adjacent chair. "I called our family lawyer to find out about Jerome's will," she said. "I'd assumed his estate would come to me as his only surviving relative. Hardly an unreasonable assumption, right?"

"And the family lawyer—"

"But that's not what happened. My *dear* brother left me the contents of this apartment and all his worldly possessions: his books, his tacky furniture, and his frigging model planes." She threw the remnants of the plane against the wall, smashing it. Then, turning to me, she grabbed my wrist, squeezing tightly, and, leaning uncomfortably close, she said: "He left all his money to his beloved department, to be used for any purpose deemed appropriate by Dr. Danziger."

My mouth had gone dry. Trying to speak in a soft voice, hoping to ratchet down her anger, I said, "All his money to Anesthesiology . . . that must have been quite a shock. How much money did he leave?"

"A million dollars, at least."

"Surely—surely not that much?"

"No, you wouldn't believe it, would you?" She let go of my wrist so she could make a sweeping disparaging gesture: "Not looking around this dump. My father did well in the stock market, and he left us each a half million when he died. And Jerome inherited Dad's talent for picking stocks."

I rubbed my wrist, sore where she'd been squeezing

it. "Do you know if Dr. Danziger knew about Jerome's will?"

"I've spoken to him—and he *says* no. But then I don't have any reason to trust him, do I? Jerome dies a violent death at work and his department picks up a bundle—rather a remarkable . . . *coincidence*."

Indeed. I couldn't believe Jerome hadn't told Austin about the bequest—another gift to lay at the feet of his beloved boss. But if Jerome had ever mentioned his will and the size of his estate, Austin certainly had good reason to deny it now. All he'd need, a story circulating about how Jerome's death in Austin's own lab brought major money into his department—a bequest that Austin had known about in advance.

Not a motive that made much sense to me, not with his eye on the Dean's office—but I could understand why it might to Verna.

Her onyx-and-rhinestone-spider pin had an unpleasant lifelike cast to it. When she saw me staring at it, she unpinned it. "Look at this," she said, pointing to the red stones set in its abdomen in the shape of an hourglass: "A black widow." And then, watching me, she added, "I don't believe I mentioned my husband is dead, did I?"

"How did he die?"

Nodding her approval, she said, "I wasn't sure you'd have the guts to ask. He drowned." Then, smiling, she said, "I was out of town, if that puts your mind at ease."

I'd wondered if Verna might have killed her brother. If Jerome's death could have been accomplished through sheer will, I'd have had no doubt about her guilt—but, realistically, she couldn't have known essential details about the lab or the power supply.

Her pin reminded me of the green worm wrapped around Kitty's enameled-apple pendant. "Did Jerome ever mention a woman named Kitty Evanston? Or Kitty Jones?''

"Not that I remember. I'd be surprised if he actually had a relationship with a woman—I always assumed that his sex life consisted of regular time with a life-size inflatable rubber doll. He never dated, as far as I knew.''

But he had asked Kitty out, according to Fred. Maybe that wasn't the kind of thing he'd discuss with Verna— or perhaps Kitty had been one of the very few women he'd approached.

"When we were teenagers, Jerome used to try to catch me undressing, and he'd try to act like he'd just 'forgotten' to knock. Or I'd find my underwear drawer with things moved around—like he didn't think I'd notice.''

Wanting to put some distance between us, I walked over and looked at the lone picture on the wall, a framed watercolor showing a small stone house, half-buried in snow, dark footprints leading away from it. I remembered what Jerome had said at Austin's party: *There's a saying about our profession: "Like a man walking in a blizzard, an anesthesiologist's footprints are erased as soon as he passes."* And then he'd looked at Nick and said, *But that doesn't apply to the anesthesiologist's memory—at least one hopes it doesn't.*

"Did Jerome mention any other names, any other information about people at work?'' I asked, my mouth suddenly dry.

"You're a little slow on the uptake, dear. The question you're supposed to be asking me next is, 'So what do you want from me?' "

Verna's pompous, self-important attitude made Jerome look good by contrast. "And?''

"You need to help me search his apartment, and the boxes from his office.'' She gestured at the cartons stacked against the wall. "Dr. Danziger didn't waste any time packing up everything—he already has someone else in Jerome's office by now, I'd expect."

"Did Jerome mention any other names, any other information about people at work?" I asked again.

"You're missing the *obvious*. Jerome needed to be right and to demonstrate that the other person was wrong. He's not—he wasn't—concerned about being liked, he just wanted to be seen as a model of virtue—all the better to impose his values on other people. And he liked to have power over people—so he collected information. He had notes on everyone who might be useful to him—even on me, he told me once."

Standing up, she said, "You'll start with the boxes from his office"—he pointed at the row against the wall—"since they may make more sense to you."

" 'Notes on everyone'?" But it made ugly sense. His pleasure in his stories about his colleagues' misdeeds, his delight in providing Austin with copies of problematic information from patient charts—of course he'd have kept copies of anything useful for himself.

"You're welcome to read anything you find," she said, as if bestowing a gift, "with the exception of my file. In return, I won't read yours if I find it first."

"You're assuming I'll help you?"

"Of course. You came here because you wanted answers. Part of it has to do with Jerome's death, the rest your own . . . personal issues."

Verna was right. I couldn't shake the feeling that Jerome's death had something to do with Kitty Evanston. And one related memory that kept coming back, a scene my mind kept replaying.

When Jerome had been talking about Kitty's surgery at the Development Fund party, the eavesdropper's light-colored head could have been Fred's bald head. Or Austin's silver hair. Or Eva's blond mane.

And, while it made no sense at all in terms of motive, there was one other possibility that kept bubbling up in my mind: Nick's corn-silk hair.

Wading through the boxes from Jerome's office was an even more depressing exercise than I'd expected. Books and journals related to anesthesiology filled about two-thirds of the cartons. The remainder contained files filled with professional articles, minutes of meetings that took place up to a decade ago, computer printouts with data from ancient studies, evaluations of medical students and residents supervised by Jerome from the beginning of time. There weren't any hospital charts in the boxes, hardly a surprise; I guessed that whoever had packed up had set them aside—which meant it was time for another trip to medical records, to make sure Kitty's file didn't contain any additional surprises.

A folder with administrative memos looked like his fun reading. The top one was the bylaws for the medical staff. Thumbing through it, I found the parts underlined that he'd quoted when he'd justified his investigation of me—the sections that gave him permission to search out information on applicants.

Another memo, re: GIFT PROCESSING POLICIES was from Chester Moats, the director for Development. Sent to deans and department chairs, it described how all external donations were to be processed through the university's Development Fund, making it clear that there could be no exceptions—sections that Jerome had underlined. *Surely he hadn't been anticipating his own death?*

The next document in the file was a list of faculty who were appointed to various college committees, another listing the unfortunates who served on each of the departmental committees. He'd inked an asterisk beside his name each time it appeared; I was only surprised he hadn't used paste-on gold stars.

Stuck in the middle of the committee listings, I found a green note card with four dates in what looked like Jerome's writing: March 14. April 10. May 19. June 24.

After replacing everything else, I took the card to the bedroom, where Verna was shaking each of his books by the spine. Handing it to her, I said, "This is the only thing I found that seems out of the ordinary."

As she studied it, she began to smile. "Did Jerome ever mention getting . . . unusual calls?"

I could have cheerfully choked her. "*You* were the anonymous caller who told him that animal-rights activists had targeted Dr. Danziger's lab? And who claimed they were getting inside information?

"Of course not. How could you assume such a thing?"

Watching her closely, I didn't say anything.

Handing back the card, she picked up a book and shook it, then four more as I stared at her.

Finally she looked back at me. "Of course *I* wasn't the one—a man I've been seeing made the calls, using the scripts I wrote. My dear brother tended to be a little paranoid anyway, and he'd mentioned the new woman who'd had trouble back in New York . . . I thought it would give him something to think about."

"These were the dates when your friend called Jerome?"

"They look about right . . ."

"What else have you done that I should know about?" My voice conveyed my irritation.

"I don't know what I'm going to do with all this," she said, looking around the room.

"Verna—"

"Nothing else, really."

Six hours later we'd gone through everything in Jerome's apartment without finding any sign of his supposed notes. Maybe they never existed, maybe someone else had already found them. Driving home, I felt dirty and sticky and itchy, as if I'd walked through spiderwebs and picked up malignant passengers who were even now seeking their revenge, crawling over me, looking for a weak spot in my defenses.

And I couldn't shake a lingering sense of unease, as if I'd overlooked something important, something Verna had said or something I'd seen—and the omission would come back to haunt me.

Chapter 24

"I'm a little better since I saw you," Lou Ramsey told me as he sat down in my office on Monday morning. "I finally made an appointment with the psychologist that Dr. Turkin recommended . . . I've seen him three times now, and he thinks I'm starting to make some progress." I was warmed by the obvious changes in the burly *Phoenix* seaman. So distraught during his first interview, the brief half smile on his weathered face seemed incongruous. Today his ivory hair and beard were neatly trimmed, and he was dressed in chinos and a green knit shirt. And—thankfully—he wasn't clutching his yellow legal pad.

A pleasure to see such a difference—but I was troubled because Willie O'Rourke, the last of the crewmen on the *Phoenix*, hadn't come to see me yet—and he hadn't responded to the message I'd left about setting another time. Whatever his reservations about a psychological evaluation, that was odd behavior for a man out of work who had money at stake.

"I'm very glad to hear it," I said, smiling. I'd spent part of my weekend preparing the final phase of my assessment for the *Phoenix* survivors. If it worked as I hoped, I'd have strong evidence about who really had PTSD—and my data wouldn't rely solely on the trustworthiness of their stories. Then, trying to make it a casual question as I was preparing the equipment, I asked, "How did you get along with the other crew members?"

"The twins are good guys. I don't have a lot of use for the rest of the bunch. Gary was on the sauce all the time—too pickled to be of much use—and Vince was a drinker, too, just not quite as bad. When Vince puts an arm around your shoulders, you better check his sleeve for a knife—same with Willie—and Davy was only a little better. They were always giving Bert grief about following orders; they wouldn't have lasted much longer if we hadn't had the accident."

"Have they been keeping in touch with you?"

Pursing his lips, he said, "They've called a few times to talk about the lawsuit."

Not a big surprise. When I'd seen Davy Crockett Bayless, he'd known that I'd interviewed Lou already, but no one else: *Vince Gambier and Willie O'Rourke, you haven't met them yet.* And I'd suspected that Vince's folder with the tape recorder—if that's what it contained—was designed to help some members of the crew reconcile answers to probable questions.

"Why weren't the twins out with you when the *Phoenix* turned over?"

"They got sick, same as me. Stomach virus, probably—I couldn't keep food down the night before. I heard they had the same."

Just a coincidence—all three with the same symptoms?

Using biofeedback equipment I'd borrowed from a colleague and adapted for my purposes, I explained that the sensors I was putting on his forehead and hand would be measuring muscle tension and heart rate, while the cuff on his arm would be inflated to check blood pressure every so often.

Lou had gotten quiet, as if steeling himself. Now he asked, "Like a lie detector?"

"No, I won't be asking you questions—I want to measure your responses to certain kinds of mental stress."

Physiological reactivity to reminders of the trauma is a key PTSD symptom. When combat veterans with and without PTSD listened to tapes of combat sounds, heart rate jumped up higher for those with PTSD, enough so that the differences were sufficiently reliable to classify 90 percent correctly; among auto-accident victims who listened to tapes describing their own wrecks, those who had developed PTSD after the collision demonstrated a similar propensity.

"First you'll sit quietly for five minutes," I said.

Next I asked him to count out loud backward by sevens. "Begin with one hundred, then the next number would be ninety-three, then what would be next?"

"Eighty-six."

The exercise, called "mental arithmetic," is a common method for inducing a minor stress response in psychological research.

After three minutes of calculations, he sat quietly for another five minutes and then I played the tape I'd made, using phrases from his own interview to describe the sinking of the *Phoenix*. "The weather was getting rough because a storm was moving in. You were just coming up from belowdecks when the boat felt like a giant hand was shaking it . . ."

When he'd been sitting with his eyes closed, his heart rate had been seventy-four, leaping up to eighty-four when he began the mental arithmetic exercise. Now, listening to the tape, it hit eighty-eight, and I watched him blinking and swallowing.

Lou Ramsey had all the necessary symptoms for PTSD—including one that was difficult to fake. That wasn't the part that I found interesting, though. When I'd said, "You're in the water, struggling," Lou's heart rate had shot up to ninety-eight. Afterward, he told me he still couldn't remember.

Thumbing through the *Houston Chronicle* on Monday evening after I got home from work, I stopped as a name jumped out at me: William O'Rourke. He'd been found dead in his apartment on Renwick, the victim of a knife attack. His body hadn't been discovered until Sunday, but it looked as if he'd been dead a week or more.

The picture of Willie, taken from his police file, made me sit up straight and peer closely. I couldn't swear to it—but I thought he was the lookout I'd spotted when Nick and I were heading toward my office in Rugton.

Vince must have found his file in my office. I felt the sweat breaking out on my face, trickling down between my shoulder blades.

In my notes, I'd raised three troublesome questions. First, PTSD symptoms weren't impressive in any crew member except Lou. Second, was it possible that the others had not made active efforts to rescue Lou during the period he'd "forgotten"? And, finally, the most serious: Could the *Phoenix* disaster have been a well-planned calamity, not a simple accident?

Willie's violent death could have simply been a remarkable coincidence—but I guessed that Vince was eliminating a possible witness who could tie him to a murder. The thought made my heart pound. Was I at risk?

Bound by confidentiality, I couldn't go to the police with my suspicions. However, under the guise that it might help fix the time of death, I called and told them about the appointment that Willie had missed. I mentioned the lawsuit as well, because it was a matter of public record—hoping the information might point them toward Vince, eventually.

I hadn't planned to do any exercise that evening, but I was so wired after reading the newspaper that I went jogging with Pavlov in tow. Derek Zellitti's brother Tony intercepted us as we were cooling down. "I understand that this girl my brother is seeing is a friend of yours," he said, barring my path on the sidewalk. "I want you to know that I don't appreciate your interference, and I'm not going to tolerate it. I'm an attorney, you know." Dressed in an expensive dark blue suit that helped minimize his chubbiness, his shoulders thrust back, he touched his striped Italian silk tie as he stared down his nose at me—but I noticed he kept his distance from Pavlov.

Resisting the impulse to roll my eyes, I said, "You think I have some special influence?" Drenched in sweat from my run, my hair a wet and tangled mess, I was wearing purple shorts and a green-and-purple T-shirt that said SEXISM IS A SOCIAL DISEASE.

"I certainly hope not," he said, pursing his mouth as his disparaging glance swept over me.

I guessed he still had no idea about my occupation, or how our paths were about to cross professionally. "Your brother is old enough to make up his own mind."

"She has a nose ring and short hair," he said.

"She has a good heart, and she's a poet, a fine one," I said, walking around him and continuing toward my house.

"I'm getting worse—things have really been going downhill," Davy Crockett Bayless said, rubbing his

buzz-cut hair as he sat in my office on Tuesday morning.
''I can't fall asleep, and when I do I've got terrible
nightmares—''

Patients who are attempting to fake or exaggerate a
disability are often quite anxious about testing—but I
didn't think that was what was troubling him.

His face was drawn, and the shadows under his eyes
looked as if he hadn't slept well for several nights. In
contrast to the skimpy shorts and top he'd worn to his
last appointment, today he was dressed in jeans and an
oversize denim shirt that camouflaged his unsightly muscles and made him look even shorter. While he'd swaggered before, now he had the look of a hunted man—
and he'd seemed positively eager to get inside my office
when I greeted him in the waiting room.

After he'd finished the memory and concentration
tests, I hooked him up to the physiological equipment.
His heart rate was high to start and went up some more
with mental arithmetic, but his response to his own story
about the *Phoenix* wasn't notable—until I came to the
part about Lou: *We were trying to pick him up and he
just kept swimming away from the raft, acting like he
didn't see us.*

And one other part that I'd added as well. ''It's half
an hour after you've left the dock. You're talking with
Vince—'' His heart rate leaped up ten beats.

As we were finishing, I said, ''You have reason to be
concerned. You're going to have to tell your story to be
safe.'' Nothing more.

Davy's only response was a wide-eyed stare just before he bolted from my office.

At noon I went to the catered luncheon in Kurt von
Reichenau's office that I'd scheduled under protest.
Wearing a beige jacket over a turquoise shirt and a tur-

quoise-and-red tie, white wisps of hair flying like flags above his ears, Burgess Coppersmith hardly looked like a serious donor.

As my boss extolled the virtues of our department, I squirmed as I pictured him in khaki shorts, a whistle on a cord around his neck, playing day-camp director. In the midst of Kurt's monologue, Burgess caught my eye and winked as he gave me a conspiratorial smile—his expression conveying only polite interest when Kurt looked at him a moment later.

Excusing myself early as I'd been ordered, Kurt's tone was aggrieved when he called me afterward: "You should have warned me that his thinking's slipping a bit."

"What do you mean?"

"After I gave him chapter and verse about our need for funds to renovate Rugton, he just talked about how he liked to outmaneuver taxi drivers on the way to the airport."

Grinning, I told myself it wasn't my business to translate if Kurt hadn't gotten the message.

"I used to be so optimistic, but now I don't want to get up in the morning," Vince Gambier said, as he sat in my office after lunch. "I don't want to face another day. The worst part is that I can't see any way out—there's no light at the end of the tunnel." Dressed in jeans and a faded black T-shirt, his expression somber, his long hair cut short, he'd arrived right on time for his appointment—and this afternoon he smelled of cigarettes but not beer.

"What makes everything look so dark?"

"The *Phoenix* disaster turned my life upside down, of course . . . and now Willie's death—maybe you read about it in the newspaper?" Looking at me closely, there was a feel of danger in the air, like smoke wafting across the room.

"Yes," I said, meeting his gaze, all too aware of the dryness in my mouth, "I'm sorry about the loss of your friend. Do you feel like going ahead with the session, or would you rather reschedule?"

"Let's get it over with."

At least we were in accord on one issue. "How have you been sleeping since I last saw you?"

"Poorly, the same as before. I still wake up screaming from my nightmares—"

He wasn't carrying his accordion folder, but he'd have no reason for a recorder today, no further need to reconcile answers. *My personal notes on my case—I don't like having them out of my sight*, he'd said. The very thing he'd have brought to this session if he'd been telling the truth the first time.

"How much coffee have you had today?" I asked a few minutes later, as I was attaching the sensors to his forehead.

"Couple of cups, maybe," he said.

Right. I'd known that Vince had already gotten word about the physiological part of the assessment when Thelma Lou buzzed me to tell me he was here—and to mention that during her lunch hour she'd seen him in the cafeteria, drinking cup after cup of coffee in gulps like bad medicine.

His strategy might have helped with a lie-detector test, but it wouldn't do him much good for my assessment.

I'd made some changes for his evaluation. At the point where the tape for Davy and Lou had described the sinking of the *Phoenix* using their own phrases, the cassette I played for Vince recounted an auto accident. Watching the equipment, I could tell Vince was wrinkling his forehead like crazy to simulate heightened muscle tension—without parallel changes in heart rate or blood pressure—before he realized he'd tuned into the wrong program.

As he was standing by the door, about to leave, he said, "I couldn't believe it when the cops showed up on my doorstep to ask about Willie."

Had they mentioned my call? "What did they want to know?" I hoped my voice didn't sound as shaky as I was feeling.

"If he had any enemies . . . I told them only those folks who were working for the insurance company, trying to block our claims."

I had goose pimples when he walked out of my office.

Chapter 25

"Nick's out of town," Sydney said, when she opened the core-lab door and saw me standing there on Wednesday morning. Under her lab coat she was wearing a green smock dress and tennis shoes. The smiling blue ceramic moon pinned on her collar contrasted with her sullen expression—and her still-livid black eye.

"Actually, I wanted to talk with you."

"What—what about?" She peered behind me, as if checking to see if anyone else was hovering within earshot.

"The day the lab got sprayed with ketchup." After Perry Urbay showed me how to check schedules on the hospital computer, I'd picked a morning when Eva and Fred were both busy to corner Sydney. Now, stepping inside, a clipboard under my arm, I pulled the door closed behind me. "I heard it was animal-rights activists harassing the lab, but parts of the story bothered me . . . Did they leave a note? Or maybe leaflets?"

"No, nothing like that—"

"That's odd—so why did Dr. Pettit assume it was the work of animal-rights types?"

"Someone had called him, told him the lab was targeted . . . at least, that's what he said." Kicking her foot front and back, staring down, she reminded me of a child wanting to run but afraid to try. "I don't have time to stand around and talk." Turning her back on me, she stalked away, and I followed, watching as she began pulling cardboard boxes about the size of thick frozen dinners out of an upright freezer.

"What's that you're working on?"

"These are patients' serum samples. I'll be measuring cytokine levels, comparing data from before and after surgery."

"I heard Dr. Pettit tried to blame you for the ketchup incident," I said.

"I wasn't there when it happened; I was over at the loading dock when they found the mess." Her voice was more confident now. "He wanted to blame me, but I could prove I wasn't anywhere close."

"That's right—the vandals pulled a plug on one of the freezers, and the alarm went off. And you were over at the dock with a cart, trying to find out who had called you about the shipment."

Opening another freezer, she said, "You probably don't even know what cytokines are."

"You got me," I said, and watched her chin lift in response, the satisfied look on her face as she launched into an explanation.

Maybe the culprits had pulled the plug because they didn't know their way around a lab and they'd hoped to leave other damage that wouldn't be detected so quickly. Or maybe they wanted to make sure someone found the sabotage rapidly—fast enough so Sydney wouldn't be implicated.

"That's very interesting," I said, when she was done. "How long does it take for an alarm to go off on a freezer, once you pull the plug?"

"Only a few minutes for the kind we have here. With minus-eighty freezers, like most of these, it's set with the thermostat—as soon as it begins to warm up, it triggers the alarm. But I'd already been gone half an hour when the alarm sounded."

"That's what caught my attention, your ironclad alibi."

Looking quickly at me, then away, she said, "I'm busy, I've got work to do—"

Sydney would have been bullied by everyone in the lab who was so inclined—probably everyone but Nick—but she'd gotten even, in the end.

"Just a few more questions," I said. "How expensive is a power supply unit for gel electrophoresis?"

"Around two thousand."

"And a Precision Balance?"

Walking over to a sheet on the counter with a stack of boxes in her hand, she looked as if she was attempting to be nonchalant as she checked off numbers on the page that corresponded to the markings on the cartons. "The one that got taken was the cheapest model in the line . . . probably cost just a bit over a thousand. Not exactly big ticket, as lab equipment goes."

"No," I said, remembering the stolen thermocyler that Austin said had been worth twenty thousand. But that was what made it all the more interesting.

When I was listening to the radio this morning as I was driving to work, a young woman had won a pair of concert tickets. "This is the first time I've ever called you," she'd squealed, her voice tight with excitement—and I'd felt bad for her. There's nothing so dangerous for someone inclined to gambling as winning the first time—if they decide they've got the touch, they'll keep trying again and again and again.

Because that was what must have happened with Sydney.

Just as he'd scolded me, Jerome had undoubtedly nagged other people about drinking coffee. A simple matter for someone in the lab to pollute the coffeepot, to act as if they were drinking along with the rest, to feign sickness and take time off work. A way to make Jerome look like the obvious culprit.

Someone like Sydney.

She'd chosen a time when Nick was away so he wouldn't get sick from the sodium fluoride. The incident made Belinda Luttrell have second thoughts about working in the lab—part of Sydney's plan to eliminate her "competition." Feigning terrible symptoms, Sydney took two days off work. And then, because she enjoyed making Jerome sweat, she'd arranged to have the lab splattered with ketchup. Not as naive as she looked— far from it.

"That shiner looks painful," I said, touching my face as I looked at hers.

Making a production of checking the numbers inked on the freezer boxes, she kept her face averted. "I walked into a door."

A Precision Balance was used for "measuring small quantities," according to Eva. Remembering the scent of marijuana when I'd passed Sydney and her long-haired ex-boyfriend in the hallway, I could see obvious uses for it outside the lab.

And I remembered what she said when he'd been shaking his fist in her face: *I kept my word.* I guessed that she'd set a time when the lab would be empty and told him where to find the Precision Balance—that much at least. And maybe more.

Looking at her fading black eye now, I wondered if her ex-boyfriend had pressed her to help him one more time after he'd gotten the Precision Balance. Perhaps he'd struck her because she'd assured him that everyone would be at Austin's party last Wednesday night—and then Fred had appeared.

"Let me tell you what I've figured out about your role in the lab accidents," I said.

Her head came up and her eyes opened wide. "I don't have to listen to anything from you—"

"No, you don't. But I thought I'd offer you the courtesy of talking with you first, before I tell anyone else."

As I walked her through my reasoning, I watched the color ebb from her face.

"Well?" I asked, when I was done.

"You're all wrong. I didn't have anything to do with it."

Her quick glance at me, the way her eyes scanned my face, told me I'd guessed something of the truth. Something close at least.

"That's possible," I said, "but I see it differently. Did you put the isotope in the watercooler?"

Surely Sydney wouldn't have dumped the isotope in the cooler, then drunk the water deliberately? Hard to believe . . . but it would have been one way to strike back at Eva while making herself look like another unfortunate victim. And, predictably, the incident drove away Belinda, the second technician—so that Sydney's services became more valuable to Nick.

"Are you crazy? I'm not about to make myself sick— I didn't have anything to do with that!"

Anything to do with *that*—an interesting choice of words. Looking at her, I believed her—at least about the isotope. "Did you help steal Dr. Aarastadt's power supply—"

"No! I don't know how that happened!"

"Did you have anything to do with rigging the electrical problem in Dr. Verlin's old power supply—?"

"What do you mean? Everyone said Dr. Pettit's death was an accident! You can't blame that on me—what do you want from me?"

Her face was red and blotchy, her expression venomous. Probably telling the truth—but I couldn't be sure now, not when she was so upset.

"I need answers to questions about other people in the lab."

"And if I say no?"

"Then I'll talk with each of the faculty members from the core lab—starting with Nick—and tell them my concerns about you."

"You'll do that anyway, no matter what—you're just jealous."

Do I have reason to be? I looked at her and didn't say anything for a minute—but I was wondering if she was right, and if I had reason to worry—but it wasn't related to Sydney.

"If you'll help me with my questions, I'll try not to say anything," I said. "But if anything else happens, any other 'accidents' or any more thefts, then I'll tell everyone, including the police—so you need to make sure your ex-boyfriend knows the risks if he tries to lean on you again."

As she stared sullenly at the floor, I asked, "Are we in agreement?"

"What do you want to know?"

"Did you know that Dr. Pettit was trying to develop new research skills?"

"Not really . . ."

"Sydney, our deal doesn't hold if you lie to me. Let's try one more time: Did you know Dr. Pettit was trying to develop new research skills?"

She directed an angry look at my feet, not meeting

my eyes. "Belinda spotted his application for Woods Hole in the lab—she was laughing about it, so I went over to take a look."

"Anyone else see it?"

"Don't know," she said, rolling her eyes. "I don't read minds."

"When did you last use Dr. Verlin's power supply?"

"Jeez," she said, setting one of the cardboard boxes down forcefully, "how much of this do I have to put up with?"

"When did you last use Dr. Verlin's power supply?"

"Back just before Belinda left. And it was working just fine, and no, I didn't have any problems with it. Dr. Pettit couldn't even run simple molecular studies, but he was always acting like he knew it all—and then look what happened to him."

"Dr. Aarastadt hadn't used it in the interim?"

"Not that I know of—but she's a royal bitch," she said. "If you want someone who causes problems, you should be talking to her."

"What kinds of problems?"

"She got real nasty with Dr. Verlin. She told him she was tired of him following her around, watching every move she made—like he was stalking her. Everyone knew about his arrest for soliciting a prostitute, she said—and she wasn't interested in 'that kind of man.' "

I couldn't help wincing for Fred as Sydney described the scene. "When did this happen?"

"Back in June, when Dr. Pettit was out of town. I was working in Nick's lab with the door closed, maybe they thought I couldn't hear—but those doors aren't that heavy."

Fred might have felt bruised enough to rig the power supply for Eva or Jerome—he certainly had the knowledge. But I could see other possibilities, not so obvious:

Eva might have wanted to provoke Fred to go after Jerome. Or she might have wanted to make sure Fred kept his distance so she could carry out her own plans without worrying about his appearance at an inopportune time. Or she might have wanted to give Fred an apparent motive for Jerome's murder.

"Dr. Aarastadt got roses right after their fight," Sydney said. "They delivered them to the lab when she wasn't here. The note with them said, 'Last chance.' No name on the card, but I wondered if it was Dr. Verlin."

Last chance. The wilted roses I'd seen on the floor in the corner of her office? Surely Fred wouldn't have kept pursuing her, not when she'd been so deliberately cruel—but then, watching him at the Development Fund party, he'd certainly looked lovesick. Who was Eva's persistent admirer, if it wasn't Fred—and was it the same one who sent her the roses earlier?

And the key question: Were the roses—and the message—related to the "accident" with the power supply, and had it been intended for Eva? If so, the link would mean it had to be one of four men: Jerome, Fred, Austin . . . or Nick.

"You overheard conversations in the lab pretty often?"

"Sometimes they'd forget I was even there when I was working in the next room—like I was part of the woodwork."

"You were there when Nick told Dr. Pettit that I was interested in lie detection, weren't you?"

"What—what do you mean?"

Setting my clipboard on the lab counter, pointing at the blank page, I said, "I'd like you to print something for me—in block letters."

She crossed her arms over her chest and stepped back from me. "What do you want from me?"

"You didn't ask what I wanted you to print—or why." The very questions she should have asked, if she wasn't responsible.

Jerome had challenged me at the party the day after I'd talked with Nick in the library. Maybe Sydney was already nervous because she'd heard Jerome making jokes about my interest in the lab sabotage; perhaps she'd picked up on Nick's interest in me.

Letting the silence stretch, I studied her face before I finally said, "Maybe you even hoped I'd think Dr. Pettit was responsible when you decorated my office door— or Nick."

"I don't know what you're talking about—and I have work to do."

Following Sydney as she walked into the outer room of the core lab, I flinched as we rounded the corner: Jerome's watch was still sitting on the counter against the wall.

Smirking as she turned and caught sight of my face, Sydney said, "That'll get packed up with the rest of his personal things once we can get into his lab."

" 'Get into his lab'?"

"Dr. Pettit got the lock changed just before his death. He didn't tell anyone the combination—and now the hospital locksmiths can't find the record. Dr. Danziger was furious. He told them if they can't find it by Monday, they'll have to drill it out and put on a new one at no cost."

If his dossiers really existed, if they hadn't already been lifted from his office files, that's where they'd be. Safe and secure from prying eyes.

And what would Sydney's dossier say? "Any reason Dr. Pettit might have wanted to get rid of you?"

She gave me a quick worried glance, then stared at the floor. "Don't know."

"You're not going to claim you had absolutely no problems with him, are you?"

"He made up stories about me. Once I called in sick because I was bleeding so badly and had terrible cramps. My doctor said it wasn't anything serious, just a bad period and my IUD had fallen out.

"One of the secretaries asked if I was OK, so I told her what the doctor had said. She must've told Dr. Pettit, because he went around saying it wasn't clear to him what a missing IUD had to do with working as a lab technician—I heard him talking with Nick about it." Her face was flushed, her expression rageful.

Nick had told me that Jerome had acted as if Sydney was trying to get out of work when she'd mentioned a possible electrical short, and then he'd sent her the memo about lab safety. Maybe he'd reacted so strongly because she'd caught him trying to rig an accident for someone else. Perhaps he'd caught Sydney preparing some mischief of her own—or helping her boyfriend steal drugs. "Dr. Pettit was giving you a hard time about lab safety problems."

"But he's not going to be pointing a finger at me—" Her hand covered her mouth. I felt sure she'd stopped herself before she said "anymore" in a voice warm with satisfaction.

Chapter 26

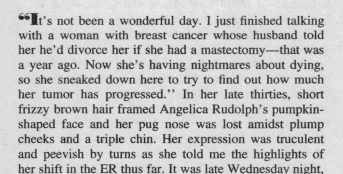

"It's not been a wonderful day. I just finished talking with a woman with breast cancer whose husband told her he'd divorce her if she had a mastectomy—that was a year ago. Now she's having nightmares about dying, so she sneaked down here to try to find out how much her tumor has progressed." In her late thirties, short frizzy brown hair framed Angelica Rudolph's pumpkin-shaped face and her pug nose was lost amidst plump cheeks and a triple chin. Her expression was truculent and peevish by turns as she told me the highlights of her shift in the ER thus far. It was late Wednesday night, and I'd finally tracked her down, after considerable effort.

"Before her, I had a drunk at the desk who puked all over my shoe," she was saying. Five-four and weighing somewhere over two hundred pounds, her white nurse's uniform at least a size too small, she looked like an overripe fruit, ready to split its skin.

I hear the voices of two men—one on my left, one on my right, Kitty Evanston had said—but only one man had been scheduled as part of her surgical team. Had she been wrong—or had someone else been part of her surgery, someone whose name didn't appear on the list?

Kitty's chart still had not resurfaced—which made me wonder if it ever would. I'd tried to track down the nurses who were involved. After a series of confusing phone calls to the personnel office, who assured me that there was no Maria Tsai anywhere in nursing and never had been, I learned her real name had been Hai Ying Tsai—and she'd returned to Taiwan in the spring after finishing her master's degree. Angelica, the surgical nurse, looked like my last hope.

If she could confirm specific details from Kitty's surgery—the barbershop music, the conversation—maybe I'd get some answers, finally, about the accuracy of her memories. Except that now, looking at oversize woman in front of me, I had serious doubts that Kitty's story could have had any basis in fact. Kitty had claimed her surgeon said it was like operating on the Goodyear blimp—but she'd only been thirty pounds overweight; compared to Angelica, she'd been thin.

"I've never had much use for psychological research," Angelica said. "It tells us everything we already know."

I'd told her I was considering a research project on memory and anesthesia, my cover story for questioning her about Kitty Evanston's surgery.

"So why me?" she asked. "Why'd you seek out me for your . . . source?"

"A patient who had gall bladder surgery on Valentine's Day remembered some details from her operation. You were the nurse—"

"Who was the surgeon?"

"Dr. Redman. I understand he—"

"The infamous Dr. Redman—the bastard who stroked out in the spring. And that's the reason you're badgering me and not him.

"Or maybe you'd still be after me even if he was available—because you wouldn't want to take up his precious time with all your questions—and you assume I have nothing better to do." She wagged her head in disgust.

Her name might be Angelica, but I couldn't see her as an angel. "Ms. Rudolph, I realize you're a busy woman. If another time would be better—"

"And you're hoping I'll recall specific details from February—one surgery among hundreds before and after. What made this particular operation so memorable?"

"The patient said she heard barbershop music playing during her surgery—"

Blinking, she stared off to her left. "Anything else?"

Bingo. "Her anesthesiologist was Dr. Eva Aarastadt, a tall blond—"

"No," she said, her tone definite. "That's not the one I remember."

"Do you mean that Dr. Aarastadt's not the anesthesiologist you remember, or—"

"I'm *sure* you'll excuse me to take care of my work," she said, pausing just outside a room where the door was half-open. From inside, I heard a woman whimpering. "We've got a woman in here who seems to be having terrible stomach pain, but no one's figured out what language she's speaking so far—

"You're still here?" Angelica asked when she came out of the patient's room five minutes later.

"If another time would be better—"

Shrugging, she said, "Fine with me if you want to follow me around all night—no place else I plan to go."

"Just before you went in the room, I thought you were saying that Dr. Aarastadt, a tall blond woman, wasn't the anesthesiologist you remembered—"

"That's right."

"But—but you did remember barbershop music?"

"Sure—Redman played that stuff all the time, the same tapes, over and over."

Just like Fred's story—so Kitty could have known about Redman's barbershop tapes before her surgery. The kind of specific detail she could have used to make her claim sound genuine—even if it wasn't. My shoulders sagged.

"So if there's nothing else—"

"What songs were on the tapes, do you remember?"

"Grasping at straws, aren't you? 'Take Me Out to the Ball Game,' that was one of his favorites."

"Any others?"

" 'You're Nobody 'Til Somebody Loves You.' "

I took a deep breath and let it out slowly. "That's a song the patient remembered. Her name was Katherine Evanston—Kitty Evanston. She was thirty, but she looked closer to twenty. She had short dark curly hair and dimples, medium height—" Looking at Angelica, I caught myself just in time before I added the last word: plump.

The silence stretched so long that I'd almost given up hope when she finally spoke. "I might remember the patient—but her anesthesiologist wasn't a woman . . . now I remember, Redman said he was supposed to get the blond for Valentine's Day. He'd been looking forward to her."

Not Eva? "Who was the anesthesiologist?"

"Redman's stroke wasn't exactly a surprise. He may have had a heartbeat, but any EEG would have shown he was already brain-dead . . . a sexist pig who treated nurses like pond scum."

"Who was the anesthesiologist?"

"Can't think of his name. But he's tall, light hair—"

"Excuse me, can you tell me anything about my husband's condition?" The white-haired woman who grabbed Angelica's arm had been pacing up and down the corridor, a rosary clutched in her hands, her lips moving as tears streamed down her face. "In there," she pointed to a room at the end.

"He's not my patient, but I'll find someone for you," she told the older woman, speaking gently, solicitously, "if you'll come with me." And then, to me, her tone cold, she said, "Wait here," as she walked past me with the rolling, wide-legged gait of someone whose thighs are rubbing together.

Through the open door of a nearby room, I watched the cardiac monitor beside the bed tracing the heartbeat, heard its soft beeping. *Tall and light-haired.*

My own heart was racing as I reminded myself that Nick hadn't arrived until March. Telling me how much he was looking forward to seeing me on his return, he'd phoned me from Paris earlier today, the fourth time he'd called since he left. The unmistakable warmth in his voice had made my breath catch in my throat.

When I'd seen Thelma Lou this afternoon, she'd finally remembered the story she had forgotten. Just before her surgery, after hearing from the secretarial grapevine that she had been blamed for the anonymous letters to faculty recruits like the one Eva had received, Kitty Evanston had gone to Austin and told him that Jerome had asked her for home addresses for three senior faculty candidates, including Eva.

As Thelma Lou told me the story, I'd pictured the department roster—bottom heavy, only a handful of full professors.

Jerome had worked hard to become Austin's right-hand man. He wouldn't take kindly to competition for Austin's attention. And fewer senior faculty meant less competition. Jerome as saboteur still made eminent sense, especially if Eva had been the scheduled anesthesiologist.

When Angelica returned, I said, "You said the anesthesiologist was tall and light haired. Could it have been Dr. Danziger—"

Two medical students walked past us, talking loudly. "Then my next patient was a guy who'd gotten thrown through a plate-glass window. You should have seen the blood—"

"That's it," Angelica said. "Dr. Danziger, who acts like God himself."

I let out the breath I'd been holding. But was she remembering the right surgery? Looking at the oversize woman in front of me, I couldn't see any way I could politely ask if Kitty's memory had been correct. "Was there anything else about the surgery that stuck in your mind? Anything at all?"

"Like I said, Redman was a sexist pig, and we'd already clashed during other surgeries. I'd heard the story of how he'd gotten an intestinal bypass because he hadn't been able to lose weight any other way. So after he'd dropped two hundred pounds, he had the zeal of the newly reformed—cracks about everyone else's weight, particularly women."

"Something he said during *this* surgery . . . ?"

"He kept complaining about how fat the patient was, how it made surgery more difficult—but he looked at me each time he said something."

I was wrong—she was an angel. "The patient remembered being compared to the Goodyear blimp—"

"Yeah, that was one of his lines. And he called her a beached whale."

Austin had been Kitty's anesthesiologist. Austin, the department chair, a man who didn't handle routine cases, had taken Eva's place as the anesthesiologist at Kitty's surgery. *Why?*

And then Angelica turned her head and I saw her expression—and I wondered if I could trust anything she'd told me: She was smiling, her expression full of remembered pleasure.

"You've been working the ER since early March . . ." I'd had trouble tracking her down at first because she'd moved from surgical nursing to the ER.

"What do you mean?" But her voice had gone up.

"You switched jobs after the surgery. Something made this operation memorable for you—?"

"Only a small thing. A very small thing."

"Yes?"

"When we were all done, I asked Dr. Redman if he might want to try this abdominal exerciser I'd been using—and I glanced down at his belly when I said it. If you could have seen his face—"

We stood in the corridor, laughing together so hard that my sides were aching.

Chapter 27

"You," Eva Aarastadt said as she opened her front door and saw me on Thursday evening. She stood silently, looking at me. Her blond hair was tied back in a messy knot, and she was wearing a worn chenille robe, once blue, now closer to gray. Her eyes were red, her cheeks blotchy.

When I'd stopped by her office in the afternoon, the first time I'd been free since speaking to Angelica Rudolph last night, I was told she'd left work early because of an appointment elsewhere; Austin's secretary had obligingly provided Eva's home address.

Thanks to Angelica, now I knew the truth—or at the least part of it: Kitty, paralyzed, in excruciating pain, had heard and remembered—and, shoving it in a corner of her mind, made herself forget—because the memory of the experience, the incredible agony, was, quite simply, too terrible.

Murray Snelling had been right all along: Kitty's surgical memories were authentic.

What I didn't know was why Eva, scheduled as Kitty's anesthesiologist, had not taken part—or how Austin Danziger came to serve in Eva's place. If I could

find out why he'd substituted, then I might know if
Kitty's anesthetic problems had indeed been deliberate—
including the whisper at the end.

And I had questions about Eva's roses—even though
I was afraid of the answers.

"I should have guessed you'd come," she said.

I expected her to be irate, to say this was a bad time,
to demand an explanation for my appearance.

Turning her back on me, she walked away from the
door, leaving it open behind her.

Shutting it as I followed her, I was wondering if I
should turn around and leave, as the pit in my stomach
was strongly suggesting. It felt like I'd stumbled into a
house visited recently by death—as if I'd intruded on
Eva's mourning.

A black-ceramic planter sat on a carved wooden ped-
estal in the foyer. It was filled with hyacinths and daf-
fodils forced into bloom outside their natural season;
now past their prime, the petals were darkening and the
heavy scent was cloying.

Turning to face me, she said, "Of all days for you to
appear . . . how did you know today was the day?" Her
voice was strained, her expression desolate.

Looking up quickly, I suddenly guessed what she
meant—what had happened today, why she'd left work
early—hardly a routine appointment. I pictured the patient I'd remembered just after Eva had left my office,
the image of her despairing face etched in my memory—
a woman who had come to see me after she'd gotten
her Huntington's disease diagnosis confirmed through
genetic testing. Now I stared at Eva, reflexively raising
my hand to cover my open mouth, trying desperately to
think what to say as I felt my face heating with shame.
"Oh no—"

Realizing how remarkably intrusive I must seem, how

terribly inappropriate, I watched her take in my response.

"No, you didn't know, did you—that's something, at least."

She'd been drinking I could tell, something she avoided normally. My chest tightened in sympathy—and a profound sense of mortified embarrassment. "I'm sorry, I really had no idea about the timing, I'll get out—"

"It won't be better later. It's time we had a talk, I suppose—I might as well get all the bad news at once."

Following her reluctantly into her living room, I found myself staring at the portrait on the wall: Eva in a floor-length evening gown, black, low-cut, a pendant with an enormous ruby lying between the sloping tops of her breasts. The painter had captured her classic face with its high cheekbones, the thrust of the jaw—her air of hauteur. An uncommonly beautiful woman. A remarkably proud woman.

She saw me look from the picture to her. I thought she winced, but I wasn't sure—she was good at hiding certain kinds of responses.

Standing at the edge of the room, I took a deep breath as I looked away. "I had no idea this was the day . . . Jerome dropped hints, but he never actually told me—I only guessed your secret after you came to my office. I feel like such an intrusive cretin, appearing here tonight." I'd assumed she'd gotten tested long ago.

Waving me toward a chair, she said, "I thought you knew. Your expression when you looked at me in your office—I could read the pity in it."

I shook my head no, remembering. Eva had mistaken envy for pity. Not something she'd be able to hear, not now.

I saw the bleakness in her face.

"Eva, I'm sorry. Truly."

In the silence I could hear birds chirping outside, like a cruel chorus singing about how life goes on. Through her window I could see the sun, almost down, red, a fire in the sky.

Last week, after I thought I'd guessed her secret, I'd looked through my reference books to check the accuracy of my memory.

Early to midforties is the most common time for onset of Huntington's chorea, I'd read. Caused by a single mutation on chromosome four, the course is downhill— there's no treatment, no remission, no miraculous cure. The symptoms appear gradually, with a ten-to-twenty-year duration before death.

Unpredictable spontaneous movements are characteristic, often appearing initially in the face and arms. Because they resemble normal restlessness at first, patients may be able to suppress the tics and twitches in the early stages, or hide them by blending with normal movements—but the problems can become more conspicuous when patients are stressed.

The disease will be accompanied by behavior and personality disorders about half the time, with aggression as the most common symptom, and personality disturbances may precede other illness symptoms by as much as twenty years. Depression can become severe as the disease progresses; other psychiatric symptoms may include severe mood swings, morbid jealousy (one woman who had divorced her husband years earlier kept breaking into his new house and burying his clothes in the garden), delusions—and explosive temper outbursts.

Intellectual losses are progressive, with short-term memory problems typically appearing first. Patients experience increasing difficulties learning new material. For Eva, this was perhaps the most central and horrifying specter—since it meant the end of her professional life might loom all too soon.

There's a blood test that can tell you whether you have the disease.

Eva must have gotten her results today.

"I hadn't wanted to know," she said. "I thought I could live without knowing. Then I realized I'd gotten to be a hypochondriac, alert for every small symptom, every little change. The odds are fifty-fifty, genetic Russian roulette. Flip a coin, what's it going to be?

"You'd asked why I moved here. I came to town to be tested where I could have some privacy, a place where I wasn't well-known. To find out what my genes had programmed for me. Which way my coin had flipped.

"I made a deal with myself. If I was safe, I'd give up smoking."

In the silence I watched her light a cigarette.

"You have Huntington's disease?"

Nodding, Eva turned away from me, but I caught a glimpse of the wetness shining on her cheek.

In response, I felt the tears puddling in my eyes.

Wiping my eyes, I looked around, trying to find something else to focus on. Across from me I saw a terra-cotta sculpture of a Japanese warrior, his hair pulled up in a topknot, straining to hold the reins of a prancing horse. One of several pieces of expensive artwork around her contemporary living room—a cold place, all too much like a furniture showroom, without personal touches that would engage or comfort. Maybe her aloof air came naturally, from so much time spent staring into the black abyss.

Eventually she said, "What did you come here to find out?"

"What happened on February 14—but this is obviously not a good time to be asking—"

"Valentine's Day—how very ironic. The beginning of the end." Picking up an empty wineglass from the end table beside her chair, pointing toward a doorway, she said, "There's wine in the fridge, extra glasses in the cabinet beside it." And then, catching my eye, "I'll be damned if I'll be prudent today."

When I was seated again, I could hear baroque music playing from unseen speakers, too intricate, crowding the room. Taking a sip of her wine, she said, "On Valentine's Day, Jerome spotted me as I was about to go over to the surgery floor. He flagged me down and told me that a florist had just delivered a box with a dozen roses for me to the department office. When I started to walk away, he grabbed my arm and said, 'Bet your boyfriend doesn't know about your medical problems—or he'd think twice about you.' Then he just stood there, smirking, waiting for my reaction."

Running her tongue over her lips, she stared at an oversize painting that showed falling leaves, swirling, five-lobed like hands, reaching out toward us. One, tinged with red, looked like a bloody fist, ready to strike.

"I felt like the floor had just collapsed under me," she said, a catch in her voice. "I didn't know what to say or do. When I started back to my office, my legs were trembling so badly that I could barely walk.

"I called Austin and told him I'd taken ill—I asked him to cover for me. Stress makes my symptoms worse, I get clumsy—more tics and twitches. I couldn't take the chance that someone might notice. I couldn't risk harming a patient because I couldn't function properly."

She laughed, a harsh cackle without any humor behind it, and I felt chilled by the sound. "Afterward, I realized Jerome was probably just fishing, looking for confirmation—and I'd handed it to him on a silver platter.''

She'd called Austin—why? And why did he drop whatever he was doing?

As I was about to ask, her right hand began to tremble. She looked up at me, checking to see if I had noticed—and if I was going to turn away. With an effort, a real effort, I kept my eyes on hers as she set down her wineglass before subduing her right hand with her left.

''Your turn,'' she said. ''What's the reason for your interest in February 14?''

I told her Kitty Evanston's story, from the beginning.

Together, we reconstructed what must have happened. Jerome, in charge of scheduling, had very deliberately booked Eva as Kitty's anesthesiologist. Under the guise of his Quality Assurance duties, he could have reviewed her charts from similar patients and pinpointed her probable anesthetic choices.

Jerome knew about Kitty's previous malpractice suit when he rigged her anesthetic, and he knew about her fight with Eva. He must have hoped to create a highly visible problem for Eva—a way to discredit her, to cast doubt on her clinical skills. As a bonus, he could get his revenge on Kitty at the same time.

While there was no way to be sure so long after the fact, Eva said that Jerome could easily have found Kitty in the recovery room after her surgery and whispered in her ear.

Jerome must have already known that Austin substituted for Eva long before I raised the issue—he'd have gotten Kitty's chart after her surgery to see if any problems had been noted. And then, when he knew I'd be hunting for it, he got her chart again to make sure it didn't fall into my hands, belatedly ''protecting'' Austin so I wouldn't discover he'd been Kitty's anesthesiologist.

"Did Austin ever say anything to you about Kitty's surgery?" I asked Eva.

"No—nothing."

But Austin wouldn't necessarily have had any objective way to know that something had gone wrong during Kitty's surgery.

"How did you know Austin?" I asked.

She answered too quickly, as if she'd been waiting for the question: "He was on the faculty in Philadelphia when I did my residency there."

Jerome couldn't be sure what had happened with Kitty. He couldn't be sure that Austin would have chosen the same anesthetics as Eva—not until he checked the chart.

But Eva had trained with Austin, so the choices might well be similar.

"You're probably the only person in the department who would have asked him to cover," I said.

"We've known each other a long time . . ."

"Just because you were a resident with him?"

"We were lovers," she said, shrugging. "Off and on, over the years."

Possible—even probable. But there was more to her story, something she wasn't saying.

"All day, I've been thinking about my father," she said. "He died of Huntington's—I watched this glorious, brilliant man disintegrate. When I was living in New York and my parents were up in Connecticut, I never introduced anyone to them, never told anyone about him. I've kept everyone in my life separate from them, so people would never make the connection.

"I don't want people knowing, watching me for every little sign, so if I'm clumsy or stiff or rude they'll automatically assume it's another symptom, more evidence I'm getting worse.''

What she was already doing to herself.

"How'd Jerome find out?" I asked.

"He was so terribly jealous of my friendship with Austin—he hired a private detective who tracked down my family and questioned the neighbors.''

"Did Jerome tell Austin?"

"No—but he was about to. If he'd lived, he would have told him.''

Jerome had discovered Eva's secret. How would this proud woman have reacted to losing control over her privacy? Could she have killed him in a fit of rage? If she wanted her last years to go according to her own script, if she really didn't have anything else to lose, maybe murder wouldn't have been a big obstacle.

"You'd not told anyone else?" I asked.

Shaking her head no, she looked away.

At that moment, I could feel the loneliness pooled around her, deep enough to drown. I understood why she was talking with me now.

"I don't know why I'm telling you any of this now. Maybe that's just part of the mantle you've learned to wear—an instant confessor for people." Anger, fear in her voice. "I can trust you won't tell anyone else?"

I nodded, not confident I could speak without a quiver in my voice.

Looking away, lighting another cigarette, she coughed after she inhaled. "It's amazing how you can lie to yourself, making excuses, telling yourself you really don't have any hard symptoms—how the test is going to come back clean, and then you'll make plans for the rest of your life." Picking up an empty matchbook cover, she began ripping off tiny pieces, piling them neatly on the end table beside her.

"Hell is knowing all the ways you can change in the next ten to twenty years: uncontrollable jerking and writhing, suicidal depression, an inability to put complex thoughts together. Knowing there's nothing but a long slide ahead of you, not knowing how fast you'll travel down, what parts of yourself will disappear first.

"Here's one of the real kickers: Insight and orientation can last undamaged until death—so you know just how far you've fallen, how much of yourself you've lost." She took a drag of her cigarette. "But I won't let myself go all the way down."

As I was trying to think what to say, how I could possibly respond, she looked over at me and said, "Bring the wine in here, would you? Open another bottle if you need to. I'm going to get drunk tonight—I'm already far enough gone to answer the questions you haven't asked yet—the ones about Nick and me."

I felt the conversation moving well beyond my control, like driving a car with faulty brakes. I'd been expecting it, but I couldn't help drawing back.

In the kitchen, trying not to think about Eva and Nick, I willed myself to focus on Jerome as I opened another bottle of wine.

If we were correct about Jerome's role in Kitty's anesthetic problems, then I'd been wrong—there wasn't any obvious link between her surgery and Jerome's death, none that I could see. It wasn't a comforting thought—because it meant that just because Nick didn't have any role in Kitty's surgery, I couldn't eliminate him from the roster of lab members who had access to the power supply. And Nick and Eva . . .

"Nick sent you the roses on Valentine's Day?" I asked, as I sat down again.

"Jerome must have told the story of how I threw them against the wall in the department office."

When I nodded, she said, "Nick moved here partly because of me. We'd started seeing each other when his marriage was breaking up—we'd had a commuter affair. We were discreet—that was one of my ground rules. He knew I'd seen Austin off and on over the years, and he was afraid we'd rekindle old flames. I didn't have any intention of starting up again with Austin, not when he was my boss—but I've never been monogamous, never promised to be faithful. When Nick sent the roses to the department office rather than my home, I felt like he was marking his territory—or trying to—and I blamed him for making me give away the show with Jerome. I told him I didn't want to see him for a while.

"Nick wants to be married again. He told me he wouldn't wait for me if I wouldn't make some kind of commitment to him."

And then he must have sent her the roses, the ones with the card that read "Last chance."

After that, Nick had made sure that Eva knew about his interest in me. When I'd been standing at the entrance to Denton, talking with Eva, he made a point of saying he'd call. He'd taken me to Austin's party for our first real date. Maybe he was hoping that Eva would arrive and stumble upon us when we stopped at the lab before heading out for Galveston.

A former lover never looks quite so attractive as when he's interested in someone else.

There are an amazing number of synonyms for lie: conceal, deceive, delude, distort, dupe, equivocate, evade, falsify, fabricate, misinform, mislead, pretend, prevaricate.

"Betray" was the one that came closest for me right now.

"You care about him, don't you?" she asked.

"More than I should, certainly," I said, my voice

breaking despite myself. The wine I'd just sipped burned the back of my throat.

"You told him my diagnosis, didn't you?"

"No. I didn't say anything to him—or anyone."

"But you will now, won't you?"

I imagined myself telling Nick about Eva's secret. I wanted him to hear the pain she'd kept silent, to know how she'd shut him out. I wanted him to know how little she'd shared with him—what lay in wait for her, for anyone who traveled with her.

"No," I said.

We locked eyes for a very long minute, and then she said, "I believe you. I don't know why, but I believe you. So I'll give you something in return. When I saw him at the hospital just before he left, I told him I wanted to get back together . . . he said he wasn't interested anymore—because of you."

I didn't know what to say, not a clue how to answer.

"Don't break into a chorus of 'You'll Never Walk Alone,' " Eva said. "The kind of men who want me aren't the kind who'll stick around when I start going downhill."

After a long silence, she began to talk about her father; he sounded very much like her in his earlier life. She drank more wine, and I switched to water. Her eyelids drooped, then finally closed. I got the comforter from her bed and covered her with it after I was sure she was sound asleep. As I let myself out of her house, I kept hearing one of the last things she'd said: "Think how it feels to know that all the lights in your brain will be going out, one by one, leaving behind darkness and spreading decay." When I closed her door behind me, I had tears streaming down my face.

Chapter 28

People respond to stress in different ways. Some acquire physical symptoms: headaches, backaches, stomach pain. Some grow angry, lashing out at the least provocation. Some become depressed and withdrawn; some get wired and rush around without sleeping, living on the edge with caffeine and adrenaline.

I do something out of the ordinary, at least for an adult: I walk in my sleep.

I'd begun sleepwalking after I was hospitalized the first time as a teenager. Usually I'd only go small distances, from my bedroom to the living room, occasionally going as far as the backyard. Once my father found me ambling down the street, my eyes wide-open. At various times Ian had found me sitting mindlessly in front of my computer, getting dressed, or running water for a bath.

The frequency varied. Last month, after hearing Murray Snelling's story of Kitty's surgery, Pavlov's anxious whining roused me as I was stepping out on my back porch twice within a week.

Now I awoke in Nick Treece's living room at two o'clock on Saturday morning, staring at a canvas sideshow banner: THE GREAT WALDO. Earlier, his arm around my waist, Nick had given me an enthusiastic explanation: "He could swallow things like lemons and peaches whole, and then disgorge them at will. At the climax of his act he'd swallow a live mouse and regurgitate it for the audience." Pictured in a tuxedo, the handsome dark-haired man with a handlebar moustache was leering at the apple in his hand.

"What an unpleasant way to make a living," I'd said.

Just back from his trip, Nick had grilled steaks for our dinner after we'd gone to an early movie. When he'd asked me over, he'd said, "I'd like to show you my place—and it would be nice to have at least one date where we don't stumble onto a disaster."

Later, as we were lying in his bed, he said, "I'm not supposed to say anything, but I just have to tell you. When I was working on Jerome's schedule with Dr. Danziger before I left town, he told me that he'd like me to take his place as chair, once he becomes Dean."

"How flattering—how very nice for you," I said.

"Maybe—maybe nice for us . . . it would mean I'd have a permanent position here, a good one."

It had been a fine evening with everything I could have wanted in romance and passion and companionship. Only now, when I'd awakened in his living room, trembling and fearful, trying to pinpoint what was troubling me, my mind had started replaying Nick's words after we'd found Jerome's body.

When I was newly widowed, sometimes my chest would be filled with so much pain that I thought my heart would stop. A pain so intense that it was like acid, gnawing through to leave a gaping hole. Now, standing in Nick's living room, shivering, I felt it all over again.

I'd wanted so badly to believe in Nick. I wanted to believe in Santa Claus and the tooth fairy and a future where I had a partner again. But I should have known that Nicholas Treece wasn't Saint Nicholas, and my life wasn't going to turn into a perpetual holiday because we'd met.

Tiptoeing back into the bedroom, I found his wallet on the bureau. I didn't feel good about searching it, but I couldn't have asked him for what I needed.

He was still sleeping soundly when I finished dressing and let myself out. I didn't leave a note—there was no easy way to say that I was worried about his involvement in a murder.

In the year after my mother's death, grieving, I'd been bothered by the feeling that nothing important could ever be predicted, let alone controlled. When those thoughts became too intrusive, I did dangerous things—maybe trying to show I could control the darkness, maybe simply tempting fate. Remembering all too well the way I'd felt back then, I headed for the medical center, for Austin's lab. To look for things I wasn't at all sure I wanted to find.

Sometimes it's easier to be afraid than to feel pain.

The parking garage beside Denton was nearly deserted when I arrived. Trying to ignore its emptiness, I told myself how nice it was to get one of the best spots, beside the entrance, how brightly the paths outside were lighted.

The building's main door was locked, so I took a detour through the emergency room next door, flashing my ID at the guard and then making my way through one of the tunnels that honeycombed the hospital complex. The corridor felt unusually cool, as if the normal presence of people warmed the hallways, and their absence left a chill.

Once I was inside Denton, the elevator came immediately, its speed a reminder of the building's emptiness.

Using the numbers I'd gotten from the card in Nick's wallet, I unlocked the door to the core lab—and stopped before I stopped inside. The lights were on, just like the morning when we'd found Jerome's body. Surely no one would be here at this time of night. Standing quietly, my hand on the knob, I waited for someone to challenge me.

No sound.

I thought seriously about shutting the door and walking away. Remembering what a good time I'd had with Nick, I pictured myself getting in my car and driving back to his apartment—making up an excuse for my sudden departure. Climbing back in his bed, feeling his arms warm around me.

Don't let your fear beat you back, I told myself now, my old litany after my mother's death.

I stepped inside the lab, closing the door behind me. No sound, no one around. Walking softly, I made my way around the front room of the lab, then the back, looking in all the places where someone could be hiding, telling myself that I was being ridiculous even as I was crouching and opening cabinets that were too small to conceal anyone.

I'd copied the combinations for Nick's door as well as Fred's. Feeling absurd, I opened both their labs, turned on the lights, and looked around: nothing.

Despite the evidence, I couldn't shake the feeling that I wasn't alone.

Jerome's watch was sitting in the corner of the counter where I'd seen it when I visited Sydney. Picking it up, remembering how he'd died so very near the spot where I was standing, I felt a chill.

It was the same brand as the one worn by the entomologist I'd dated, a Casio; I was hoping that Jerome would have bought such an elaborate gadget for exactly the same reason—a place to stow certain personal data so close to his heart. If I was right, that's where he'd recorded his new combination. Now I tried to reconstruct the sequence of buttons my date had punched to display my phone number.

After a half dozen tries, nothing had worked. Either I didn't have a clue about how it worked, or I'd guessed wrong. One more shot, and I'd be reasonable and head home. Home to safety.

The digital display came up with the words "MYLAB" followed by a six-digit number. At least some parts of my memory still functioned—those that hadn't been fatally mesmerized by Nick Treece.

The labs for Jerome and Eva were in the inner room. Punching the numbered sequence in the buttons on Jerome's lab door, I started to go inside and paused. Had I heard something behind me somewhere? Surely it was only the sound of one of the freezers, humming to life. Standing with the cold metal knob in my hand, my heart beating fast, I listened long enough to reassure myself.

Predictably, his small lab was only marginally neater than his office or apartment. Looking around, it was obvious why he'd chosen to work in the core lab; here, there was no free space on the counters. Making my way to a small desk in the corner, I opened its lone file drawer.

It was jammed full of folders—research materials, from the titles. Pulling out the one labeled "cytokine assays," I leafed through journal articles and promotional material from suppliers. Ten more folders were equally uninformative.

Did Jerome's secret dossiers only exist in Verna's imagination?

About to close the drawer, increasingly eager to leave, I wondered why three labels were typed, the remainder

handwritten. I took a closer look at the typed labels:
TOXINS. CATALYSTS. BIOHAZARDS.

Opening "TOXINS," I found typed pages, names at
the top. Arranged in alphabetical order, from the looks
of it: Aarastadt, Eva, on the top page. *Jerome's dossiers.*

The notes on Nick were in the "TOXINS" file as
well, and included a report from a private detective.

Nick was an only child, and his father was a well-
known surgeon who died when he was thirteen, the report said. Growing up, his mother kept telling him he'd
be a surgeon, just like his father. Nick chose anesthesiology, but he told his mother he was a surgeon. Until
her death, whenever he visited her, he told her stories
about his successful surgical career.

Nick's colorful stories, Jerome had said. Even now,
when I'd already guessed some of Nick's flaws, I was
wincing as I realized how much I'd willed myself to
overlook.

Time for reading later, I told myself, closing the
folder. Clutching the three files, I let myself out of Jerome's lab, shutting the door softly behind me, checking
to make sure it was locked again.

Like an echo, I heard a clicking noise, and then I
realized what it was: *The sound of someone punching
buttons at the core lab's main door.*

I grabbed Jerome's door knob, but it was well and
truly locked. I didn't remember the combination and
there was no time to retrieve it from Jerome's watch
again.

Hide the folders. If I didn't have the files, maybe I
could talk my way out. I needed to put them somewhere
safe, someplace where I could find them but no one else
was likely to chance upon them quickly—and then try
to bluff my way out of the lab.

How to camouflage them so they wouldn't be obvi-

ous? I thought of the cabinets, rejected them—far too
obvious, and I had no idea which were most frequently
used. Then I remembered when Sydney had been hunting for her serum samples. *Under the boxes in the
freezer.* She wouldn't be likely to be working this weekend—I could come back later and retrieve them.

Moving to the unit nearest me, I opened the door and
shoved a folder under the cardboard stacks on each of
three different shelves, closing it as softly as possible
before I crouched in a corner.

I heard footsteps, a heavy tread, and I took a deep
breath. A man, not Eva or Sydney. But the chances were
still two out of three that it wouldn't be Jerome's murderer. As if he could sense the path I'd taken, I heard
him walk over and try the knob on Jerome's door. Then
a kind of shuffling noise.

Then a soft laugh.

Cowering in the corner, my blouse damp with sweat,
I was weak from the adrenaline surge.

"Haley," he called out, "I know you're here. There's
no light under Jerome's door, so you're somewhere in
the main lab. We do need to talk."

Chapter 29

Like freshly poured concrete hardening in the sun, I felt myself frozen by his voice. Nicely spoken—not harsh, sounding as if he expected there might be a defensible excuse for my presence in the lab at this time of night. Waiting for me to tell him what it might be.

"There's only the one entrance to the lab," he continued, speaking in the same oh-so-reasonable voice, "and I know my way around here much better than you. We can work out our differences, don't you think?"

He had a remarkably seductive manner. Crouched down, listening to him, I could appreciate how his faculty came to obey—the impulse was nearly irresistible. I felt my breath coming fast.

Looking beside me, I saw the cord for one of the freezers plugged into a socket. *Freezer alarm.*

From the sound of his footsteps I guessed he was walking around as he talked, looking in corners, checking out all the possible hiding places—just as I'd done earlier. An octopus hides behind the inky screen it manufactures, I remembered. I was wishing I had the same talent as I heard his footsteps moving closer.

Trying to make myself as small as possible, I heard

him coming. Waiting until the last possible instant, I pulled the plug. His steps stopped and I was staring at shoes encased in the throwaway protective coverings worn for surgery.

Feeling oddly embarrassed, I moved from my crouch to a standing position, all too aware that he was so much taller than I.

"That's better," he said. "You must have rather sore knees." And he seemed so solicitous, his voice so very even. Such a fine manner with patients, I remembered, so reassuring.

Austin Danziger was carrying a blue gym bag. He was dressed in a surgeon's paper robe over green hospital scrubs, a disposable cap concealing his silver hair. But what held my attention were his hands, encased in surgical gloves.

My mouth was dry as I stared at him.

"Fred said you never work in the core lab," I heard myself saying—and then cursed myself for my clumsiness.

"It was fortunate timing. They'd called me in because Verbrugge had been complaining about pain after his bypass surgery—even ex-Deans get special treatment. I was talking with him when I looked out the window and spotted you walking out of the Denton Hall parking garage. No reason for you to be here at this time of night—unless you were after Jerome's files. His sister told you about them after the service, I gather."

He seated himself in a chair near the door to the inner lab, setting his gym bag on the floor. His movements were unhurried, his expression bland—but he'd positioned his bag so it blocked the exit.

Like paths in a labyrinth—with only one exit. And now the minotaur was guarding the only way out.

Gesturing at a nearby chair, he said, "Why don't you sit down while we talk."

Austin stood six-three, and he had the muscular build of a man in good condition. We both knew I couldn't win a physical contest with him.

"I'm more comfortable standing," I said, and watched his mouth twitch. He wasn't a man who tolerated defiance comfortably, even on small issues.

"As you wish," he said, getting up, his voice still deceptively calm. "But that means I'll have to stand as well."

Making sure he could grab me if I made any sudden moves. Scanning the area, there wasn't anything close to use as a weapon—nothing that I could snatch in time before he'd reach me. I could only hope he'd be startled enough when the freezer alarm went off to give me a chance to make a run for it. Leaning on the door to Eva's lab, I clutched the knob for support.

"You were in Jerome's lab," he said.

"No—"

"There's a German proverb: 'Lies have short legs—it is easy to catch up with them.'" Smiling, he glanced down at my legs, pausing long enough for his double meaning to be obvious before he added, "I put a couple of matchsticks in his door so I'd know if anyone got in. They were there earlier, they're gone now."

I wanted to scream, but that wasn't a smart idea. The walls were thick and solid. Shouts wouldn't be audible any farther than the immediate hallway, and the corridor was sure to be deserted, just as it was when I'd arrived. By shrieking now, I'd only succeed in galvanizing Austin into action that much earlier.

"You must have found Jerome's files, or you'd still be in there," he said. "That means you've hidden them somewhere in the lab. Where did you stash them?"

"I'm sorry I can't be helpful," I said, moving toward him. "But it's late and I should be heading—"

Barring my way, his hands poised to grab me, he said, "Sydney mentioned that she saw you lurking down the hall on the morning after Jerome's death, pretending to read a newspaper. Nick told me how he found you talking with Belinda in the gift shop; when I stopped there for a candy bar, she told me how you'd been grilling her while pretending to be her replacement. And then"— he paused, looking closely at me—"let's just say that your appearance here, at this time of night, doesn't suggest that your intentions are benign."

He couldn't afford to let me walk out because he didn't know what I'd read about him in Jerome's files, not on top of what I'd already guessed. He'd already tried to warn me off, and I'd ignored him—so if he let me go now, he would have to assume I'd keep looking— and maybe come up with whatever was in the files on my own.

And then— As the final kicker, he thought I knew something else.

The fact that he was dressed in scrubs meant he'd taken the time to change out of his street clothes after he saw Verbrugge. Not much of a risk; he'd probably made the switch in his office down the hall, leaving the door open so he wouldn't miss me on my way out. What made it hard to breathe was the realization that he'd taken the time to prepare himself before hunting me down. He'd made the decision about killing me when he saw me walking out of the parking garage.

He probably had his clothes in the bag. He'd dump the scrubs he was wearing in the hospital laundry once he'd finished with me—if there happened to be blood on them, or other physical traces, it wouldn't attract any attention.

When I didn't answer, he said, "Perhaps we can trade information, since you seem to have such a curious mind. Where did you get the combination to Jerome's door?"

Keep him talking, try to think of something. "His watch. He'd programmed the numbers in his watch, like a man I dated once." I was hoping it was hard for Austin to think of killing me directly—not the act itself, but the fact that he would need to use his hands. He'd engineered Jerome's death at an antiseptic distance, but something subtle like an accident with the power supply wouldn't be possible for me.

Looking down, I found myself staring at his hands. No reason for Austin to worry about fingerprints in his own lab. He was wearing gloves so he wouldn't leave any traces on my body. I felt hot, then I began sweating, drops forming on my forehead and face.

"Clever," he said. "That should have occurred to me—"

"You overheard Jerome talking about Kitty Evanston's surgery at the Development Fund party," I said, "and you were her anesthesiologist on February 14." *Keep him talking.*

"When I saw him bending over her in the recovery room, I asked him if anything was wrong, and he denied it—but he was so clearly unnerved when he spotted me that I didn't believe him. I confronted him after you started asking questions . . . he tried to tell me that Eva must have set a trap for me, but I knew she'd never cross me."

So Jerome had indeed been the whispered voice. "He wanted to be your second-in-command," I said.

Nodding, he said, "He told me that he wanted me to appoint him as associate dean for Academic Affairs when I became Dean. He'd help me 'shape up' the medical school''—he grimaced—''and he made it clear he wanted to have a say in all the major decisions. I told him I couldn't put someone who was only an associate professor in such a senior role. He told me he was 'confident' I'd find a way to get him promoted from associate to full, he knew I could manage it—because it was so important that we continue to work closely together.

''I told him he'd have to publish at least a couple more papers if he wanted me to get him promoted,'' he said. ''He wasn't happy with it, but he did see the logic. When he mentioned the course at Woods Hole, I encouraged him. We discussed the experiments he would run, and he kept me informed about his progress.''

In exquisite detail, no doubt. Jerome would have wanted to make sure Austin knew exactly how hard he was trying—day by day. Making it easy for Austin to set the stage.

Austin had known how to rig the power supply because of his hobby—he'd spent hours rewiring the animated figures in his penny-arcade collection.

Wiping the sweat from my face with my hand, I caught the scent of Nick's aftershave, and I closed my eyes for an instant. *I could have been lying beside him in his bed right now—safe.* ''Nick saw you with the power supply, didn't he?'' I asked.

When I'd awakened in Nick's living room, staring at his sideshow banner, my mind had started replaying the things he'd said when we'd found Jerome's body—and I realized what I'd overlooked: *Austin, he'd called him. Not Dr. Danziger.* Not once, but three times.

Then Nick had left a careful message with Austin's secretary—all the details of Jerome's death. A message that made it effortless for Austin—he didn't need to feign surprise or shock, only grief.

Leaning forward, his voice sharp, Austin said, "Surely he didn't tell you that?"

"No. I'm not sure he knows it himself, consciously." Nick had gone into anesthesiology because of Austin—he'd admired him so much that he'd even adopted his boss's hobby as his own. And Austin had tried to make sure of Nick's loyalty—and silence—by telling him he'd inherit his position as chair when he became Dean.

He nodded, reassured. But he hadn't said that Nick hadn't seen him with the power supply—he'd only asked if he'd mentioned it. How comforting to have guessed correctly.

Austin didn't like being challenged by anyone—and I'd done it repeatedly. This moment had a particular sweetness for him, I realized—he could show me just how clever he'd been, how little I'd known. He could enjoy preening in front of me before he killed me.

"You were responsible for the isotope in the water-cooler," I said.

"A simple matter to have one more trick among the series."

"Another death in your lab won't help your candidacy for Dean."

"You should learn to listen more closely. Perhaps you missed it earlier when I referred to Verbrugge as our 'ex-Dean.' The Board of Trustees will announce my appointment at a news conference this afternoon."

I froze, seeing the picture in color for the first time. Austin already knew exactly how I would die—and how my body wouldn't be found until sometime early next week, at best. Derek had been delighted when I'd asked him if he'd take Pavlov for the night; he wouldn't know there was a problem until late tomorrow—and he'd have no idea where to look. Nor would Nick—even if he were so inclined after my abrupt disappearance. My legs felt weak and tremulous.

My only hope, admittedly weak, was running past Austin when the freezer alarm startled him—not a strong prospect. Trying to remember what I knew of self-defense for the fast-approaching moment when he was going to grab me, I thought of gouging his eyes or Adam's apple, stomping on his instep, kicking his crotch.

Looking down, judging angles, I could see the outline of an erection through his scrubs. How stimulating he was finding the moment, having me at his mercy.

"Jerome changed the lock on his lab door without telling me," he said. "That was when I knew he'd found out something about me. Now that we've had our little chat, I do need to know where you've hidden the files."

"I don't believe that's possible." Once he had them, I was dead. *Why didn't the alarm ring?*

"Did anyone ever give you a real tour of the core lab?"

No, I shook my head. I ran my tongue over my dry lips.

"Each of the faculty in my research group has a lab in here, and we have shared resources as well. One of those is the cold room. It's what the name implies—a refrigerated room. The temperature inside is carefully regulated at two degrees—that's centigrade, of course.

"You'll be spending some time inside until you feel more like talking . . . unless, of course, you want to tell me now where you've hidden the files, and save yourself the unpleasantness."

I shook my head.

"I can't imagine that it will be difficult for me to find them, anyway—there aren't that many hiding places, af-

ter all. Pity for you that you don't have much body fat.
It won't take all that long—''

I didn't have any more time left. Lunging, I aimed for
the gap between him and the doorframe.

In one smooth motion he grabbed my arm and spun
me around so my back was to him; putting his right arm
around my neck in a choke hold, holding my left arm
with his, he began dragging me. The moves I'd been
rehearsing to fight back were absolutely useless. He was
pulling me in such a way that I was off-balance, and I
couldn't get a grip with my feet as my heels slid on the
slippery linoleum. As he squeezed my throat tightly with
his arm, I was struggling to breath. With my free arm I
was clawing at the arm that was holding me and I was
straining to reach his face, but I might as well have been
scratching at a lamppost.

A few seconds later he stopped and released my left
arm. Opening a metal door, he thrust me inside with
such force that I fell heavily against a section of the
metal wall opposite the door, my shoulder exploding in
pain.

''I wouldn't advise touching the bottles on the
shelves—it's not the safest of places,'' he said. As he
was closing the door I could hear a high-pitched sound
in the background—probably the freezer alarm. The
sound was cut off abruptly as the door thudded shut.

The small window in the door gave off enough light
for me to glimpse my surroundings as I jumped up,
wincing at the ache in my shoulder. A small room,
maybe nine by five feet, with metal shelves that were
filled with glass bottles, some holding clear liquids, others red or orange, the groups sorted according to color.
A sink and counter ran along the far wall, a stack of
paper towels beside the single faucet. A light fixture
overhead, not turned on, no light switch on the wall

inside. I tried pushing against the door, then pulling. Nothing.

Of course there had to be a safety lever. On the surface of the metal door, nothing. Maybe at the edge? A white lever on the left. I pulled it with all my strength. I tried the door again. I tried everything twice more. Nothing. Either he'd disabled the safety, or he'd anchored the door on the outside.

Dressing for my date with Nick, I'd worn a short-sleeved green blouse, cream-colored silk slacks, and green flats—a fine choice for a hot summer night. I'd sweated enough to dampen my shirt during my interlude with Austin. Now I was shivering fiercely.

Looking out the window, I caught sight of him walking toward the door, something white in his hand. Inside, the sound of an exhaust fan overhead was so loud that I couldn't hear his footsteps, wouldn't have known he was coming if I hadn't seen him. He reached up, and then the light was gone.

He'd covered the window to leave me in the darkness. My breath was coming in gasps, my heart racing.

As cold as I was feeling now, I didn't have much time before my fingers got so stiff and clumsy that I wouldn't be able to do much. *The bottles.* At this point, it didn't much matter what was in them; Austin could kill me faster than any microbe—if I didn't die from hypothermia first.

Feeling my way toward the sink, I stumbled into the shelves, heard the bottles clanging, one falling and breaking as I struggled to keep my balance. *Already getting clumsy from the chill?* Or wobbly from fear.

I seized the first bottle that came to hand. Its frigid surface made me shiver all the harder and I had to force myself to keep hold of it after I touched it. Reaching out, I found the edge of the sink, and then, after an eternity, the stack of paper towels. It seemed to take forever to wrap several around the glass.

Gripping the bottle by the screw-cap end, I headed for the dim outline of light on the door. Like a batter trying for a home run, I checked my swing, trying to position myself for maximum impact. I'd hoped to use one arm to cover my face and eyes, but the bottle was heavy enough that I couldn't protect myself and still have enough force behind my glass bat to do the trick. Stepping back, I took careful aim and closed my eyes at the last second, crying out when glass and icy liquid from the bottle sprayed over me.

The window was still intact—or at least the dim outline of light around it hadn't changed materially. Probably safety glass—hopefully not reinforced with steel net.

So far I'd only made things worse—spraying myself with who-knows-what had left me easier prey for the cold. I wanted to curl up in a corner and wrap my arms around myself and cry.

Keep moving. Good judgment goes by the wayside with hypothermia, I reminded myself. Not wanting to step directly on pieces of jagged glass as I went for another bottle and more paper towels, I slid my feet along the floor.

How long would Austin search before he found the folders? Maybe he'd already spotted them and left. Perhaps he'd decide to come back tomorrow and search at his leisure. If he looked long enough, he'd surely find them.

I set aside the remnants of the first bottle on the counter close to hand, easily grabable—a weapon if Austin opened the door. Wrapping the second, I wondered what he'd thought I must know, what he'd been thinking when he stopped himself: *And then—*

I recalled the way he'd tried to get me to resign from the project—and suddenly I understood.

Remembering when he'd spotted me talking with Coppersmith at the party, it made a kind of crazy sense. *I made a donation through the Anesthesiology Research Foundation so he could hire a couple of faculty*, Burgess had said.

Bypassing the Development Office to avoid paying them a share, Austin had used Coppersmith's money to fund salary lines for Eva and Nick—and Jerome had found out, somehow. The memo on the topic that I'd seen in Jerome's files wasn't related to plans for his own estate—it reflected his outraged jealousy.

As I wrapped the bottle, I was trying to walk in place, trying to keep moving, keep up my body temperature. I could tell that my thinking was already beginning to slow—I was finding it harder to put thoughts together.

Austin probably didn't think he'd taken much of a risk until the Board of Trustees began investigating Verbrugge's financial dealings in March. At that point Austin realized that if he was caught using Coppersmith's donation out of channels, he'd lose his shot at being Dean—but by then it was too late for him to change what he'd done, as Jerome knew well.

On Friday, Kurt von Reichenau had told me he'd called Austin to brag about our luncheon with Coppersmith.

Austin must have thought I was following in Jerome's footsteps. Once he saw me looking for Jerome's files, he knew I suspected him of Jerome's murder.

Less risky to kill me—especially with all the prior "accidents" in the lab to obscure the real motive—than to leave me alive and allow me to continue to search. The cover story for my death would be straightforward: Having no legitimate business in the lab in the first place, I must have ducked into the freezer when I heard someone enter—and then found myself trapped.

Shivering, I thought about how polar bears lurk outside the breathing holes used by seals. Waiting patiently until they came within reach, then grabbing them with their teeth and claws. What would I do even if I broke the window? At least I'd have enough light to look around and see if there was anything else I could use to get myself out.

At least I wouldn't die in the dark.

Ready with another bottle wrapped in paper towels, I positioned myself for a second swing at the window in the door. Closer this time, for a more forceful impact. Closing my eyes, I swung with all my remaining strength—and felt myself falling forward, bright lights in my face, plunging through the door as it was opening. Unable to stop myself, I was crashing on the floor, screaming as I landed on my right shoulder again, trying to decide if I could be in such pain and still be delirious as I watched the bottle rolling away from me, unbroken.

"Haley, I have a gun."

A woman's voice. I must be far gone.

The light was so bright after the darkness, the change so sudden, I couldn't focus for a very long moment.

Then I saw that Eva Aarastadt was standing in front of me, a gun in her right hand, an anguished look on her face. Wearing jeans and a blue T-shirt, she was looking at me, then away. As I stared up at her I saw her right hand trembling, saw her reach to grip the gun with both hands.

"Don't move, Austin," she said, her voice sharp.

Looking over, I saw him standing as if poised to spring. Speaking in his oh-so-reasonable voice, he said, "Jerome kept notes on everyone and she found them. If she dies, the secrets are safe." The same soothing tone I'd heard earlier.

A stillness as we both awaited her answer.

"I know," she said. "I'm well aware."

"There's more at stake than you may think. Jerome told me about you," he said. "I know—"

"*No*," Eva said, shaking her head, her expression desolate.

"If you ever need help, I'll be there for you," he said, "if you won't get in my way this time." And he seemed so solicitous, his voice so very even and comforting.

Offering her a safety net, exactly what she so desperately wanted and needed—and she knew he'd keep his word, because he'd already come through for her.

Her former lover, appealing for her help. A man offering her salvation on demand.

What goes around, comes around.

Sitting up, wincing at the pain in my shoulder, I closed my eyes, trying to stifle tears. Knowing that any second she'd tell him it was OK to shove me back in the cold room, and I was too stiff and too tired to fight any longer.

Knowing that together they could concoct an unbreakable mutual alibi.

Then Eva said, "I'm sorry, Austin, I can't let you kill her."

Epilogue

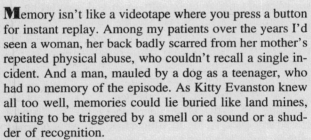

Memory isn't like a videotape where you press a button for instant replay. Among my patients over the years I'd seen a woman, her back badly scarred from her mother's repeated physical abuse, who couldn't recall a single incident. And a man, mauled by a dog as a teenager, who had no memory of the episode. As Kitty Evanston knew all too well, memories could lie buried like land mines, waiting to be triggered by a smell or a sound or a shudder of recognition.

I wish I could voluntarily entomb some of my own memories, seal them firmly out of reach. For weeks after my confinement in the cold room, I'd get panicky whenever I felt chilly.

Sometimes the ability to forget is a blessing. For Eva Aarastadt, it's a curse.

Unable to sleep, Eva had come to her lab, trying to bury her fears in her work. When she'd first heard me moving around, she'd assumed it was Fred, hanging around, hoping to "run into her" as he'd done so often before. Then she'd listened to the conversation between Austin and me as we stood outside her door—and agonized about what to do. Initially she thought she could simply let me out after Austin left; when Austin showed no signs of leaving, she was forced to confront him with the gun she'd gotten because she hadn't felt safe working late by herself—the weapon Jerome had indeed seen in her lab.

Eva and I became friends and, eventually, she told me Austin's real secret—the one he worried Jerome had uncovered—a saga involving drug addiction and the deliberate administration of inadequate anesthesia.

Austin had discovered that his mentor in Philadelphia had become hooked on painkillers after an auto accident. To feed his habit, he'd begun stealing narcotics—providing less than the necessary anesthetic dosage in intravenous bags of patients undergoing surgery. In the final stages of interviewing for the chair in Houston, afraid the revelation would damage the credibility of the recommendation written on his behalf, Austin kept silent. Eva, working as a resident under Austin's supervision, came to him when she had begun to be concerned as well. Assuring her he'd investigate, Austin had persuaded Eva to keep quiet for another week while he explored the problem. When she discovered Austin's duplicity and confronted him after his mentor's arrest, he promised he'd help her if she ever needed something in exchange for her continued silence. Eva had asked Austin to return the favor by creating a job for her in Houston.

Jerome, jealous of the newcomer's obvious ease with Austin, had learned that Austin had misused funds to make her appointment possible. He'd threatened his boss with exposure if he didn't find a way to make him his second-in-command. Then, during a department meeting, Jerome presented Austin with the framed picture that was hanging in the Anesthesiology conference room, the pen-and-ink drawing ''Before Anesthesia'' that showed the terrified patient, tied down—and he'd changed the combination on his lab door at the same time.

After Jerome's files were impounded by the police, I never heard anything more about their contents.

Austin was arrested and charged with the attack on me, as well as Jerome's murder. The Board of Trustees got the news just before they were about to announce his appointment as Dean.

One of the more satisfying moments occurred when Tony Zellitti came to my office for a deposition in August, his opportunity as the attorney for the *Phoenix* plaintiffs to ask questions about my opinions as an expert witness after reading my reports. We arrived at the front door of Rugton simultaneously; he looked me up and down as he smoothed his blond hair. "You look very familiar," he said, smiling. "Have we met?"

Dressed in a navy suit, white blouse, and heels, I said, "I'm your brother's neighbor. The last time we spoke, you told me that you weren't going to tolerate my interference with him." Nodding neutrally, I walked past him up the stairs as he stood glowering at the building directory beside the elevator.

Several minutes later, he'd finally found his way to the conference room where the two attorneys for the insurance company were already seated. I'd gone to my office first, so I entered the room behind him. After the lawyers introduced themselves, one said, "And Dr. McAlister is standing behind you." When he turned and spotted me, his jaw dropped, and his face turned bright red. I liked to think he was remembering my damning reports about all but one of his clients.

Davy Crockett Bayless and Vince Gambier were charged with the murder of Bert, the captain of the *Phoenix*, and Vince's indictment included a second mur-

der as well, that of Willie O'Rourke; after Vince read
my notes, he got worried about leaving witnesses who
might be easily broken—especially since he feared I
might have recognized Willie. Convinced that he was
the next victim after reading of Willie's death, remembering I'd said that he had to tell his story to be safe,
Davy had gone to the police and confessed as part of a
plea bargain, naming Vince as the mastermind.

Angry with the captain, visions of large insurance set-
tlements dancing in their heads, the trio had doctored
food for the twins and Lou Ramsey the day before the
accident with the hope that they wouldn't be able to
work. Timing it when the nets were full and the skipper
and Lou were belowdecks, they'd deliberately snagged
the anchor to overturn the boat, Vince assuring the others that the two would be able to climb out. As I'd suspected, Lou's shipmates were paddling away from him
in the life raft while he was struggling in the water,
pretending not to hear his cries for help until the *Vantage*
was within range.

Nick Treece felt like I'd left him out at sea, all the
more so because I never explained why I'd walked out
so precipitously when things had been going so well. In
some ways I couldn't blame him for his behavior with
Austin; given his history, he could no more have escaped
Austin's influence than a planet could have willingly
torn itself out of its rotation around the sun. But his
cover-up, if that's what it was, had been a symptom of
a larger problem—a man with such well-practiced lies
for his mother almost certainly did the same with other
women. I couldn't believe his ex-wife's fits of rage were
simply random events.

After we parted, Nick sent me one of his beloved
canvas banners: THE AMAZING RUBBER SKINNED GIRL.
His accompanying note asked me to remember the eve-

ning I'd seen it hanging in his living room—and to call if I ever changed my mind. Standing close together that night, his arm tight around my waist, he'd given me an enthusiastic explanation: ''She had Ehlers-Danlos syndrome, a collagen disorder—she could pull her skin so it stretched as much as a foot from almost any part of her body.'' Pictured in a skimpy pink bikini, the buxom blonde was beaming as she extended skin from her thigh with one hand, from her midriff with the other.

The blonde looked a lot like Eva. They'd gotten back together, so maybe Nick didn't need the banner, once he had the real thing—but I thought it was more likely that she'd already made it plain she wasn't going to stretch to fit any man, no matter how great her need.

While I never told Nick why I left, I think he had his suspicions—I guessed his parting gift was a message that he'd changed his ways and no longer admired Austin.

In August I hung Nick's banner in my spare bedroom after signing a lease that committed me to the house in Montrose for another year. It wasn't that I'd decided there weren't any perfect homes, any more than there weren't any perfect men—certain delusions are so very well fixed for me—only that it wasn't wise to rush into action in either case.

Acknowledgments

I am grateful to many people. Phil Marucha and John Sheridan provided valuable advice about laboratory "safety." Certain plot issues were suggested by Suzanne Felten, and her thoughtful comments on the manuscript led to helpful revisions. Enid Light has had a profound influence on my scholarly work over the last decade; her insightful comment about anesthesiologists sparked a key thread in this novel. Haley's recent deception research was inspired by Jamie Pennebaker's observations on the analysis of speech content. Jack McDonald kindly tolerated endless odd questions about medical issues. I appreciated Ann McKay Thoroman's astute observations on the manuscript, and her support during the final revisions. "Some evidence for heightened sexual attraction under conditions of high anxiety," the research report by Donald Dutton and Arthur Aron using the Capilano Canyon Suspension Bridge, appeared in the *Journal of Personality and Social Psychology* in 1974. Gerald Rosen's scholarly article on survivors of a maritime disaster prompted the evaluation of the *Phoenix* survivors, while Ed Blanchard's studies of psychophysiology and PTSD imagery suggested a useful assessment strategy.

297

As always, Ron Glaser was unfailing helpful in answering numerous questions about everything from cars to dogs—and his support and encouragement lit the road and eased the long journey.

Rhode Island
State Facts

Nickname: The Ocean State

Date Entered Union: May 29, 1790
(the 13th state)

Motto: Hope

Rhode Island Men: Spalding Gray, *writer, performist*
David Hartman, *TV newscaster*
Anthony Quinn, *actor*
Gilbert Stuart, *painter*

State Flower: Violet

State Tree: Red maple

Fun Fact: The first circus in the U.S. was in Newport, in 1774.

Rhode Island was the last of the original 13 colonies to become a state.

"I have to find out the truth," Allison said.

"I suppose you're right." Gabe smiled grimly. "No matter who gets hurt."

"You must think I'm a monster! I'd never willingly add to anyone's misery."

"I wasn't referring to anyone else. I was thinking of you," Gabe said quietly. "You've had a lot of disappointment in your life. I wouldn't like to see you go through any more."

His husky voice warmed Allison. Very few people had ever been concerned about her—certainly no one like Gabe. Was he being sincere? Or was it just a tactic to get rid of her?

"Why should you care what happens to me?" she asked hesitantly.

"I can understand why you don't trust me." He reached over and captured her hand.

Gabe's warm touch sent a tingle up her arm. She tried not to let herself imagine what it would be like if circumstances were different and he really *was* interested in her....

American

HEROES

AGAINST ALL ODDS

Tracy
SINCLAIR

Does Anybody Know
Who Allison Is?

Silhouette Books

Published by Silhouette Books
America's Publisher of Contemporary Romance

SILHOUETTE BOOKS
300 East 42nd St.,
New York, N. Y. 10017

ISBN 0-373-82237-5

DOES ANYBODY KNOW WHO ALLISON IS?

About the Author

Tracy Sinclair began her career as a photojournalist for national magazines and newspapers. Extensive travel all over the world has provided this California resident with countless fascinating experiences, settings and acquaintances to draw on in plotting her romances. After writing over fifty novels for Silhouette, she still has stories she can't wait to tell.

Books by Tracy Sinclair

Silhouette Special Edition

Never Give Your Heart #12
Mixed Blessing #34
Designed for Love #52
Castles in the Air #68
Fair Exchange #105
Winter of Love #140
The Tangled Web #153
The Harvest Is Love #183
Pride's Folly #208
Intrigue in Venice #232
A Love So Tender #249
Dream Girl #287
Preview of Paradise #309
Forgive and Forget #355
Mandrego #386
No Room for Doubt #421
More Precious than Jewels #453
Champagne for Breakfast #481
Proof Positive #493
Sky High #512
King of Hearts #531
Miss Robinson Crusoe #565
Willing Partners #584
Golden Adventure #605

The Girl Most Likely To #619
A Change of Place #672
The Man She Married #701
If the Truth Be Told #725
*Dreamboat and the
    Western World* #746
*The Cat That Lived
    on Park Avenue* #791
Romance on the Menu #821
Grand Prize Winner! #847
Marry Me Kate #868
The Sultan's Wives #943
*Does Anybody Know
    Who Allison Is?* #957
*What She Did on Her
    Summer Vacation* #976
For Love of Her Child #1018
*Thank Heaven for Little Girls
    #1058
Mandy Meets a Millionaire #1072
Please Take Care of Willie #1101
The Princess Who Gets Engaged #1133
Lucky in Love #1167
The Bachelor King #1278

Silhouette Romance

Paradise Island #39
Holiday in Jamaica #123
Flight to Romance #174
Stars in Her Eyes #244
Catch a Rising Star #345
Love Is Forever #459
Anything But Marriage #892
The Best Is Yet To Be #1006
An Eligible Stranger #1439

Silhouette Books

Silhouette Christmas Stories 1986
"Under the Mistletoe"

*World's Most Eligible Bachelors
The Seductive Sheik*

*Cupid's Little Helpers

Dear Reader,

Allison's story starts in Newport, Rhode Island, a summer resort frequented by America's wealthiest and most influential families. Back in the 1800s they built magnificent mansions that they quaintly called "cottages." The Vanderbilts had a four-story seventy-room "cottage" with gardens and pools and stables—everything money could buy.

As I was touring one of these luxurious American castles I thought, what if a young woman like Allison had been given up by her mother at birth and was desperately trying to find out who her parents were? And what if she traced her mother to a place like this? Would there be a joyous reunion—maybe even romance with a handsome friend of the family? Or would she stumble across dark secrets best left undisturbed?

This is one of my favorite books. I became very involved in Allison's life, shared her sorrow and rejoiced when she finally found happiness. I hope you'll enjoy reading her story as much as I enjoyed writing it.

With all best wishes,

Tracy Sinclair

Please address questions and book requests to:
Silhouette Reader Service
U.S.: 3010 Walden Ave., P.O. Box 1325, Buffalo, NY 14269
Canadian: P.O. Box 609, Fort Erie, Ont. L2A 5X3

Chapter One

Allison Riley had always wondered who her parents were, like all the other children at the orphanage. It was merely a matter of speculation, however, until she was twenty-five years old and living on her own. Finding out who she was became a top priority the night Bruce broke their engagement.

He'd skirted the issue, but the real reason was her "uncertain background," as his parents so delicately put it. They vigorously opposed what they considered an unsuitable marriage.

"This doesn't mean we have to stop seeing each other," Bruce had said uncomfortably.

"As long as your mommy and daddy don't find out," she'd answered bitterly.

"That isn't fair, Allie! You know I work for my dad. It wouldn't do either of us any good for me to openly defy him. We can't get married if I don't have a job."

"You could get a job with another firm. You're thirty-three years old. Isn't it time you left the nest?"

"Investment banking is in a recession right now. It wouldn't be easy to find a comparable position somewhere else. If you'll just be patient, I'll try to smooth things over with Mother and Dad.''

"What if they don't change their minds?''

When Bruce had failed to assure her of their future together, no matter what, Allison's illusions died. He was a spoiled rich man's son, and his parents were shallow social climbers who expected him to marry a debutante—which he would undoubtedly do.

It was a shock to realize, once she started to think rationally rather than emotionally, that she honestly didn't care. Her pride was hurt naturally, but the reason for her rejection was the really crushing blow. Allison vowed at that moment that she'd never again let herself be dismissed as a shadowy figure without a past, or even a name of her own.

The search for her identity had taken her to a hospital in Philadelphia where she was born. And now, here, to a mansion in Newport, Rhode Island.

Butterflies were beating their wings in Allison's stomach as she stood outside the imposing double doors of Rosewood Manor. Was the missing piece of the puzzle within reach? If so, would she be welcome? Or would her mother be horrified that the daughter she gave away so many years ago had suddenly turned up to intrude on her life?

There was only one way to find out. Allison drew a deep breath and rang the bell.

A butler with an impassive face answered the door. His carefully blank expression was replaced by startled surprise when she asked to see Monica Van Ruyder. After an instant, his mask descended once more.

"Whom shall I say is calling?''

"She doesn't know...I mean...'' Allison paused to compose herself. "My name is Allison Riley.''

He allowed her into the entry hall, but no farther. She glanced around in awe at the marble columns and arches below the twenty-foot ceiling. Beyond the pillars was a sweeping staircase with ornate wrought-iron railings that curved on both sides before fanning out to a second floor.

As her dazzled eyes swept over paintings, antique wall sconces and rose-colored damask draperies, the butler returned with a younger man, somewhere in his forties. He had a weak chin and thin lips compressed in a straight line.

The man greeted her with a menacing scowl. "What do you want here?"

It was a startlingly rude reception, but Allison tried not to let it bother her. "I'd like to see Monica Van Ruyder."

"What about?"

"Well, I...it's personal."

"I'm her brother, Martin Van Ruyder. You can tell me."

"It's about something that happened a long time ago," Allison said reluctantly.

"I suppose you're going to claim she owed you money. All right, submit an itemized bill and we'll pay it if it isn't too outrageous. Don't be greedy. I'm sure she doesn't owe you a cent, but we'll write it off to nuisance value."

"I didn't come here for money! I'd just like to talk to her. I'm sure she'll want to hear what I have to say." Allison lied out of desperation.

A nasty smile curved his mouth. "That proves you don't know the first thing about Monica. Women never interested her."

Allison hadn't come this far to be turned away. Her nails made crescent marks in her damp palms. "I really must insist on seeing your sister."

"Okay, that's it! I don't know what your game is, but if you're not out of here in two seconds, I'm going to call the police."

Allison stared at him in bewilderment. "Why won't you let me see her? You don't even know why I came."

"I'm sure you have a very plausible story prepared—one involving money. You scam artists come out of the woodwork when somebody wealthy dies."

Allison's first reaction was incredulity. "You mean she's—I don't believe you! You're just saying that to get rid of me. She can't be dead!"

"What difference does it make to *you?* You couldn't have been on very close terms if you didn't even know she died."

Allison felt a crushing sense of defeat as the news sank in. It wasn't fair to have arrived too late. "Was it an accident?" she whispered.

"What difference does it make?" he asked curtly.

"Please, I'd like to know."

"Why?"

"I think Monica Van Ruyder was my mother."

"What?" Martin's face flushed with anger. "You're really going for the gold, aren't you? Which marriage is supposed to have produced you? My sister had three husbands. That was written up in the newspaper. It's a funny thing, though, nobody ever heard of her having any children."

Allison was instantly sorry for her bald statement. She never would have blurted out her suspicion if she hadn't been so upset over the news of Monica's death.

"I suppose you've concocted some wild story to get around the facts," he taunted. "All right, try it out on me. Why am I supposed to believe Monica was your mother?"

"I'm not sure she was," Allison answered slowly. "That's what I came to find out."

"Oh, so now you're having second thoughts about getting away with it. At least you realize your scheme won't work. If you're smart, you'll go back to wherever you came from and try to fleece an easier mark."

"I'm not trying to deceive anybody. All I want is information. I was raised in an orphanage and I never knew who my parents were."

"That's very touching." He sneered. "How did you arrive at Monica?"

"I spent a lot of time going through the records at the hospital in Philadelphia where I was born. There were two other possibilities, but she seemed the most likely."

"And as long as you had a choice, why not pick the richest one?" Martin's voice was heavy with irony.

"No! I didn't want anything from her."

"Then you won't be disappointed, because that's exactly what you're going to get. You'd better leave now."

"Could I just see a picture of her?" Allison pleaded.

His teeth clicked together. "No, you may not! I want you out of this house. If you try to pursue your outrageous fraud I'll have you thrown in jail. Is that quite clear?" Without waiting for an answer, he strode to the door and flung it open.

She had no choice. In all fairness, Allison could see why Monica's brother would think she was a fortune hunter. The family was unimaginably rich. If only he realized that she didn't want a cent from them, just confirmation, one way or the other.

An attractive older woman was coming down the staircase as Allison went out the door. "Who was that pretty girl, Martin?"

"Nobody, Mother," he answered briefly.

Mary Louise Van Ruyder gazed at her son with raised eyebrows. She was in her sixties, but her figure was still trim and her face relatively unlined. She obviously took good care of herself, yet she wasn't one of those foolish women who try to deny the passage of time by following fashion's dictates, however unsuitable. Her short gray hair was simply styled, and her navy linen dress was elegantly understated.

"My eyesight is still excellent," she remarked dryly. "I distinctly saw a young woman in the hallway. What did she want?"

"Nothing to concern yourself over," he answered dismissively.

"If you're trying to whet my curiosity, you've succeeded. How many more times must I ask you?"

"It was just some woman with a wild story about Monica. I didn't want you to be upset by it, that's all. She won't be back, I guarantee you," Martin said grimly.

"How did she know Monica?"

"She didn't. That's what makes her visit so outrageous. The whole thing is really quite absurd, not worth repeating." When Mary Louise gave him a level stare, he continued reluctantly, "She had some weird idea that Monica might have been her mother. You see, I told you it was all a lot of rubbish."

"What made her think that? She must have had a reason."

"These scam artists make up their own reasons. I knew she was a phony when she claimed to have tracked Monica to a hospital in Philadelphia. Remember how Monica hated that town? She wouldn't even go with us to Aunt Jane's funeral. Father was furious."

An unreadable expression crossed Mary Louise's face. "I'd like to talk to the girl," she said quietly.

"That would be very foolish. Haven't you been through enough grief?"

"I'm not a delicate flower, Martin. You don't have to shield me from the hard facts of life."

"Father always did. I'm only trying to do what he would have wanted me to," Martin said righteously.

"Your father was a good husband, but he was somewhat overly protective. Since he's been gone, I've learned to think for myself. Kindly permit me to continue to do so."

"Excuse me for saying this, Mother, but you aren't always astute about people. You've been sheltered all your life so it's understandable that you take everybody at face value. You don't know how devious fortune hunters can be."

"Are we still speaking about that young woman?"

"The same applies to anyone who tries to take advantage of a credulous woman," Martin answered primly.

"You make me sound like a doddering old lady."

"I didn't say that. But you *are* in your sixties."

"That doesn't automatically affect the mind," Mary Louise said ironically.

"You have to be realistic, Mother. You're a very wealthy woman. All sorts of people are attracted by your money, and you aren't even aware of it. You've already proved how gullible you are."

"I assume you're referring to Sergei. I do wish you weren't so close minded about him."

"I'm sorry, but I can't help feeling that your friendship is quite unsuitable. Besides being five years younger than you, the man is a decorator, for heaven's sake! That's a hobby, not a job."

"Sergei is an interior designer, and a very successful one. It happens to be a profession requiring intensive training. Members of the association have to meet rigid standards."

"Then he has less excuse for trying to use you than that girl who was just here."

"I'm capable of making up my own mind about her. Ask her to come back."

"I couldn't if I wanted to. She didn't give me her name."

"It's Allison Riley, madam." The butler, who had been lurking unobtrusively in the background informed her.

"Thank you, Jordan." She ignored the baleful look her son shot at the butler. "Invite her to tea tomorrow, Martin."

"How am I supposed to find her?"

"You might try phoning all the hotels in town. There aren't that many."

"What if she's staying at one of those bed and breakfast places?"

"That will take a little longer, so I suggest you get started." Mary Louise smiled pleasantly. "Will you have the car brought around, Jordan? I'm going out."

After his mother left, Martin stalked into the library and slammed the door. He pulled up a chair to the exquisite Louis XVI desk and dialed the phone, but the call wasn't to a hotel.

Burton Rockford sat in his plush office high in a Manhattan skyscraper, having a quiet talk with his son, Gabriel. It was a pleasure that didn't occur often enough in the older man's opinion. He enjoyed his son's company.

As head of the venerable law firm of Rockford, Rockford, Collingsworth and Strand, Burton handled only the most prestigious clients. But Gabe had a full caseload, in addition to an active social life.

"Your mother would like you to come over for dinner sometime before your fortieth birthday," Burton remarked mildly.

"That gives me five years." Gabe's gray eyes sparkled with merriment as he laughed, showing even white teeth in a tanned face.

Burton regarded his tall, athletic son with the pride he always felt. Even sprawled in a chair with his long legs outstretched, Gabe had a natural grace. The lithe body coupled with a ruggedly handsome face worked like catnip on women, his father reflected. Maybe that was the reason Gabe was taking so long to settle down. His mother kept dropping not-so-subtle hints about grandchildren, but so far he hadn't shown any signs of cooperating.

"Is that why you asked me into your inner sanctum today?" Gabe grinned. "To find out how I'm spending my nights?"

"I have a pretty fair idea." Burton smiled. "I was young once, myself, although you might find that hard to believe."

"You could still give me a run for my money," Gabe said fondly.

"Thank heaven I'm too old for those games. There's a lot to be said for marriage."

"And you've said it all," Gabe teased.

"It doesn't seem to have fallen on fertile ground," Burton commented dryly. "What are you looking for in a wife?"

"Who said I was looking?" Gabe's laughing face sobered. "That isn't strictly true. I'd like to get married. The problem is, I've never met the right girl."

"You must be very hard to please. All the young ladies I've seen you with have been real beauties."

"The chemistry always seems to be missing." Gabe got up to stand by the window, jingling coins in his pocket as he looked down at the traffic far below. "Maybe I'm being unrealistic. What if I never meet the one who makes bells ring?"

"I don't think you have to worry. Sometimes when you least—" Burton broke off as his buzzer sounded. He switched on the intercom, saying irritably, "I told you I didn't want to be disturbed."

His private secretary's voice sounded slightly harried. "I'm sorry, Mr. Rockford. Mr. Van Ruyder is on the line. He's calling from Newport. I told him you were in conference, but he insists on speaking to you."

"All right, put him on. Pompous little ass," Burton said before picking up the receiver. "God save me from rich men's sons who couldn't get a job if their daddies didn't give them one."

"Careful there." Gabe chuckled. "I might have to go to work for another law firm to prove I didn't make partner through nepotism."

"You're not putting yourself in the same class with that little twit?" Burton picked up the receiver. "Hello Martin, what can I do for you?" he asked smoothly.

"You can catch the first plane to Newport and talk some sense into my mother!" Martin's voice was high and strained.

"What seems to be the problem?"

"I swear, she's getting senile! Any slick con artist can sell her a bill of goods."

"I think you're being a little hard on her."

"Am I? That man, Sergei Yousitoff is proof enough. He got Mother to introduce him to all her friends, and now he's the toast of Newport. She refuses to see how he's using her."

Burton suppressed a sigh. "I understand Mr. Yousitoff was an established designer here in New York City before he took Newport by storm. You might not care for the chap, but I've always found him to be quite pleasant."

"Do you consider it proper for him to be staying here as a guest in the house? The man is little better than a tradesman! What do you think her friends are saying?"

"I imagine some of them are quite envious. Now, if you'll excuse me, Martin, you caught me in the middle of a conference."

"I haven't told you why I called yet!" Martin exclaimed indignantly.

"I'm glad to hear you had a more compelling reason."

"Wait until you hear!" Martin was too wound up to hear the irony in the older man's voice. "Some woman came to the house today claiming to be Monica's long lost daughter."

"You're not serious?"

"Why do you think I'm in such a stew? Can you believe the nerve of some people? Before I threw her out, she practically admitted she was a fraud."

"I realize these incidents are upsetting, but unfortunately there are unscrupulous people in the world who prey on the grief of others. My advice is to put it out of your mind."

"That's exactly what I would have done, but Mother insists on listening to her story. She's making me scour the town until I find the wretched woman and invite her here for tea tomorrow afternoon."

"I don't quite understand. The girl was at your house, but Mary Louise didn't speak to her?"

"I wouldn't permit it. I was afraid something like this would happen. You know how Mother feels about not having any grandchildren. You'd think Monica and I deprived her of them on purpose! It isn't *my* fault that Laura can't have children. God knows we've tried everything." Martin's voice rose to an unpleasant whine.

"It's natural for a parent to want grandchildren." Burton slanted a glance at Gabe. "But I'm sure Mary Louise doesn't blame either you or your wife."

"That doesn't mean she's resigned to the fact. You should have seen her face when I told her this perfect stranger was claiming to be Monica's daughter. Any sensible person would know it couldn't possibly be true, but Mother wants to believe in fairy tales.''

''I think you're underestimating her. There must be more to this than you're telling me. Surely the girl offered some kind of proof to back up her claim.''

''Absolutely nothing except a theory. She claims a woman named Monica Van Ruyder had a baby at a hospital in Philadelphia on the same date as this Allison person was born. There were probably a dozen other babies born that day, but you can bet none of the other mothers were as rich as Monica. The woman is clearly an opportunist!''

Burton was lost in thought. ''Most likely,'' he said finally.

''You can't believe there's any truth to her story!'' Martin exclaimed. ''Look at the facts. Can you see our Monica with a baby? She couldn't stand the little ankle biters. That's what she always called them. And then there's another thing. Even if you were willing to suspend credulity, why on earth would she go to Philadelphia to have the kid?''

''Your father had a sister who lived there, didn't he?''

''Aunt Jane. All the more reason why Monica would have avoided the place like poison. She didn't get along with the old girl.''

''Well, if that's all this young woman has to go on, I don't believe you have anything to worry about.''

''Still, I don't like the idea of letting her come here to tea. Who knows what sob story she'll give Mother?''

''You'll be there, too, I assume?''

''You better believe it! I wouldn't leave those two alone for an instant. Fraud or no fraud, this could be serious. If Mother was convinced she had a granddaughter, she'd start thinking about a new will!''

''Mary Louise is too sensible to do anything that precipitous, but I do think it's a good idea for the entire family to be present for moral support. This is bound to be painful for your mother.''

''I tried to shield her from it,'' Martin said piously. ''I try to be the man of the house now that father is gone, but she treats me like an adolescent. That's why you have to be here to expose the woman. Tea isn't until three. You'll have plenty of time to make it by then.''

"I'm sure you can handle the situation without my help. I work mainly on corporate matters these days."

"I need action, and I want it fast! May I remind you that the Van Ruyder family is one of your biggest clients," Martin said imperiously. "I'd hate to see you blow the account—to put it succinctly."

The older man's eyes cooled, but his tone remained cordial. "We pride ourselves on having only satisfied clients. If you're no longer comfortable here, I'll be glad to supply you with a list of capable attorneys. I'll have it delivered to you by messenger."

Martin backed down hastily. "Don't fly off the handle, Burton. I'm sorry if I was out of line, but this thing has got me crazy! Please come and help me out. I don't know what that woman might have up her sleeve, or how Mother might react. There's a lot at stake here."

"That's true, but you don't need me. It shouldn't be difficult to expose the woman. All you have to do is point out the discrepancies in her story. She'll discredit herself."

"Only if Mother listens to logic instead of her emotions. The hell of it is, this girl looks like Monica. Well, no, maybe that's not entirely true, but she has Monica's coloring. You know, long black hair and big blue eyes with those thick black lashes. Except that Allison's don't look fake."

"She sounds like a real beauty," Burton commented. "Does she have Monica's figure?"

Gabe's rather bored expression changed to interest as he glanced up from the magazine he was leafing through.

"She isn't as well endowed, if you know what I mean. But I guess she has a pretty good figure," Martin said unenthusiastically. "She's also clever enough not to come on too strong, which is another thing that worries me. I voiced my suspicions in no uncertain terms, but if I tear into her to prove them, Mother's sympathies might be aroused."

"That would be a mistake, I agree." Burton glanced over at his son. "I'll tell you what I'll do, Martin. I'll send Gabriel there to help you out. He's quite good at sensing when witnesses are lying."

"What are you volunteering me for?" Gabe asked suspiciously. "I can't go anywhere right now. I have—" He stopped in midsentence when his father waved him to silence.

"That's great!" Martin exclaimed. "I'll have a room made up for him. How soon can he get here?"

"I'll ask my secretary to look up the airline schedule and call you back."

As soon as his father hung up, Gabe said, "Whatever it is, I can't do it."

"Don't be so negative. I thought you'd like a nice vacation in Newport. The weather is beautiful at this time of year, and you can indulge in all those sports you pursue so tirelessly."

"If it's such a rare treat, why didn't *you* jump at the chance?"

"The most strenuous sport I engage in these days is chasing clues in a mystery novel." Burton smiled.

"As much as I appreciate your generous offer, I'll have to pass. I really can't get away right now. I just got stuck with the Beckwith divorce case." Gabe made a wry face. "I can't say I'm looking forward to it. They're an unappetizing pair."

"Then you'll be pleased to have an excuse to get out of it. I'll have Farnsworth take over for you."

Gabe gave his father a curious look. "Why the sudden rush to accommodate that little pip-squeak, Martin? You got a bit testy with him there for a minute. What did he do, threaten to take his business elsewhere?"

"The boy doesn't have the authority to fire a gardener's helper," Burton said disgustedly. "I suppose I should be more understanding. Martin blusters to make up for his own ineptitude. But sometimes I can't help getting impatient."

"Then why are you sending me to smooth the heir apparent's path? If Mary Louise is smart, she'll leave her fortune to a home for wayward poodles."

"I want to make sure she doesn't do something equally foolish with it." Burton relayed to his son what Martin had told him. "Your job is to see that this young woman doesn't get away with it."

"She sounds like an amateur," Gabe said dismissively.

"Perhaps, but this is an emotional issue. Monica caused her parents a lot of heartache. She could be captivating one moment and a little witch the next."

"You can speak plainer than that." Gabe joked.

Burton barely heard him. His mind was focused on the past. "She was very beautiful and high spirited, so people tended to make allowances for her escapades. Everyone except her father. Peter and I got along well, but he was a strange duck in many ways—almost mid-Victorian in his thinking. He was very strict with his children, yet he treated Mary Louise like a pampered pet, shielding her from anything that might upset her.''

''She doesn't strike me as a shrinking violet.''

''She's really emerged from her cocoon since Peter isn't here to do her thinking for her anymore. The lasting damage was to the children. I can't help wondering if they might have turned out differently if their father hadn't been so rigid with them.''

''Or maybe they were just bad seeds. I can't say I really knew Monica, because she was ten years older than I, but I remember she had a reputation for being wild.''

Burton nodded. ''I helped Peter get her out of many a scrape.''

''Is there any chance this girl's story is true? *Could* Monica have had an illegitimate child somewhere down the line?''

After an almost imperceptible pause, Burton said, ''You're an attorney. You know there has to be evidence to prove any allegation.''

Gabe's gaze sharpened. ''That doesn't answer my question. Do you know something I don't know?''

The older man smiled. ''I like to think I've acquired a little more knowledge through the years.''

''In other words, you aren't going to tell me. Why not? It would make my job a lot easier.''

''I want you to go there without any preconceived ideas.''

''So you do think it's a possibility,'' Gabe said slowly.

''If you insist on having my opinion, I'd say the girl is probably a fraud. It seems too coincidental for her to come forward just a short time after Monica's death. Where has she been all these years? Undoubtedly she's prepared to answer that. It will be up to you to decide if her story is credible or not.''

''From your end of the conversation I gather that she's very attractive. Aren't you afraid that will color my judgment?'' Gabe grinned mischievously.

''You haven't let a beautiful woman talk you into anything so far,'' his father answered dryly.

''I should have quit while I was ahead.'' Gabe laughed. Then his face sobered. ''If this girl *is* on the up-and-up, I feel sorry for her. It's going to be quite a shock to find out what her mother was really like.''

''Unfortunately we don't get to pick our relatives. I'll have someone check the records at the hospital in Philadelphia. That part of her story should be easy to verify. The rest is up to you. Stop on the way out and have Eleanor make a plane reservation for you. Plan to be at the Van Ruyder's by three o'clock tomorrow.''

''It might take me several days to make up my mind about the girl,'' Gabe said with an innocent expression. ''I don't want to make any snap judgments.''

Burton smiled. ''You can take the entire week—and your tennis racket. You deserve a little vacation.''

''I might prefer one that doesn't include Martin, but I suppose nothing in life is perfect.''

Burton's eyes twinkled. ''As you young people say, you've got that right. Keep me informed.''

Allison's spirits were at low ebb when she left the Van Ruyder house. She hadn't expected to be welcomed with open arms, but Martin's aggressive hostility was hurtful. The worst part, however, was learning of Monica's death. That the woman had died such a short time ago, seemed like a very cruel twist of fate.

Would Monica's reception have been any different than her brother's, though? She'd succeeded in keeping her baby a secret from the family all these years. It would have been a shock to be confronted by a past she'd thought was safely buried.

Maybe it was wrong to have come here. What right did she have to disrupt the lives of these strangers—even if they *were* family. But were they? The question would always nag her if she didn't resolve her own doubts.

What would be the harm in trying to find out, as long as she did it discreetly and didn't bother the Van Ruyders again? They were prominent members of the community, and Newport was a little town, except for the yearly influx of summer tourists. People in a small community usually knew everybody's secrets. A little prudent questioning of the natives might uncover something. It was certainly worth a shot.

Allison knew just where to start. The proprietor of her hotel was born in Newport and had lived there all of his life. He'd told her that—and much more—while she was checking in. If anyone knew about Monica's earlier life, it would be Mr. Jensen.

John Jensen was at the front desk, reading the postcards left by the hotel's guests for him to mail. When Allison entered the lobby, he gathered them together hastily and pushed them into a drawer.

"Back so soon?" he asked.

"I just went for a little ride today," she replied. "Tomorrow I intend to get up early and do some serious sight-seeing, starting with The Breakers. I can't wait to see those fabulous old mansions."

"That's the most famous one, but if you ask me, Marble House is more elegant. It was built by another one of the Vanderbilts, back in the late eighteen hundreds. They called their summer homes cottages. Some cottage! Marble House was modeled after the Petit Trianon at Versailles and cost eleven million to build in *those* days. Can you imagine what that would mean in today's dollars?"

"It boggles the mind," Allison murmured obediently.

"You can't believe how those people lived. The family only stayed at Marble House for six or seven weeks a year. They brought a regular staff of thirty-six when they came to town, but for big parties they hired extra help."

Allison made appropriate sounds of amazement as John Jensen related tidbits of information about the illustrious former inhabitants of Newport. Under different circumstances her interest would have been genuine, but for now she was more concerned with his knowledge of present-day residents.

"You certainly know a lot about Newport's history. It must have been very glamorous in those days. Too bad none of the big old homes are occupied anymore," she remarked artlessly.

"Well now, that's not exactly true. The eight most famous houses are maintained by the Preservation Society, but some of the old line families still live on the smaller estates. They aren't quite as grand as The Elms or Rosecliff, but they're pretty posh all the same."

"Who can afford the upkeep on even a smaller version?"

"The Van Ruyders for one. Peter Van Ruyder is dead now, but his family still comes to Rosewood Manor every summer—what's left of them, that is. Peter's great grandfather was a big banking tycoon. That's where the family fortune came from originally, then his grandfather branched out into all kinds of other things. By now the money just comes rolling in. Martin won't have to do a lick of work for the rest of his life, which is just as well. The boy can't even bait a fishhook," Jensen said disdainfully.

"I seem to remember reading about a Monica Van Ruyder in the society columns," Allison remarked casually. "Would she be a relative of this family?"

"That was Martin's sister. She died about a month ago."

"How sad. She must have been quite young."

"Monica would have been in her middle forties by now, although it's hard to believe. I still think of her as a pretty little teenager, screeching around town in her red convertible and driving the boys wild. She was a proper little hellion in those days, always getting into one scrape or other. It made her father furious, but she was the one person he couldn't control."

"She sounds very...colorful."

He chuckled. "She was that, all right. But don't get me wrong. She wasn't a bad kid, just full of the devil. Monica lit up a room when she came into it, and everybody crowded around her. Naturally she was spoiled. It's my personal opinion that Peter was too strict with her—or at least he tried to be. I think that's why she ran off and got married so young the first time. Still in her teens she was."

Allison's breath caught in her throat. "Who did she marry?"

"A local boy. The name wouldn't mean anything to you."

She wondered if Monica was married here in Newport, but that wouldn't be something that would interest a tourist. Maybe there were records at City Hall. "Was she—did she have any children with him?"

"It might have settled her down a mite if she had, but three marriages didn't produce any offspring. Poor Mary Louise didn't have much luck with her children. Monica never had any, and neither did Martin."

"Is he married?"

"He's on his second marriage, but give him time," Jensen said dryly. "He's young yet."

"Younger than Monica?"

"No, a couple of years older. He's all Mary Louise has left now. We all thought when Peter died a couple of years ago she'd sell the old place. Monica didn't come home much and Mary Louise rattled around in that big house with only Martin and his wife Laura for company. But she's been coming back every summer, as regular as clockwork. Of course we're all happy to have her here. Mary Louise is a nice lady—no airs at all. She does a lot of work for charity, too."

"It must have been a great shock when her daughter died. Was it an accident?"

"Funny thing, but nobody knows exactly how Monica died."

"That seems strange. The family is so prominent."

"When you've got their kind of money, you can hush things up."

"You mean there's some kind of scandal connected with her death?"

"If there was, it never came out."

"You must have some theory about how she died," Allison persisted.

John Jensen looked at her speculatively. "You seem mighty curious. Did you happen to know Monica?"

"No, I...I guess I just got caught up in your story." She forced a smile. "It's like reading a book and wanting to know the ending. You make the Van Ruyders sound so interesting. You really should be a writer."

He looked mollified. "They're tame compared to some of the people around here. I can't mention any names this time, but there's a certain family that spends every summer here. They bring a nanny along to take care of the children. At least that's what she's supposed to do, but I happen to know—" The telephone rang cutting him off in midsentence. Allison had gotten all the information she could safely probe for, but as she turned away, Jensen held out the receiver to her. "It's for you."

She looked at him blankly. "Are you sure? Nobody knows I'm here."

"Somebody does," he answered laconically.

Allison took the receiver from Mr. Jensen and said tentatively, "Hello?"

"Miss Riley, this is Martin Van Ruyder. I've been phoning all over town looking for you." His voice managed to sound cold and petulant at the same time.

"Why?" she asked in bewilderment.

"It wasn't *my* idea, it was my mother's. She wants to meet you."

"You told her about me? She believes my story?"

"I didn't say that. I'm still convinced that you're a fraud."

"But your mother doesn't think so." Allison was filled with excitement. She wasn't wrong after all!

"My mother is grasping at straws. She wants to believe her daughter isn't really gone, that she left behind something of herself. But you and I know that isn't true. You're perpetrating a cruel hoax."

"If you really believe that, why did you call me?"

"Because she insists on seeing you. I can't prevent it, but you can. If you have any decency at all you'll go away and leave us alone. I'll tell her you realized you were mistaken."

"But I don't know that! All I want is a chance to find out for sure."

"I could make it worth your while. Just name your price—anything within reason," he added prudently. "I'll write you a check and you can pick up a nice little profit without any hassle."

"I wish I could convince you that I don't want anything from you or your family."

"Yeah, sure," he answered sardonically. "You'd better reconsider. You're passing up a good thing."

"The answer is no," she said firmly.

"All right, we'll play out your little charade, but don't think you're going to get away with it. When our lawyers get through with you, you'll wish you'd taken the money and run."

Allison felt a slight chill. "You didn't need to call a lawyer. I'm not asking for anything."

"I thought that would shake you up." Martin gave a nasty laugh. "We have the best legal advice money can buy, so be prepared. If you still insist on going through with your shakedown, come to the house at three o'clock tomorrow afternoon for tea—but don't expect any sympathy," he added mockingly.

John Jensen stared curiously at Allison as she slowly replaced the receiver. "Is everything all right?"

"I don't know," she answered in a muted voice. "I have a feeling I just opened Pandora's box."

Chapter Two

Allison paused for a long moment outside the imposing front
door of Rosewood Manor. This was the last chance to change
her mind. Should she take Martin's advice and leave the Van
Ruyders alone? Maybe he was right. If she was mistaken about
Monica, it would cause his mother further pain for no good reason.

Allison's indecision changed to determination. She'd lived too
long as a non-person, somebody without parents or a past. The
Van Ruyders might not want to accept her—in fact, from what
she'd seen of Martin, she wasn't too thrilled with *them*—but she
had to know the truth.

The butler opened the door with the same impassive counte-
nance he'd worn the day before. It was impossible to tell if he
shared his employer's opinion of her. Not that it mattered, Allison told herself. She didn't expect to find any friends here.

Jordon preceded her down a long hall, past a huge drawing
room and a paneled den to a charming sitting room filled with
bowls and vases of flowers. Tall French windows looked out on
a manicured lawn that stretched out beyond a flagstone terrace.

Allison had only a fleeting impression of luxury. Her attention immediately focused on the four people in the room, who were regarding her with the same keen interest. She braced herself for hostility, needlessly as it turned out.

The older woman rose from a down-filled, floral patterned couch and smiled pleasantly. "I'm so glad you could join us for tea, Miss Riley. I'm Mary Louise Van Ruyder."

"It was very kind of you to invite me," Allison murmured.

"You've met my son, Martin. This is his wife, Laura."

Allison exchanged polite greetings with a very thin, very chic blond woman wearing a deceptively simple green cotton dress. Everything about her spelled money, from her perfect hairstyle and long polished nails to her aloof manner. Or maybe that was an echo of her husband's disapproval, although she hid it better than he did. Martin was having trouble masking his dislike. He had merely nodded curtly.

She didn't have time to dwell on it because Mary Louise was introducing her to the fourth occupant of the room, the most dazzling specimen of manhood Allison had ever seen. His features were rugged rather than conventionally handsome, but they made his face more interesting. Perfection was reserved for his tall, athletic physique, which couldn't have been improved upon. That should have been enough good fortune for any man, but this one was more than just a centerfold. Intelligence shone out of his penetrating gray eyes.

"And this is Gabriel Rockford, a dear friend of the family," Mary Louise concluded.

"He's our attorney," Martin said tersely.

Gabe stood and took Allison's hand, smiling charmingly. "I hope you won't hold that against me. Everybody has to do something."

She wasn't fooled by his easy manner or the male admiration in his eyes. Gabe had been brought in to prove she was a fraud. He was more polished about it than Martin, but he was the enemy, nonetheless. She withdrew her hand, realizing he could tell by her icy fingers how nervous she was. In his eyes that probably made her automatically guilty.

"Okay, we're all here," Martin said. "Let's get down to business."

"Where are your manners?" his mother asked. "Miss Riley was invited to tea." She looked inquiringly at Allison over the exquisite antique tea service on the table in front of her. "Do you take lemon or cream?"

"Neither, thank you," Allison replied.

A uniformed maid brought the delicate teacup and saucer after Mary Louise had poured. She placed it along with a monogrammed linen napkin on a table next to Allison, then passed a tray of small tea sandwiches.

"Is this your first visit to Newport?" Mary Louise asked.

"Yes, I've always wanted to visit Cape Cod, but somehow I never got around to it."

"Aren't we lucky that you finally found time," Martin commented sarcastically.

"Where is your home?" Gabe cut in smoothly.

"I live in New York City," Allison answered.

"That gives us all something in common," Mary Louise said pleasantly. "Gabriel's office is there, and our family home is on Park Avenue."

"I'm sure she's aware of *that*," Martin remarked.

His mother continued as though she hadn't heard him. "I do love New York, although not necessarily in the summer. When it gets hot and humid in the city I escape to Cape Cod."

"You're very fortunate. It was stifling when I left." Allison wondered when they were going to get past polite generalities.

Laura joined the conversation for the first time. "Do you have a job in the city, Miss Riley?"

"Yes, I'm a buyer in the better sportswear department at Maison Blanc." It was an upscale women's store.

"Really! I buy quite a few things there. Mrs. Frasier takes care of me. Perhaps you know her?"

"Oh, yes. She's been with us for many years. Her customers won't let anyone else wait on them."

"That's because she isn't pushy. So many saleswomen tell you everything looks good on you because they're only interested in making a sale. Mrs. Frasier never does that." Laura had become almost animated.

"Oh, for—!" Martin swore pungently under his breath. "How much longer are we going to keep up this charade?" He turned on Gabe. "Why aren't you asking her some questions? That's what you're here for!"

Mary Louise's pleasant expression didn't waver as she gazed

at her son. "Much as we're enjoying your company, Martin dear, your presence here isn't required. Why don't you and Laura drive over to the tennis club? I'm sure Gabriel and Miss Riley will excuse you."

Martin wilted under his mother's calm scrutiny. "No, I'll stay," he muttered.

"Then perhaps you'll offer our guest some cake." She held out an antique china serving platter filled with several kinds of cookies, slices of poppyseed cake and assorted petit fours. He took the plate reluctantly as Mary Louise said to the maid, "We can manage by ourselves now, Florence."

When Allison refused the pastries, Gabe said, "You really should try those little chocolate things. They're fantastic."

"And a million calories in every bite," Laura remarked.

"None of you ladies have to worry about your figures," he answered gallantly, but his gray eyes were on Allison.

She steeled herself against the rush of pleasure his attention gave her. Gabe had the faculty of making a woman feel special, as if he couldn't wait to be alone with her. What female wouldn't be flattered? But she mustn't be fooled by his potent male appeal. Behind that beguiling manner was a keen legal mind that had already judged her and found her guilty.

When the maid had left them alone, Mary Louise said to Allison, "Martin tells me that you came to Newport to see my daughter, Monica."

"Yes, but I didn't know she was...that she had passed away. I hope my unexpected visit didn't cause you more pain. That wasn't my intention," Allison said earnestly.

"I'm sure that's true. You seem like a very nice young woman. Had you ever met my daughter?"

"No, I was hoping to."

"Because you think she was your mother?"

Allison took a deep breath. "I think it's a possibility, yes."

"Can you give us some reason why you believe that?" Unlike Martin, Mary Louise's tone wasn't challenging. She sounded as if she honestly wanted to know. "To my knowledge, Monica never had any children."

"This is very difficult. The last thing I want to do is hurt you." Allison was tempted to give it up. How could she disillusion this poor woman who had just lost her daughter? As unlikely as it seemed, Mary Louise didn't seem to know Monica had been pregnant and borne a child.

"I loved my daughter very much, but we didn't have as close a relationship as I would have liked. Monica didn't allow anyone into her confidence completely. If you have information on the part of her life I didn't share, I would like very much to hear it." When Allison continued to hesitate, Mary Louise said, "You've made a serious assertion. You can't simply leave it at that. Unless of course, you're having second thoughts about the validity of your claim."

"I can tell what you're thinking, but you're wrong. I didn't come here to try to get money from you, or intrude on your lives in any way. I'm sorry if this comes as a shock, but your daughter had a baby when she was eighteen. I just want to find out if I was that child."

"I assume you have some kind of proof that Monica was the person involved?" Gabe asked. "Couldn't you have made an honest mistake?" He was giving her a chance to recant gracefully.

"I saw the records at Our Lady of Mercy Hospital in Philadelphia. Monica Van Ruyder had a baby girl on May 27, the year I was born. She was eighteen at the time."

"Either you're lying, or it was somebody else by the same name," Martin said.

"Her address was listed as Park Avenue, New York," Allison answered simply.

"What was the father's name?" Gabe asked.

"It was left blank."

"I think you'd better start at the beginning," Mary Louise said. "What led you to Philadelphia in the first place?"

"I recently decided to look for my parents," Allison began. "I'm an orphan and I never knew who they were."

"You didn't feel the need to know before now?" Gabe asked.

"I was curious, naturally. It's something an orphan always wonders about."

"But you never did anything about it until recently. Why is that?"

"Good question," Martin said with satisfaction.

"My reasons are personal," Allison said firmly. "What matters is that I did start to search for them. I'd been told I was born in Philadelphia. That's all the information I had."

"The orphanage told you that, but not your mother's name?" Gabe asked.

"They didn't have any records on me. I was told by my mother—or I should say, the woman I thought was my mother."

"Wait a minute!" Martin exclaimed. "What kind of nonsense is this? You decided you didn't like the mother you had, so you chose Monica instead?"

"Let me explain. For the first nine years of my life I lived with a family named Riley. I always thought they were my parents and their five younger children were my brothers and sisters. We were a typical working-class family, although it was always a struggle to make ends meet. Tim Riley was a construction worker—a laborer actually—and Nora, his wife had been a cook at a big duplex on Fifth Avenue. But after the children started to come along, she had to quit."

"Do we have to sit through this soap opera?" Martin sneered. "What does any of this have to do with Monica?"

"Stop interrupting, Martin," Mary Louise ordered impatiently. "Go on, Miss Riley."

"I suppose it does sound like a bad movie," Allison said wryly. "I'll try to speed it up."

"No, I want to hear everything," Mary Louise said.

"There isn't much more to tell. The construction industry hit a slump and Tim was out of work for a long time. Money got really tight with so many mouths to feed and, well..." Allison stared down at her tightly clasped hands as the old hurt surfaced. "That's when they told me I wasn't really their child and they couldn't keep me any longer."

"They raised you from infancy and then just dumped you in an orphanage when the going got rough?" Gabe asked incredulously.

"Our situation was really grim. I didn't realize it at the time, but I do now. It took me a while to get over feeling abandoned although as I got older I understood that their own children had to come first. I wasn't their flesh and blood."

"It must have been quite a shock to find out you were adopted," Mary Louise said gently.

"Yes, but children are resilient. And the orphanage wasn't like something out of *Oliver Twist*. After I stopped feeling sorry for myself I made a lot of friends, and the people who ran the place were very decent.''

"Did your family—the Rileys, that is—come to visit you?'' Mary Louise asked.

"It was discouraged during the first couple of months. After that they phoned a few times, but we were never really close again.''

"They probably felt guilty about what they'd done,'' Gabe said. "If they didn't, they should have!''

"Don't judge them too harshly. None of us knows what we might do in a similar situation. If Monica was my mother, she chose to give me up, too.'' Allison tried to diffuse the emotional atmosphere. "I guess I'm not much of a prize.'' Her laughter had a catch in it.

After assessing his mother's misty eyes and Gabe's touched expression, Martin whispered rapidly to his wife.

Laura obediently followed his instructions. "I'm sure we're very sorry for your unhappy life,'' she began.

"I appreciate your sympathy, but it's misplaced,'' Allison cut in. "I have a great life. I went to night school and got a college degree, which led to an excellent job. My standard of living isn't anything like yours, but I have a nice apartment and lots of friends. I'm really a very happy person.''

"Then why do you want to disrupt other people's lives?'' Martin burst out.

"I don't. Whether I'm right or wrong about your sister, I won't ever bother you again after I leave here.''

"That's very noble, but you know Mother wouldn't permit that.''

"We're being a trifle premature,'' Gabe said. "Let's go back a little. Do you have a copy of Monica's hospital record, including the reason for her stay there?'' he asked Allison.

"No, but you can ask to see it,'' she answered. "They have everything on microfilm.''

"That kind of information is usually confidential. You just asked for it and they gave it to you?''

"Not exactly. I telephoned first, but they wouldn't tell me anything, so I became a hospital volunteer.''

Gabe stared at her. "But you live in New York.''

"Philadelphia is only a short train ride away. I did volunteer work on the weekends. They're shorthanded on Saturdays and Sundays, so they were glad to get me."

Martin frowned at her disapprovingly. "You're admitting you lied to the hospital authorities so you could break into their secret files. Besides being a criminal act, it shows what kind of a person you are. If you lied to the hospital, why should we believe you're telling the truth now?"

"I didn't lie to anybody," Allison protested. "I was a very competent worker. I did all sorts of things the nurses didn't have time for. And I didn't break into any files. I became friendly with a woman in the office. I told her my story and she looked up the information for me."

"That doesn't make it any better. It just shows how you use people for your own devious purposes."

"I don't think that's the issue right now." Mary Louise frowned. She turned to Allison. "I assume the Rileys told you the date of your birth, but there must have been more than one baby born on that date. Why are you so sure you were Monica's?"

"By the process of elimination. Nora Riley told me my mother was an unmarried teenager. That's why she had to give me up. There were three women who had baby girls that day, but one was married, and the other was twenty-two."

"One could have been lying about being married, for appearance sake, and the other might have passed for a teenager," Gabe said pointedly. "Your foster mother could have made an honest mistake."

"I realize that, so I looked for further indications. Another reason that seemed to point to Monica, was her address. I told you Nora worked for a very social family on Fifth Avenue—the Charlton Langerfelds. Did you know them?" she asked Mary Louise.

"I might have heard the name, but even if I knew them, why would that be significant?"

Allison hesitated. "Giving up a baby for adoption must be very traumatic for everyone involved, even if keeping the infant isn't an acceptable alternative. It would be only natural to want to keep track of the child, to see how it turned out."

"I see," Mary Louise said thoughtfully. "And what better way than placing the baby with somebody you knew—not personally, but someone you could keep in touch with, in a casual way, like an acquaintance's household help. Yes, I can understand your reasoning.''

"Well, *I* can't," Martin stated. "If Monica *had* given birth to a baby, she wouldn't have given it to somebody's cook!"

"What if no debutantes were available?" Gabe asked sardonically.

Allison ignored them and appealed to Mary Louise. "Now you can see why I said I wasn't sure. Can you think of anything that might tip the balance one way or the other? Do I look like your daughter? Can you see anything of her in me?"

"You're asking my mother to prove your case for you?" Martin asked incredulously.

"Or to disprove it," Allison answered despairingly.

"Judge for yourself." Mary Louise picked up a photograph in a silver frame and handed it to her.

Allison's breath caught in her throat. "Is this my—your daughter?"

The picture showed a laughing woman with dark hair and blue eyes. She was wearing a brief white bathing suit and had her arm around the waist of a very handsome man.

"I prefer this snapshot to the more formal studio portraits," Mary Louise said. "It captures her vitality and zest for living."

Allison studied the picture avidly. The woman's coloring was similar to hers, but it was difficult to tell from the candid snap if they actually looked alike. Monica's nose was short and straight like her own, her eyes were wide and thickly lashed. But something about her expression indicated a difference between them, an attitude perhaps. There was a challenging quality in the bold way she faced the camera with her head thrown back, almost as if she were inviting criticism. Was there also something a little dissatisfied in her expression? The photographer must have caught her at a bad angle. By all accounts, Monica had had everything.

"Is this a recent photo?" Allison asked.

"It was taken last summer."

"Is that her husband with her?"

"No, she was divorced. He couldn't be your father, in case

you're wondering," Mary Louise said quietly. "She'd only known him a few weeks."

"That didn't occur to me. I was just...I don't know, maybe trying to gather all the information I could about her. So I could tell if we were anything alike."

"It might be interesting to find out." Mary Louise looked at her reflectively. "I have an idea. Newport is so dreadfully crowded at this time of year. I don't know what your accommodations are like, but I'm sure you'd be more comfortable here. Why don't you stay with us for a few days?"

"Have you lost your mind, Mother?" Martin said thunderously. "We already know the woman is a con artist. This might be what she's been angling for all along. If you let her in this house she could steal us blind!"

"Martin is only thinking of you," Laura said nervously, with a somewhat apologetic glance at Allison. "What you're considering is rather rash."

"It pains me to have to remind both of you that this is my home," Mary Louise replied evenly. "If either of you feels it would be too crowded to have another houseguest in residence, my feelings won't be hurt if you make other arrangements for yourselves."

"I don't believe this! Gabe!" Martin appealed to his lawyer.

"Your mother does have a point. She can invite anyone she likes. Besides, if I cross her, she might send me packing, too." Gabe grinned.

"A lot of good *you* are," Martin muttered.

"I'm sure we'll all have a lovely time getting to know one another." Mary Louise's face was imperturbable. "I hope I'm not being premature, Miss Riley. You will join us, won't you?"

Allison was slightly dazed at this turn of events. So many emotions coursed through her that it would take time to sort them all out. But that could come later. Right now she seized the opportunity presented to her.

"I'd be delighted to accept your kind invitation. And please call me Allison."

"That would be a lot more friendly. And do call me Mary Louise. I'll tell Florence to prepare a room for you."

After his mother had left, Martin confronted Allison furiously. "I suppose you're pretty proud of yourself, worming your way in here. But it won't do you any good. You'll never get a red cent out of Mother if I can prevent it.''

Allison knew it was useless to argue with him. "I'm sure you'll be able to. I don't expect to leave here any richer than when I came. Now if you'll excuse me, I'm going back to the hotel for my things.''

Gabe followed her outside. "I'm sorry about Martin's rudeness.''

"You aren't responsible for his behavior," she answered curtly. "Anyway, you probably agree with him. Your manners are merely better.''

"That's no compliment." He smiled. "Anybody could fit that description.''

"I don't know why it's so difficult to convince him that I'm not a fortune hunter. His mother is willing to keep an open mind. That's all I ask.''

"Don't be fooled by Mary Louise. Under that old world charm is a very shrewd lady.''

"Is that a warning?" Allison thrust her chin out pugnaciously. "Perhaps you'd better go inside and inventory the silver before I get back.''

"I'm not your enemy," Gabe said gently.

"Am I supposed to consider you a friend? Martin brought you here to discredit me. He was quite open about it.''

"That might have been *his* purpose. Mine is to discover the truth. You, yourself, admit you have doubts. There's a lot at stake here, and not only monetarily. I would hate to see Mary Louise hurt needlessly.''

Allison's animosity drained away. "I would, too. She's a really nice person. I wonder how she ever produced a son like Martin.''

"Mary Louise didn't have much say in her childrens' upbringing. Her husband was a very strong man with rigid convictions. That could be why both kids grew up with problems.''

"Monica, too?''

Gabe shrugged. "She went through three husbands. That indicates a certain restlessness, if nothing else.''

"It's hard to believe. She and her brother had every advantage. What was Monica looking for?''

"The same thing everyone else is, I presume. True love.''

"If such a thing exists."

Gabe's eyes wandered over her delicate face, lingering on her soft mouth. "You're very young to be so cynical."

Allison was suddenly aware of him as a man, rather than an adversary. A man to beware of, she reminded herself. The glow in his eyes was part of the act he was putting on to win her confidence so he could trip her up.

"Girls learn at an early age that love means something entirely different to women than it does to men," she said tersely.

"Obviously you've met the wrong men."

"Possibly, but I'm not interested in finding out. So if you're going to suggest furthering my education, you can save your energy. It won't get you anywhere."

"You should never challenge a man unless you're prepared for the consequences," he said softly.

"It wasn't a challenge, merely a statement of fact."

"You never expect to fall in love again?"

"I didn't say I ever was in love."

"You didn't have to. What happened, Allison, did he leave you for another woman? Although I can't conceive of it."

"How many women have you fed that line to?" she asked derisively.

"I don't believe in playing games," he answered quietly. "I've always been truthful in my relationships."

"That's hard to believe. Men make extravagant promises to get what they want—and foolish women believe them. It's standard operating procedure."

Gabe's sober expression changed to amusement. "If you're referring to sex, I assure you I've never made any promises to entice a woman into bed."

He wouldn't have to. That hard body must have given great pleasure to a lot of women. Allison's cheeks warmed as she had a sudden, vivid picture of what it would be like to lie naked in his arms.

"I'm sure you lead a very active sex life, but I'd prefer not to discuss it," she said primly.

"We'll have to do something about those inhibitions of yours," he teased. "Sex is a normal, healthy part of life."

"But not a subject for discussion."

His eyes sparkled with laughter. "I didn't intend to supply details."

"Will you tell me how we got on the subject of sex?" she demanded. "We hardly know each other."

"I hope to become a lot better acquainted," he murmured.

"You've just proved my point about men being different from women," she said angrily. "You wouldn't hesitate to make love to me for the sake of your clients. It's all part of the job."

"Have you ever looked in a mirror?"

"Please don't add insult to injury by telling me how beautiful I am! I'm not as gullible as your girlfriends."

Gabe gazed at her with an unreadable expression. "I guess I've met my match. Since you've figured out my game plan, I'm no danger to you."

"Exactly." Allison hoped she sounded more confident than she felt.

"Does this mean there won't be any romantic kisses in the moonlight?"

"You've got *that* right."

"And I suppose skinny-dipping in the pool at three in the morning is out. Too bad." A little smile curved his firm mouth as his eyes swept over her curved body. "You'd be enchanting by starlight."

Her pulse rate speeded up—as he knew it would. Gabe *wanted* her to picture their nude bodies linked together while the cool water gently rocked them against each other. Their lips would meet and then part. Until he gathered her close for the ultimate embrace.

"I have to get my things from the hotel," she said abruptly, getting into her car and slamming the door.

Gabe's face was enigmatic as he watched the car disappear down the driveway.

"Well, what did you think of her?" Mary Louise asked when Gabe returned to the house.

"She's very lovely."

"That much is evident. You know what I'm asking. Do you agree with Martin that she's an opportunist?"

"You evidently don't think so, or you wouldn't have invited her to be a guest."

"Lawyers!" Mary Louise exclaimed. "They will never give you a straightforward answer."

"That's because there isn't one. I can't make a judgment without knowing her better, any more than you can."

"It's the reason I invited her here." Mary Louise frowned thoughtfully. "She does bear a resemblance to Monica—that beautiful glossy black hair and porcelain skin. She has Monica's deep blue eyes, too."

"There must be thousands of girls with the same coloring. All it takes is an Irish ancestor somewhere in the family tree."

"Then you don't think it's significant?"

"I didn't say that. I was only playing devil's advocate. There are other things that are more significant. I don't see how Monica could have had a baby without your knowledge."

Mary Louise's eyes were sad. "It displays a lack of trust on her part. That's difficult to live with."

Gabe's gaze sharpened. "Are you saying it's possible?"

"How can I be certain? Monica went away to school, she went to summer camp. My generation turned their children over to other people to raise, because we were told it was the thing to do. It was called providing them with every advantage."

"Then Allison's story could be true," he mused.

"That's what I want you to help me find out. Do you know what it would mean to me to have a grandchild?" Mary Louise's face was radiant. "This time I wouldn't let anyone come between us. We'd have the kind of relationship I've always wanted."

"You mustn't substitute wishful thinking for common sense," Gabe said gently. "You're too intelligent for that."

Mary Louise sighed. "You agree with Martin. You think I'm an addled old woman."

"On the contrary. I think what you did was remarkably astute. We should have an interesting few days, if nothing else." After a look at her downcast face Gabe added, "And who knows? They may change our entire lives."

A man appeared in the doorway of the sitting room. Sergei Yousitoff was around sixty, tall and distinguished looking, with a full head of dark hair sprinkled with gray. He was wearing casual clothes, but he would have looked equally at home in white tie and tails. He had the self-confidence and sophistication of an ambassador, or perhaps a captain of industry.

"Am I interrupting anything?" he asked.

"No, do come in," Mary Louise said. "How was your meeting with Nancy Buffington?"

"Long," Sergei answered tersely. "I feel the urgent need for a drink."

"I'll make you one." Gabe walked over to an inlaid rosewood cabinet where a silver tray held Baccarat decanters filled with a variety of spirits.

"Make it a double," Sergei called. "I know Nancy is a friend of yours, Mary Louise, but I can't take her job, even for you. Besides having more money than taste, she's the kind of idle, empty-headed woman I can't abide."

"I always had a feeling you were prejudiced against the rich," Mary Louise teased.

"Not at all. I find money very useful when it isn't excessive. If you had a few less millions I'd ask you to marry me."

"Doesn't that prove you're prejudiced?"

"No, it simply means I have an aversion to being considered a fortune hunter."

Her smile faltered. "I must apologize for my son's behavior last night. I really don't know why you put up with it."

He touched her hair lightly, gazing into her eyes. "Don't you?"

Gabe strolled over and handed Sergei a glass. "Would you like to offer me a dollar to go to the movies?" he asked with a grin.

"Gladly. How much more would it cost for you to take Martin with you?"

"Now you're getting up into big money." Gabe laughed, then slanted a chagrined glance at Mary Louise. "Martin is just a little overly protective. I'm sure it's nothing personal."

"You're probably right," Sergei answered politely.

"Well, at least you won't be the primary target for the next few days," Mary Louise said brightly. "We have a new houseguest. I'll be interested in your opinion of her."

"Not another potential client?" Sergei asked warily.

"I wish I could afford to turn away clients like you do," Gabe joked. "You're pretty exclusive."

"I've reached the stage of life where I can afford to be. I have more than enough money, a successful career and good friends."

"You're a lucky man."

"It would seem that way, wouldn't it?" Sergei glanced at Mary Louise, suppressing a sigh.

"Allison should be back soon," she said. "I want you to meet her."

"Who is Allison? Tell me about her."

As Mary Louise started to, Florence came into the room. "You have a telephone call, Mr. Rockford," she said.

"Thanks, Florence. I'll take it in the library."

"What do you have to report?" Burton Rockford asked his son.

"You haven't given me much time," Gabe protested. "I just met the girl a couple of hours ago."

"I know what a fast worker you are," his father answered dryly.

"The circumstances are a little different in this case."

"Granted. So, what did you think of her?"

"I honestly don't know what to tell you. She's either very clever, or incredibly naive. She admitted to having doubts about Monica being her mother."

"That sounds like she has very little proof, so she's playing on the family's sympathy instead."

"Not successfully with Martin. He never passes up an opportunity to bully her, which of course enlists Mary Louise's sympathy. How can he be so stupid?"

"Through long practice. Other than being sympathetic, how does Mary Louise feel about the girl? Does she believe her story?"

"She'd like to. She invited Allison to stay here."

Burton gave a startled exclamation. "Didn't you try to dissuade her?"

"Martin did, needless to say. Actually I think it's a good idea. If Allison is a phony, she's apt to reveal the fact in some way. Like referring to incidents in Monica's past that she'd have no reason to know about unless she'd been reading up on her. Monica's exploits were widely covered in the society columns. Like the time she fed caviar canapés to the chimps in the Central Park Zoo.''

''As a matter of fact, she wasn't responsible for that. It was her style, but she was in Jamaica at the time,'' Burton said.

''That's the point I'm making. It's just the kind of colorful story that could trip Allison up.''

''Then you're inclined to believe she's a fraud.''

''What really nudges me in that direction is the improbability of Monica being able to have a baby without her parents' knowledge. How could they not know she was pregnant? It's not something that's easy to hide. Mary Louise said Monica was away from home a lot, but *somebody* must have known.''

''Perhaps they didn't see fit to tell Mary Louise,'' Burton remarked.

''Monica went to exclusive schools and camps. They'd be out of business if they helped her conceal a serious thing like that.''

''Only if the secret got out.''

''So *you* think Allison is on the up-and-up?''

''Not necessarily. I just want you to consider all of the possibilities.''

''It's a heavy responsibility,'' Gabe answered soberly. ''Mary Louise is a levelheaded lady, but she desperately wants to believe Allison's story.''

''She's tougher than she looks. If it's not true, she'll survive.''

''That's remarkably insensitive of you!'' Gabe exclaimed. ''Whatever happened to compassion and fair play? In spite of my loyalties being with Mary Louise, I don't relish the prospect of trying to trap Allison. You evidently wouldn't have any problem with that.''

Burton chuckled. ''At my age I'm fairly immune to big blue eyes. I gather this Allison is your type, although I always thought you were partial to blondes.''

''She makes them pale by comparison.''

''Perhaps I should have handled the situation myself. Remember that you're representing a client. Just tell yourself the girl is a hostile witness and treat her accordingly.''

''If I ever faced a witness like Allison I'd lose the case,'' Gabe said wryly. ''When I look into those big blue eyes you're immune to, I see Snow White, not the Wicked Witch.''

''I've known some very cold-blooded criminals who were also

beautiful women. Although I'm not saying it's necessarily so in this case, Mary Louise doesn't deserve to be exploited,'' Burton said quietly.

''I'm just afraid her hopes are already too high. The trouble is, she's a woman with a lot of love to give, and nobody worthwhile to give it to.'' Gabe paused for a moment. ''How do you feel about Sergei Yousitoff? He's another houseguest.''

''I've always found him to be a very nice fellow.''

''I think he's in love with Mary Louise. He was joking about marrying her, but I got the impression that he was serious.''

''If she's smart, she'll snap him up. Sergei is intelligent, well educated and amusing. He even moves in the same circles that she does, through his business connections. They could have a good life together.''

''Maybe he's concerned that people would think he married her for her money.''

''That's nonsense. Sergei is independently wealthy. He doesn't have the kind of money Mary Louise does, but few people do.''

''Another obstacle is Martin. He guards the family fortune as zealously as if he made it himself.''

''There's plenty to go around. Your job is to see that it goes to people who deserve it.''

''Using that yardstick, Allison has already worked harder for it than Martin ever did,'' Gabe said derisively.

''I'm becoming concerned, Gabriel. Are you sure you can remain impartial?''

''Not to worry. What does Allison have besides a beautiful face, an enticing body and a way of looking at a man that makes him want to carry her off to bed.'' Gabe laughed at the sudden silence on the line. ''I'm only pulling your leg, Dad. She's all of that and more, but I don't approve of people who try to profit from the tragedy of others. If that's what Allison is aiming to do, I won't hesitate to nail her.''

''I certainly hope so.''

''Relax, I won't let you down.''

Long after he'd hung up the phone, Burton Rockford continued to look grave.

Chapter Three

Allison was excited by the prospect of staying at Rosewood Manor. Who wouldn't be? It was the most elegant, still privately owned and occupied mansion in Newport.

She entered a different world when she returned with her luggage and was shown to a luxurious guest room on the second floor. It was spacious and airy, with French doors leading to a balcony large enough for a round glass table and a couple of white wrought-iron chairs.

The balcony overlooked an oval swimming pool that sparkled like an aquamarine set in green velvet. The pool area and tennis court took up only a fraction of the spacious grounds. Extensive, carefully tended lawns bordered flower beds and surrounded a white gazebo whose latticed walls were covered with climbing roses.

Allison was gazing at everything with delight when there was a light tap at the door. The maid who'd shown her to her room had come to tell her the family was having cocktails in the library. Allison ran a comb through her hair and freshened her lipstick before going downstairs.

She was dismayed to find her hostess and Laura had changed

for dinner. Mary Louise wore a jade green silk dress with a magnificent diamond and emerald pin on the shoulder, and Laura was wearing a red faille cocktail suit. The men had on suits and ties. Allison felt terribly out of place in the same white linen skirt and navy-and-white striped blouse she'd worn all day.

With supreme tact, Mary Louise didn't appear to notice. "Were you provided with everything you need?"

"Yes, my room is lovely, thank you," Allison answered.

"We want you to be comfortable here. I'd like you to meet my good friend, Sergei Yousitoff."

If he was curious about her, Sergei concealed it well. He was as charming as he would have been to any other guest.

After they'd exchanged pleasantries, Allison felt some apology was due her hostess. "I didn't know you dressed for dinner. I'm sorry."

"It's quite all right, my dear," Mary Louise said graciously. "We're fairly casual usually, but tonight Sergei and I have to go to a charity bazaar. It's something I simply couldn't get out of."

"I wouldn't want you to," Allison said. "Please don't change any of your plans for me. I don't expect to be entertained."

"You're very understanding. Unfortunately Martin and Laura have a previous engagement, too, but Gabriel will dine with you."

Allison's nerves knotted at the prospect of an intimate dinner for two. "I'm sure you have other plans," she told him. "I'll be quite all right on my own."

"I planned to spend the evening with you." He gave her a melting smile. "I didn't expect to be lucky enough to have you all to myself."

"That's settled then," Mary Louise said. "Fix Allison a drink, Sergei."

"I envy you and Gabe," he told Allison as he mixed her drink. "I wish we could stay home and have a quiet dinner and some interesting conversation, but Mary Louise has this compulsion to do good deeds."

"Stop complaining, you sound like a husband," Mary Louise said lightly.

"He doesn't sound anything at all like *Father*." Martin glowered at the older man.

"That's true. Your father didn't argue, he simply refused to go anyplace," she said.

"How can you say that?" Martin protested. "You and Father had a very active social life. He had a world of friends, all very influential people."

"Yes, dear." Mary Louise looked at her watch. "Hadn't you and Laura better be running along? We must go, too. I've told the staff to serve your dinner in the morning room," she told Gabe. "It's so much cozier. You don't want to be shouting to each other down that long table in the dining room."

Allison felt self-conscious with Gabe after everyone had gone. She didn't normally have trouble talking to people, but this man left her tongue-tied. They had nothing in common. His custom-tailored suit, the very costly gold watch on his wrist, his expensively styled hair—these were only superficial things, but they put him in a world that was foreign to her.

"Mary Louise is a very thoughtful hostess," Gabe remarked. "Besides providing me with a lovely dinner companion, she chose congenial surroundings as well."

"There are certainly a lot of rooms in this house," Allison commented brightly. "I don't even know what a morning room is."

"If you're ready for dinner I'll show you."

He led the way to an informal room furnished with wicker furniture and brightly printed cushions. The floor was tiled, and two walls were glass from floor to ceiling. They looked out on floodlit gardens that were echoed inside by pots and tubs of blooming plants.

Despite the informal atmosphere, a glass-topped hexagonal table was set with yellow-and-white organdy place mats, heavy sterling flatware and crystal wineglasses. In a centerpiece of fragrant yellow roses was a thick round candle.

"What a perfectly charming room," Allison exclaimed. "This house is unbelievable."

Gabe nodded. "Not many of us can afford to live like this anymore."

A uniformed maid entered carrying a tray with two delicate soup bowls set on matching saucers. The bowls contained cold avocado soup topped with a dollop of sour cream and a sprig of watercress.

When the woman had served them and left the room, Allison said, "I never saw her before. How many servants are there?"

"I don't know. It takes a large staff to run a place this size. The crew of gardeners and maintenance workers is probably as extensive as the household help."

Allison gazed out at the flower beds drenched in moonlight. "It must be like living in a fairyland. All you have to do is ask and your wish is granted."

"Not every wish. It's a trite saying, but money can't buy love or happiness."

"The Van Ruyders look happy to me."

"Appearances can be deceiving."

"That was insensitive of me," Allison said penitently. "Monica's death must have been devastating to her mother. And to Martin, too. It explains why he's so hostile toward me."

"Rudeness is never excusable."

"It's understandable, though, if he thought I was making baseless accusations his sister couldn't deny. I shouldn't have said anything after he told me she passed away. But at first I thought he was just trying to keep me from seeing her, and then I was so shocked that I didn't realize how my claim would affect the family."

Gabe shrugged. "Martin has always been his own worst enemy."

"That doesn't make me feel any better. I still wish I hadn't come."

He looked at her enigmatically. "You can always call it off. You said you have doubts about your relationship to Monica."

"It's too late to back away now. I've raised questions in her mother's mind as well. For all our sakes, I have to find out the truth."

"I suppose you're right. No matter who gets hurt."

"You must think I'm a monster! I barely know Mary Louise, but I can tell she's a kind, generous person. I'd never willingly add to her misery."

"I wasn't referring to Mary Louise. I was thinking of you," Gabe said quietly. "You've had a lot of disappointment in your life. I wouldn't like to see you go through any more."

His husky voice warmed Allison. Very few people had ever been concerned about her—certainly no one like Gabe. Was he being sincere? Or was it just a tactic to get rid of her? Bruce had left a legacy of distrust along with disillusion.

"Why should you care what happens to me?" she asked hesitantly. "It would be easier for you if I retracted the whole story and left quietly. You could go back to your law office and your debutante girlfriends."

"I'm too old to date debutantes." He smiled. "Besides, I've never cared for women whose main concern was their appearance and where the next party will be."

"You're only interested in women who can hold an intelligent conversation?"

He laughed. "I didn't say that. After all, I'm a healthy adult male. I do appreciate intelligence, but if the woman is as beautiful as you, I might become distracted."

"I don't think so." Allison gave him a level look. "I think you know exactly what you're doing."

"I can understand why you don't trust me." He reached over and captured her hand. "Poor little Allison. You haven't had much reason to trust people."

Gabe's warm hand sent a tingle up her arm. She tried not to let herself imagine what it would be like if circumstances were different and he was really interested in her. That was impossible, of course. Even if Gabe wasn't predisposed against her, he knew women a lot more glamorous than she.

Allison withdrew her hand and sat back. "You don't have to feel sorry for me. I've learned to take care of myself. I don't need anyone."

"No one is completely self sufficient. We all need somebody."

"That's what pets are for," she answered lightly.

"Cuddling with a cocker spaniel doesn't do it."

"They have redeeming features. Dogs are loyal and faithful. They don't question your motives, and they're always there when you need them."

"All very noble qualities, but how about someone to hold you in his arms and kiss away the problems of the day?"

"What good is that? It's only a temporary solution at best."

"You've been even more deprived than I realized," he said in a deep velvet voice. "Obviously you've never known a real man. Someone whose only priority was to make love to you and bring you more pleasure than you've ever known.''

Allison could almost feel Gabe's mouth on hers, his hands moving sensuously over her body. Bruce had never stirred her senses this easily. She stared at him, unable to look away.

He leaned toward her, his eyes incandescent in the candlelight. Fortunately there was a distraction.

The maid had removed their soup plates and the salad that followed it. She returned now with the main course, breast of herbed chicken, wild rice and fresh asparagus.

''This looks delicious,'' Allison said brightly, struggling to regain her poise.

Gabe didn't continue his subtle seduction. ''Mary Louise has a great chef. Her invitations are seldom turned down.''

''It's nice that she has a lot of company. It would get very lonely in this big house otherwise. Do her son and daughter-in-law visit often?''

''They live here.''

''All summer? Doesn't Martin work?''

''He's self-employed.'' Gabe's lip curled sardonically. ''Martin has appointed himself the full-time job of keeping Mary Louise from remarrying.''

''Did his father die recently? It's traumatic for the whole family at first. Children are often jealous of anyone taking a parent's place.''

''Peter Van Ruyder died years ago.''

''Then isn't it rather mean-spirited of Martin to deny his mother companionship? She's a remarkably young-looking woman, and very attractive.''

''I doubt if Martin sees her as a person. To him, she's the guardian of his inheritance and he's dedicated to making sure nobody else gets a share of it. You must have noticed how he treated Sergei.''

''I didn't realize there was anything going on between Mary Louise and Sergei. I simply thought he was being charming to his hostess.''

''He would like their relationship to be a lot closer than that. I believe Sergei is in love with Mary Louise, but he won't ask her to marry him because people would think he married her for her money.''

"Are you sure that's not the reason?"

"Great wealth can be a powerful aphrodisiac," Gabe acknowledged. "But he doesn't fit the profile. Besides being independently wealthy, Sergei is an intelligent and interesting man. He's very much in demand. If he didn't truly care about Mary Louise, he wouldn't put up with Martin for five minutes."

"How does she feel about *him?*"

"It's hard to tell. Her generation was taught to hide their emotions. She's pleasant to everybody, but whether it goes deeper with Sergei is anybody's guess. I do know that she enjoys his company. He's a regular visitor here."

"If she does care about him it would be a shame to let Martin spoil things for them. But having lost one child, I suppose she's especially close to her only remaining one."

"That's a possibility," Gabe answered noncommittally.

"I didn't like to ask the family, but you can tell me. How did Monica die?"

"I'm glad you didn't bring it up in front of them. Her death was quite recent. Mary Louise is holding up magnificently, but I'm sure she has some bad moments when she's alone."

"You don't have to warn me. I would never be so insensitive as to ask questions."

"I know you wouldn't." Gabe smiled winningly. "Some-body taught you very good manners."

Allison had the feeling she was getting the runaround. "At the risk of spoiling your good opinion of me, I'm going to be persistent. You didn't answer my question."

The uniformed maid entered at that very inconvenient moment. This time she lingered, pouring coffee from a silver pot into fragile china cups, then passing sugar and cream. After that she served each of them a crystal bowl containing a perfect mound of crème brûlée with a rosette of whipped cream on top.

Gabe smiled at the woman. "That looks delicious, Anita, but I'll have to jog for an hour to work off all the calories."

She returned his smile. "Would you like red raspberries instead? They're very tasty."

"How about in addition to? I can't pass up Armand's crème brûlée."

"I'll bring them right away, Mr. Gabriel."

"I don't know where Mary Louise gets her produce, but it's terrific," he told Allison. "You have to taste the berries."

There was no point in trying to get him back on the subject of Monica, since the maid would return at any moment. "I'm sure they're very good, but I can't eat two desserts. I'm stuffed already."

"Don't make any snap decisions."

Anita returned with a bowl of ripe red berries that did look delicious. On the tray was a pitcher of cream, extra fine sugar and a bowl of whipped cream.

Gabe speared a berry and held it out to Allison. "You have to try one."

She tasted it and licked her lips. "Mmm, you're right, they're heavenly."

"We'll each have some, Anita."

"But no cream on mine," Allison said. "I have to draw the line somewhere."

He looked at her admiringly. "You don't have to worry about your figure."

"I will if I keep eating like this. I wonder how society ladies stay so thin."

"By being on a constant diet."

"It's kind of sad. They can afford anything they want, but they won't let themselves enjoy it."

"Are you sure that's the kind of world you want to move into?" Gabe asked quietly.

Allison sighed. "You're convinced that's why I came here, but you're so wrong. I couldn't fit into this world even if I wanted to."

"What gives you that impression?"

"So many things. I haven't been to the places they've been, I didn't go to fancy schools. I couldn't hold up my end of a conversation."

"You didn't have any trouble tonight."

"That's different. You're being especially nice to gain my confidence."

"Do you honestly think I've been putting on an act?"

"It's all right. You have a job to do. I understand that."

He stared at her in silence for a moment. "You really don't trust anyone, do you? Well, I guess it's understandable. I wasn't talking about dinner tonight, though. I was referring to the cocktail hour earlier. You didn't have any trouble talking to Sergei and Mary Louise, or even Laura, who isn't the easiest person in the world to warm up. Martin was annoyed at how animated she got with you.''

Allison laughed. "Aren't you getting a little confused? You're supposed to be arguing for the prosecution, not the defense."

"I wish you didn't regard me as an adversary," he said soberly. "I only want to get at the truth, the same as you do. No matter how this thing is resolved, I'd like to be friends."

"Even if your suspicions about me are correct?"

He hesitated imperceptibly before replying, "I'm a lawyer, not a judge."

"You're also very adept at not answering questions," she said dryly.

"And *you* should have been an attorney. You'd be dynamite at cross-examination. You remind me of a prosecutor I once faced. My client was accused of tax evasion, but by the time she got through with him, the jury was ready to send him to the electric chair. I was no match for that lady." He chuckled.

"That's because you confronted her in a courtroom instead of over a candlelit dinner table."

He smiled wryly. "It hasn't done me much good with *you*."

"I'm a special case," she said lightly.

"You are indeed."

The now familiar glow in his eyes alerted Allison. She folded her napkin and placed it on the table. "I can't eat another bite."

"Me, either. I need to get physical. How about it?"

She gave him a startled look. Regardless of their differences, Gabe had been a perfect gentleman up until now. It was hard to believe he'd proposition her that crudely.

Before she could react, he said, "There are some dance clubs in town. Just what we need to work off our dinner. How does that sound?"

Allison felt exceedingly foolish. "It sounds great. I'll change clothes and be right down."

"You look fine just as you are."

"We aren't exactly a matched pair. You have on a suit and tie."

"Which I'll be happy to take off—the tie, that is." He grinned, removing his tie and unbuttoning the top few buttons of his shirt. "There, is that better? Instant casual."

Hardly, Allison thought. Gabe still looked elegant and assured, like one of those men in the ads selling expensive cars or luxury cruises. He also looked wildly masculine. The opening in his shirt revealed a wedge of tanned chest covered with a sprinkling of dark, crisp hair.

"Nobody will be dressed up," he assured her. "You'll fit in perfectly."

Gabe didn't mislead her. Everyone in the crowded, noisy disco was dressed casually, most a lot more so than Allison. The younger patrons wore jeans and T-shirts printed with flip sayings.

They were the tourists, mostly college kids on vacation from New York, Boston and Philadelphia. The rest of the crowd were summer people whose families had homes in Newport.

Gabe was familiar with all of them. He was stopped and greeted repeatedly as they made their way to one of the small tables that ringed the room.

Allison commented on the fact. "You certainly know a lot of people."

"My parents used to have a home in Newport. We spent the summers here when I was growing up, and so did the people I just said hello to. The regulars made up a small, tight-knit community. All the families knew each other."

"Did you have an estate like the Van Ruyder's?"

"Nothing that grand," he said dismissively.

"This must be a wonderful place to spend the summer. Why did your parents stop coming here?"

Gabe shrugged. "Mother got tired of the hassle. Summer help became increasingly difficult to get, both household and gardening, and she had to deal with it on her own. Dad was often tied up in the city all week. She decided it wasn't worth it, once I was off on my own."

So their house wasn't exactly modest, Allison speculated. She'd suspected as much, since they belonged to Mary Louise's crowd.

"The property is still in the family, so to speak," Gabe continued. "They sold it to Dad's brother, my uncle Herb. We all have a standing invitation to visit anytime. I even have a key to the place. I'll show it to you if you like.''

Before Allison could answer, a young blond waitress appeared to take their orders. Gabe had to shout to make himself heard over the sudden blast of noise. The combo had returned from their break to resume playing.

When the waitress left, Allison remarked, ''This is certainly a popular place.''

''What?'' Gabe put his arm around her shoulder and leaned forward to speak into her ear. ''I can't hear you.''

When she turned her head to repeat the remark, their faces were so close that her lips brushed his. Gabe's arm tightened reflexively. Allison's heart started to race as she stared into his gray eyes. The clean masculine scent of his after-shave was like an aphrodisiac, heightened by the close proximity to his hard body. Her lips parted unconsciously as his face lowered to hers, almost in slow motion.

Suddenly one of the wildly gyrating couples spun off the dance floor and collided with their table, bringing Allison to her senses. She drew away, avoiding Gabe's eyes as the youngsters made a laughing apology before dancing away. Gabe seemed uncharacteristically disconcerted, too.

Luckily a group of his friends stopped by. After chatting for a few moments they pulled up chairs for a more lengthy visit. Gabe introduced Allison and her tension lessened as the conversation became general.

When one of the couples got up to dance a little later, Gabe turned to Allison. ''I haven't asked you to dance yet. Shall we give it a go?''

''Sure. We came for some exercise.'' She was completely relaxed with him now. Besides, nobody could get romantic to rock music.

They joined the crowd of uninhibited couples writhing on the dance floor. Allison loved to dance, and the compelling beat dispelled any remaining tension. She was sorry when the music stopped and the guitarist took the microphone for an announcement.

''Okay, kids, here comes a slow one to cool you off. Just one for the older folks,'' he said over a chorus of protests.

''There *is* a God who looks after us older folk,'' Gabe groaned, taking her in his arms. "That was more strenuous than racquet-ball."

"Don't tell me you never go dancing. You're too good at it."

"Memories of my youth."

She smiled. "You're not over-the-hill yet."

"I'm glad you noticed," he murmured, drawing her closer.

Suddenly Allison's tension was back. This time she didn't have to imagine how it would feel to be in Gabe's arms. His taut body was as seductive as she'd known it would be. The broad shoulders, hard chest and muscular thighs brushing against hers created a feverish need that ignored all reason.

When she tried to put distance between them, Gabe's embrace tightened. "We have a problem," he said in a husky voice.

"I don't know what you mean," she answered, holding herself stiffly.

"In case you haven't noticed, there's an awesome chemistry between us."

"You're really incredible! Isn't there *anything* you won't do for a client?" she asked angrily.

"Denying it won't change the facts, Allison. We might as well be honest with each other."

"Is this where I'm supposed to say, you're right, darling, I want you, let's go home and make love?"

"I don't expect to be that fortunate. While I'm convinced the desire between us is mutual, I don't think you'll allow yourself to satisfy it."

"Well, at least we agree on *one* thing."

He smoothed the silky hair off her forehead with caressing fingers. "Nothing is written in stone. You just might change your mind."

"Don't bank on it. I'm sure you've had great success with women, but if I *were* attracted to you, it still wouldn't change my decision. I have a deep aversion to being used. Why don't you just put all your energies into proving I'm a fraud? It would be a lot more honorable."

"At this moment, I don't give a damn who or what you are."

"You'll come to your senses when you remember the fat re-tainer Martin is paying you to expose me," she said derisively.

The slow number ended and the combo switched to a raucous

beat. Allison moved out of Gabe's arms.

"I'd like to leave now," she said.

Allison overslept the next morning after lying awake half the night fuming over Gabe. He was as bad as Bruce—just a little smoother at it, that's all. How long after they made love would it have taken until Gabe started urging her to drop her claim? Men were all alike. Not one of them could be trusted!

After she'd showered and dressed in white pants and a sky blue pullover that matched her eyes, Allison went downstairs to breakfast, hoping she wasn't terribly late. Nobody had told her what time meals were served. It would be embarrassing if everyone else had finished and the staff was waiting to serve her. She'd never been a houseguest before, and certainly never in a place this grand.

The formal dining room was empty, so she went to the morning room, which proved to be the correct place. A long buffet was filled with covered silver dishes, pitchers of fruit juice and baskets of muffins and toast. The room was deserted except for Gabe, who was sipping coffee and reading a newspaper.

Allison hovered uncertainly in the doorway. She desperately wanted a cup of coffee, but was another confrontation with Gabe worth it?

He looked up and smiled at her. "Good morning. Did you sleep well?"

"Very well, thank you." She glanced at the table that held only one other place setting besides his. "Has everyone else eaten?"

"Mary Louise and Sergei have. Martin and Laura have breakfast in their suite. There are hot dishes on the buffet. Help yourself. I can recommend the French toast. Armand makes it out of sourdough bread."

"It sounds delicious, but I think I'll skip breakfast." Allison couldn't match Gabe's imperturbability. Her blood pressure had shot up the minute she spotted him.

"You can't avoid me completely," he said calmly. "Why not relax and try to enjoy yourself?"

"I didn't come here to enjoy myself."

"Then you're off to a good start." He grinned. "Don't go,"

he called as she turned away. "I promise not to make any personal remarks again. Sit down and have some breakfast."

"Well, maybe just a quick cup of coffee." What Gabe said was true. She couldn't avoid him for the entire visit.

"You're missing a treat if you don't try the French toast. There's real maple syrup, too."

"I don't know how you can eat like you do and stay so trim," she remarked without thinking.

"A compliment is the last thing I'd expect from you." He smiled.

Allison was annoyed that she was the one who'd gotten personal. Gabe was a magnificent male specimen, though. No doubt about it. A well-tailored suit can conceal a lot of flaws, but he didn't have any. His thin cotton T-shirt showed off broad shoulders that didn't need any additional padding. The rest of him was lean and fit, also. His taut jeans spanned a flat stomach and the impressive legs of an athlete.

"I think I will have something to eat," she said, walking over to the buffet.

Under the silver covers were scrambled eggs and crisp bacon, in addition to the French toast Gabe recommended. There was also cereal and fruit. Everything looked appetizing, but Allison's stomach was tied up in knots. She selected a blueberry muffin and poured herself a cup of coffee from a magnificent Georgian urn.

"Would you like to visit some of the old mansions this morning?" he asked.

"No, thanks. I have things to do, and I'm sure you do, too."

"You're my reason for being here." His mouth curved sardonically. "Whither thou goest..."

"Surely you don't expect to follow me around everywhere I go!" she exclaimed in outrage.

"Why not? You don't have anything to hide, do you?"

"That's not the point. I don't want to spend all of my time arguing with you."

"I'll try not to be offensive. But as you pointed out, I have to earn my retainer."

"Why don't you just go chase an ambulance?" she muttered.

His eyes sparkled with amusement. "Rockford, Rockford, Collingsworth and Strand is a very prestigious law firm. We don't chase ambulances. There isn't enough money in it.''

"Seriously, Gabe, can't we call a truce? If you were sincere about being attracted to me, I'm flattered. But you can see we're totally unsuited to each other, even if you didn't have doubts about my motives. We come from different worlds.''

His expression softened as he gazed at her lovely, pleading face. The sleepless night had left lavender shadows under her eyes, highlighting the fragility of her clear skin.

"Isn't there room in your world for me?'' he asked in a husky voice.

"You know it's the other way around.''

"For a scrappy kid who refused to give in to adversity, you have remarkably little self-confidence.''

"You couldn't be more off base. I'm simply a realist. I've learned to push hard to get ahead, but I have no desire to go where I'm not wanted. *That's* self-esteem.''

"Maybe you just don't realize when someone is sincere about wanting you,'' he said softly.

"Your kind of acceptance isn't difficult to achieve.''

Gabe looked at her searchingly. "Would you have felt the same about me if we'd met under different circumstances?''

"Our paths never would have crossed, so the question is academic.''

Before he could answer, Anita entered the room carrying a cordless telephone. "You have a long-distance call, Mr. Gabriel.''

After a moment's hesitation he said, "I'll take it in the den.''

The maid glanced at the buffet. "Can I get you anything else, Miss Riley?''

"No, thank you. I'm all finished.''

As the woman began to clear away the food, Allison rose and went through the French doors into the garden. She didn't want to be there when Gabe returned.

Several paths led from the terrace. Allison took the one away from the pool and tennis court area. It cut through thick green lawns and weed-free flower beds to a fragrant rose garden. Scores of bushes were covered with blooms in glorious, vibrant colors. A little farther up the path, Mary Louise was clipping off dead blossoms and putting them in the straw basket over her arm.

She waved and called, "Good morning. Isn't it a glorious day?"

"Beautiful," Allison answered. "I'm sorry I was late for breakfast."

"We don't have any set time. Everyone eats when he feels like it. That's why we serve buffet." Mary Louise took off her gardening gloves. "Did you and Gabriel have a good time last night? He said you went into town."

"Yes, it was very nice," Allison answered without enthusiasm.

"Isn't he a charmer? I wonder why some lucky girl hasn't snapped him up by now. I'm sure it isn't from lack of trying."

"Maybe he's just a confirmed bachelor," Allison remarked, since some kind of reply seemed indicated.

Mary Louise smiled mischievously. "All men are until we change their minds for them. Gabriel is wily, though, he dates a number of girls. If one of them does have the edge it would be Hester. From what I hear from his mother, he sees her more often than the others."

"Hester?"

"The granddaughter of friends of ours. Hester Danville. She's a photographic model."

Allison didn't need to hear anymore. She had a mental image of a tall, sexy blonde with a drop-dead figure and a vocabulary that didn't include the word no. That would be just his type, she thought waspishly.

Mary Louise was looking at her quizzically. "How about you? Why isn't a pretty girl like you married? I realize that's a dreadfully sexist remark nowadays. You'll have to excuse me, my dear. I'm hopelessly old-fashioned."

"You're not at all," Allison protested.

"You don't have to be polite. I've accepted the fact that I'm a dinosaur. In my day, marriage was every girl's goal. To achieve that admirable state we were taught to be submissive." The older woman's voice had a mocking undertone. "When we married, our husbands shielded us from the harsher realities of life. They thought we were too delicate to face them."

"Times really *have* changed. Now women hold down a job in addition to raising a family. A lot of women do, anyway." Allison added. Not anyone Mary Louise was likely to know.

"They're probably closer to their children than I was. Mine never shared their little disappointments with me. They were told by their father to spare me any unpleasantness."

"He must have loved you very much," Allison said awkwardly, since the older woman was obviously regretting her lost opportunity.

"Yes." Mary Louise turned away. "Let's sit on that bench under the tree. The sun is getting quite warm. I suppose that's why the roses thrive so well. They need a lot of sun."

Allison didn't want her to change the subject now that they'd finally gotten around to Monica. There were so many things she wanted to ask. She paused to frame her questions sensitively.

Mary Louise didn't give her a chance. "Gabriel tells me he met a lot of old friends at the disco last night. We'll have to invite them over for a party. I love having young people around."

"Gabe would thank you for that description." Allison smiled. "He kept referring to himself as being one of the older folks."

"That's patently ridiculous. The man is a heartbreaker."

"I know he's younger than your children, but was Gabe friendly with them?" Allison asked artlessly.

"They knew each other, but there was a good ten years difference in their ages. That's a lot when you're young. What am I saying?" Mary Louise gave a slight laugh. "It's an important difference when you get older, too."

Allison knew she was thinking of Sergei. "I wouldn't say that. I think compatibility and companionship are a lot more important, especially when you get older."

Mary Louise smiled wryly. "Has Gabriel been gossiping?"

"He's very fond of you," Allison answered evasively. "He likes Sergei, too."

Mary Louise sighed. "Everybody but Martin likes Sergei."

"I probably shouldn't say this, but Martin is a grown man with his own life to lead. You deserve to be happy, too."

"It isn't that simple. I've always done what was expected of me. When my husband was alive I gave grand parties for business tycoons and political figures. I was on the board of numerous charities, opened our home for worthy causes and lent my name to cultural organizations. I was a credit to my husband and a responsible citizen." Mary Louise gazed out at the distant water, almost oblivious to Allison's presence.

"I'm sure it was a very rewarding life," Allison said, not at all convinced. "But now you've fulfilled your obligations. You've earned the right to explore a different life-style. It would be very foolish to pass up a warm relationship because of a silly thing like age difference. Nobody could even tell there was one. You and Sergei look like you're the same age."

"I'm five years older than he."

"Big deal! Men marry women half their ages, and everybody says, way to go. Why should it be any different for women?"

"I guess we haven't come as far as we think we have."

"Nonsense! Age is a state of mind. You're a vital, caring woman with years of living to do. Take my advice and latch onto him before somebody else does."

"My inhibitions aren't the only problem. Sergei has his own reservations. I have so much more money than he."

"I was told he doesn't exactly have to worry about where his next meal is coming from."

"Most people would consider him rich, but not compared to me. Sergei knows how he would be perceived."

"Your friends wouldn't be influenced by gossip—not if they're true friends. And why would you worry about anyone too mean-spirited to be happy for you?"

"You don't suppose people would think I was a silly old woman?"

"Gabe doesn't, and *I* don't—although my opinion doesn't count for anything." Allison gave a slight laugh, embarrassed that she'd gone too far in her enthusiasm.

"You're wrong, my dear. I value your opinion very much. You're the only one around me who has no reason to be biased."

"I hope I've at least helped to put things into the proper perspective."

"You've given me something to think about, anyway." Mary Louise gazed at her with a slight trace of surprise. "I've never spoken this frankly with anyone before. I'm normally a very private person. I didn't even discuss my feelings with my husband."

"Sometimes it's easier with a stranger. You know you'll never see them again, so you can get it all off your chest."

"Surely you're not thinking of leaving so soon?"

"I don't want to wear out my welcome, but I can stay for a week if you don't mind putting up with me that long."

"It would be my pleasure. I'd really like to know more about you."

"What I'd prefer to talk about is Monica. Unless it would upset you too much," Allison said hesitantly.

Mary Louise smiled faintly. "I've come down from the ivory tower Peter built for me." She reached out to the nearest rose-bush and stroked a creamy white blossom with her forefinger. "Monica had skin like this rose petal. She was a beautiful baby, and she grew into an enchanting little girl. Everybody made a fuss over her."

The older woman was silent for so long that Allison murmured, "She must have been an adorable child."

Mary Louise nodded. "I hated to see her grow up, but Monica couldn't wait to do everything—drive a car, go to college, see the world. She wanted to sample everything life had to offer."

"I guess all young people feel that way."

"I suppose so." Mary Louise's expression softened. "I'll never forget her first date. She wore too much lipstick and almost tripped in her first pair of high heels. She looked like a little girl playing dress-up, but her young man was completely dazzled." After a long pause, Mary Louise dragged herself back to the present. "That's how I like to remember her." She looked at her watch and rose. "Goodness, I had no idea it was so late. I have a garden club meeting in half an hour."

Allison felt as if somebody had slammed a door in her face. It was interesting to hear about Monica's childhood, but her early years weren't the ones that counted. Was that all Mary Louise intended to talk about? She hadn't come this far to be put off so easily.

"Could I go to the meeting with you?" Allison asked hastily. "I love flowers."

"You'd be terribly bored, my dear. The name garden club is a misnomer." Mary Louise laughed. "Mostly we discuss fund-raising projects and appoint committees. I guess old habits die hard." She picked up her basket as Gabe sauntered down the path toward them.

"Can I be of any help?" he asked. "I'm looking for something to do."

"You can take Allison sight-seeing," Mary Louise said. "I feel terrible about constantly running out on you," she told her. "But we'll spend the evening together, I promise."

Gabe waited until their hostess was out of hearing before saying mockingly, "I guess you're stuck with me whether you like it or not."

Chapter Four

When Allison didn't snap back after his comment, Gabe looked at her more closely. "Is anything wrong?"

"No, I'm just disappointed, that's all. I got Mary Louise to talk to me a little bit this morning, but mostly about when Monica was a child. She said it was the way she wanted to remember her."

"That's understandable." He smiled. "Parents are fondest of the times when they were in complete control."

"But how am I going to get at the truth if Mary Louise refuses to face it? Why did she ask me to stay here if she doesn't want to know?"

"I'm sure she does, but you have to understand that it's difficult for her to speak about the adult Monica."

"*Why?* What did she do that was so terrible?"

Gabe paused to choose his words carefully. "Monica was perhaps too blessed. She had everything life had to offer. There weren't any challenges."

"Mary Louise said she wanted to experience everything, but is that so bad? What's wrong with having a zest for living?"

"It's fine if you don't concentrate solely on your own pleasure.

I doubt if Monica ever gave a thought to the people she hurt, the ones who loved her.''

"If you're referring to her divorces, they're seldom the fault of only one spouse."

"That's certainly true," he answered neutrally.

"Maybe somebody hurt *her* badly when she was young and impressionable. She was only seventeen when she became pregnant." Gabe's silence wasn't lost on Allison. "I know you won't believe it until you actually see the records, but let's just say I'm right. The father didn't marry her. Perhaps he even claimed he wasn't responsible. Think how traumatic it must have been to have a baby all alone and then have to give it up for adoption."

"Mary Louise would never have turned her out, as you seem to be implying. Nor would she have allowed the baby to be adopted. You know a little about her. Can you see that happening?"

"Obviously she didn't know," Allison said uncertainly. "It's the only explanation."

"How would a seventeen-year-old manage on her own?"

"I don't know. I only know Monica Van Ruyder gave birth to a baby in a Philadelphia hospital. How do you explain *that?*"

"I can't. We seem to be at a stalemate."

"You might be willing to leave it at that, I'm not. I have a lot of questions, and I intend to get answers—starting with who the father was. I'll bet even after all these years, Mary Louise can still remember the names of the boys Monica dated when she was seventeen."

"Possibly, but they could be scattered all over the country by now. And even if you did track them down, do you think the guilty party would admit to having fathered an illegitimate child twenty some years ago?"

Everything Gabe said was true. Dejection weighed Allison down, but she refused to give in to it. "Maybe I can tell by his reaction if he's lying."

"I'm a trained interrogator, and even *I* can't tell when someone is lying."

She squared her shoulders and faced him determinedly. "You can try to discourage me all you want. I'm not giving up."

"I don't want to rain on your parade, honey," he said quietly. "I just want you to be realistic. You're facing a daunting task."

"I know," she said forlornly.

Gabe wanted to hold her and stroke her gently, but he knew better than to make any overt gesture. "Who knows, maybe you'll be lucky and they'll all be visiting Newport this summer."

She flared up immediately, misinterpreting the light tone he used to mask his sympathy. "I didn't say it would be easy, but if everyone had your attitude, we'd all still be riding around in horse-drawn carriages."

"Well, you can't invent the automobile until you get some help from Mary Louise, so let's take her advice and go sight-seeing."

"How do you expect me to concentrate on purely frivolous things when I have so much on my mind?"

"The Breakers will make you forget everything else, I guarantee it."

After a little coaxing, Allison let herself be persuaded. There really wasn't anything she could do without some clues from Mary Louise.

The Breakers was a huge Italian Renaissance mansion set on a dozen acres of oceanfront property. A pair of thirty-foot-high wrought-iron gates guarded the entrance. They were open now, and a gravel driveway led through a park filled with giant trees. Squirrels scampered around gathering acorns, adding to the park-like atmosphere.

"It's hard to believe this was a family home," Allison remarked, staring at the arches and pillars and rounded balconies. "It looks like a doge's palace, or some terribly posh hotel."

"It could easily be one of those," Gabe said. "There are seventy rooms inside."

"How could anybody possibly use seventy rooms?"

"Thirty-three of them were set aside for the servants, as well as the maids and valets of guests."

"Now that's what I call considerate houseguests, the kind who bring their own help to clean up after them."

"That wasn't one of their duties." Gabe smiled. "Servants had a strict pecking order in those days. A valet drew the master's bath, but he didn't clean out the tub afterward."

"What do you bet it was considered woman's work?"

"You're not suckering me into *that* controversy." Gabe chuckled. "Come on, let's go inside."

The Grand Entry Hall was forty-five feet tall, roughly five stories. Allison stared up in openmouthed amazement at the ornate gilt cornice surrounding a ceiling painted to represent blue sky. Garlands of carved flowers held by golden cherubs were swagged above marble pillars and curved archways. A stained-glass skylight illuminated a huge Flemish tapestry dominating the stairwell of the red carpeted main staircase.

"I don't know where to look first," Allison said, marveling. "There's so much to see."

"This is only the beginning. Wait until we get to the dining room."

Gabe led her to a room even more embellished than the Great Hall. This room was only two stories high, but the vaulted ceiling rose in carved, painted and gilt stages to an elaborately framed painting on the ceiling of Aurora, goddess of dawn.

"Those people must have spent a lot of time staring at the ceiling," Allison remarked.

"Maybe they wanted to be sure the chandeliers didn't fall on their heads."

Two massive Baccarat chandeliers strung with thousands of crystal prisms and beads illuminated a carved oak table inlaid with lemon wood. It was surrounded by twelve chairs upholstered in red damask. Additional chairs were spaced between twelve enormous freestanding rose alabaster columns.

"Why did they need so many extra chairs?" Allison asked.

"The table could be extended to seat thirty-four."

"If they'd used folding chairs, they could have stored them away in a closet."

"You have a very practical mind," Gabe teased. "Would you have recommended paper napkins, too?"

"You bet, if I had thirty-four people for dinner."

They wandered through the oval music room with its grand piano, the library paneled with gold embossed green Spanish leather, a billiard room that had pale grey-green marble walls and carved yellow alabaster arches.

Each room had its own color and personality. The morning room was furnished with sixteenth-century-style chairs and settees covered in rose silk brocade, and Mrs. Vanderbilt's oval bedroom was a mixture of coral and beige flowered wall covering and cream colored moldings.

After all the opulence and almost overwhelming display of wealth, it was restful to return to the loggia on the lower floor. Through Palladian arches, beyond a lush green lawn was the ocean.

"What a beautiful, peaceful view," Allison commented.

"Do you want to walk down to the water before we push on? I thought we'd go to Kingscote next for a change of pace. It isn't as ostentatiously grand as The Breakers, but it's interesting for its Gothic Revival architecture."

"No more," she groaned. "I'm having trouble remembering everything I just saw."

"It's a lot to take in all at once," Gabe agreed. "Okay, we'll space them out, one historic house a day. How's that?"

"There are eight of them, aren't there? I'm afraid I'll have to skip a couple. I'll only be here a week."

He slanted a glance at her. "You expect to accomplish your purpose by the end of the week?"

"Whether I do or not, I'll have to leave. I can't impose on Mary Louise for any longer than that. Besides, I have to get back to work."

"Surely it's more important to remain here as long as it takes."

"You're implying that I won't have to work if I pull this off?" Allison's blue eyes sparkled angrily.

"That wasn't what I meant, but it *is* true."

"I still have to hedge my bets," she answered mockingly. "If you succeed in proving I'm a fraud, I'll need my job to fall back on."

"I didn't come here with any preconceived ideas," he said quietly.

"That's hard to believe, but I won't argue the point."

Gabe smiled. "You never backed off from an argument before."

"What's the use? I'll never convince you anyway."

"You haven't tried very hard," he said softly.

"There are limits to what even a scam artist will do for money. Let's go back to the car." She stalked off without waiting for an answer.

As he walked alongside her, Gabe remarked, "That's quite a chip you have on your shoulder."

"You'll only have to put up with it for a week. Then you can go home to all the girlfriends who tell you how wonderful you are."

"It will be a nice change." He grinned.

"Well, hang in there. Better times are coming."

"I don't know about that. I'll miss our pitched battles."

"Are *all* of your women compliant?"

"How do you know there are that many?"

"Just an educated guess," she answered dryly.

"You sound like an authority on the male animal."

"I'm not, trust me. I don't know the first thing about men."

"That's hard to believe." Gabe's eyes swept over her admiringly. "You must have made a lot of strong men weak."

"Oh, sure. They can't live without me."

"I can believe it. You could easily become addictive," he said in a silky voice.

His sensuous tone infuriated Allison—because for one crazy minute she couldn't help wishing he meant it. "Is that the kind of line you use to keep Hester happy?" she asked waspishly.

"Somebody has been telling tales out of school."

"It doesn't matter. I knew there would be a Hester."

He didn't deny it. "Is there a Hector in *your* life?"

"Dozens of them," she replied airily. "I play the field, like you do."

"You've never considered getting married?"

"Lots of times. I've also considered moving to a cave, but I decided it was equally impractical." They'd reached the car and Allison ended the conversation by getting in.

Gabe slid into the driver's seat. As they drove out the gates he looked at her inquiringly. "Where would you like to go now?"

"I have an errand to run. You can just drop me off in town."

"It's okay, I'll wait for you."

"That won't be necessary. I don't know how long it will take."

"No problem. I don't have anything else to do."

"I'm sure you can find something more stimulating than following me around day and night. I really hate the feeling of being watched every minute.''

"That's the only part of the job I enjoy." He smiled.

"Flattery won't get you anywhere. You can't come with me," she said firmly.

"Now you've piqued my curiosity. What do you plan to do that's so clandestine?''

"Nothing secret, merely personal. I have to buy panty hose, and I don't need a spectator.''

"I've been in a lingerie department before. My palms don't turn sweaty with embarrassment.''

Allison could believe that. Gabe probably knew more about lingerie than she did—the sexy kind, anyway.

"Pull over to the curb here," she ordered as they drove through the middle of town. When he complied, she got out of the car. "Thanks for the tour. I'll see you later.''

"How will you get back to the house? Give me a call when you're finished and I'll come and pick you up.''

"You don't have to do that. I'll take a cab.''

Traffic started to back up behind him on the narrow street and Gabe had to drive on. She waited until he was out of sight before going into a store to ask directions.

Allison spent a long weary afternoon at the Newport City Hall, going through twenty-five-year-old records. The Van Ruyder name didn't turn up in any of them. None of Monica's three marriages had taken place here.

It was probably too much to hope for, and there was no reason to believe Monica had eventually married the father of her child. She might have told one of the husbands about her youthful affair, though. Since that idea hadn't panned out, Allison's only other option was to question Mary Louise about Monica's boyfriends. The major problem there was the older woman's evasiveness. She didn't really want to talk about her daughter. It seemed strange.

The afternoon had been a waste of time. Allison walked slowly back to the main shopping street, feeling a familiar sense of discouragement. It was difficult enough to trace someone after twenty-five years, but when you didn't know who you were looking for and everyone was conspiring to make sure you didn't find out, the task was almost impossible. Somewhere out there was the man who had fathered her. He could supply the missing pieces of the puzzle, but would she ever find him?

Allison wandered past the shops, reluctant to go back to the house and face more of Gabe's questions. He was upsetting enough without that. As she was passing a beauty shop, Laura emerged, inspecting her right hand.

"Well, hello," Allison said in surprise. "I didn't expect to run into anybody I knew."

"You can hardly avoid it in a town this size," Laura said. "Did you come to shop? The Sporting Life has some nice casual things, although you probably have plenty of clothes."

"It's always fun to look. You don't seem to have bought anything."

"No, I just came to have a nail patched." Laura lifted her hand again. "They're not as good at it as my manicurist in New York, but it will have to do."

"Are you going home from here? I could use a lift."

"Certainly. How did you get downtown?"

"Gabe dropped me off."

"Isn't he a hunk? I suppose that sounds terrible, but what woman wouldn't notice? Like the saying goes—I'm married, not dead." Laura giggled.

Allison didn't want to pursue the subject. "Can I buy you a cup of coffee before we start back?"

Laura consulted her watch. "Why not? We've missed tea, and dinner isn't until eight."

As they walked to a coffeehouse, Allison said, "Maybe I should have gone shopping after all. Do you dress for dinner every night? I'm afraid I didn't bring anything suitable."

"I wouldn't worry about it. We're fairly casual except on the weekends. Tell me frankly," Laura said, once they were seated. "Do you think I'm too old to wear those ultraminiskirts?"

Allison judged her to be quite a bit younger than her husband, maybe only in her early thirties. "I think they'd look great on you. You have an excellent figure."

"I work at it," Laura said matter-of-factly. "I really love short skirts, but Martin is so conservative. He's always afraid of offending his mother."

"Mary Louise seems very open-minded to me."

"Yes, but she's such a perfect lady. You'd never know if she disapproved of something. She always says the right thing and never raises her voice or loses her temper."

"I suppose that's the way she was raised."

"Or else she's a saint. Monica used to use the most outrageous language—words that would impress a marine sergeant. I think she did it to see how far she could go before her mother snapped back. But Mary Louise never did."

Allison held her breath, afraid of saying something that would put Laura on guard. She was so different away from Martin, so much friendlier.

"I'm really surprised," Allison remarked casually. "From the way I've heard Monica described, she was a fantastic person. Everybody loved her."

"The men did—and their feelings were reciprocated. It didn't matter to Monica if they were married or single, either. She liked variety."

"Perhaps she was rebelling against what she felt was a harsh upbringing," Allison said slowly. "I heard her father was quite strict."

"As far as I'm concerned, that psychological jargon is hogwash," Laura said impatiently. "I heard how strict her father was, but that didn't stop her from doing anything she wanted. Did you also hear that he was constantly getting her out of trouble? Monica thought rules were for other people."

"Did you see much of her?"

"More than I wanted to. When she deigned to pay a visit, the whole household was put on alert. We planned our schedules around her. If Monica wanted dinner at ten o'clock, that's when it was served." Laura's eyes sparkled with anger. "It didn't matter what *we* wanted. You wouldn't think Martin was a member of the family. His sister was the only one who mattered."

Laura had obviously resented Monica. The bitterness still remained, making her evaluation of her sister-in-law suspect. Monica was everything Martin wasn't. Maybe she was what Laura wanted to be, too. Nobody was neutral about Monica. She'd evidently had a great impact on people.

Laura gave an embarrassed laugh, suddenly realizing she'd gotten carried away. "I didn't mean to imply that Monica was intentionally malicious, or anything like that. She was really just high-spirited. It's true that she liked to have her own way, but don't we all?''

"How true. It must have been difficult for you, though. A mother always takes her daughter's side over her daughter-in-law.''

Laura wasn't about to commit any more indiscretions. "Oh, no, Mary Louise is a perfect mother-in-law.'' She pushed her coffee cup away. "If you're finished, I'd like to start back.''

Allison dressed for dinner that night in a simple blue linen sheath, hoping it would be acceptable. To compensate for her plain outfit she created an elaborate hairstyle, pinning her long hair to her crown, then letting it cascade down in a shining spill of waves and curls.

She took equal pains with her makeup, applying blue eye shadow, tipping her long lashes with mascara and highlighting her mouth with a slick of pink lip gloss.

Her appearance produced mixed results when she joined the others in the den for cocktails. The men's reaction was predictable. Martin scowled at her, while Sergei registered normal admiration for an attractive woman. Gabe's eyes conveyed more than that. They glowed like a predator's sighting a particularly desirable prey.

Mary Louise's expression was the only unexpected one. Her face was wistful as she gazed at Allison. "Monica wore her hair like that to her high school prom,'' she said softly. "She pinned a single rosebud at her crown. It matched her pink organdy formal.''

"Too bad you didn't think to add a rose,'' Martin said mockingly to Allison.

She ignored him, turning to her hostess. "I took you at your word when you said dinner would be casual.''

"You look charming, my dear. We like to be comfortable at home.'' Mary Louise and Laura wore thin summer dresses.

"I'm glad to hear you admit those charity bashes are uncomfortable,'' Sergei teased.

"You men look so handsome in your dinner jackets,'' she said. "I can't imagine why you complain.''

"It's a defense mechanism." Gabe smiled. "If we admit we enjoy dressing up occasionally, you ladies will remind us of it when we'd prefer to wear jeans and go to a basketball game."

"Don't you men get enough sports during the daytime?" Laura asked.

"Some of us have to work," Sergei answered.

It was an innocent remark, but Martin took it personally. "I'm sure *you'd* prefer to retire and live off the fat of the land," he said nastily.

"That's an interesting expression." Sergei was unruffled. "I've always wondered where it originated."

"From someone not very bright, obviously," Gabe said. "A fathead?"

After a look at her husband's furious face, Laura said hastily, "Do I have time for another drink before dinner?"

Mary Louise consulted her watch. "It should be ready about now."

Dinner was served in the dining room that night, a formal room with tall, damask-draped windows and Louis VI furnishings. Despite Mary Louise's claim that they dined informally, the table was set exquisitely with a lovely floral centerpiece of garden flowers and tall candles in silver candle holders.

Monogrammed linen place mats held Ainsley china serving plates that were flanked by an array of sterling flatware. At the point of each knife was a water goblet. Next to it were two different size wineglasses, one for red and the other for white. All of the crystal was Waterford.

During the first course, Gabe gazed across the table at Allison. "It's an interesting phenomenon that candlelight can make a beautiful woman look even more enchanting."

Martin's eyes narrowed as he glanced from one to the other. "Your girlfriend Hester doesn't need any help in that department. When are you going to pop the question, Gabe? Or have you already? Let us in on it."

"You'll be the first to know, I assure you," Gabe answered ironically.

"It's funny how weddings seem to be catching." Sergei's voice was bland. "People who have been teetering on the brink, suddenly make up their minds to get married when romance is in the air."

His glance at Mary Louise wasn't lost on Martin. "Are you speaking for yourself? I wouldn't think a man of your age would be interested in marriage—unless he had a powerful incentive, of course."

"Love isn't reserved solely for the young," Sergei answered.

"They think it is." Mary Louise's voice had an unaccustomed edge to it.

"Not all of the young are that shortsighted, if I can be permitted to include myself in that category," Gabe said.

Sergei's eyes twinkled. "I would give a great deal to have your youth and my experience."

"Most people are satisfied to just grow old gracefully," Martin said primly.

"And a lot of people are never satisfied with their lives, no matter what age they are," Gabe commented.

It was not a relaxed dinner, due to Martin's constant sniping and Gabe's refusal to let him get away with it. Allison couldn't enjoy the excellent food and wine, even though she wasn't the object of Martin's malice, for once. She became his target when Mary Louise suggested giving a party to introduce Allison to some of the young people in town. Her purpose may have been merely to change the subject to neutral ground, but Martin reacted furiously.

"Do you want to set off a full-blown scandal? How are you going to explain who she is and what she's doing here?"

"She's our guest," Mary Louise replied. "Well-bred people don't ask questions."

"Get real, Mother! The news is probably all over town by now."

"Then we won't be telling people anything they don't already know."

"We'll be a laughingstock when they find out we were taken in by a—"

"Martin!" Mary Louise interrupted him sharply.

Sergei intervened tactfully. "Will the party be just for young people, or can I come, too?"

"Somebody has to be there to chaperone. Otherwise there's no telling what these kids will be up to." Gabe grinned.

"Who do you think you're kidding with that pious act?" Allison said. "Face it, pal, you're one of us."

"Don't argue, children, there's room for everybody." Mary Louise smiled. "That gives me an idea. We'll make it a multigenerational party. I'll invite my friends and their children and grandchildren. We'll have it this Saturday."

"Isn't that awfully short notice?" Laura asked.

"People aren't booked up every night like they are in New York. There isn't as much to do here. I think we can gather a nice little crowd."

"You're making a mistake," Martin insisted. "Think what Father would say. He'd never permit you to do anything this foolish."

"Unfortunately your father is no longer with us," Mary Louise answered. "If everyone is finished, shall we adjourn to the library for coffee?"

"I don't want any coffee." Martin's mouth was sulky. "Laura and I are going out."

The mood of the evening showed a definite improvement after he left. The others talked and joked easily, with no barbed undertones. Even Allison relaxed and enjoyed the company, including Gabe's. He was so charming that it was easy to forget he was an adversary.

After they finished their coffee, Mary Louise suggested a game of bridge.

"I'm sorry," Allison said regretfully. "I never learned to play."

"You didn't miss anything." Gabe chuckled. "Bridge is responsible for more divorces than infidelity or snoring."

"People do tend to take it too seriously," Mary Louise agreed. "I'll never forget the time my mind wandered and I trumped Peter's ace. He kept me up half the night lecturing me."

"Definitely a man with the wrong priorities," Sergei murmured.

"I saw a game of Trivial Pursuit on the shelf over there," Gabe remarked. "We could play that."

The suggestion met with everyone's approval. Gabe spread the game board on the coffee table and they pulled up chairs around it. Minor squabbling took place over who should ask the questions, but they settled the problem by agreeing to take turns.

Gabe began by asking Allison, "What was the first ready-to-eat cereal?"

"Cornflakes," she answered.

"Wrong, it was shredded wheat. Okay, try this. Where in London are the Crown Jewels located?"

"The Tower of London. Thanks for picking one from the easy category. I'd be mortified if I missed two in a row."

"He's playing favorites," Sergei declared in mock complaint.

"I can't believe Gabriel would take liberties with the rules." Mary Louise smiled.

"To make points with a beautiful woman? He'd be crazy if he didn't." Sergei laughed. "Okay, it's my turn to ask the questions. Who was Howdy Doody's twin brother?"

"It's a trick question," Gabe said. "He didn't have one."

"Wrong. His brother's name was Double Doody."

"You're putting me on!"

"Look for yourself." Sergei brandished the card. "I'll give you another chance. What two U.S. public officials aren't allowed to travel together?"

"A Democrat and a Republican." Gabe grinned. "They'd both want to sit in the driver's seat."

"I believe the correct answer is the president and the vice president," Mary Louise said.

"Correct. See what you get for being a smart aleck?" Sergei said to Gabe. "Mary Louise went ahead of you. Here's one you're bound to know. Who appeared on the first cover of *Playboy* magazine?"

"It was Marilyn Monroe, but I resent your implication."

"You knew the answer, didn't you?" Allison asked dryly.

"My father told me."

"And I'll bet he bought the magazine for the articles."

"This game is getting as controversial as bridge," Gabe complained. "Let's all go into town for a pizza. I'm hungry."

"I can have Florence fix us some sandwiches," Mary Louise offered.

"Don't bother," Sergei said. "I vote with Gabe. It's such a nice night. Let's go out and get some fresh air."

"But it's so late."

"Later than you think. Discover the joy of being spontaneous."

"I never have been," she answered hesitantly.

"All the more reason to start now," Gabe said. "I'll bet

you've never even had a pizza. We'll tell them to serve yours with a knife and fork so the culture shock isn't too great," he teased.

After she let herself be persuaded, Mary Louise was enthusiastic. Her eyes sparkled as she glanced around the noisy pizza parlor crowded with young people.

"I can't get over it. A whole world goes on while I've been wasting time sleeping," she commented.

"Stick with us, we'll show you how the other half lives," Gabe joked.

"As if you'd know," Allison scoffed.

Mary Louise covered her hand briefly. "We'll teach each other," she said softly.

They were all hilarious when the pizza arrived and Mary Louise tried to deal with hers. After watching the others covertly, she picked up a slice in her fingers, then looked aghast when long strings of cheese remained attached to the next piece.

An attractive girl about Allison's age stopped by their table. "Mrs. Van Ruyder?" Her voice was incredulous. "I wasn't sure it was you."

"Pinky dear, how nice to see you. I didn't know you were in town. I heard you were working at your father's advertising agency."

"I'm on vacation. It helps to know the boss." She grinned.

Mary Louse introduced her to the others. "I'm so glad we ran into you. I'm having a little party Saturday night and I'd like you and your parents to come. I'll telephone your mother tomorrow. I hope you can make it on such short notice."

"I can't speak for them, but I'd love to."

"Splendid. I want all of you young people to meet Allison. She's visiting us."

"How nice." Pinky glanced mischievously from Allison to Gabe. "Shall I bring a date, or is Gabe up for grabs?"

"He's taken," Allison said. "I believe her name is Hester."

"Bring anyone you like," Mary Louise said, before he could comment. "I hope it's going to be a large gathering."

After Pinky left, Gabe had a chance to deny his relationship with Hester, or at least try to minimize it, but he didn't. That was a good sign, Allison assured herself. Maybe he'd decided to stop coming on to *her*.

Suddenly the high went out of the evening. She was tired and she wanted to go home, but Mary Louise was having such a good time that Allison didn't want to spoil her fun.

"I'm so glad we ran into Pinky," Mary Louise said. "I'd like you to get to know her. She's a dear child. Her mother is Sandra Mayhew—at least that's the way I always think of her, only it's Sandra Gresham now. Anyway, she was Monica's best friend. The two girls were inseparable in high school."

Allison felt a shot of adrenaline. "Will Sandra be at the party Saturday night?"

"I certainly hope so. I'll phone her first thing in the morning. Her parents, too. Curtis and Elinor Mayhew are among my oldest friends."

"Oldest in terms of age, or length of time you've known them?" Sergei asked warily. "Your elderly dowager friends always back me into a corner at parties. The last one wanted to talk about the propriety of putting what she considered risqué oriental prints in the bathroom. They always want me to side with them over their husbands."

"You don't have to worry about the Mayhews. They're more apt to talk sports than erotic art. She's an avid golfer, and he's a fine tennis player."

"That's a relief!"

"They're a very attractive couple. I think Curtis is more handsome now than he was as a young man. He's still tall and trim, and he has the most distinguished looking gray hair."

"Are you trying to make me jealous?" Sergei asked.

"Scarcely. Their marriage is of long duration. Although I must say, Curtis was quite a ladies' man in his youth."

"Don't tell me people of your generation played around?" Gabe teased.

"I wasn't implying anything of the sort!" Mary Louise said indignantly. "Curtis was a bit of a flirt, but he didn't mean anything by it. He and Elinor are a very devoted couple."

"I'm sure they are." Gabe's eyes danced with the amusement he was suppressing. "Behind every happy marriage is a discreet husband."

"I don't consider that funny, Gabriel."

"He wasn't trying to be funny," Allison said. "Gabe simply can't conceive of a man being faithful to one woman."

"I thought you said you weren't an authority on men," he drawled.

Noticing the tension between the two, Sergei intervened smoothly. "You ladies are being too hard on the poor boy. Where is your sense of humor?"

"I'm sorry." Mary Louise smiled ruefully. "Evidently I'm not as 'with it' as I supposed."

"You're doing fine. Would you like anything else to eat?"

"Not another bite. But what is in the tall glasses those youngsters are drinking?" she asked.

"I believe they're called Slurpees or Slushies, or something equally descriptive. Would you like one?"

"I shouldn't. I won't sleep all night."

"I'd like to be the cause of that," Sergei said softly.

Mary Louise's cheeks turned pink and she glanced away. "Oh well, why not? You only live once. Let's all have one of those strangely named drinks."

Allison groaned inwardly. She couldn't put another thing in her stomach; it was already knotted with tension. Would this evening ever end?

Mary Louise chattered on happily about the party and who she planned to invite. Finally Sergei suggested they leave.

"If you can't think of any other concoction you'd like to try, I have a rather early appointment in the morning," he said.

They all said good-night in the downstairs hall, but when Allison started to follow Mary Louise up the stairs, Gabe took her arm.

"I want to talk to you," he said.

"It's late and I'm tired," she answered.

"I won't keep you long. I just want to set the record straight." He held on to her arm, preventing her from following the others. "I didn't appreciate that crack in the restaurant. What makes you think I'm promiscuous?"

"Possibly the way you've been coming on to me when you have a fianceé at home." She tried to pull her arm away, but he wouldn't release her. "Don't bother to deny it! Mary Louise told me about Hester, and Martin confirmed the fact at dinner tonight."

"Did either of them tell you I'm engaged?"

"Well, maybe not in so many words, but I didn't need it spelled out for me."

"You just automatically assumed that when the cat's not around, the rat will play," Gabe said sarcastically.

"Isn't that what you're doing with me? Whether you're engaged or not, you're dating some woman back home on a regular basis. This trip might be business, but that doesn't stop you from trying to have a little fun on the side."

"I'm not succeeding spectacularly," he said grimly.

"I'm sorry for being so uncooperative."

"Has anyone ever told you that you're a very infuriating woman?" he rasped.

"Why? Because I prefer not to be your summer amusement?"

"So far, you're more aggravating than amusing. I've never made love to any woman simply because I was bored and she was available."

"Fortunately I'm not. You don't have to worry about spoiling your perfect record."

"In your case I'll make an exception." He jerked her forward and kissed her hard.

Allison tried to push him away, but he wrapped his arms around her, imprisoning her against his taut body. She struggled, uttering little cries of outrage that did no good. All of Gabe's anger was expressed in his punishing kiss.

Gradually, though, his mouth softened against hers. His arms loosened slightly and one hand curved around her nape in a caress rather than a restraint. Allison held herself rigid, trying to resist his potent attraction. But her struggles ceased as he parted her lips for an arousing kiss that made her legs feel boneless. When he deepened the kiss she clung to him mindlessly, aware only of his lithe body pressed against hers. Their hips and thighs were joined as if they were one person—which she suddenly longed to be.

Gabe finally dragged his mouth away and buried his face in her hair, still holding her close. Allison knew she should move away, but her body didn't agree. This was what she'd known it would be like—only it was even better.

Gabe was the one who ended it. Placing his hands on her shoulders, he put her away firmly. "Go to bed, Allison."

For a moment she stared at him in bewilderment at his harsh tone. Perhaps she *had* provoked him, but after his initial anger faded, didn't that kiss mean anything to him? Was she the only one who entered a magic kingdom?

Allison averted her head and turned toward the stairs. Gabe had really paid her back for her accusation. He showed her how easy it would be for him to score if he felt like it. And then he pushed her away to show he didn't want to.

"Good night, Allison." Gabe's voice was gentle now.

Why not? He'd proved his point. She ran up the stairs without answering.

Chapter Five

Allison had intended to skip breakfast the next day, to avoid meeting Gabe. But when she peeked cautiously into the morning room before slipping past into the garden, Mary Louise was sitting alone at the table.

She glanced up and smiled. "Good morning, dear. Did you have as good a time as I did last night?"

"I...yes, it was a lot of fun." Allision had trouble getting the lie out, considering how the evening had ended.

"I've been on the phone for hours inviting people to the party, and I'm happy to say most of them can come."

"Including Monica's friend, Sandra?" Allison asked casually.

"Yes, and her parents, too, *my* contemporaries. I must say this is a revelation to me. I've always planned these affairs weeks in advance. It took endless conferences with the caterer and the florist, not to mention with my own staff over what china to use and what wine to serve—although Peter always handled that. Everything had to be perfect, especially when he was alive. Suddenly I've discovered that you don't need engraved invitations sent a month ahead, and if there are a few mishaps it won't be a tragedy."

"Welcome to the world of reality." Allison smiled.

"I must seem like a very shallow woman to you."

"Not at all! I didn't mean to imply anything of the kind. You do a lot of good with your money. Why shouldn't you enjoy it, too?"

"You've brought a breath of fresh air into my life. I'm so glad you came," Mary Louise said impulsively.

"I am, too, but time is flying by and we haven't discussed my reason for being here. We really have to talk about Monica."

"I suppose so, but not today. Let's wait until after the party."

"I'll have to leave right afterward," Allison said helplessly.

"Not so soon! You've only been here a few days."

"It will be almost a week on Saturday."

"Can't you ask for more time off from your job?"

"It won't get any less painful to have our talk. I realize you'd rather not believe your daughter had an illegitimate child, but—"

"That would be hurtful, certainly. But what I find difficult to accept is the idea that Monica didn't feel she could confide in me."

"Perhaps she felt you'd be disappointed in her. Teenagers don't always think clearly, especially in circumstances that are traumatic. Maybe she felt she was doing the adult thing by handling it herself."

"We'll never know now." Mary Louise sighed.

"Not what went on in her mind, but we need to find out what happened to her baby. It can have an impact on both our lives. The only person I can think of who might give us the answer is the father of Monica's child."

"You think he'd admit to anything after letting her go through an experience like that all alone?" Mary Louise asked indignantly.

"Somebody must have helped her—with money, if nothing else. The hospital had to be paid."

"Monica had a trust fund from her grandmother. Money wouldn't have been a problem."

Allison refused to let herself become disheartened. "Okay, but she couldn't come and go as she pleased at seventeen. You said she was away at private schools and camps much of the time. She couldn't have left there for a period of months without your knowing, could she?"

"No."

Something in the tone of Mary Louise's voice made Allison look at her sharply. "You don't sound so sure."

"Monica went through a rebellious period when she was seventeen," Mary Louise said slowly. "She broke a number of rules and the school said they couldn't deal with her. I'm sure she was simply influenced by some of the older girls. I wanted to enroll her in another school, but Peter said Monica needed a firmer hand. He sent her to stay with his sister and hired private tutors to come to the house. Poor Monica. It must have seemed like a prison. My sister-in-law was a joyless person. We didn't get along very well." Mary Louise's smile was more of a grimace. "Jane considered me frivolous."

Allison had a premonition. "Where does your sister-in-law live?"

"She died many years ago." After a pause, Mary Louise said, "She lived in Philadelphia."

Allison felt a flash of triumph that she attempted to mask in deference to the older woman's feelings. "All of these things can't be dismissed as coincidence. Do you honestly doubt that somehow or other, Monica had a baby without your knowing about it?"

"No, I suppose I have to agree with you. The possibility occurred to me when Martin said you were born in Philadelphia. He took it as proof that Monica couldn't be your mother, but I began to wonder. That could have been the reason Peter sent her to his sister's for six months and refused to let me contact her. It would have been like him to tidy up the mess without telling me."

"I'm sorry," Allison said in a muted voice.

"I am, too. It's a difficult thing to forgive, but dwelling on it would be futile. My regret now is the years I missed with my grandchild."

"Then help me find out the rest of the story. You don't want to waste any more time." Allison was in the strange position of hedging on her own parentage, something she was almost sure of. But it would be cruel to raise Mary Louise's expectations if there was a chance she was wrong.

The older woman gazed at her silently for a long moment. When she finally answered, it wasn't directly. "Sons are wonderful, but I was so thrilled when I had a daughter, too. I looked forward to sharing all of Monica's little triumphs. I thought we'd go shopping for her prom dress and giggle together about her boyfriends. It didn't happen that way. When I watched my friends with *their* daughters, I realized what a failure I was.''

"Oh, no! You're being too hard on yourself.''

Mary Louise shook her head. "I was an excellent wife but a terrible mother. I allowed my husband to make all the decisions concerning the children. I don't think Monica ever forgave me for it.''

"Your husband was a very strong man,'' Allison said diffidently.

"And I never challenged him, even when I felt he was wrong. It wasn't until after Peter was gone that I grew into a person in my own right. It's too late to make things up to my children, but I've been given a second chance. I don't intend to make the same mistakes this time.''

"I can understand how you feel. That's why it's important to know who the father of Monica's baby was. He's the only one who can tell us what happened to it.''

"Perhaps he didn't know.''

"I can hardly believe that. It was his child, too, even if it was an inconvenient accident. After the baby was put up for adoption and he was off the hook, he had to be curious about it. If only to be sure it wouldn't turn into his liability. Our problem is tracking him down.''

"Sometimes it's best to let sleeping dogs lie.'' Mary Louise held up her hand as Allison opened her mouth to protest. "Allow me the pleasure of believing I have a grandchild.''

"But you *do* have! We just agreed on that. Don't you want to know who she is?''

"You've made a very convincing case for yourself.''

"Suppose I'm wrong?''

"I prefer to believe you're not,'' Mary Louise answered calmly. "All my life I've been sensible and predictable. Just for once I want to indulge myself. And if my dream turns out to be a fantasy, well, I haven't lost anything, have I?'' She pushed back her chair. "Excuse me, my dear. I have to invite a few more people to the party. I don't dare phone some of my friends before eleven.''

Allison remained lost in thought. In a way she understood Mary Louise's reluctance to face reality, but without the older woman's cooperation, how could she ever arrive at the truth?

Gabe hesitated in the entry for a moment before coming in. "You look as if you're wrestling with a weighty problem," he commented.

"I am."

"Anything I can do to help?"

Allison had been so involved in her thoughts that she'd forgotten about the state of warfare between them. She was suddenly reminded of it. "You don't solve problems, you create them," she answered with a scowl.

"For what it's worth, I'm sorry about last night."

"You should be! I'd made it clear that your advances weren't welcome."

"I'm not sorry about kissing you. It was a revelation." He grinned. "Under that prim exterior, you're a very warm, passionate woman."

She couldn't deny her response, inexplicable as it was. "Then what are you apologizing for?"

"I shouldn't have overreacted when you accused me of being a womanizer."

"So, you're admitting it."

"No, I am not." He bit off each word. "I'm merely saying I should have laughed it off. Anybody who knows me, realizes it isn't true."

"Does that include the women you hit on?"

"Are you *trying* to start another argument?" Gabe came nearer and leaned over her, gripping both arms of the chair. "If you want me to kiss you, just ask. It isn't necessary to provoke me. Unless it makes you feel better to pretend I forced myself on you. Is that it?"

"You did!"

"At first, maybe, then I got enthusiastic cooperation."

"You're a very experienced man," she said defensively. "You know how to make a woman respond to you. That doesn't mean I wanted to."

"Let me get this straight. You enjoyed kissing me, but you're not happy about it?"

"Well, of course I—I mean, I didn't—" She paused and drew a deep breath. "You're just trying to mix me up."

"I don't believe I'm responsible for that." His expression gentled as he traced the curve of her cheek with a long forefinger. "I think you're afraid to show any honest emotion because too many people have let you down in the past."

Mary Louise entered the room scanning some sheets of paper in her hand. Gabe straightened up and Allison rose gratefully from the chair. Her pulse was racing, and she had the uncomfortable feeling that he knew it.

"Good morning, Gabriel," Mary Louise said when she glanced up and noticed him. "We missed you at breakfast."

"I decided to go jogging instead." He patted his flat midsection. "Had to work off that pizza from last night."

"You must be ravenous. I'll have Armand fix you something."

"Don't bother, I'll have an early lunch."

"Have you and Allison made plans?" Mary Louise asked tentatively.

"No." Allison spoke up before Gabe could. "I thought I'd go shopping in the village."

The older woman brightened. "That's just what I was going to suggest! Would you like company?"

"I'd welcome it."

"Splendid. I'll get my purse."

Allison started to follow her out of the room, not wanting to be left alone with Gabe. "I need to get mine, too."

As she walked by him, he murmured, "You can run, but you can't hide."

Allison was disturbed by her instant reaction every time Gabe touched her. The man was awesome! Bruce had never elicited such a response, but that was because she never really loved him. Not that she loved Gabe! That would really be letting herself in for heartbreak.

Allison tried to put the whole thing out of her mind for the afternoon and give Mary Louise her full attention. The older woman was so delighted to be with her. They wandered in and out of shops where Mary Louise urged Allison to buy everything she looked at, however briefly.

"I don't really need any casual clothes," Allison said. "What I'm looking for is a dress to wear to the party."

"They don't carry many dressy clothes. This is strictly a resort area. A lot of these shops close when the season is over."

"I'd better find *something,* or I'll be the only one there in jeans."

"I'm sure it won't come to that. If you don't find anything, you can always wear something of Monica's. I haven't gotten around to giving away the clothes she left here when she visited."

Before Allison could answer, Mary Louise was distracted by an outfit on a mannequin. It was a white handkerchief linen skirt paired with a matching strapless top that had rows of vertical ruffles separated by lines of faggoting. The outfit was pulled together by a gold sash, wrapped and tied in a bow.

"You'd look adorable in that," Mary Louise exclaimed.

"I wouldn't have anyplace to wear it at home."

"But you'd get a lot of use out of it while you're here."

Allison's eyebrows rose when she looked at the price tag. "I'd have to wear it day and night to get my money's worth."

"You must let me buy it for you."

"Oh, no! I wasn't hinting."

"I know you weren't, my dear. I want to."

She was so insistent that Allison had to give in. While the clerk was wrapping the package, an attractive older woman in golf clothes entered the shop. She and Mary Louise greeted each other fondly.

"You're the last person I'd expect to find out shopping," Mary Louise remarked.

"As you can see, I just came from the golf course." The woman laughed.

Mary Louise introduced her to Allison. "You've heard me speak of Elinor. This is Sandra's mother and Pinky's grandmother."

"That makes me feel positively matriarchal," Elinor said.

Was the woman's smile perfunctory, or was she just imagining things, Allison wondered? Elinor was certainly examining her closely. Could Martin be correct, for once? Had the reason for her visit spread all over town? No doubt. The Van Ruyder servants knew. That's all it would take.

After a few minutes of small talk, the two older women began to discuss a friend's operation. Allison murmured an excuse and went next door to a gift shop she'd noticed. It was a cut above the usual T-shirt and souvenir stores. In a corner was a group of canvases by local artists.

One in particular caught Allison's eye. It was a small oil painting of a woman sitting on a daisy-filled lawn with a group of little girls gathered around her in a semicircle. Allison was charmed by it, and she had a feeling Mary Louise would be, too. She gave it to her when they were seated in a tearoom.

"You didn't have to buy me a present," Mary Louise objected.

"I wanted to. There's no law that says you have to wait till after you go home to send a hostess gift," Allison said lightly.

"I wish you wouldn't talk about going home."

"All right, but open your package. I hope you like it, but the shop owner said it's exchangeable. If you'd prefer something else, my feelings won't be hurt."

Mary Louise's eyes were misty as she gazed at the small canvas. "Oh, my dear, I love it! This is the most thoughtful present I've ever received."

That afternoon together stirred strong feelings in both women. Allison wanted to know what happened to Monica's child as much for Mary Louise's sake now, as her own. The subject wasn't mentioned for the rest of the day, though. They talked and laughed like two old friends—or close relatives.

Martin was less than pleased when he noticed the change in his mother's attitude from that day on. Allison couldn't worry about him, though. She was having too much trouble trying to stay away from Gabe, which was proving to be virtually impossible. Mary Louise, quite innocently, kept throwing them together. She had so many details to take care of for the party that it didn't leave her with much free time.

"I don't want you to get bored," she said, after suggesting that Gabe take Allison to see some of the other Great Houses.

"I'd rather stay here and help you," Allison pleaded.

"There's really nothing you can do, dear. Run along and have fun with Gabe."

"Shall we be on our way, then?" he asked. Only the sardonic expression on his face betrayed his amusement.

"I suppose so." Allison suppressed a sigh, following him outside.

"Your enthusiasm is underwhelming," he remarked as he helped her into the car. "Sydney Carton was more cheerful on the way to the guillotine."

"That's because he knew his punishment would be swift."

"Do you honestly think I want to make you unhappy?" Gabe leaned over her for a moment, examining her flawless features. "You really *don't* know much about men." He walked around to the driver's side before she could answer.

They rode in silence for a while. But when Allison noticed that they seemed to be heading out of town she said, "Where are we going? Aren't most of the houses along Bellevue Avenue?"

"I thought we'd go to Green Animals instead. It's in Portsmouth on the shores of Narragansett Bay. This is the only one of the Preservation properties that isn't actually in Newport."

She was intrigued in spite of herself. "Why would anybody name a house Green Animals?"

"The name refers to a topiary garden begun in the eighteen hundreds by a man named Thomas Brayton. His daughter gave it that name."

"Doesn't topiary mean the practice of clipping bushes into geometric shapes?"

"It started that way with the mazes you still see in Europe. But Brayton took the art a step further. His seven acres of gardens are filled with boxwood shrubs pruned and trained into animal shapes like an ostrich and a unicorn, among others."

"It sounds fascinating."

"I think you'll find it unique. It's one of the few topiary gardens in this country."

Gabe's description didn't begin to do the place justice. Allison exclaimed over the perfectly sculpted camel and elephant whose smooth shapes were formed by carefully clipped bushes. Across a formal garden bordered by low boxwood hedges, a boar and a bear faced each other, both on raised, circular green platforms made from the same kind of bushes.

"What's that one supposed to be?" Allison seized Gabe's hand and pulled him along. "It looks like a giraffe, but its neck is too short."

"You're right, it's a giraffe. Originally the neck was longer, but it was damaged in the 1950s by a hurricane. In the interest of safety, the neck was shortened. It takes several years for a topiary figure to reach maturity, and pieces damaged by the weather can take many seasons to recover."

"That would make this giraffe over forty years old," she marveled.

Gabe had slipped his arm casually around her shoulders. "That's older than you are."

"I hope I'll be in as good shape when I reach that age. Although, probably not. I don't have as many people taking care of me." She turned a laughing face up to him.

"Poor little Allison. You've never had *anybody* to take care of you."

She was suddenly aware of his arm around her and the deepened quality of his voice. Moving out of his embrace she said lightly, "It builds character. There's something to be said for knowing you can make it on your own."

"But it's a lot nicer to curl up in somebody's arms at the end of a long hard day."

"I'll have to take your word for it."

"I could show you if you'd let me," he murmured.

"Don't you ever give up?" she asked in exasperation. "We were getting along fine for a change. Why do you insist on spoiling things?"

"I'm trying to make them better." He smiled.

"For whom? Certainly not me!"

"That's not true. I have a feeling you've never met a man who appreciated you. I'd like to make love to you the way you deserve, with caring and tenderness." He cupped her chin in his palm and tilted her face up. "I want to undress you slowly and kiss every inch of your beautiful body. And when you hold out your arms to me, I want to gather you close and satisfy you completely."

Allison was powerless to move away, hypnotized by his sensuous voice. She could imagine everything he was describing—and all the things he'd left out. His scorching mouth stringing kisses across her breasts, his seductive hands, searching out every vulnerable part of her.

Mercifully a voice broke the spell. "Excuse me, can I get through?" They were standing in the middle of the path and a gardener wanted to get by with his equipment.

Allison hadn't even heard the man approaching. That was how completely Gabe engrossed her. But it had to stop. She turned to face him squarely.

"I suppose it's too much to appeal to your better nature, but I'm going to try. Could you please knock it off? I'll only be here for a few more days."

He gazed at her speculatively. "I might be open to a deal. Can I see you when we both get back to New York?"

"Why not? The three of us can pal around together."

"I'm not engaged to Hester," Gabe said quietly.

Even if that were true, it didn't make him any more accessible. Allison faced the fact that she could easily fall in love with Gabe. Her attraction to him was more than merely physical. She enjoyed just being with him. He made every minute together special.

But no meaningful relationship could ever develop between them. Gabe came from the same social background as the Van Ruyders. His parents would be just as opposed to her as Bruce's parents had been. Only this time more than her pride would be hurt.

Gabe interrupted her reverie. "It's taking you a long time to make up your mind."

"Why don't we just play it by ear?" she answered evasively.

Gabe was on his good behavior after that and Allison relaxed and enjoyed his company while she could. It wouldn't be for much longer, she thought wistfully.

He took her to Marble House, the result of William Vanderbilt's instructions to build "the very best living accommodations that money can buy." The eleven-million-dollar house was Newport's most ornate and expensive "cottage."

Rosecliff, where *The Great Gatsby* was filmed, rivaled it in opulence. "Just think, I could be walking in the exact spot where Robert Redford walked," Allison said.

"You could be following in the footsteps of a lot of illustrious people," Gabe said. "The house changed hands several times after the original owners died."

She gazed around the eighty-foot-long ballroom with its French marble mantelpiece and crystal and ormolu chandeliers. "How could so many people have so much money?"

"They didn't have to pay taxes. The income tax wasn't introduced until 1913."

"They were still tycoons. Even if I didn't have to pay taxes, all I could afford to build would be a birdhouse."

"They do say money isn't everything." Gabe chuckled.

"Those are the people who already have it."

The remaining days until the party flew by since Allison spent them with Gabe. He was a charming companion and for once, there was no friction between them.

On Friday, the day before the party, Gabe suggested going to the country club for a change of pace, but Allison declined. They were having breakfast with Mary Louise and Sergei.

"I absolutely have to buy a dress today. The party is tomorrow! It's already the last minute."

"I really don't think you're going to find anything," Mary Louise said. "Why don't you look through Monica's things? She had excellent taste in clothes."

"I'm sure she did, but I wouldn't feel right about it."

"It would please me very much, my dear," Mary Louise said quietly.

After her protests proved futile, Allison allowed herself to be persuaded. With mixed emotions, she followed Mary Louise up the stairs and into Monica's room.

The closet in the large bedroom was crammed with clothes. Monica must have had an unbelievable wardrobe if these were the things she left at Rosewood Manor for infrequent visits.

Mary Louise pushed aside a group of long, glamorous gowns. "We don't need to bother with these, since the party will be quite informal."

Allison wasn't convinced. She'd seen the preparations going on all over the house. Florists had turned the ballroom into an indoor garden and banked the entry with masses of blossoms. If that was casual, what would a formal party be like? She decided to let her hostess make the selection.

"Either of these would do." Mary Louise glanced from a short green chemise with billowy organdy sleeves, to a pair of white silk pants with a navy organza tank top. The accompanying jacket was edged in gold braid in a sunburst pattern. "Does either one appeal to you?"

"They're both gorgeous." Allison's attention was riveted on the pantsuit with longing. "I'd be hesitant about wearing the white one, though. I'm afraid I'd spill something on it."

"White silk always has to be cleaned after every wearing. Don't give it another thought."

"Well, if you're really sure." Allison touched the luxurious fabric gently. "I'm just afraid it might bring back memories for you."

Mary Louise's face was expressionless. "Many things remind me of my daughter. This will be one of the happier ones."

On the night of the party Allison took special care with her appearance. Monica's pants and jacket fit Allison perfectly, though the top was a little large. Her high, firm breasts were evidently smaller than the generously endowed Monica.

Other than that, Allison was quite happy with how she looked. The elegant outfit made her look chic and glamorous—as though she actually belonged here. Telling herself not to indulge in foolish fantasies, she sprayed herself with perfume and went downstairs where the family was already gathered.

Gabe's reaction was the one that mattered to Allison and it was most satisfactory. His eyes gleamed as they roamed from her long black hair and finely boned face, to her curved figure. "I won't be able to get near you tonight."

"You have enough girlfriends," Mary Louise chided. "Let the other young men have a chance."

"Thanks a lot," Gabe said wryly.

The guests started arriving soon after, dozens of them. Allison was introduced to so many people that she stopped trying to remember all the names. The one she was most interested in meeting was Sandra Gresham, Monica's best friend.

Allison was chatting with Pinky and a group of her friends when Pinky remarked, "There's my mother and dad." She waved at a couple entering the room.

Sandra was a fashionably thin woman, poised and expensively dressed. Her jewelry was impressive but tasteful, and her hair and nails were perfect. She had everything privilege could confer, yet her expression was faintly dissatisfied.

When Pinky introduced Allison, Sandra's gaze sharpened. "I heard Mary Louise had a houseguest."

"Allison is from New York," Pinky volunteered. "I told her we'd have to get together in the city. She works at Maison Blanc, which isn't far from my office."

Sandra's attention remained riveted on Allison. "How did you happen to come to Newport?"

Allison hesitated for only an instant. "I'd never been here before and I'd heard so much about the area."

"How do you know Mary Louise? I've never heard her mention you before."

"Really, Mother," Pinky protested. "You're giving the poor girl the third degree."

"I'm sure Allison realizes I'm only expressing friendly interest," Sandra answered smoothly. "Besides, people with nothing to hide don't mind answering questions. Isn't that right, my dear?"

"Absolutely." Allison was puzzled by the woman's covert hostility, but she managed a smile.

"So how *do* you know Mary Louise?"

"We met rather unexpectedly and she invited me for a visit." That could have taken place at any time, Allison thought.

"How nice for you. Are you staying all summer?"

"Oh, no, I have to get back to my job."

"Too bad you don't work for your dad." Pinky grinned.

"Who *is* your father?" Sandra asked casually. "Perhaps I know your family."

"I'm an orphan. I'm afraid I never knew who my parents were."

"That's unfortunate, but it can't make any difference at this stage of your life."

Allison was startled by the raw emotion on the older woman's face. It was almost like hatred, although how could that be? "I guess everybody in my situation wonders about their background," she said slowly.

"Maybe you're better off not knowing. Did you ever think of that?"

"I don't agree," Pinky said. "Anybody would be curious, if nothing else."

"That's not reason enough to dwell on something that happened a long time ago. It's pointless to live in the past."

"That's funny coming from you. Mother is the most tradition-bound woman I know," Pinky told Allison. "She still shops in the same stores her mother did—and has the same saleswomen wait on her. She's never changed dry cleaners. She even has the same friends she made in kindergarten!"

That was the opening Allison had been waiting for. "Mary Louise says you were her daughter's best friend," she said to Sandra.

"Is that what she told you? We were friendly for a time, but we drifted apart after high school."

"Have you kept in touch with any of Monica's friends?" Allison asked innocently.

Sandra's smile was unpleasant. "They were mostly male—and usually traumatized after a relationship with her."

"My goodness, that sounds intriguing. Are any of them here tonight?"

"It would be impossible to go anyplace where there aren't. Excuse me, I haven't said hello to my hostess yet."

"I wonder what got into Mother. She's not usually this testy. One of her committee members must have screwed up." Pinky laughed.

Gabe joined them and took Allison's hand. "I believe this is our dance."

She followed him onto the floor, trying to figure out Sandra's behavior. Mary Louise was certainly wrong about the friendship. Sandra detested Monica. Had Monica taken a boyfriend away from her? But surely she wouldn't hold a grudge all these years. And what could she possibly have against *her,* Allison wondered.

"You're very quiet," Gabe commented.

"I just had the strangest meeting with Pinky's mother. She took an instant dislike to me."

"That's hard to believe." Gabe's embrace tightened and his lips brushed her forehead.

She was too distracted to notice. "It's true. I know I didn't imagine it."

"What did she say to you?"

"It was her expression and the tone of her voice as much as anything else. But she asked me a lot of questions about why I was here. I think she knows."

"It wouldn't surprise me. Everybody at the party probably does, too. Servants talk, or Martin might even be responsible. He never knows when to keep his mouth shut. Sandra is probably interested in the gossip, like everybody else."

"It doesn't account for her hostility."

"What you told me doesn't sound too offensive."

"I didn't tell you all of it. She asked about my family, and when I told her I didn't have any she advised me not to go looking for them."

"It could be she's not too fond of *hers*." He grinned.

"I'm serious, Gabe! When I asked if any of Monica's former boyfriends were here tonight, she put me off with a nasty remark. I simply have to find out."

"You think one of them is your father?"

"It's possible. That would explain Sandra's behavior. He could be an old friend from way back. These people don't like anyone to rock the boat. He's undoubtedly married now, and she's afraid I'm going to cause a scandal by making his affair public after all these years."

Gabe's eyes narrowed momentarily. "What *do* you want?"

"Only to talk to him. To find out for sure. I don't want to be a faceless person for the rest of my life."

"A face like yours is a gift from heaven," he said in a husky voice. "But okay, honey, I know what you mean. I'll see what I can find out."

"I'd appreciate it so much. I'm not getting very far on my own."

"This is the first time you've asked for my help."

"It's in your own interest, too. You were sent here to find out the truth about me."

"Does that mean you finally realize I didn't come to do a hatchet job?"

She hesitated. "It doesn't really matter. We have a common goal."

He tipped her chin up and looked deeply into her eyes. "I only wish that were true."

"How can you get romantic when we're finally making progress?" Allison asked impatiently.

"It might have something to do with the perfume you're wearing and the way you fit into my arms," he answered lightly.

"Kindly try to concentrate on what's important."

"That depends on your point of view." He nibbled gently on her ear.

She raised her shoulder to dislodge his mouth. "Be serious, Gabe! We need to circulate and talk to as many people as we can."

"How is that going to help?"

"I don't know. We'll steer the conversation around to Monica and hope they let something slip."

Allison got various reactions, none of them helpful. Mary Louise's friends closed ranks. They were polite, but wary. Did everyone but Monica's mother know what had happened twenty-five years ago? More likely, their reticence was because of her mysterious death. If they knew how it happened, they weren't talking publicly about that, either.

Some of the guests reserved judgment about Allison, but Pinky's grandparents were charming to her. Curtis Mayhew, Elinor's husband, was as dashing as Mary Louise had said. He was still a very handsome man. His tanned face was surprisingly young looking, despite his silvery hair, and his lean physique was a tribute to the amount of tennis he played.

"It's always a pleasure to see a pretty new face," he told Allison jovially. "I hope you plan to be around for a while."

"I'm afraid not," she answered. "This is certainly a wonderful place for a vacation, though."

"I'm trying to persuade her to stay on," Mary Louise said.

"There's a great deal to see," Elinor remarked.

"I know," Allison agreed. "Gabe took me through a lot of the historic houses."

"It was Mary Louise's idea." Gabe chuckled. "I could have been much more creative."

"It's something tourists are required to do before enjoying the things they came for," Curtis said. "Are you a tennis player, my dear?'' he asked Allison. "You're welcome to be my guest at the club anytime."

Sandra joined their group. "Up to your old tricks, Father?" she drawled. "I knew I'd find you with the prettiest new face. He worships youth," she told Allison.

"I wouldn't put it that strongly," Curtis protested mildly. "I don't see anything wrong with enjoying the company of young people, though. You can be certain they won't talk about their arthritis or latest gastric upset."

His wife smiled. "You're so intolerant, darling. Some of us get old and achy. We don't all have your secret of eternal youth."

"Father's secret is the right kind of exercise." Sandra's nasty smile made the innocent remark sound snide.

In just a few moments she'd destroyed the festive mood of the group. Sandra's parents were too well-bred to tell her to knock off whatever was eating her, but Elinor looked pained and Curtis's face was carefully expressionless.

Allison knew she wasn't going to find out anything with Sandra there, and she preferred not to put up with her bad temper. "Will you excuse us?" she asked. "I want to sample some of those great looking hors d'oeuvres."

When they were out of hearing, she said to Gabe, "If that woman were *my* daughter, I'd disown her!"

"She's certainly not a barrel of laughs, is she?" he asked.

"*Now* do you believe she disliked me from the moment we met?"

"I wouldn't take it personally. She obviously has a chip on her shoulder. Maybe she had a fight with her husband before she got here."

"In which case, she should have stayed home."

The evening was great fun, even though Allison didn't find out anything new about Monica. There were long periods when she forgot that was her goal. The times she danced with Gabe, for instance. It felt so right in his arms. When he molded her body to his and rested his lips on her temple she was filled with an aching kind of happiness.

Pinky and her friends weren't a source of information, but Allison enjoyed being with them. They were amusing, and they accepted her without question.

"If you're not doing anything on Monday, why don't you and

Gabe come over to my house for lunch and swimming?'' Pinky suggested.

"I'd love to, but I have to go home no later than Monday. I'm due back on the job Tuesday.''

"You only work a four-day week? I'll have to speak to my father about that,'' Pinky joked.

"When I put in for vacation time I planned on an extra day at home to do the laundry and take my clothes to the cleaners—all those things you have to do after a trip.''

"Too bad. Well, how about tomorrow? A bunch of us are going to the yacht club for some sailing and windsurfing.''

"It sounds great, but I have to wait and find out if Mary Louise has anything planned. Can I let you know?''

"Sure, but not too early.'' Pinky grinned.

The party didn't break up until late, but Allison wasn't a bit tired. She didn't want the night to end.

After the last guest had left, Gabe loosened his tie and said, "Let's get some air. It was hot in there with all those people.''

Allison followed him into the garden, inhaling the rose-scented air. "But wasn't it a glorious evening? I've never been to a party like that. I thought they only existed in the movies.''

"So you think you could get used to this way of life,'' he remarked casually.

"Who couldn't?'' She laughed. "I've almost forgotten about the world of the subway and the supermarket. It's a good thing I'm going home Monday.''

"Without getting what you came for?'' Gabe's face was enigmatic in the filtered moonlight.

"I'm not happy about it, but I don't know what more I can do. Mary Louise won't tell me anything, and I struck out with her friends. I finally convinced her that Monica did have a baby, but maybe it's just too soon for her to want to know all the circumstances. I can only hope that in time she'll want to find out.''

"That kind of leaves you in limbo, doesn't it? Or do you plan to follow up on the other possibilities?''

"No. I don't want to disrupt any more lives. I'm afraid I was only thinking of myself. I didn't realize the kind of heartache I could cause.'' She lowered her head and touched a rosebud gently. "If I never find out who my parents were, people will just have to accept me for what I am."

"I can't imagine anyone rejecting you for any reason." Gabe framed her face in his palms and looked deeply into her eyes. "You're as near perfection as a mortal woman can get."

"Isn't that a little extravagant?" She smiled tentatively, aware of his sudden change of mood.

"It doesn't begin to do you justice," he answered huskily.

Putting his arms around her waist, he drew her close. Allison didn't put up even a token struggle. This might be the last time she was alone with Gabe. She wanted to feel his firm mouth on hers, his urgent body promising more joy than she'd ever known.

"Sweet Allison, you're driving me crazy," he groaned, stringing hungry kisses over her face. "I want to make love to you."

"It's late," she murmured. "We should go to bed."

"You're right." He urged her hips closer to his. "It's inevitable. You know that, don't you?"

"No." Her answer was a faint whisper. The warmth of Gabe's body was lighting a fire deep inside Allison, seducing her will to resist.

"Don't fight it, angel. There's something very powerful between us. I felt it the first day we met." His warm mouth slid down her neck. "Don't tell me you didn't feel it, too?"

"I..." She drew a sharp breath as Gabe's hand curved around her breast. A bolt of electricity jolted through her as his thumb gently circled the sensitive tip, turning her liquid with desire. She clung to him, unable to stand alone.

"You do want me," he said exultantly.

His deep kiss raised the level of excitement almost unbearably. Allison moved against him, uttering tiny sounds of pleasure. As his hand slipped under the hem of her tank top and she reached up to unbutton his shirt, Mary Louise called to them from the house.

"Gabriel, will you lock up when you and Allison come inside? I'm going to bed."

Her voice brought Allison back to reality with a jolt. She averted her face and moved out of Gabe's arms. How could she have gotten so carried away? In another moment she would have made love to him right there in the garden!

"Allison? Are you two still out there?" Mary Louise called again.

"Yes, we...we're coming right in," Allison answered hastily.

Gabe put his hand on her arm. "Don't go. We can't leave it like this."

She took a deep breath to steady herself. "What almost happened would have been a mistake. I'm very attracted to you, but I don't do this sort of thing."

"This sort of thing?" He gripped her shoulders hard. "I want to make love to you, not just have sex!"

She gazed up at him uncertainly. "I wish I could believe that."

"Who made you too afraid to believe somebody could care about you? All men aren't like him."

"Good night, children," Mary Louise called. "I'm going upstairs."

"Wait! I'll go with you." Allison practically ran toward the house.

For just a moment she'd teetered on the brink—until Gabe reminded her of Bruce. She'd believed him, too. When would she ever learn?

Gabe didn't try to stop her. When she looked back she saw that he remained motionless, staring after her. In the moonlight his features looked carved out of stone.

Chapter Six

Gabe's attitude changed drastically after the emotionally charged incident in the garden. When Allison joined him and the others at breakfast on Sunday morning, he glanced up and smiled sardonically.

"There she is, last night's winner," he said with veiled sarcasm.

"Everybody did find her adorable. I got so many nice comments," Mary Louise said happily, unaware of his true meaning.

Sergei was more astute. He glanced covertly at the young pair. "It was a nice party, but I think we were all a little tired at the end."

"Not me. I could have partied all night if I'd had somebody to keep me company," Gabe said. "I almost had Allison convinced, but she chickened out on me."

"You young people never know when to go to bed," Mary Louise commented.

"Don't include Allison," Gabe drawled. "She was a good girl."

Fortunately Mary Louise rang the bell to summon the maid.

'What would you like for breakfast?" she asked Allison. "On Sundays we dispense with the buffet."

"Just coffee will be fine," Allison said.

"You have to eat something. Try one of Armand's mushroom omelets. They're delicious."

"All right, that sounds good."

Allison would have agreed to anything. She just wanted to finish breakfast and get out of there. Gabe was only warming up with those hidden barbs and mocking amusement. Things were bound to get worse. He had the upper hand because he knew she couldn't snap back at him.

Sergei tried to lighten the tension by talking about last night's party. Mary Louise joined in and for a short, blessed time, Gabe behaved himself.

Allison was trying to force down some of her omelet when Anita came to tell her she had a telephone call.

"Bring her the cordless phone," Mary Louise instructed. "Her eggs will get cold if she takes it in the other room."

The call was from Pinky. "I'm going to leave for the club in fifteen minutes, so I thought I'd better call you. Are you coming?"

"I haven't talked to Mary Louise yet," Allison said.

"About what, dear?" the older woman asked.

"I wondered if you had any plans for today—some that included me, I mean."

"Sergei and I plan to spend a relaxing day by the pool. You're welcome to join us of course, if you have nothing else to do."

"Pinky and her friends are going to the Yacht Club," Allison said tentatively.

"Then by all means go with them. You'll have a lovely time."

After Allison had accepted, Pinky said, "The invitation includes Gabe, too."

Allison gave him a quick glance before lowering her voice and turning away slightly. "He might have something else to do."

"You won't know until you ask him."

"I'd rather not. He might think he has to accept."

Allison's furtive behavior automatically drew Gabe's attention, leaving no doubt that she was discussing him. "If you're talking about me, don't worry. I'm willing to take a chance on anything.

Unlike some people." Raising his voice he said, "Tell Pinky I'd be delighted to come."

His voice carried, as he expected it to. "That's great!" Pinky said. "Don't hurry. I'll see you when you get there."

Allison's mood was stormy as she changed into her bathing suit and pulled on jeans and a T-shirt over it. By the time she went downstairs where Gabe was already waiting, she was spoiling for a fight. It was hard to contain herself until they were in the car driving away.

"This is a good day for surfing," he remarked. "Just enough wind."

"How can you sit there and make small talk after the way you acted?" she demanded.

"Which time? I seem to have committed a lot of indiscretions with you."

"You certainly have, but I was referring to breakfast this morning. Why didn't you come right out and tell Mary Louise and Sergei what happened last night?"

"Because nothing did. It would have made a very dull story."

"Aren't you a little old to sulk?" Allison asked caustically. "You must have been a real brat when someone tried to take away your teddy bear."

"Actually I was very generous with my toys. But I did get a little cranky when somebody raised my expectations with no intention of gratifying them."

"Are you implying that I'm a tease?" she asked indignantly. "*You're* the one who wouldn't stop coming on to *me!* I told you I wasn't interested."

"That wasn't the message I got in the garden last night."

She turned her head away and stared out of the window, unable to deny it. "Last night was a mistake," she said in a low voice.

"What's the matter, Allison, did I almost make you lose sight of your goal?"

"I don't know what you're talking about."

"It's always nice to have a contingency plan in case your first one doesn't work out. In one of your few moments of honesty, you admitted to a hankering for the good life. If you can't make your claim to be Monica's daughter stick, you can always marry a wealthy man. There were plenty of them there last night. You're missing a bet by not putting me on the list, though. I'm not exactly poor.''

"You are absolutely loathsome!"

"I have to agree. A gentleman doesn't try to force a lady to admit the truth.''

"Is that why you insisted on coming today? To make sure I don't get my hooks into some poor unsuspecting millionaire's son?''

"Why else would I be here?'' Gabe's face was impassive.

"You could have saved yourself the trouble. Even *I'm* not tricky enough to snare my victim in one day. That's all I have, since I'm going home tomorrow.''

"I'll believe *that* when I see it, too. I don't think this week will ever end,'' he said grimly.

"I'm sorry you're not enjoying yourself,'' she said sarcastically. "*I* am. You've no idea how much fun it is to have someone harass you constantly.''

"You haven't exactly made *my* life a garden of earthly delights, either.''

Allison had an instant flashback to a moonlit garden and Gabe's hands caressing her body. His mouth wasn't compressed into a thin line then. It had been warm and seductive against hers. How completely she'd been fooled. This was how he really felt about her.

Gabe's expression softened as he glanced over at her averted face. "May I make a suggestion? How about a truce for today? We can resume hostilities tomorrow on the way to the airport.''

"I'd like that—I mean, the part about the truce.''

He reached over and took her hand. "Okay, it's a deal. No more recriminations.''

Allison was relieved as they drove into the entrance to the yacht club, even if it was only a temporary respite. Gabe's opinion of her shouldn't matter, but it did—and there was nothing she could do to change it. She stole a look at his handsome profile. At least this last day with him wouldn't be marred by bitterness.

Pinky and her friends were milling around the big lounge deciding who wanted to go sailing and who preferred windsurfing.

She and the people who had been at the previous night's party welcomed the newcomers exuberantly. They were all vocal about how much they'd enjoyed themselves.

"You see what you missed by frolicking out in Hollywood with all those starlets?" Pinky said to a handsome blond young man. "Stu just flew in this morning," she explained to Allison. "Meet Stuart Harrison the Third."

"Stop trying to make me sound stuffy." He took Allison's hand and held onto it. "I'm really a fun guy. Please call me Stu."

"Is that a name, or a perpetual condition?" Gabe asked.

"Gabe, old man!" Stuart clapped him on the shoulder. "I haven't seen you in a dog's age. How the heck are you?"

"Still working for a living. We can't all live on our trust funds."

Gabe's voice had a slight edge. It wasn't difficult to deduce that he didn't care much for Stuart. Allison found him amusing, though. The fuss Stuart made over her was flattering, too.

"Hey, I'm doing a service to the economy." Stuart laughed. "Why should I take a job from somebody who really needs it?"

"That's very noble, but how much call is there for a guy whose greatest talent is mixing a perfect martini?" Pinky joked.

"Do you want the art to die out?" Stuart chuckled.

"Are we going sailing, or are we going to stick around here all day?" one of the young men demanded.

"I vote for sailing." Candace Weatherby linked her arm with Gabe's. She was a curvy blonde with big brown eyes and a sensuous mouth. "How would you like to crew for me?"

"You make it sound very tempting." He gazed down at her and smiled.

"Okay, that takes care of Gabe," Pinky said. "How about you, Allison? Do you want to crew or windsurf?"

"I'm afraid I've never done either one. Couldn't I just go along for the ride?"

"Sure, I guess so," Pinky answered after a moment's hesitation.

"That puts an extra person on somebody's boat," Candace objected. "If we're going to race, we have to give that boat some kind of advantage."

"I didn't realize it would be a problem," Allison said. "Go ahead with your race. I'll just watch and cheer everybody on."

"That wouldn't be much fun for you," Pinky said.

"I'll take Allison on my boat, and you don't have to give me a handicap," Stuart said.

Allison grew increasingly embarrassed at the fuss she was causing as everyone joined in the discussion, offering various solutions.

Gabe settled the matter decisively. "I'll give Allison a wind-surfing lesson while the rest of you race."

"You're supposed to crew for me." Candace pouted.

"I'll make it up to you," he promised with a melting smile.

Allison's gratitude toward him evaporated. After they left the others and were walking toward the beach she said, "You didn't have to baby-sit me. I would have been okay on my own."

"That wouldn't have been polite. None of us would have been comfortable about leaving you out."

Allison was annoyed to discover she was an obligation. "You didn't have to be a martyr and volunteer," she said stiffly.

"What makes you think it was a duty?"

"What else could it be? You had the chance to go sailing with a buxom blonde."

Gabe grinned. "She *is* rather well endowed."

"I certainly can't compete in *that* department—even if I wanted to." Allison pulled her T-shirt over her head and flung it on the sand. Underneath she was wearing a relatively modest blue tank suit, the color of her stormy eyes.

His gaze was appraising as she unzipped her jeans and cast those aside, too. "Quality is as important as quantity."

"You don't have to be polite," she said curtly. "I know my own shortcomings."

"I can't see that you have any—except for a very short fuse."

Allison was suddenly ashamed of herself. Gabe had put his own pleasure aside for her, and she was behaving like a shrew. All because she was jealous of Candace. Why not admit it? To herself, at least.

"I'm sorry," she murmured. "I don't know why I'm always so defensive. I guess old habits die hard."

Gabe's expression was gentle as he gazed at her bowed head. "You can relax, honey, you're among friends."

That was the best he had to offer her, Allison thought poignantly. But it was better than nothing.

She didn't have time to dwell on it after Gabe started to teach her to windsurf. It was a lot harder than it looked. He was very patient, but after half an hour she hadn't made much progress. The board was slippery and she had trouble keeping her balance.

"Hold onto the mast and shift your weight when the board tilts." He was positioned behind her with one arm around her waist.

"Easy for *you* to say," she panted. "This thing is as unpredictable as the stock market."

"Don't worry, I won't let you fall off." His arm tightened as a swell lifted the board.

Allison was suddenly conscious of their closely contoured bodies, locked together spoon fashion. The intimate feeling of Gabe's bare chest against her equally bare back brought visions of a different kind of coupling. The clean, salty smell of his skin worked as a kind of added aphrodisiac. She rested her head on his solid shoulder and tilted her head to look up at his strong features.

"Hey, pay attention or we—" The laughing complaint broke off sharply. His breath caught as he gazed at her lambent face.

Almost in slow motion, his head descended, blotting out the sunshine. But his mouth supplied all the warmth Allison would ever need. She parted her lips, welcoming the sensuous invasion of his tongue. Gabe shifted her in his arms, wrapping her so closely to his taut frame that she was unmistakably aware of his desire. Her own desire rose joyously to meet it.

For one exquisite moment they were oblivious to everything except each other. Then a gust of air filled the sail, causing the board to heel sharply. They were pitched off, still clasped in a heated embrace.

The cool water brought Allison to her senses. She bobbed to the surface, coughing and sputtering.

Gabe surfaced beside her. "Are you all right?"

"Yes, I...I guess I lost my grip on the mast."

"Windsurfing takes concentration," he said softly, reaching out to brush the wet hair off her forehead. "What distracted you?"

"Nothing, I...my arms got tired."

"Why is it so difficult for you to admit your feelings?"

"I just did. I told you. I got tired." She started to swim for shore. "I've had enough instruction for today."

Gabe stared after her for a moment. "I've almost given up hope of ever teaching you anything," he muttered under his breath.

When they got back to the clubhouse, Allison was relieved to find the others had returned also. During the general milling around it was easy to distance herself from Gabe.

He didn't seem to mind. Possibly because Candace made a beeline for him. That made up for any disappointment he might have suffered, Allison thought waspishly. He was giving the curvy blonde the same seductive smile he'd used on *her*.

Allison turned abruptly to the man standing next to her. "Who won the race?" she asked.

"*I* did, naturally." Stuart's teasing smile took the arrogance out of his statement.

"Then it's lucky Gabe took me off your hands."

"I would gladly have settled for last place if I'd had *you* aboard."

"You don't really mean that. I'll bet you hate to lose."

"Everybody does, but I give it my best effort when the prize is a beautiful woman. How involved are you and Gabe?"

"Not at all."

Stuart looked skeptical. "He brought you here today. You're both staying at Rosewood Manor."

"That's why we drove over together. Does it look like we're involved?" Allison waved negligently at the couple across the room. They were engaged in what looked like an intimate conversation.

"I guess I jumped to conclusions."

"Obviously. Gabe and I don't even get along very well."

"The man's a fool if he doesn't appreciate you."

"You can't win 'em all," she answered lightly.

"Since Gabe is out of the picture, how about a date tonight? There's a dance at the country club every Sunday."

"Well…" She glanced over again at the other couple. This was her last night in Newport and she'd counted on spending it with Gabe—frustrating though it might be.

"I see." Stuart raised an eyebrow. "You two are a little more involved than you're admitting."

"You're wrong." Her jaw set as she watched Candace hook an arm around Gabe's neck and whisper something in his ear. Allison turned back to Stuart with a forced smile. "I'd love to go to the dance with you. The only reason I hesitated was because I didn't know if my hostess had anything planned for tonight."

"I'm sure she'd let you out of it."

"I'll have to check with her."

Allison was already regretting the momentary annoyance with Gabe that prompted her to accept a date with Stuart. This was her last night with Mary Louise, too. She really should make a final stab at convincing her to face reality.

"No second thoughts. You said you'd go to the dance with me and I intend to hold you to it," Stuart said playfully.

Pinky came over to join them. "How did the windsurfing go?" she asked Allison.

"Not great. I couldn't seem to get the hang of it."

"This was only your first lesson. You'll catch on. It's easier than waterskiing."

"I wouldn't even attempt *that.*"

Stuart gave her a surprised look. "You don't water-ski? I can see I have a lot to teach you." He gave her an intimate smile.

"Lots of luck," Gabe said dryly. He had strolled over to their group, with Candace clinging to his hand. "I tried, but I didn't get anywhere."

"Maybe there's something wrong with your technique." Stuart put his arm around Allison's shoulders.

"Nothing that *I* can see." Candace laughed.

A young man named Jason came over to talk to Pinky. "I have a couple of errands to do after I drop you off. Are you ready to leave, or do you want to catch a ride with somebody else?"

"No, I have to go home, too." Pinky turned to include Allison and Gabe. "If you two aren't doing anything tonight, we're all going to the country club."

"I already invited Allison," Stuart said. "She's going with *me.*"

Candace gazed through her lashes at Gabe. "Poor Gabe. Does that leave you at loose ends?"

"Not if you'll go to the dance with me," he answered.

"I thought you'd never ask." She laughed.

"That's all settled then," Pinky said. "I'll see you both tonight."

They all began to leave at once and everyone regrouped in the parking lot, discussing plans for the evening. Allison and Gabe didn't have anything to say to each other, which suited her fine. She had no interest in fencing with him.

After they'd driven in silence for a few blocks, he slanted a glance at her set profile and remarked, "You did all right for yourself today."

"You know I didn't," she answered coolly. "Windsurfing isn't my sport."

"I guess you'll just have to stick to hunting."

She whipped her head around to look at him indignantly. "I never shot anything in my life!"

"I was referring to a different kind of hunting. You have an unerring gift for setting your sights on big money. Did you know Stu was loaded, or did I give it away when I mentioned his trust fund?"

Allison felt a stab of pain that she didn't allow to show. "That gave me my first clue, and then I confirmed it by talking to him."

"A girl can't be too careful," Gabe said mockingly. "You know how many phonies there are in the world."

"I'm not in any danger of being taken in by them. That's for amateurs like you people."

He frowned when she didn't flare up at him. "Your act isn't very convincing, Allison. You're not as tough as you sound."

"I don't let very many people see this side of me, but I don't have to keep up a front with you," she taunted. "You knew I was a fortune hunter from the very beginning."

"Not from personal experience. What's the matter, don't I have enough money for you?"

"You're not a good prospect," she answered carelessly. "Too much competition."

"A woman with your charms doesn't have to worry about that." The glance he raked over her body was insolent.

Allison struggled to hang on to her temper. "There's always

someone with more bountiful charms. You didn't have any trouble switching your attention today."

Something flared in Gabe's eyes and was masked instantly. "A man likes to hear a few words of appreciation every now and then."

"I'm sure you'll find Candace very accommodating," she replied stiffly.

"It does look like a promising evening."

"For both of us," she snapped as he braked to a stop in front of the Van Ruyder mansion.

Allison was out of the car instantly. She went into the house without a backward glance at Gabe, who followed with a thoughtful look on his face.

Mary Louise was coming down the staircase. "Did you and Gabriel have a nice day?" she asked.

"*He* did, anyway." When the older woman looked at her with a slight frown, Allison managed a smile. "I'm afraid I disgraced myself. I fell off the surfboard."

Mary Louise's brow cleared. "I'll have to speak to Gabriel about that. He should have taken better care of you."

"He was too busy making out with a blonde named Candace."

Gabe came into the house in time to hear Allison's statement. "That's not what happened at all," he told Mary Louise. "I was completely at the mercy of a predatory female."

Her laughing eyes appraised his tall, broad-shouldered frame. "You look as if you can defend yourself."

"*If* he wanted to," Allison said.

"Gabriel does have a lot of women running after him. Let's give him the benefit of a doubt."

"That's something Allison has never done," he said. "I was merely making a date with the young lady so I'd have somebody to take to the dance, as long as she accepted a date with Stu Harrison."

"You're both going out? I must tell Anita to serve dinner in the morning room, since there will just be Sergei and myself," Mary Louise said. "Martin and Laura have an engagement, too."

"I don't really want to go to the dance," Allison said truthfully. It wouldn't be any great joy to watch Candace wind herself around Gabe all night. "I'll stay home with you."

"Nonsense, child. I'm delighted that you're enjoying yourself."

"We haven't spent much time together," Allison persisted.

"We will tomorrow," Mary Louise promised.

"I have a noon flight, which means I'll have to leave here no later than eleven. That doesn't give us any time to speak of."

"Won't you reconsider and stay longer?" Mary Louise pleaded.

Allison hesitated. "I guess I could reschedule and take an evening flight." She was conscious of Gabe's enigmatic gaze. He was sure this was only a show of reluctance before letting herself be persuaded to stay. "It's such a lot of bother for just a few hours, though. Besides, Gabe would never forgive me," she said mockingly.

Mary Louise looked puzzled. "What does Gabriel have to do with it?"

"We planned to keep each other company on the plane," he cut in smoothly. "Don't give it another thought," he told Allison. "I could force myself to stay another week."

"I thought you might." She turned to the older woman. "If you're sure you don't mind my going out tonight, I'd better go wash my hair."

Allison's temper simmered all the time she was blow-drying her hair and putting on makeup. Her blue eyes smoldered as she applied eye shadow and mascara. She let her long hair hang loose around her shoulders, but her face got the full treatment—blush on her high cheekbones, pink gloss over deep pink lipstick, the works. Gabe was about to see what he was missing, she thought grimly.

The dress Mary Louise had bought her was perfect for an informal summer dance. The ruffled top was softly feminine, and the gauzy fabric was subtly sexy. Allison went downstairs complacently anticipating Gabe's reaction.

She had to settle for Stuart's. Gabe had already left.

Stuart was properly impressed, however. "You look fantastic!" He held her arms out from her sides, gazing at her slender body with avid eyes. "What did you do to yourself?"

"Took a shower and washed my hair," she answered briefly.

His admiration wasn't as satisfying as Gabe's, somehow. "I'll say goodnight to Mary Louise and be with you in a minute."

The older couple were having cocktails in the library. They both checked her out with approval. "You look lovely, dear," Mary Louise said. "You'd better take a sweater, though. It might get cool later. Do you have your key?"

"It's in my purse." Allison laughed. "What time do I have to be home?"

"I know you're joking, but you do need your rest. You were up until all hours last night."

"You'd better run along before she reminds you to buckle your seat belt and phone if you're going to be late." Sergei chuckled.

Mary Louise's smile was misty. "You'll have to excuse me. It's been a long time since I've seen one of my children off on a date. I was always a worrier and old habits die hard."

"She'll be perfectly safe at the country club," Sergei teased, taking her hand. "And I'll be here to watch the clock with you."

Allison felt misty-eyed herself as she waved goodbye. Nobody had ever cared when—or even if—she came home.

The country club was crowded and very festive. Pinky and her crowd were already there, seated at a long table. She beckoned to them.

"Where have you been?" Pinky indicated the chairs next to her. "I saved you a place."

Allison wasn't thrilled to find herself sitting next to Gabe. Candace was on the other side of him, looking very sexy in a halter-neck dress that plunged deeply to show a lot of cleavage. She was monopolizing his attention, which didn't bother him in the least. He was smiling at her with amused tolerance.

Gabe did glance around after Allison was seated. "I see you finally made it," he remarked. "We thought maybe you stopped off someplace."

"Stu was a little late picking me up."

"That's not very promising." Gabe smiled mockingly. "He wasn't exactly counting the minutes till he saw you again."

She forced herself to match his tone instead of lashing back.

"The night's young yet. He'll be putty in my hands by the time it's over."

"Stu has a reputation as a smooth operator. Make sure it's not the other way around."

"I can take care of myself."

"You haven't shown very good judgment so far."

"Because I wasn't taken in by *your* line? That only proves my point."

"I must be losing my touch," he said lightly.

"At least you're finally admitting it was all an act," she said, hiding her hurt.

"Not the part about wanting to make love to you." His voice deepened. "I still do."

Stuart put his arm around Allison's shoulder. "Stop hitting on my girl, Gabe. You have your own date."

"I couldn't cut you out if I tried." Gabe's smile was humorless. "Allison knows what she wants."

"That makes two of us." Stuart's embrace tightened. "What can I get you to drink, angel eyes?"

"Just a glass of white wine. No, wait." She looked directly at Gabe. "Make that champagne. I'm going for the gold tonight."

"Whatever your little heart desires." Stuart signaled to a waiter.

"Good hunting," Gabe murmured as Candace poutingly reclaimed his attention.

Allison tried to ignore him and enjoy herself, but it was difficult. She was conscious of his eyes following her, misinterpreting her every move.

Stuart was another problem. After Gabe's assurance that he had the inside track, Stuart was determined to pursue it. He held her in a tight embrace on the dance floor, and slid kisses over her cheek. She tried to put distance between them, with little success.

"You'll never get away from me, baby doll," he murmured. "We were made for each other."

"How can you tell on such short acquaintance?"

"I knew it the minute I laid eyes on you." He massaged the back of her neck. "You're the girl I've been looking for all my life."

"You must be very hard to satisfy," she said lightly. "I was told you've dated scores of them."

"Don't believe everything you hear about me. Rumors spring up because I don't lead a conventional life, holding down a regular job like most people. They think all I do is chase girls."

"But it isn't true?"

"Certainly not." He grinned. "I play tennis and golf, too. They're very time-consuming."

Gabe appeared next to them with Candace in his arms. He took note of Stuart's close embrace. "I see you're making progress," he commented sardonically.

"I'm trying to." Stuart chuckled.

He thought Gabe's remark was directed at him, but Allison knew better.

She found Stuart pleasant enough company when he didn't come on too strongly. He was amusing, and his admiration was a welcome antidote to Gabe's barbed comments. The only thing that bothered her slightly was the amount of Scotch he put away over the course of the evening. But it didn't seem to affect him, and it wasn't up to her to deliver a lecture.

All of the group were close friends. They changed partners and cut in on each other frequently. Allison danced with everyone except Gabe, which was a pure plus. They always got into an argument, so what was the use? Gabe evidently shared her view, since he didn't come near her.

It was almost midnight before he finally did ask her to dance. Maybe because he thought it would look strange, otherwise. He'd danced with all the other girls. Allison had kept track.

She rejected the belated invitation coolly. "You don't have to be polite. The evening is almost over, anyway."

"The orchestra is still playing," he answered mildly.

She shrugged. "Oh, all right."

"I *could* say, if it's such a chore, forget it," he remarked mockingly. "But I won't."

Allison walked stiffly beside Gabe to the dance floor, very conscious of his hand on her waist.

She was even more tense when he put his arms around her. It brought back memories of another time he'd held her close—for a different reason. His body had been urgent with desire then, and his mouth was a flame that ignited her own passion. The disturbing vision was dissipated by his derisive question.

"How are you making out with Stu?"

"Just dandy. I don't have to ask how you're doing with Candace. She's been clinging to you like ivy."

"It looks like we both struck gold. Do you plan to continue your romance with Stu in New York?"

"I haven't told him yet that I'm leaving tomorrow."

"It shouldn't be any problem. He spends a lot of time in the city. I'll call you for a progress report," Gabe said casually.

"I can't imagine why that would be of any interest to you. Your only concern was protecting the Van Ruyder fortune, and you've done that. Mary Louise didn't fall prey to my evil scheme. You won. We don't need to have any further contact."

"She's become very fond of you."

"And you think I'll use that to keep the pressure on?" Allison gave a harsh laugh. "That really presents you with a problem, doesn't it? You can't keep an eye on me every minute. Maybe you can tap my phone and hire a private detective to tail me."

"I was going to suggest that you accept Mary Louise's invitation to stay on until we resolve this matter. It would make things easier all around."

"I have no desire to make things easier for you," she replied hotly.

"Tell me something I *don't* know."

She stared at him suspiciously. "Why are you urging me to stay all of a sudden? On the way to the yacht club today, you said you couldn't wait to get out of here."

He smiled smugly. "That was before I met Candace."

Allison's flash of anger almost surpassed her feeling of rejection. "You'll just have to conduct your own long-distance romance," she said curtly. "Unlike the rest of you, I have to work for a living."

Stuart tapped Gabe on the shoulder. "I said you could *borrow* my girl. That means you're supposed to bring her back within a reasonable time."

"Nothing about Allison is reasonable." Gabe's smile was derisive, even though he added urbanely, "Every encounter with her is an unforgettable experience."

* * *

The evening ended soon after that. As a group of them stood under the outdoor canopy waiting for their cars to be brought around, Allison thanked Pinky for her hospitality.

"I'm glad we got to spend the day together, anyway. I wish you weren't going home tomorrow," Pinky said.

"What's all this?" Stuart demanded. "It's the first I've heard of it. You can't leave now," he told Allison. "We just met."

"I know. It's too bad," she said with simulated regret.

"Where are you going? Maybe I'll come, too."

"I'm returning to the working world. You wouldn't want to expose yourself to that," she joked.

"Not if I can help it." He grinned. "Life is too short to spend it with your nose to the grindstone. Stay here and play with me."

"Sorry, I used up all my playtime."

Stuart's car was brought around. It was a low, racy sports car, customized with all sorts of extras. Allison thought the discussion was over, but he brought it up again as they drove away.

"I really don't want you to go, Allie."

"That's very flattering, but I have to."

"Let's go have a drink and discuss it."

"It's after closing time. Nothing will be open."

"I know of an after-hours joint."

"I don't want any more to drink, Stu, and it's getting late. I really have to go home."

Allison had difficulty persuading him, but he finally took her back to Rosewood Manor. Instead of parking in front of the entrance, however, he stopped the car on a curve in the driveway under a large tree that cast a deep shadow. Even moonlight didn't filter through the thick branches.

When Stuart cut the engine she said lightly, "Is this my punishment? You're making me walk the rest of the way?"

"I don't play rough. I'm a lover, not a fighter." He snaked an arm around her waist and cupped her chin in his hand, urging her face toward his.

The liquor on his breath was unpleasant. Allison turned her head away. "I really have to go in, Stu."

"Not yet." He jerked her toward him and mashed his mouth against hers.

She struggled, but he had a grip like steel. When she finally managed to pull away slightly, his rasping breath told her he was aroused and potentially dangerous.

She tried to defuse the situation. "Come on, Stu, we're too old to make out in a car like teenagers. This car isn't built for it, anyway."

"You're right, gorgeous." He slid his hand under the hem of her skirt and caressed her thigh. "Let's take a stroll around to the pool and find one of those nice padded chaises."

She pushed his hand away. "Are you crazy? The whole family is at home!"

"Yeah, I guess it would be a little public." He gave a lewd laugh. "How about under this big tree? It's sort of kinky, but why not?"

She shoved him away and reached for the door handle. "You're disgusting!"

"Okay, so we'll go back to my place." He grabbed her arm and yanked her back, catching her off balance. As she sprawled at an angle across the seat, he curved a hand around her breast and strung wet kisses down her neck. "Anyplace you say, baby."

"Take your hands off me! Don't you understand the meaning of the word no?"

"Not when you've been sending me signals all night." His expression turned ugly. "There's a word for women like you."

"And there's one for men like *you*, but I don't use that kind of language."

Allison struggled upright and reached for the door again, but Stuart grabbed her roughly. "You've been asking for it and you're going to get it. No woman makes a fool out of Stu Harrison."

"That's because God got there ahead of us." She gritted the words through clenched teeth.

He swore pungently and gripped the front of her dress. With a swift movement he ripped her bodice to the waist. Allison gasped at the realization that he was out of control.

She fought him furiously. Stuart was stronger than she, but the sports car was an unlikely ally. A wide console separated the bucket seats, hindering his attempt to drag her onto his lap. By scratching and clawing until one arm was free, Allison finally managed to grab the door handle and turn it. She hung on as the heavy door swung open, tumbling her onto the ground.

She was on her feet in an instant, running for the house, but Stuart was right behind her. With a sinking feeling, Allison realized she'd never be able to get inside before he caught her. It seemed like a miracle when the front door opened and Gabe was silhouetted by the light.

She ran into his arms, clasping him tightly around the waist and burying her face in his shoulder. Gabe's arms closed around her as Stuart came pounding up.

"What the hell is going on?" Gabe demanded.

"Stay out of it," Stuart rasped. "This is between Allison and me. It's none of your business."

Gabe's face was flinty. "I'm making it my business. What did you do to her?"

Allison reluctantly withdrew from his comforting embrace. This was her mess to clean up. "It's all right. We just had a misunderstanding."

Gabe's expression darkened even more when he noticed her torn dress. She hastily pulled the two sides together, her cheeks warming.

"Leave us alone, Gabe," Stuart ordered. "I have a few things to say to Allison."

"I hope you can talk without any teeth," Gabe answered. "Because I'm going to knock yours out if you're not off the property in ten seconds."

Stuart blustered, but he wasn't reckless enough to ignore the rage in Gabe's eyes. With exaggerated nonchalance he returned to his car and revved the engine loudly as an act of defiance before driving away.

Allison went into the house silently, with Gabe following. She didn't want to discuss what had happened, but she was sure he did. Well, he was entitled.

"Are you all right?" He lifted her chin to look at her searchingly. "Did he hurt you?"

"No, I'm okay. I'm just glad you were here."

"I am, too." He smoothed her ruffled hair gently.

"What were you doing downstairs at this hour? Not that I'm complaining, but why weren't you in bed?"

"I was waiting to lock up. I thought you might forget."

There was something evasive about his answer. "You were

waiting for me to come home, weren't you?'' she asked quietly. "You expected something like this to happen.''

"I know Stu better than you do.''

"You might have warned me.''

"Would it have done any good?''

"Of course it would! I'd have been able to discourage him ahead of time without hurting his feelings.''

"That's very important, isn't it?'' Gabe asked mockingly. "It wouldn't do for Stuart Harrison the Third to get his feelings hurt.''

"I simply meant the situation wouldn't have gotten out of hand if I'd set him straight tactfully.''

"What you really mean is, you're afraid I've scared him off permanently.'' Gabe's taut body radiated fury. "Maybe you didn't welcome my intervention after all.''

The emotional scene she'd been through with Stuart had left Allison defenseless. She couldn't snap back at Gabe as she normally would have. Let him think whatever he wanted about her. He would anyway.

Gabe's anger drained away as he gazed at her tear-bright eyes and drooping shoulders. He reached out a hand to her face, then dropped it abruptly. "Go to bed, Allison, before I do something I'll regret,'' he said harshly.

Chapter Seven

Allison got out of bed reluctantly the next morning. She groaned at the prospect of all she had to do—pack, stand in line at the airport, go through the hassle of getting a cab in New York City. What she tried to avoid thinking about was Gabe and last night's fiasco.

Why did he misinterpret everything she said or did? It was so frustrating. First he showed concern over the horrendous incident with Stu, then he practically accused her of inviting it! She couldn't seem to do anything to please him.

Mary Louise and Sergei greeted Allison pleasantly when she went in to breakfast. Gabe merely nodded.

"How was the dance last night?" Mary Louise asked. "Did you enjoy yourself?"

"Yes, it was very nice," Allison answered politely. "The coffee smells heavenly," she remarked, hoping to divert her hostess.

"Armand made eggs Benedict this morning. Try some," Mary Louise urged, only momentarily distracted. "What time did you get home?"

Sergei smiled. "Are you going to ground her for breaking curfew?"

"Don't be absurd. I thought I heard voices during the night. I simply wondered what time it was."

Gabe spoke up for the first time. "That must have been the three of us saying good-night. Stu and Allison came home right after I did. I'm sorry we were so noisy."

"I wasn't complaining," Mary Louise said with a smile. "It feels good to have young people around again, coming and going at all hours."

"Speaking of going—I'd better phone the airport and see if I can change my ticket to a later flight," Allison said.

"Won't you please stay longer?" Mary Louise pleaded. "At least for another week."

Allison shook her head. "I wish I could, but I have to go back to work."

"You can telephone your place of business and tell them you're going to be unavoidably detained."

Allison smiled wryly. "They might tell me I'm unavoidably fired."

"I'm sure they wouldn't be that unreasonable. You could at least ask," Mary Louise coaxed.

"What do you have to lose?" Gabe surprised her by asking.

Allison couldn't imagine what he was up to. Maybe disagreeing with her had just gotten to be a habit, but she couldn't hold out against all of them. Sergei sided with the others. Finally she agreed to make the call, just to end the argument.

Carla Fenton was Allison's friend, as well as her boss. She knew Allison's whole story, including why she'd gone to Newport.

"I'm so glad to hear from you!" Carla exclaimed. "I've been dying of curiosity. What happened? Was your mission accomplished?"

"No, the woman I came to see died a month ago."

"Oh, I'm so sorry! Is this the end of the line, or were you able to find out if she really was your mother? I guess you could hardly question her relatives, under the circumstances."

"It was a little sticky at first. Monica's brother was ready to call the police, but his mother listened to my story. She's a wonderful woman. She actually invited me to stay here at the Van Ruyder estate. That's where I'm calling from.''

"Wonderful! That must mean she believes you're her grand-daughter.''

"Not necessarily.'' Allison sighed. "She's so desperate for a grandchild that she's willing to accept me, no questions asked.''

"Don't fight it.'' Carla laughed. "You're an heiress. They are *the* Van Ruyder family, aren't they? The Park Avenue ones?''

"Yes, but that part isn't important. All I want from them is the truth.''

"You have something against being rich?'' Carla asked skeptically.

"I can't even conceive of it—at least, not this rich. You have no idea how these people live. The house is a mansion, and there are servants to do everything but cut up your meat.''

"That's bad? I'll bet you could get used to it.''

"You don't understand. It wouldn't answer my questions. I came here to find out who my parents were, so I don't always have to write down 'unknown.' That might not sound like a big deal, but I found out the hard way that it is to some people.''

"Bruce is a jerk and so are his parents,'' Carla said succinctly. "You're well rid of him, but I understand what you're saying.''

"Unfortunately Mary Louise doesn't want to dig any deeper. I believe she's afraid to find out anything that will prove I'm wrong.''

"Do you think you are?''

"I honestly don't, but I'm up against a wall of silence. She's wonderful to me in every other way. That's the reason I'm calling. Mary Louise wants me to stay longer. I told her it was impossible, but she insisted on my asking.''

"No problem. Business is always slow during the summer months. Our kind of customers are all vacationing at one resort or another. Some of the salespeople have been asked to take voluntary time off.''

Allison had mixed emotions, thinking of Gabe. "It would really be all right if I took another week?''

"Absolutely. You'd be crazy to pass up an opportunity like this. Take lots of snapshots so I can see how the other half lives.'' Carla laughed. "That's probably as close as I'll ever get.''

Allison met Gabe when she came out of the library where

she'd gone to use the phone. She braced herself for another confrontation, but he surprised her.

"I want to apologize for my behavior last night," he said quietly. "I shouldn't have hassled you about Stu."

"It's all right," she murmured. "You were there when I needed you. That's what counts."

"You've very forgiving." After a moment's hesitation he said, "Did you change to a later flight?"

"No, my boss said I could stay." She gave him a lopsided smile. "It looks like we're stuck with each other for another week. Unless you're willing to leave me here without supervision."

Gabe's smile suffused his entire face. "Who would ride to your rescue if I wasn't around?"

"You don't have to worry. I intend to stay far away from Stuart Harrison the Third."

His expression changed. "Do you *want* me to leave, Allison?"

She glanced down to pick an invisible piece of lint off her blouse so he wouldn't read the truth in her eyes. Another week with Gabe wouldn't change their relationship, but it was like a gift from heaven.

His jaw set as he stared at her bowed head. "I guess I got my answer."

She looked up quickly. "You can't leave me now. I have terrible judgment about men. What if I meet up with another Stu?"

Gabe's taut body relaxed and he frowned at her with mock severity. "Okay, but I don't intend to lose any more sleep over you. You'll just have to hang out with *me* this week."

Mary Louise joined them in time to hear his joking remark. Her face lit up. "Does this mean you're going to stay?" she asked Allison.

"For another week. That will give us lots of time to talk," Allison added deliberately.

"That's wonderful, dear! I'm so pleased."

"I am, too. Why don't we sit down now over another cup of coffee?"

"I wish I could, but I have a committee meeting this morning and I must make a few phone calls first. We'll get together later this afternoon."

As Mary Louise bustled off, Allison said to Gabe, "I don't know what to do with her. Why did she insist that I stay if she doesn't plan to spend any time with me?"

"You have a whole week to wear her down."

One of the maids came into the hall to tell Allison she had a telephone call. Stuart phoning to apologize? She couldn't think who else it could be.

Gabe's face was grim as the same thought occurred to him. "You don't have to talk to him—unless you want to."

She didn't. "Tell the gentleman I've gone out."

"That's giving him the benefit of the doubt," Gabe muttered.

"It's Miss Gresham on the phone," Florence informed her.

"It was so hectic last night that I forgot to give you my phone number in the city," Pinky said after Allison picked up the receiver. "I'm glad I caught you before you left."

"I'm not leaving after all. I managed to get another week's vacation."

"That's super! Will I see you today? The gang was going to drop over here for a pool party, but we decided to go to the club for a few sets of tennis instead. I can have Stu pick you up."

"No, thanks, that didn't work out."

"Did he get out of line last night? What a geek!" Pinky said disgustedly. "Well, no problem. I can stop by and pick you up, or maybe Gabe could give you a lift. If he doesn't have a date with Candace. They got really chummy last night."

"*She* did, anyway," Allison said coolly. "The poor man couldn't get away from her."

"He didn't seem to be trying too hard." Pinky laughed. "Candace knows all the right moves."

"She and Stu would make a good pair."

"They've already been that route. She's out for fresh game. Listen, I have to run. Shall I pick you up?"

"No, thanks, I'll get there on my own if I can make it," Allison said.

"Get where?" Gabe had come into the library looking for her.

"Pinky and her crowd are going to the tennis club."

"It sounds like fun. Do you want to go?"

"No, but don't let that stop *you*. Candace will undoubtedly be there," Allison couldn't help adding.

"Then you have to come, too." He grinned. "It's your turn to protect *me*."

"Are you sure you want protection?"

"I'm not crazy about predatory females. I'm just perverse enough to want the ones I can't have."

Allison felt immensely better. "That certainly rules out Candace."

"So, why don't you want to go to the tennis club?"

"It certainly doesn't have anything to do with *her*."

"Okay, then I repeat, why don't you want to go?"

"I have some things to do," she answered vaguely.

"Like what?"

"Do you have to know every move I make?" she demanded.

"I do when you're acting strangely. What do you plan to do today?"

"Nothing special." Allison knew Gabe wouldn't give up until she gave him a valid reason. Since she couldn't think of one he'd accept, she had to tell the truth. "I don't know how to play tennis," she muttered.

"Is that all? What's the big deal?"

"It's just one more reminder that I don't belong here." Allison's frustration boiled over. "I don't play tennis, I can't windsurf or sail. I don't even know why I agreed to stay another week. Mary Louise won't sit down and talk openly to me. If I had any sense I'd get on a plane and go home tonight."

Gabe folded his arms and gazed at her calmly. "Are you through feeling sorry for yourself?"

"As usual, you're totally wrong about me! I have a very positive attitude about myself. Maybe I don't excel at a lot of the sports you people are proficient in, but that's only because I never had an opportunity to learn."

"I couldn't have said it better myself." His hand closed around her wrist. "Come with me."

"Where are you taking me?" She had to trot to keep up with his long strides as they left the house and began walking across the green lawn.

"I'm going to make a tennis player out of you, since you seem to regard it as some sort of Holy Grail."

"That was only an example. It won't work, Gabe. You tried to teach me how to windsurf, and look what happened."

His pace slowed as he gazed down at her. "What happened had nothing to do with your ability. I won't try to teach you contact sports from now on."

"Windsurfing isn't a contact sport," she murmured.

"It isn't supposed to be. That's how we got into trouble," he said wryly. They had reached the tennis court where he took two rackets and a can of balls out of an equipment box. "Okay, first we'll work on your forehand."

Gabe lobbed easy balls across the net in the beginning, so Allison could return them and build her confidence. He taught her how to serve and how to stroke fluidly.

She was panting by the end of the lesson and her muscles ached, but she was exhilarated.

"You did great." Gabe put his arm around her shoulders as they walked off the court. "You could be an excellent tennis player if you kept at it."

"You're just saying that."

"Why would I?"

Allison gazed up at his handsome face. "Because you're a very nice man," she said softly.

His arm tightened, drawing her against his lithe body. After a brief moment he released her, saying lightly, "Too bad good guys finish last."

The next couple of days were a pure delight. Allison and Gabe hung out with Pinky and her crowd at private clubs, eating, drinking and being waited on. It was a once-in-a-lifetime vacation. That's the way Allison resigned herself to thinking of her visit.

On the occasions when she and Gabe had dinner with Mary Louise and Sergei, Martin was mercifully absent so the evenings were very pleasant. Mary Louise couldn't do enough for Allison, but she resisted every effort to turn the conversation to Monica.

"I'm ready to give up," Allison remarked to Gabe as they returned to the house on Wednesday afternoon. "I'll never be able to pin Mary Louise down."

"You still have time left." He stopped the car in front of the door. "She might be out in the garden. See if you can corner her there. I have some phone calls to make. I'll see you later."

Allison wandered into the garden without much hope. There

was no sign of Mary Louise, but she lingered to enjoy the beautiful surroundings. After strolling along a brick path for a while Allison sat on a wrought-iron bench under a flowering tree, gazing at a bed of purple and white petunias.

Footsteps on the path turned out to be Sergei's. "You're looking very pensive," he said. "Is anything wrong?"

"Nothing is allowed to go wrong at Rosewood Manor." She smiled ruefully. "Mary Louise doesn't permit it."

"Can you blame her for not wanting to face reality? None of us would if we didn't have to. Let her have her fantasies," Sergei said gently. "She hasn't had a lot to make her happy, in spite of what you might think."

"You love her very much, don't you?"

"More than anyone will ever know," he answered quietly.

"Then why on earth don't you ask her to marry you?"

"I'm sure you know why."

"She's in love with you," Allison said bluntly. "Isn't that more important than the opinion of a few mean-spirited people?"

Sergei looked startled. "You're wrong about Mary Louise. She likes having me around, but only as a friend. I provide her with companionship and make her laugh when she gets discouraged. If she knew how I felt, she'd be uncomfortable. I wouldn't even have her friendship anymore."

"She does know how you feel—or at least she guesses."

"How do you know that?" he asked intently. "She's never given me any indication."

"If she were my age, Mary Louise would probably propose to *you*. Women go after what they want in today's world. But you have to realize that Mary Louise was raised with all kinds of silly inhibitions. She'll wait for you to tell her you love her— and you'll blow it because you're afraid of public opinion."

"Do you think that would stop me if I really thought she loved me?" he demanded.

Allison smiled. "Take my advice and go for it, pal."

Sergei's eyes gleamed with excitement. "Thanks, I might just do that! How about you?"

"I don't know what you mean."

"In spite of my advanced years, my eyesight is still excellent. I've watched you and Gabe together. You light up a room."

"Your eyesight might be good, but you jumped to the wrong

conclusion. It's different with Gabe and me. The only thing involved is sex."

"Are you admitting the feeling is mutual?" Gabe had approached so silently that neither of them heard him.

After a glance at their faces, Sergei rose from the bench. "This seems to be the day for letting it all hang out. I'm going back to the house to do some serious thinking."

There was a moment of silence after he left. Gabe broke it. "You haven't answered my question."

"We've been getting along so well. Why rock the boat?"

As she started to walk by him, back to the house, he put his hands on her arms. "It's time we were up-front with each other about our feelings."

"I'm not sure that's a good idea," Allison answered carefully. "It will only lead to an argument."

"Maybe not, if we both feel the same way," he said softly.

"I already know how you feel, but it hasn't changed your opinion of me. You still think I came here under false pretenses. You're just willing to overlook it for a few passion-filled hours." Bitterness colored her voice.

Gabe cupped her cheek gently in his palm. "An entire week with you wouldn't be enough. I don't care anymore why you came here. I'm just glad you did."

Allison stared at him, feeling a dawning happiness that warmed her like sunshine. Was it possible that Gabe really cared about her?

As they gazed at each other wordlessly, Anita came down the path. "There's a gentleman to see you, Miss Riley."

Gabe's bemused expression changed to a scowl. "Stu again? What does it take to discourage the jerk?"

"It's a Mr. Bruce Dunham," the maid said. "Shall I bring him out here, or show him into the drawing room?"

A chill raced up Allison's spine. How had Bruce found her—and why? Gabe mustn't be allowed to meet him! She couldn't bear to have him find out about her humiliating rejection.

"Tell the gentleman I'll be right with him," she said hastily.

Gabe's hand closed around her wrist, preventing her from leaving. "No, bring him out here."

The maid couldn't fail to notice the sudden tension between the two, but she was too well trained to question a direct order.

Especially since Gabe's was delivered with greater authority. After a moment's hesitation, Anita returned to the house.

"You had no right to do that," Allison said in a low voice. "This has nothing to do with you."

All the former tenderness was gone from his face, leaving it cynical. "Everything you do concerns me. I'm the Van Ruyder watchdog, remember? I'd like to meet your confederate."

"It's typical of you to jump to conclusions, but you happen to be wrong. Bruce is...he's just someone I used to know."

"He evidently prizes the relationship more than you do," Gabe drawled. "He couldn't wait another week to see you. Or did he come for a progress report?"

"I have no idea why he came," Allison answered truthfully.

"A glitch in plans?" Gabe asked sardonically. "From the look on your face, this is obviously a departure from your original strategy. It will be interesting to hear his explanation for this unexpected appearance."

"My hostess might require one, but I don't have to answer to you." Allison jerked her wrist away and turned toward the house.

It was too late. Bruce was hurrying along the path toward them.

He looked a little surprised to see Gabe, but his face lit up at the sight of Allison. "It's great to see you, Allie! I've missed you like the very devil."

"What are you doing here, Bruce?" she asked tautly.

He looked slightly taken aback, but not for long. "I've been phoning you for days. I was getting worried when I couldn't get you, so I called Carla at the store. She told me where you were and I decided to hop over and pay you a surprise visit."

Knowing Carla's opinion of him, Allison could figure out what happened. Carla couldn't resist the opportunity to rub it in. She wanted Bruce to know what he'd missed out on—the chance to marry an heiress. She probably told him it was an accepted fact.

"It's been too long, Allie," Bruce said in a deepened voice.

"We can't talk now," she said. "Tell me where you're staying and I'll phone you."

"Why don't you ask Mary Louise to put him up here?" Gabe asked mockingly. "There's plenty of room and she'd do anything you asked. Allison has made a lot of progress in a short time," he told Bruce.

"That would be fantastic!" Bruce's eyes shone with excitement. "I'd love to meet the Van Ruyders."

"Gabe was only joking," she said sharply. "I couldn't possibly ask Mary Louise to let you stay here."

"Let her work on it. Allison prefers the subtler approach." Gabe looked appraisingly at the other man. "Since she won't introduce us, we'll have to do it ourselves. I'm Gabe Rockford." He didn't extend his hand.

"Nice to meet you, Rockford. I'm Bruce Dunham, Allison's fiancé."

Gabe's jaw tightened. "I see. Well, it's nice to keep your little scheme in the family."

"He is not my fiancé," Allison stated grimly. "How could you tell him a thing like that?" she asked Bruce.

"Don't be angry at me, darling." He gave Gabe a humorous wink. "We had a little falling out. You know how it is."

"No, I'm afraid I don't," Gabe replied. "Why don't you tell me? What did you and Allison argue about?"

"It isn't important." She cut in swiftly, before saying to Bruce in a determined voice, "We have nothing further to discuss—and certainly not here."

"I know you were hurt, sweetheart. I handled things badly and I'm sorry. But everything's going to be all right now."

Allison stared at him, wondering how she'd ever considered herself in love with Bruce. He was handsome enough, blond and athletic, the perennial college boy even in his thirties. It was strange that she'd never noticed how weak his chin and mouth were. Or how superficial he was. Bruce was practically salivating at the prospect of being part of the Van Ruyder family.

"Why didn't you tell me you were related to the Van Ruyders?" he asked.

"Allison is full of little secrets," Gabe drawled. "You never know for sure what she's up to."

"You can say *that* again! I was knocked for a loop when Carla told me the news. This solves everything!"

"That's the nice thing about money," Gabe remarked satirically.

"This is about more than money. The Van Ruyders are the cream of society. There won't be any opposition to our wedding now," Bruce told Allison.

Gabe's eyes narrowed. "Somebody objected?"

Bruce barely heard him. He was glancing toward the imposing mansion. "Maybe we could have the wedding right here. Wouldn't that be spectacular?"

Allison was so furious that she no longer cared who knew the shameful story of her broken engagement. Did Bruce honestly think she'd excuse his parents' unforgivable behavior and his own spineless failure to stand by her?

"I wouldn't get your hopes too high," she said bitingly.

"You could at least mention it. You never know if you don't ask."

"I'm sure your mother would love to get her toe in the door, but I can't help her climb the social ladder."

"Don't be bitter, darling. Mother really likes you. She's just a little old-fashioned about some things. I know you'll get to be great friends after we're married."

"There isn't going to be any marriage," Allison said bluntly. "Monica Van Ruyder was not my mother."

"But Carla said—"

"Carla was just pulling your chain."

"I don't understand. You're a guest here. How can that be if you're not related to them? They wouldn't invite a perfect stranger into the house. You didn't know them before, did you?"

"It's a long, involved story." Allison just wanted to get rid of him. Bruce had already done his damage. "Take my word for it, I'm as unacceptable now as I was before."

He looked distressed, yet unwilling to give up. "Maybe not. The Van Ruyders must like you," he said thoughtfully. "That should count for something."

"Go away, Bruce," she said tautly. "It's over."

"I don't intend to give up this easily."

"Why not? You did last time."

"I never saw this side of you," he complained. "You've changed."

"*You* haven't."

"Don't be that way. We can work this out, Allie." He reached for her hand.

Gabe stepped between them. "I think the lady asked you to leave."

Bruce's weak mouth curled. "Now I'm beginning to get it. You found a better prospect," he said to Allison.

Gabe answered for her. "*Any* man would fit the description."

"I don't have to take that from you!" Bruce flared.

"You do if you don't get out of here." Gabe's eyes glittered dangerously, although his voice remained calm. "The choice is up to you. Either leave of your own free will, or I'll take great pleasure in throwing you out."

"Is that what you want?" Bruce demanded of Allison.

"Just leave," she said wearily.

"Okay, but this time I won't be back," he blustered.

The only sound in the silence that fell was Bruce's footsteps receding down the path. Allison wished Gabe would leave her alone, too, but he stayed.

"Why didn't you tell me?" he said finally.

Her mouth twisted in self-mockery. "If you were once engaged to someone like Bruce, would you brag about it?"

"How long ago did all this happen?" Gabe asked quietly.

"A couple of months ago. He called me a few times afterward, but I haven't seen him until today."

"He let his parents break you up? That seems incredible."

She shrugged. "I told you I was a lousy judge of men."

"What objection could they possibly find with you?"

"That should be fairly obvious. I'm a nobody of uncertain parentage—although I'm sure they spoke more graphically among themselves." She smiled sardonically.

A look of pain crossed Gabe's face. He made an imperceptible movement toward her, but something about her stiff posture warned him off.

"I didn't want you to know," she continued in an unemotional voice. "It isn't something I'm proud of. That's why I was so upset when Bruce turned up here, not because he was a conspirator in some nefarious scheme."

"I'm sorry. I was way out of line."

"It doesn't matter. You've always been suspicious of me. Why should today be any different?"

"Seeing Bruce again upset you. I can understand that. But you're not being fair. I came here with an open mind."

"Why do men find it impossible to tell the truth?" she asked angrily. "You had doubts then, and you still do."

"Certainly things bothered me in the beginning," he admitted. "Like your timing. It seemed a little questionable that you only decided to look into your background after Monica was gone and couldn't confirm or deny your claim. Now I understand why your visit came when it did, and what motivated it."

"How did she die?" Allison asked abruptly. "No one would ever tell me that, either."

"Her death was enough of a tragedy for the family," he said evasively. "Talking about it is painful."

"You see? You still don't trust me!"

"She died of alcohol and enough pills to stock a pharmacy," Gabe answered reluctantly. "How she accomplished it is a mystery, because she was in a rehab center at the time. Monica was a master at manipulating people, no doubt about it. She talked somebody into supplying her needs."

"How did you manage to keep a thing like that a secret?"

"I suppose most of Mary Louise's friends had their suspicions, but a lot of them have skeletons in their own closets. They banded together in a code of silence, and some influential people were successful in keeping the cause of death out of the newspapers. You can see why the family doesn't want the circumstances to become known."

"Was it suicide?"

"Who knows? Although I doubt it. In my personal opinion, Monica was too fond of life to exit willingly. She might just have been rebelling against the rules of the sanatorium, the way she broke rules all her life. To show she could do it. Unfortunately this time she didn't get away with it."

"What a terrible waste."

"Yes, she was living proof that money can't buy happiness."

Allison stiffened. "Is that directed at me? You never quit, do you?"

"Aren't you overreacting rather drastically? It was just a general statement, and not a very original one at that."

"You'd be sensitive, too, in my position," she answered heatedly. "Ask Sergei what it's like to have people suspect your every motive. If Mary Louise would only cooperate with me, I'd be out of here like a shot. All I want is to know who I am. Why can't anyone understand that?"

"I do, honey," he answered gently. "I didn't before, but after finding out what that clown Bruce put you through, I do now."

He moved toward her, but she backed away. "I don't need pity."

Gabe's face darkened as he grabbed her by the shoulders and jerked her toward him. "Has anybody ever told you that you're a very aggravating woman?"

"Add that to the list of all the other things you don't like about me."

His jaw set. "You sure don't make it easy for somebody to be on your side."

"When were you ever?" she scoffed.

"If you weren't so busy fighting the whole world, you might have noticed that I care about you."

"I'll bet you also brought home stray dogs and cats when you were a little boy. Well, thanks, but I don't need anybody's help. I can fight my own battles."

Gabe swore under his breath. "I can't seem to make a dent in that stubborn little mind of yours, so maybe I can get through to you this way."

He jerked her into an almost bruising embrace and kissed her so hard she was breathless. Allison made indignant little sounds of protest, which he ignored. His arms were wrapped around her, welding her body to his taut frame. Struggling was useless. She was completely helpless in his arms.

Gradually Gabe's fury lessened and the pressure of his mouth was no longer punishing. His kiss became sensually provocative, sparking a response from Allison. She stopped struggling when his tongue teased her lips apart for a stirring exploration of the moist interior.

Gabe's tight grip had loosened, becoming an embrace instead of a restraint. His hands caressed her back, wandering down to cup her buttocks and urge her even closer to his hardened loins.

Allison's response was immediate. She curled her arms around his neck and returned his kiss with the same urgency. She wanted to get even closer than this, to feel his nude body against hers, filling her with joy.

Gabe finally dragged his mouth away and buried his face in her hair. "Why do we always argue, when all I want to do is make love to you?" He kissed her temple, her closed eyelids, each corner of her mouth. "I never thought I could love anyone this much. You have me bewitched."

Allison tensed, sure that she'd heard what she *wanted* to hear. "What did you say?"

He lifted his head to smile at her. "I said you're bewitching."

"No, before that."

"I can't remember. You see how befuddled you've made me?"

Allison knew it was too good to be true. He'd gotten carried away in the heat of passion, but he wasn't about to repeat the error.

Gabe stroked her hair tenderly. "All I can think about is how much I love you."

She stared at him incredulously. "Do you really mean it?"

"Don't tell me you didn't know. Haven't I made a complete idiot of myself, getting jealous and making a scene over every man who comes near you?"

"They're both such jerks," she said uncertainly. "I didn't think it was anything personal."

"How about my unremitting suggestions that we make love?" he teased. "Didn't that give you a clue?"

"Not really. That doesn't necessarily involve love."

"It does with me. I want more than your body, sweetheart, I want all of you." His kiss this time held great tenderness. After a satisfying few moments he tilted her chin up. "I haven't heard a similar commitment from you. Am I just kidding myself?"

"Is this answer enough?" She pulled his head down for a passionate kiss.

When he could speak, Gabe said huskily, "We're going to have a marriage made in heaven."

Allison could only stare at him. "You're asking me to marry you?"

"Of course I am. Haven't you been listening?"

"Yes, but I thought you only wanted..."

"I do." He chuckled wickedly. "Constantly. Our life together will be one long honeymoon."

Allison came down to earth with a thud. "We can't get married, Gabe."

"Give me one good reason."

"The same one that broke off my engagement to Bruce. I have

no background, no family, even my name doesn't belong to me. I know you'll say it doesn't matter, but it will to your parents. Trust me.''

''You're right about it not mattering to me, and it won't to my parents, either. They aren't the kind of narrow-minded bigots that spawned a wimp like Bruce.''

''I'm sure they're kinder and more intelligent, but they still won't approve.''

''I think they will, but that's really beside the point. I'm a grown man. The choice is up to me.''

Allison turned away. ''You're very close to your parents. I've heard the affection in your voice when you talk about them. It must be wonderful to have a relationship like that,'' she said wistfully. ''I would never want to spoil it for you.''

''You couldn't be anything but a blessing.'' Gabe smoothed her hair gently. ''I wish I could give you what you've missed, darling. It isn't possible to change the past, but from now on you'll have a family that cares about you. My parents will love you as much as I do.''

''I wish I could believe that,'' she said somberly.

''Wait and see.'' He took her hand. ''We'll phone them right now with the good news.''

''No.'' She pulled her hand away. ''Let's wait until we get back to New York.''

''You have nothing to be afraid of, angel. They're wonderful people.''

''I'm sure of that, but I'd just rather meet them in person first.''

Gabe wasn't satisfied, but after a lot of coaxing he finally agreed. ''Okay, you win. I guess I'll have to settle for Mary Louise and Sergei. I have to tell *somebody* we're engaged.''

''I'd rather you didn't, Gabe.''

''Listen to me, Allison. I don't intend to let you get away,'' he said firmly. ''We are going to get married.''

''I want to so much that I'm afraid to believe it will actually come true. Let's just keep this our secret for a little while. If nobody knows, nothing can happen to spoil things.''

''My dearest love, what can I do to assure you that my feelings will never change?''

''Just keep on loving me,'' she whispered yearningly.

"That's the easy part." He sighed. "I can see you need more assurance than mere words, so I'll have to give it to you."

"What do you mean?"

"I'm going to find out who your parents were."

"I'm beginning to think that's impossible. Mary Louise is the only person who might have a clue, but she refuses to tell me anything. Her friends clam up when Monica's name is mentioned, and the father of the baby has kept the secret all these years. He isn't about to admit it now. What more can I do?"

"You can leave it to me. Cross-examining witnesses is my field of expertise. I don't let them off the hook—as you've noticed." He grinned.

Allison gazed at him with pure love in her eyes. "I'll bet you've never had a witness so willing to cooperate."

"I'll remind you of that later tonight," Gabe murmured.

Chapter Eight

Gabe took Allison out to dinner that night to celebrate their engagement, although they didn't tell anybody that was the reason.

"I think Sergei guesses," Gabe remarked as they were having champagne to toast the occasion.

"I hope it gives him ideas," Allison said. "We had a talk this afternoon and I advised him to propose to Mary Louise."

"What did he say to that?"

"He said he'd consider it, but I'm not so sure. I understand how he feels."

"*I* don't," Gabe said impatiently. "When two people love each other, that's all that matters. Even more so in their case. They aren't getting any younger."

"Is that why you asked me to marry you?" Allison teased. "Because you're afraid of advancing old age?"

The candle's flame was reflected in his eyes as he gazed across the table at her. "Would you like proof of my virility?"

"I wasn't questioning that," she answered softly.

His hand tightened on hers. "It's going to be so good with us, sweetheart."

Allison didn't have to be told that. She couldn't wait to lie naked and uninhibited in Gabe's arms. Her whole body throbbed in anticipation of his torrid caresses.

Drawing a shaky breath, she said, "We'd better talk about something else."

"You're right, what I have in mind for us is very private. This is not the place."

"So...what would you like to do after dinner?" she asked brightly.

He chuckled. "I wouldn't call that changing the subject."

"You're not cooperating," she complained.

"Okay, angel, let's talk about our wedding. Do you want a big one with all the trimmings? The only trouble is, those things take time to organize. If it was solely up to me we'd get married right away, but I realize a bride wants the full treatment."

"I'll have to think about it," she replied.

"I don't like the sound of that. We're getting married if I have to drag you to the altar," he warned.

Allison decided she was being foolish. Even if history repeated itself and their marriage never took place, why deny herself the joy of planning for it? Who knows? Maybe her luck would change.

"Where will we live afterward?" she asked. "Do you have an apartment? I know so little about your everyday life. We always seem to talk about me."

"Ask me anything you like. I have an apartment we can use for now, but we'll undoubtedly want more space. Until we find something, you can redecorate my place any way you please."

"I wouldn't know how to go about it."

"My mother will be glad to help. She's good at that sort of thing. At one time they had an apartment in London, their town house in New York and the home here. She finally decided it was a lot easier to stay in a hotel when they traveled. They have a standing invitation to stay with Dad's brother when they come to Newport, though. I do, too. There's plenty of room."

"Do you feel sad about going back to your old home? Is that why you stayed with Mary Louise instead of your uncle?"

"He happens to be out of town, but I stayed at Rosewood Manor so I could keep an eye on *you*." He laughed. "I didn't know you'd turn into a commitment for life."

"That sounds like a sentence," she complained.

"I couldn't ask for a more perfect cellmate."

"Would you have come if you'd known?" she asked softly.

"Like a shot. You're the woman I've been searching for all my life."

They were gazing wordlessly into each other's eyes when the waiter arrived with their first course.

During dinner, Gabe told Allison about the summers he spent in Newport as a boy, and later a teenager.

"Was Monica here when you were?" Allison asked.

He nodded. "I used to see her racing around town in a red convertible. My friends and I all thought she was really cool, although we were too young to understand the whispered gossip about her." Gabe laughed. "I'll never forget the look on my mother's face when I asked her what skinny-dipping meant."

"Did she tell you?" Allison smiled.

"No, she sent me out to pick strawberries for dinner, figuring I'd forget about it by the time I got through. We had a kitchen garden in those days. You don't know what a tomato tastes like until you've eaten one right from the vine."

"I wish I could have seen your summer home."

"Would you like to stop by after dinner?"

"I thought you said your uncle is out of town."

"He is, but I have a key. I'm welcome to use it anytime."

Gabe's former home wasn't as opulent as Rosewood Manor, but it was by no means average. A tall iron fence enclosed the extensive grounds that surrounded the three-story, rough-cut granite home. On one side, an open porch stretched the length of the house, with a line of spaced pillars supporting the sheltering roof.

"I didn't expect anything this grand," Allison gasped.

"It's modest compared to the Van Ruyder place. Come inside, I'll show you around."

Her eyes widened at the polished parquet floors covered with oriental rugs in the double drawing room, the expanse of Tiffany glass bricks and tiles that formed one wall of the dining room.

The bedrooms upstairs were equally spacious and luxuriously

furnished. Most of them served as guest rooms now, Gabe explained, since his cousins were grown and had left home.

"Which room was yours?" Allison asked.

He led her to a bedroom at the back of the house, overlooking a rectangular swimming pool that was an opalescent glimmer in the moonlight. The pool lights had been turned off, since nobody was in residence. Allison stood by the window, entranced.

"It looks so mysterious in the dark," she remarked. "Like an enchanted lake in a fairy tale."

"I can turn on the pool lights. Would you like to go swimming?"

"We don't have our bathing suits with us."

"All the better. I'll leave the lights off and we'll go skinny-dipping. Since I've grown up, I found out what that meant."

Excitement fizzed through her as Gabe put his arm around her waist and slowly slid her zipper down. "I've never gone skinny-dipping," she murmured.

"It's easy." He slipped the dress off her shoulders and unhooked her bra. "First you take off all your clothes."

"You're doing it for me," she said faintly.

"I'll let you return the favor in a minute." He lowered his head to string a line of kisses across her breasts.

Allison uttered a delighted cry as his tongue circled one of her sensitive nipples. He heightened the pleasure by capturing one little bud between his lips while her dress slithered to the floor.

Molten desire filled her as his fingers slipped inside the waistband of her panty hose. She could barely stand while he rolled them down her hips, sinking to his knees in front of her. When she was completely nude, he caressed her thighs lingeringly.

"You're so exquisite." He stared at her with glittering eyes. "This is the way I've dreamed of seeing you."

"I dreamed about you, too," she murmured.

"Did you, darling? Was I doing this?" He kissed the soft skin of his stomach, then moved lower for an intimate kiss that destroyed all of her inhibitions.

Allison sank to the floor beside him and unfastened his tie. Her fingers were shaking as she impatiently tore open his shirt while Gabe fueled the flames by caressing her breasts.

"My wonderful, passionate Allison," he said huskily. "Tell me you're mine."

"Now and forever," she promised fervently. "There will never be anyone else for me."

"I intend to make sure of that." He kicked free of the slacks she'd unzipped and gathered her in his arms.

The sensation of their bare bodies joined together was so arousing that she moved against him restlessly, asking wordlessly for the ultimate embrace. Gabe's passion equaled hers. He parted her legs and plunged deeply, sheathing himself inside her.

They were consumed by their need for each other, almost wild in their desire to give and receive pleasure. Their bodies were taut with the rapture brought by every driving stroke. The flame that devoured them burned brighter and brighter until it was finally extinguished in a gush of satisfaction. Their tense bodies relaxed and they clung together, utterly at peace.

"You are the love of my life," Gabe murmured, when his breathing slowed.

"And you are mine," she whispered.

They were quiet in each other's arms for long moments. Then Gabe began to chuckle. "I had a lot of fantasies in this bedroom when I was a little boy, but I never dreamed one like this would come true."

"You must have been a very precocious little boy." She smiled.

"About average. All little boys think about sex—big ones, too. What did you fantasize about?"

"Not sex. I was a late bloomer."

"What *did* you dream about?" he persisted.

"Oh, the usual girl things," she answered evasively.

"They must be really wicked if you don't want to talk about them," he teased. "You might as well tell me, because I don't intend to let you off the hook."

Allison knew he meant it. "I used to dream that my parents would come to get me one day," she said reluctantly. "They'd hug me and explain that I was kidnapped when I was a baby, and they'd been searching for me ever since."

Gabe's face sobered. "I'm sorry," he said in a muted voice.

"I knew you would be. That's why I didn't want to tell you. You're feeling guilty because you grew up in a mansion, but it's okay. You have to play the cards fate deals you, and look what happened. We both wound up in the same place. That's kind of ironic.''

"It just proves we were meant to be. Although I would have found you no matter where you were.''

"Maybe, but you must admit I made it easier for you.'' She tried to jolly him out of his subdued mood. "Didn't I hear you mention something about skinny-dipping?''

"Right. You took my mind off it temporarily.''

"Well, I should hope so.'' She laughed, reaching for her clothes.

"What are you doing? I thought we were going for a moonlight swim.''

"We are, but I have to put on something to wear out to the pool.''

"Why? You're only going to get undressed again.'' He took her hand and led her out of the bedroom.

"This feels totally decadent,'' Allison protested as she and Gabe walked naked down the stairs.

"We merely shed our inhibitions.'' He stroked her bare bottom. "What's wrong with that?''

"What if your uncle should come home unexpectedly?''

"In the middle of the night?''

"It could happen. How would you explain what we're doing here completely nude?''

"Very simply. I'd just tell him a band of roving Gypsies stole our clothes.''

"Gypsies in Newport, Rhode Island?''

"That's as likely as Uncle Herb turning up at two in the morning.'' Gabe opened the door to the outside patio. "Come on, let's go swimming.''

The water felt unbelievably sensuous on Allison's bare body. While he swam the length of the pool, she floated languidly, letting the buoyant water hold her in its embrace. The ripples Gabe churned up lapped over her, like fleeting caresses.

He surfaced beside her, sprinkling her playfully with drops of water. "Are you just going to lie there and look gorgeous?''

She smiled enticingly. "What would you like me to do?''

"A leading question if ever I heard one.'' He leaned forward and touched his tongue to a drop of water on her shoulder, then to the one on the slope of her breast.

"You haven't answered it," she murmured.

"Does this give you a clue?"

His mouth glided over her breasts while his fingers traced an erotic pattern on her inner thighs. Allison's body sprang to instant life in response to his intimate caresses.

"I never get tired of touching you," he said huskily. "I want to know every secret inch of you."

She responded by searching out the hard male proof of his passion, wanting to know him in the same way. Gabe uttered a hoarse cry and gathered her in his arms, capturing her mouth for a deep kiss that she returned just as urgently.

When the water caused their bodies to sway apart, Allison wound her legs around his waist. She couldn't bear to be parted from him, even for an instant. For long moments they clung together, kissing almost frantically and murmuring unintelligible words of love.

Then Gabe gripped her hips and completed their union. It was like nothing she could have imagined. The heat from their joined bodies was so intense that it warmed the water that streamed over them, heightening the molten pleasure. Their ecstasy built like the tidal wave that finally engulfed them.

When it was over, Gabe carried Allison out of the pool and lowered her gently to a padded chaise. He dried her tenderly with some large towels he took from a wooden chest, then lay down beside her and took her in his arms again. No words were needed. They were content to lie quietly and savor the aftermath of their love.

Finally Allison stirred. "This has been so wonderful. I wish we could stay all night."

"We can, if you like. I suggest we go upstairs to bed, though." He chuckled. "That's the only place we haven't made love, but the night isn't over yet."

She stroked his face lovingly. "It's very tempting, but we have to go back to Rosewood Manor."

"Why?"

"Because we do. You know how it would look if they knew we'd stayed out all night."

"Everyone would guess we made love, which we did. I don't care who knows it. I'd like to tell the whole world how much I love you."

"That's so sweet, darling, but Mary Louise wouldn't understand. She lives by a very rigid code of ethics."

"I'm not so sure. After being exposed to us and Sergei, I think she's becoming liberated." Gabe grinned. "Besides, she'll make allowances when we tell her we're engaged."

"You promised you wouldn't!"

"After tonight, do you honestly think I'd let anyone or anything come between us?" When she looked at him with large, reproachful eyes, Gabe groaned. "Okay, angel, whatever you say. I don't know why I even bother. I've yet to win an argument with you."

"You can't have any complaints about tonight. We were both winners," she said softly.

He answered by kissing her with exquisite tenderness.

Gabe was up early the next morning, in spite of the fact that he'd had only a few hours sleep. On his way down to breakfast he stopped at Allison's door. When she didn't answer his light tap, he went inside.

She was curled up in the big bed sound asleep. He stood over her for a moment with a face softened by love. She opened her eyes when he leaned down to kiss her.

"I didn't mean to wake you, darling." He stroked her cheek. "Go back to sleep."

She gazed up at him with shining eyes. "Just tell me one thing. Was last night a dream?"

He reached under the covers to stroke her sleep-warm body. "I couldn't have imagined such perfection."

She made a soft sound of contentment. "When is your uncle Herb coming home? I could be persuaded to go back there."

"I'll take you up on your offer later. First I have something to do." He tucked the covers around her and kissed her tenderly. "Go back to sleep, angel."

Mary Louise and Sergei were having breakfast when Gabe joined them in the morning room.

She greeted him with a smile. "Good morning, Gabriel. Did you and Allison have a pleasant evening together?"

"It was very nice," he answered with admirable restraint.

"Where did you go for dinner?"

"To the Mariner's Roost for seafood."

"You should have told me that's what you wanted. Armand makes a divine lobster thermidor."

"Perhaps they felt like going out," Sergei remarked.

"They're certainly free to do whatever they like. Where did you go afterward?" she asked Gabe.

Sergei groaned. "Mary Louise, sweetheart, you're going to drive them away if you keep checking up on them."

"I'm only expressing interest," she answered defensively. "I want to be sure they're enjoying themselves."

"You're a perfect hostess. Nobody could question that. But maybe you should concentrate your energies on Sergei," Gabe said smoothly. "There are a lot of ladies around who would appreciate all he has to offer."

She gave the older man a special smile. "Sergei knows how much his friendship means to me."

"That's my claim to fame—good old Sergei, everybody's best friend." He rose, suppressing a sigh. "If you'll excuse me, I have an appointment this morning. I'll see you later."

Gabe slanted a covert look at her as she watched Sergei walk out the door. "One day he'll leave and he won't come back. Have you thought about that?"

"I've gotten used to people leaving me." Her wistful expression turned ironic. "Only Martin remains a constant in my life."

"This is presumptuous of me, but perhaps you'd be better off if you nudged him out of the nest."

"He's all I have left," Mary Louise said simply.

Gabe tried to suppress his impatience. "Children shouldn't be your whole life after they're grown. You could have a great deal more if you wanted."

"Nobody has offered me anything."

"You know Sergei is in love with you."

"Not enough to brave public opinion," she said sadly. "So I guess it isn't really love. He enjoys my company, but he doesn't want the headaches that go with marrying a Van Ruyder. And who can blame him?"

"I've heard him mention the possibility—and he didn't cringe at the thought."

"He was only joking. I was supposed to understand that."

"Answer me this. If Sergei asked you, would you marry him?"

"We used to play the what-if game when we were children. It always concerned things that were never going to happen. Like, what if you were the Queen of England?"

"That's a defeatist attitude. Anything is possible if you want it badly enough."

"Perhaps at your age."

"At any age. You just have to seize the opportunity when it comes along. I hate to see you and Sergei pass up a chance at happiness because neither of you is willing to be candid about your feelings."

"The man has to express himself first."

"Not anymore. The world has changed, Mary Louise."

"Not my world, I'm afraid." She sighed. "Or Sergei's, either. We still live by the old rules. You young people are lucky. You don't have a lot of silly hang-ups. My generation put too much emphasis on unimportant things—everything from money and family, to the correct attire for each occasion. It's different today, I'm happy to say. People aren't bound by tradition as we were."

Gabe was reminded of Allison's humiliation with Bruce, and her reluctance to chance another rejection. "We're more liberated, but certain things still matter. Like family. Allison has a burning need to know who her parents were."

Mary Louise's expression brightened. "She's such a darling girl. I felt an instant rapport with her."

"Then why won't you talk to her?"

"I don't know what you mean. We've had some lovely conversations together."

"You do know what I mean, Mary Louise," Gabe said quietly. "I realize it's painful to talk about Monica, but Allison needs to find out the truth, and you're the only hope she has. You should want to know, too."

After a long pause, the older woman said, "All my life I've been shielded from the truth. Perhaps Peter was right. It's better not to know."

"Forgive me for saying this, but that's a very selfish attitude. You're condemning Allison to limbo."

"Try to understand, Gabriel. If I had conjured up the perfect granddaughter, it would be Allison. She's warm and caring and open with me, everything my daughter wasn't. I already love her like my own. I hope she'll let me treat her like a granddaughter. I want to do so much for her."

"As hard as it is to believe, Allison doesn't want a penny from you."

"I do believe it, which makes her all the more special."

"Then give her the greatest gift possible, her own identity."

Mary Louise's face was expressionless. "What happens if we pursue this and discover that Monica was not her mother?"

"I guess it's back to square one. Allison said there were two other possibilities."

"Exactly. Then she disappears from my life and some other woman gains a grandchild. Perhaps somebody who isn't even happy about the news." She looked at him squarely. "Allison deserves more than she's ever gotten out of life. I intend to make up to her for all the unhappy things that happened to her in the past."

"It isn't that simple. Suppose she wants to get married? What if objections were raised because of her lack of background?"

"Any man who would let that bother him isn't worthy of her," Mary Louise said scornfully.

"I agree with you. But other people might voice objections— like maybe his parents." Gabe walked a fine line, hampered by his promise not to reveal their engagement.

She looked at him with a frown. "Are you telling me it happened to the poor girl?"

"I didn't say that," he answered quickly. "I was just pointing out what *could* happen."

"It seems remarkably unlikely to me." She looked at him consideringly. "There's something you're not telling me."

He laughed ruefully. "Mothers are all alike. You always think we're keeping something from you."

"And we're usually right. What did Allison tell you last night? *Is* she engaged?"

"She expressed her frustration at having to go home without finding what she came for," Gabe answered evasively. "I told her I'd speak to you."

"If that hypothetical story you told me is true, I *have* been selfish," Mary Louise said slowly. "Poor little thing. It breaks my heart to think of her being treated like a second-class citizen because of something she wasn't even responsible for.''

His jaw set grimly. "It will never happen again." When Mary Louise looked at him with dawning interest, Gabe said swiftly, "You're the one who can make sure of that."

"How?"

"Tell me everything you know. Is there any doubt in your mind that Monica had a baby when she was eighteen?"

"I guess I have to accept the fact. Your father phoned yesterday with at least partial confirmation of Allison's story. The birth record she described does exist. He said you were to phone him when you came in, but I'm afraid I forgot to deliver the message.''

"I'll give him a call," Gabe said absently. "That seems to be pretty conclusive evidence."

"I have to agree. There could hardly have been two teenage Monica Van Ruyders. It isn't exactly a common name."

"You never suspected anything? Even if she was away at school and camp a lot, surely you didn't go for months at a time without seeing her."

"I've thought about it a great deal. The summer she must have gotten pregnant was not a happy time. Monica was always rebellious, but that summer she and her father were constantly at sword points. I tried to smooth things over, but Peter simply got angrier and Monica became more defiant. Finally he announced that she was out of control and he was sending her to his sister's to complete her final year of high school."

"Do you think Peter knew she was pregnant?"

"Looking back, I'm sure of it. That would account for his frustration, which translated into anger. Peter wasn't used to situations he couldn't control."

"Would he keep something that serious from you?"

"Without a doubt. Peter knew I would never allow him to give up the baby for adoption. In most ways I was a perfect wife. I never challenged his authority, but he must have known there were limits. So he didn't take a chance. I don't think I can ever forgive him for robbing me of my grandchild," Mary Louise said somberly.

"I'm sure he thought he was protecting you." Gabe hesitated for a moment. "One thing I don't understand. If the baby was such an embarrassment, why didn't he arrange an abortion? It would have been a lot easier all-around.''

"Peter didn't believe in abortion. His tidy solution was to send Monica to his sister's. That way nobody would find out, and the inconvenient incident—as I'm sure he thought of it—would be resolved.'' Bitterness colored Mary Louise's voice.

"Your sister-in-law was willing to go along with this deception?'' Gabe asked incredulously. "What was he blackmailing her with?''

"That wouldn't have been necessary. Jane always thought I was too permissive with my children. It's easy to criticize when you don't have any of your own. She undoubtedly welcomed a chance to apply some discipline. Poor Monica. The punishment for her indiscretion seems unduly harsh—house arrest with her aunt as warden.''

"How about Monica's schooling? Did they just pull her out for five or six months?''

"There wouldn't have been any other way to hush it up. She undoubtedly had private tutors.''

"After she returned home, did Monica ever give you a hint about what happened?''

"No, she was just more outrageous. Peter began to avoid her—whether out of guilt, or the realization that he couldn't handle her. I don't know. It was easier for everyone that way.''

Gabe was thinking deeply. "Monica's baby was born at the end of May, so it must have been conceived the latter part of August. Was she here in Newport?''

"Yes, we always opened the house on the first of July and stayed until the beginning of September. When the children were younger they went to camp for part of the summer, but Monica was seventeen that year. She'd outgrown camp.''

"So the father of her child was somebody she met here that summer.''

Mary Louise looked doubtful. "The same families came with their children every year. You know what Newport is like. We all know each other.''

"Could she have had a romance with one of the town boys? Or maybe a college kid who came here to work for the summer?''

"Anything is possible, as I'm finding out. But if it was one of those, she never brought him home. I wouldn't have a clue as to who he could be.''

Gabe refused to be discouraged, although the odds were getting longer. He could only hope Monica's affair wasn't just a brief encounter. ''Did she have a crush on any of the boys you knew? Sometimes kids who couldn't stand each other one summer, fall madly in love the next.''

''You didn't know Monica very well. She played the field. I believe that's the way you young people put it. There were always swarms of youths buzzing around her, but she didn't seem partial to any special one. I think what she enjoyed most was the attention.''

''There must have been some boys she dated more than others,'' Gabe persisted.

''It's so long ago. I only remember hordes of eager young men showing up every night to take her out. She was never without a date.''

''Think hard, Mary Louise. You knew the families of all these boys. Surely you remember some being here more than others.''

''Well, I do recall two of them. One was Daniel Wallace. We were quite friendly with his parents in the city, as well as here in Newport. He was a very polite young man. Very well brought up.''

That depends on your definition, Gabe thought cynically. ''Did he and Monica continue to see each other all summer? He didn't suddenly stop coming around?''

''I know what you're implying,'' she said quietly. ''You think he might have become scared off if Monica told him she was pregnant.''

''It's happened before.''

''You're wrong about Daniel. I'm sure he would have stood by her if that had been the case. But it's a moot point because there was never any rift between them. To my recollection, he was part of the group all summer.''

''It's possible that Monica didn't tell him she was pregnant.''

''In which case, he doesn't know to this day.'' Mary Louise looked troubled. ''Daniel is married now. He has a lovely family. What good would it do to rake up the past?''

''I don't intend to jeopardize his marriage,'' Gabe assured her.

"You can't guarantee that. We're a small community. Gossip spreads like wildfire."

"All I want to do is talk to him. There's no reason for anyone to get suspicious. You said there were two boys who seemed to have an edge," he continued, to deflect her objections. "Who was the other one?"

"It was Pembroke Clay." Mary Louise's expression changed to disapproval. "I'd say he was a lot more likely candidate than Daniel. He has a lovely mother and father, but I must say I never cared much for Pembroke."

Gabe looked interested. "I saw him at the country club dance the other night, but we didn't get a chance to talk. What didn't you like about Cokey?"

"I always detested that ridiculous nickname," she sniffed.

"You must have had other objections beside that."

"It's a terrible thing to say, but I never trusted that boy. Oh, he was always on his good behavior around Peter and me, but it was clearly an act. In my opinion, Pembroke was the instigator of those wild escapades Monica was involved in."

"That's very possible," Gabe murmured diplomatically.

"I'm not saying Monica was blameless. Perhaps they egged each other on. Who knows? He made as much of a mess out of his life as she did."

"In what way?"

"For one thing, he's been married and divorced twice."

"Unfortunately that's not unusual in today's society."

"The circumstances were," Mary Louise said with distaste. "Both divorces were messy. In one of them he was accused of having an affair with an actress. It was well publicized, so he could scarcely deny it. The other divorce was equally sordid. I'd rather not go into the details."

"Is he still a stockbroker?"

"I presume so, since his father owns the brokerage house. I see his mother now and then, but we seldom mention Pembroke."

"He sounds like a good prospect," Gabe said thoughtfully. "I'll look him up."

"Does that mean you don't have to speak to Daniel? I'd really feel very badly if any of this got back to his wife. Especially since I'm sure he and Monica weren't involved in that way."

"You can trust me to be discreet."

"You haven't left me much choice." She sighed.

"What is it you want, Mary Louise?" Gabe asked quietly. "To pretend nothing ever happened? After all, it was more than twenty-five years ago. We could just let the entire matter drop. Danny's marriage would be safe. Cokey wouldn't have any more complications in his life. That's the way Peter would handle it. The only loser would be Allison, but her expectations from other people have never been high."

Mary Louise was silent for long moments. "You make me very ashamed of myself, Gabriel. I thought I'd grown as a person since my husband died, but I'm just as much a slave to convention as he was. Peter did a cruel thing to Monica, and now I'm proposing to do the same thing to Allison."

"The circumstances are quite different, and you're acting out of love, not a misplaced sense of propriety. But I'm glad you see that the truth has to come out."

"Yes. Allison deserves that much."

"I'll talk to both men. Do you happen to know if Danny is here in Newport?"

"He and his family are staying with his parents for a couple of weeks. I ran into his mother, Marjorie, in town the other day."

"Luck is on our side for once. It won't be easy getting either one to admit responsibility, however, so I'd like to chase down any other leads you can think of."

"I really haven't a clue," Mary Louise said helplessly. "Monica never confided in me, not even little things after she reached her teens."

"How about a close girlfriend?"

"She was much more interested in boys than girls."

"She must have had at least *one* girlfriend."

"For a few years, Monica and Sandra Gresham were good friends. They went to the same schools and knew all the same people. I was very happy about it because Monica had so few girlfriends."

"Did they grow apart after the summer ended? You seem to indicate they didn't keep in touch as they grew older."

"It was more than a gradual parting of the ways. They must have had an argument sometime during the last month we were here. Sandra stopped coming over to the house and Monica never mentioned her anymore. When I questioned her about it, she said Sandra was a bore and a killjoy. I felt badly that they stopped seeing each other completely, but you can't patch up your children's squabbles for them. I'm sure Sandra's mother tried, too. Our families were close friends. It was useless, though. The girls never made up.''

"Monica didn't tell you what the argument was about?"

"No, she just said it wasn't important."

"It obviously was to Sandra," Gabe mused. "Suppose the falling out was over a boy they both liked. Perhaps Monica took him away from Sandra. That could break up a teenage friendship."

"You think he could be the boy Monica had an affair with?" Mary Louise asked dubiously. "Why is he any more of a candidate than the dozens of others she dated?"

"I don't know. It might be a long shot, but at this point I'm stumped enough to grasp at any straw. It's worth talking to Sandra about, anyway."

"She's changed a lot since she was a girl," Mary Louise said slowly. "Sandra was always so happy-go-lucky in those days. Nothing ever bothered her."

"She certainly *has* changed," Gabe agreed. "At your party Saturday night she was spoiling for a fight with *someone*."

"I wonder if her marriage is happy."

"I don't know, but it isn't our problem. I'll try to tackle her when she's in a good mood."

Mary Louise's face was troubled. "You'll tell me what you find out, won't you?"

"I'll give you a full report," Gabe promised.

After leaving Mary Louise, Gabe returned to Allison's room. He found her still in bed, fast asleep. Resisting the urge to kiss her awake, he started to leave quietly. But Allison sensed his presence.

She opened her eyes and smiled at him drowsily. "I must have gone back to sleep. Why were you up so early?"

He went over to sit on the edge of the bed. "I wanted to talk to Mary Louise before she went off to one of her meetings or luncheons."

Allison sat up in bed. "Did you tell her about us?"

"I promised I wouldn't." His smile faded. "Don't you trust me?"

"Of course I do! I don't know why I asked that." She sighed. "Why do you put up with me?"

He eased the strap of her nightgown down her arm and kissed her shoulder. "That's fairly obvious. You have the most beautiful body of any woman I've ever known."

"Is that my only attraction?"

Gabe was quick to catch the wistfulness in her voice. He raised his head to gaze at her tenderly. "I never thought I'd meet anyone as wonderful as you are in every way. I want to get married as soon as possible and live with you for the rest of my life."

"Darling Gabe." She threw her arms around his neck.

He held her closely for a minute, then began to explore her ear with the tip of his tongue. "I also want to fool around."

She gave a shaky laugh. "Well at least you're honest about it."

"Absolutely." His hand cupped around her breast. "How about it?"

"I don't feel right about making love in Mary Louise's house." Allison drew back reluctantly. "She wouldn't approve."

"She would if you'd let me announce our engagement."

"Not really. It would still make her uncomfortable—and me, too."

"All right, angel. I don't agree with you, but it has to be right for you, too." He tousled her hair playfully. "If I can't make love to you, put on something less revealing. You look much too sexy."

"I'm sorry." She smiled. "I didn't bring any granny gowns."

"You won't need them, or anything else to sleep in after we're married. I'll keep you warm."

"Married." She savored the word, gazing at him dreamily. "That sounds so wonderful."

"Stop looking at me like that, or I won't be responsible," he warned. "Get out of bed, woman. We have work to do."

"Like what?"

Gabe told her the results of his conversation with Mary Louise.

Allison's blue eyes sparkled. "Do you really think you're onto something?"

"I don't want to get your hopes too high, but it's a distinct possibility. We'll start with Danny Wallace."

"Because he's the most likely candidate?"

"No, I think Cokey Clay is a hotter prospect, but I want to check Danny out first. Mary Louise is worried that his marriage might suffer if any of this got out. I don't want her to stew about it any longer than necessary if he wasn't involved."

Allison looked troubled. "I wouldn't want to jeopardize anyone's marriage."

"Don't worry about it." Gabe's face hardened. "There's no free lunch. Monica paid the price for their indiscretion. Now it's his turn—if Danny is the right man."

"Even so, I wouldn't want to hurt his wife. She didn't have anything to do with it. I don't want to hurt *anybody*. I just want to find out the truth."

"She won't know anything unless Danny tells her, I promise. Now, hurry up and get dressed. I'm hoping we can track him down at the yacht club. He was always an avid sailor."

She hopped out of bed. "Just give me a few minutes to shower and dress, and I'll be right with you. Oh, Gabe, I'm so excited!"

He chuckled. "I'd prefer to excite you in a more rewarding fashion, but I understand. See you downstairs in half an hour."

Chapter Nine

It was almost noon when Allison and Gabe arrived at the yacht club. There weren't many people in the dining room yet, so they went into the cocktail lounge, which was busier.

The bartender finished serving a group at the end of the long polished bar, then came over to take their order. His face lit up when he saw Gabe.

"Well, if it isn't Mr. Rockford. We haven't seen you around these parts in quite a while. Where have you been keeping yourself?"

"My dad decided I'd been living the good life long enough, so he sent me out to make a living," Gabe joked before turning to Allison. "I'd like you to meet Mike, the indispensable man," he told her. "The club couldn't run without him."

"That's what I try to fool them into believing." Mike laughed.

"It's true. Your job takes a lot more know-how than just pouring drinks. Remember the time those young kids got rowdy and how you straightened them out?"

The two men chuckled as they reminisced about past summers. Gabe mentioned several people before asking about the one he was really interested in.

"I understand Danny Wallace is here with his family," he remarked casually. "Does he come around very often?"

"He's here today, working on his boat. Been out there all morning. It seems to me those yachting types get more fun out of working on their boats than sailing them." Mike grinned.

"They're a special breed," Gabe agreed. "I think we'll stroll down and say hello."

"Be careful he doesn't hand you a paintbrush," Mike advised.

As they walked down to the dock Gabe said, "I wasn't just buttering Mike up. He does know everything that goes on around here. He could have told me where to find Cokey, too, but I didn't want to arouse his suspicions unnecessarily. I can probably find out from somebody else."

"Too bad Mike wasn't around when Monica was a teenager. He wasn't, was he?"

"No, he's only been here about fifteen or sixteen years. I was just out of prep school when he started, and Monica was getting her first divorce. Any gossip he might have heard was about her more recent affairs."

They were walking along the marina past moored boats of every size, from modest to impressive. Music and laughter wafted from several where people were partying in the brilliant sunshine. Several of the groups called to Gabe and invited him aboard, but he put them off with a vague excuse.

"There's Danny up ahead," he told Allison.

Daniel Wallace's boat was a sleek racing sloop named the *Carefree*. It was deserted except for a man in cutoff dungarees sanding a section of railing.

Allison stared at him avidly as they covered the short distance. It gave her a funny feeling to think that this stranger might be her father. He was nice looking in a forgettable sort of way. About medium height and well built except for being slightly overweight. Could the flamboyant Monica have been attracted to this ordinary man? Possibly, when she was a teenager.

He didn't look up until they were standing a few feet away. "What's doing, Danny?" Gabe called.

"Gabe?" The other man looked surprised and pleased. "I

haven't seen you around these parts in ages. What are you doing in Newport?"

"Just hanging out."

"I hear your parents sold their house here."

"Yes, they got tired of the yearly hassle."

"My folks are starting to feel the same way. I'd hate to see them sell, though. We've all had a lot of good summers here. You must miss your old place. I'll bet it holds a lot of memories for you."

"Priceless ones." Gabe squeezed Allison's hand. "It's okay, though. My uncle bought the house and I can use it anytime."

"Is that where you're staying?"

"No, Allison and I are staying at Rosewood Manor." Gabe introduced them.

"Come on board for a drink," Danny said.

He fixed Bloody Marys and they sat in canvas chairs on the deck. Allison mostly listened as the men talked.

"How is Eloise?" Gabe asked politely about Danny's wife.

"She's fine. We have three children now."

"That's great."

"I never thought I'd say this, but it really is." Danny laughed. "How about you?" He included Allison in his smile. "When are you going to settle down?"

"That's what my parents keep asking me." Gabe grinned.

"So?"

"There's nothing like a reformed stud," Gabe joked. "When *you* give up la dolce vita, you want the rest of us to suffer along with you."

"You can't be talking about *me*. I wasn't a party animal."

"Don't hand me that. You ran around with Monica Van Ruyder, didn't you?"

Danny slanted an uncomfortable glance at Allison. "I took her out a couple of times, that's all."

"That's not what Mary Louise said. She remembers you being underfoot constantly."

Danny tried to change the subject. "How's Mary Louise doing? I'm surprised she's still living in that big house. Everyone thought she'd sell it after Peter died."

"I guess it's like you said, it holds a lot of memories. For you, too, undoubtedly."

Danny stood abruptly. "Let me freshen your drinks. Unless you have a lunch date," he added hopefully.

Gabe stretched out his long legs. "No, we don't have any plans," he said blandly.

When Danny had gone to mix the drinks, Allison whispered, "He doesn't want to talk about Monica. That's a good sign, isn't it?"

"Not necessarily. He might just feel constrained with you here."

"Why would he, if his conscience is clear?"

"Memories of Monica are apt to be X-rated, and he's a family man now."

"Maybe," she answered skeptically. "But you won't know unless you get him to talk about her."

"I'd have a better chance if we were alone." Gabe's expression turned innocent as Danny reappeared with their drinks. "This is really nice. I don't get to unwind much in the city."

"It's a real rat race, isn't it?" Danny agreed. "How long are you staying?"

"Only this week, which is a good thing. I think I've put on five pounds already. Armand is one great chef." Gabe snapped his fingers as if remembering something. "I forgot to tell Mary Louise we wouldn't be in for dinner tonight. Did you remember to mention it to her?" he asked Allison.

"No, I forgot, too," she said, following his lead.

"We'd better let her know. Would you phone and leave a message?" As Allison rose he said, "I'll meet you back at the clubhouse."

After she left, Danny said, "That one's a real knockout."

"Does she remind you of anyone?" Gabe asked idly.

"A movie star, you mean?"

"No, I was thinking of Monica."

Danny looked startled. "There's a certain resemblance I suppose, but Allison isn't anything like her."

"I thought you didn't know Monica that well."

Danny's eyes narrowed. "What the hell is going on, Gabe? Why all this talk about Monica after all these years?"

"Why does it bother you?" Gabe countered. "What I find even more curious is your claim that you barely knew her. Mary Louise says you dated Monica regularly."

"Maybe I did. It was a long time ago. Who can remember back that far?"

"Men don't forget a woman like Monica."

"She wasn't a woman then, for God's sake! She was a teenager."

"A remarkably precocious one."

"How would you know? You were just a little kid then."

"I heard the gossip about her. Children understand more than people give them credit for."

"Okay, so she was no goody-two-shoes. What difference does it make now? Show a little decency, man! Monica is dead. Let the past die with her."

"I'd be happy to, but she left some unfinished business behind."

"What do you mean?" Danny asked warily.

"Monica had a baby when she was eighteen. It was hushed up, and nobody ever knew about it. The infant was given up for adoption."

Danny stared at him. "Are you saying that girl Allison is Monica's daughter? Is that why you asked if she reminded me of anyone?"

"The child was conceived when Monica was seventeen," Gabe continued without answering the question. "The summer she spent here in Newport."

"You don't think that *I*...that's the most outrageous..." Danny was practically stuttering in his furious denial. "What is this, a shakedown? She'll never get away with it!"

"Relax, Allison doesn't want anything from you. She just wants to know who her father was."

"Well, it wasn't me!"

"Convince me," Gabe gazed at the other man impassively, trying to judge whether he was telling the truth or not. "It's a simple matter of deduction. You had the inside track with Monica, she got pregnant. Who else could it be?" Gabe knew it *wasn't* that simple, but he hoped to shake some facts out of the other man while he was too rattled to lie.

"You're way off base! I didn't have the inside track with her, Cokey Clay did. Although you could never be certain where you stood with Monica—she went after every boy in town. But if what you're telling me is true, you should be talking to Cokey. He's your man, not me.''

"Possibly, but only if you weren't sleeping with her, too."

Danny's eyes shifted. "That's a hell of a thing to say."

"I could phrase it more delicately, but it wouldn't change the facts. One of Monica's boyfriends fathered her child, and I intend to find out which one."

"*Why?*" Danny's voice was filled with anguish. "What good will it do to disrupt a lot of lives? Whatever happened back then is over and done with."

"Not for the child, it isn't."

"What month was Monica's baby born?" Danny asked unexpectedly.

"May 27."

A look of relief flooded Danny's face. "Then I couldn't be the father!"

"How can you be so sure?"

"First I need your word that none of this will go any further."

"You have it," Gabe assured him.

"I don't know how much you actually know about Monica." Danny was silent for a long moment, remembering. "To say she was sexually active doesn't begin to describe it. Anything and everything went with her. She taught the *guys* things!"

"You're saying she was a nymphomaniac."

"She enjoyed sex, no doubt about it, but it was also an ego trip for her. Or maybe a lot of it was about power and control. Every boy in town had to be in love with her—whether he was going with another girl or not. The rewards were great," Danny said reminiscently. "For a while, at least. Then as soon as she was sure of you, you were yesterday's news."

"That's kind of a switch on what men have been doing to women for years," Gabe remarked.

"It still hurts. But that's how I can be sure I'm not the father of Monica's baby. She set her sights on me in June, right after we both got here. Not that I'm complaining. It was fantastic while it lasted. And then, just like that it was over. Cokey arrived, and she tossed me aside like a used towel. I couldn't believe it, so I hung around, hoping she'd change her mind."

"That would explain why Mary Louise said you were always over there," Gabe mused.

"You were supposed to remain faithful even after the queen bee moved on to your successor," Danny said dryly. "After a while I got discouraged and started dating Cheryl Sturtevant. That didn't set well with Monica, so she whistled me back. We went out together a few times, even did some heavy necking, but she never slept with me again."

"It's hard to believe she could keep you dangling like that without coming across."

"Can you remember what it was like to be a seventeen-year-old boy with raging hormones? Monica was unbelievable in bed. Hell, she was better than women twice her age. God only knows where she learned it all. I would have done anything to get her to take me back."

"Can you remember the last time you slept with her?"

Danny's mouth twisted wryly. "I can remember *every* time. It was the Fourth of July, how's that for irony? The high point of the summer, climaxed by rockets going off. I wonder if she planned it that way. Anyhow, I took her home early in the morning, feeling like the king of the barnyard. Then she told me it was over."

"Did she give you a reason?"

"Monica wasn't into explaining, but I knew there was somebody else."

"Cokey Clay?"

"He moved in, so I suppose so. Although I think she was fooling around on both of us. One man wasn't enough for Monica."

Gabe shook his head in disbelief. "It's just a wonder she didn't get pregnant sooner."

"At least I wasn't responsible. If the baby was born in May, it must have been conceived in August. That puts me in the clear. I wasn't even here then. My grandfather had a stroke, and we closed up the house and went back to New York."

"I guess that's pretty conclusive," Gabe said. He set his glass down and stood.

"Do you intend to talk to Cokey?"

"He's next on my list."

"I'm sure he had the same experience with Monica that I did." Danny's face was troubled. "I didn't enjoy telling you all those things about her. It's rotten to speak ill of the dead."

"Somehow, I don't think she would have minded," Gabe said thoughtfully. "Monica's whole life seemed to be a quest for attention."

"I've often wondered if she ever really cared about *anybody*," Danny said somberly.

Gabe puzzled over the question as he walked back to the clubhouse. Was Monica's rebelliousness due to her father's overly stringent upbringing, or was she just basically selfish and self-centered? Maybe it was just as well that Allison never met her mother.

She was waiting impatiently for him on the veranda overlooking the marina. "What did you find out?" she asked before Gabe even reached her. "Did he admit anything?"

"I told you not to get your hopes too high, honey."

Her face fell. "He must have told you *something*. You were gone for ages!"

"We had a long talk. I had to lead up to it gradually."

"Okay, but what did he finally say?"

"That he dated Monica that summer, but they didn't have a physical relationship." Gabe gave Allison a highly expurgated version of what he'd learned—as much for her sake as Danny's. "It was one of those innocent high school romances."

"How do you know he was telling the truth?"

"I'm sure he was, but even if their relationship wasn't completely pure, Danny couldn't be our man. He wasn't here that August." When her mouth drooped, Gabe said, "Don't be discouraged, this is just the opening gun. I always thought Cokey fit the profile better than Danny. I'll phone around to locate him, and we'll tackle him next."

Gabe had no trouble finding out that Cokey was part of a house party at the home of one of the regular summer residents. He also learned that they would all be having dinner that night at the country club.

Before leaving for the club that evening, Gabe and Allison stopped by the library where Mary Louise and Sergei were having cocktails.

"Armand is going to think you don't like his cooking," Mary Louise joked.

"I'm sorry to keep running out on you every night, but with any luck, this will be the last time," Allison said.

Mary Louise's smile faded. Gabe had told her they were going to the country club expressly to talk to Cokey. "Let me know what you find out."

"Tomorrow," Gabe promised, taking Allison's hand. "Don't wait up. We might be late tonight."

After they left, Sergei commented, "They make a nice couple."

"I think they're falling in love," Mary Louise said softly.

"I think they already have." He chuckled.

"Wouldn't it be wonderful if they decided to get married? I'm so fond of both of them. We could have the wedding right here."

"Don't start calling the caterer. Every love affair doesn't end in marriage."

"It should. If two people are in love it's a logical conclusion."

Sergei had leaned forward to pick up his drink, so he didn't see the glance she slanted at him. "In an ideal world perhaps. But in their situation, I'm not sure they could make a go of it. Allison hasn't had the privileges Gabe has. I don't know if she'd be happy in his world."

"That's utterly ridiculous! She's a lovely, intelligent girl. The man who gets her will be very lucky."

"I agree, but people can be remarkably cruel to somebody who doesn't belong."

"Not while Gabriel is around. He'd make short work of anyone foolhardy enough to slight his wife."

"Is that the basis for a good marriage, though?" Sergei's expression turned grim. "Partners should be equal. How would a woman—or a man—feel if his spouse always had to protect him from slights?"

They both knew they were no longer discussing Allison and Gabe. "He should consider the source," Mary Louise said impatiently. "Not everybody would feel that way."

"Just one would be enough," Sergei replied harshly.

She suppressed a sigh. "Then he doesn't really love her."

"Or maybe his expectations are too high. None of it would matter if he thought she really loved *him*."

Mary Louise gazed at him in dawning delight. Before she

could answer, Martin and Laura came into the library. They were dressed to go out.

Martin glanced around the room. "Where are your house-guests?"

"Gabriel took Allison to the country club for dinner," Mary Louise answered.

"They use this place like a hotel," he complained.

"I didn't realize you missed their company," she said ironically. "I'll try to arrange a little family dinner for tomorrow night."

"Don't bother on my account. I was only thinking of you. *You're* the one who wants her around. I just hate to see her take advantage of you like this."

"I appreciate your concern, but it's misplaced. Sergei and I are looking forward to being alone tonight." She gave the older man a special smile.

Martin's eyes narrowed. "You're staying home again? It's rather unusual for you to be so reclusive. What's the matter, are you afraid to be seen in public with him?" he drawled.

Mary Louise's smile was erased by a flash of intense anger. Her voice shook with the effort to control it. "You will apologize to Sergei this instant!"

Martin was startled by the extent of his mother's fury. "I was only joking," he said placatingly.

"It is never funny to insult someone."

"Sergei knew I was only kidding around."

"That's not a suitable explanation. I am deeply ashamed of you, Martin. May I remind you that this is my house and Sergei is my guest. If you find the living conditions here intolerable, I suggest you make other arrangements."

He looked shocked. "I said I was sorry."

"Don't tell me, tell him," she said adamantly.

Martin was so chastened that his apology almost rang true. Laura was equally nervous. After making an ineffectual attempt to smooth things over, she hurried her husband out of the room.

When Mary Louise and Sergei were alone, she said, "Martin's behavior was inexcusable. There is nothing I can say except to assure you it will not happen again."

Sergei hadn't reacted to Martin's snide attack, or Mary Louise's impassioned rebuke. His face was equally impassive now. "Don't worry, it isn't that important."

"Yes, it is! I won't put up with intolerance, and certainly not in my own son."

"He's just being a little overly protective. It's understandable."

"You're far too generous. I can't tell you how embarrassed I am."

"You're making a great deal out of nothing. Martin was right about one thing. We have been staying home too much. Would Armand's feelings be mortally wounded if we went out to dinner tonight?"

"I don't suppose so, but we were going to stay home and...discuss things." She looked at him searchingly. "Wouldn't you rather do that?"

"We can settle the world's problems over dinner in a restaurant." He stood, smiling pleasantly. "You're too far away at that big table in the dining room. I'll get my jacket and be right down."

Mary Louise's expression was forlorn as she watched him go.

The country club was crowded with regulars, representing three generations. Pinky was there with a group, and some of Mary Louise's friends were dining with their children. They all greeted Allison warmly, giving her a nice feeling of acceptance.

She was distracted, however, by the more pressing need to find Cokey Clay. Gabe finally located him at the bar.

Allison disliked the man on sight, although he obviously approved of *her*. After a brief inspection of her lovely face, his gaze lingered on her curved figure.

"How do you young fellows wind up with all the beautiful girls, when we're the ones with experience?"

"Maybe we just know how to treat a lady," Gabe drawled.

"Is that the line he's been feeding you?" Cokey asked Allison. "Don't you believe it. I could make you very happy, given the chance."

"Come off it," Gabe said. "She's young enough to be your daughter."

"Not unless I was a very early bloomer."

"Which you were, as I remember. You used to hang out with Monica Van Ruyder. She wouldn't have won any merit badges in the Girl Scouts."

"Ah, Monica. She was quite a gal." Cokey's mouth curved in a reminiscent smile. "Terrible thing about her death. I heard it was some kind of accident. I must say I'm not surprised. She used to drive like a crazy woman."

"She did a lot of crazy things."

"You don't know the half of it. I could tell you stories." Cokey slanted a glance at Allison. "But that's all in the past. The poor woman is dead, and buried now."

"She was a legend in her time all right. I've always wanted to ask—" Gabe broke off and turned to Allison, "This can't be very interesting to you. Why don't you join Pinky and her crowd? I'll be with you in a few minutes."

She took her cue gratefully this time. Much as she wanted to find her father, Allison couldn't help hoping Cokey wasn't the man. Everything about him repelled her, but from all she'd heard, he was just the sort that would appeal to Monica.

Cokey watched her go. "That's one beautiful babe. Is she as good as she looks?"

Gabe's jaw set, but he kept his voice pleasant. "Not as good as Monica, from all reports."

"Oh, hell, you're talking about the solid gold Cadillac of women. I never had anybody before or since like Monica."

"She was only a kid when you dated her."

"In years maybe, but not in experience. She liked to try everything. I remember one night..."

Gabe tried to conceal his distaste as Cokey related incidents better left untold. "Did this go on all summer?" he asked.

"You better believe it! She was dating Danny Wallace, but she dumped him as soon as I came to town."

"Then you went with her until the beginning of September when it was time to close up the houses and go home?" Gabe persisted.

"You bet. It was the best summer of my life."

"Did Monica date any other boys while you two were seeing each other?"

"No way! I was quite capable of taking care of her needs," Cokey said smugly.

Gabe's eyes were cold as he dropped his act. "Where were you when her baby was born?"

"*What?*" Cokey's mouth dropped open. "What the hell are you talking about?"

"If you were as close as you say, you must have known she got pregnant that August."

"This is the first I've heard of it, I swear to God! Are you putting me on? I never heard anything about Monica having a baby."

"It was put up for adoption at birth."

Cokey continued to look dazed. "They sure kept it a secret. I wonder who the father was."

"Come off it! How can there be any doubt? You just told me she didn't see anybody else all summer."

Cokey squirmed uncomfortably. "I'm afraid I exaggerated a little."

"Am I supposed to believe you made up all those lurid stories? I didn't know you were that inventive," Gabe said mockingly.

"They were all true. What I stretched the truth about was the length of our affair. It lasted less than a month, not all summer like I said."

"But you only decided to change your story when it turns out your summer of love might have some far-reaching consequences. How convenient."

Cokey's face reddened. "I don't give a damn if you believe me or not. What business is it of yours, anyway?"

"I happen to represent Monica's daughter. You don't have to worry, though. It isn't going to cost you anything. She just wants to establish her parentage."

"You'll have to look someplace else." Cokey's lascivious manner had vanished. He was now eager to convince Gabe, even at the expense of his macho image. "What I told you about Danny is true. I did take Monica away from him, and for a few weeks it was sex city. We made love in places you wouldn't believe! I figured I was the luckiest kid on the block. Then I began to suspect she was cheating on me, like she cheated on Danny when I came on the scene. Finally she dumped me the same way. It isn't something a man likes to admit, so I pretended we kept on heating the sheets until we both had to go home. You can understand that, can't you?"

Gabe didn't bother to answer. "Who was the new favorite?"

"I never knew, and that was kind of strange. Monica always liked to talk about her new conquests—like the guys do. But that time she clammed up. All I could find out was that he was older, probably a college man."

"You'd think she'd brag about that," Gabe said thoughtfully.

"Maybe her parents wouldn't have let her go out with him if it got back to them. She was only seventeen, and he could have been twenty or more."

"That might account for it. You think she sneaked out to meet him?"

"If that's what it took. Her parents' opposition would only have made him more attractive. Anyway, he had the inside track for the rest of the summer. I couldn't get another date with her. If Danny said he did, he was lying."

"When did you and Monica break up?" Gabe asked intently.

"Early in August."

"Could you be more specific?"

"Hell, you're talking about twenty-five years ago!"

"I know, but think hard, it's important."

"You want the exact date? How can I—wait a minute! It was the third of August. I remember because my father's birthday was the next day. Some relatives were coming in for a big party my parents were throwing, and I had to pick them up at the airport. It made me late for my date with Monica, and she was gone by the time I got to her house. I told myself that was the reason for our breakup, but it only speeded things up."

"So you didn't sleep with her after roughly the second of August?"

"She wouldn't even go out with me again. I assume the next guy lasted till summer was over. That was about Monica's attention span—three weeks to a month. If she got pregnant, it was by him."

"Are you sure you don't know who he was? The same people came back every year. A newcomer would be noticed. Did somebody have a houseguest or a visiting relative?"

"They undoubtedly did, but it isn't something I'd remember. People had guests all the time. Her new love interest could just as easily have been one of the college kids who come for the summer to work in the restaurants and hotels. Monica could have met him in town. That might be the reason she was so secretive about the guy. Her father would have thrown a fit.''

Gabe sighed. ''If he was a transient I'll never track him down.''

Cokey's relief was evident. ''That means you believe I'm telling the truth.''

''I suppose so. No decent man would make up the kind of sexual exploits you bragged about.''

''It's easy to be judgmental now,'' Cokey whined. ''But you have to remember, I was only seventeen at the time.''

''And you haven't grown up since then.'' Gabe slid off the bar stool and walked away.

Allison searched Gabe's face for some clue as he approached the table. She wasn't reassured by his brooding expression, although he managed a smile when he saw her.

''You don't look like you're bringing good news,'' she said tentatively.

''That depends on your viewpoint. Cokey isn't your father, either.''

''Why do I feel like celebrating? We're back where we started, but I'm really glad I'm not related to him.''

''You have good judgment.''

''Where do we go from here?'' Allison's face was troubled. ''Mary Louise only gave you those two names.''

Gabe hesitated. ''I'm afraid you might have to face the possibility that we'll never find the man we're looking for.''

''You're giving up?'' she asked hopelessly.

''Not by choice, honey. But we're up against almost insurmountable odds. Monica dated a lot of boys that summer.'' He only hoped Allison never discovered the extent of her activities.

''The one she became pregnant by couldn't have been just a casual date. Didn't Danny or Cokey give you any clue as to who it could be? You said all the summer people knew each other.''

''That doesn't narrow the field. Cokey suggested it might have been one of the transients who worked here briefly that summer.''

''Oh, no! That *would* make finding him impossible.''

''It doesn't matter, darling.'' Gabe squeezed her hand tightly. ''I love *you*. I don't give a damn who your parents were, and neither will my mother and father.''

"You might be right," she said unemotionally.

Gabe sighed. "I could prove it if you'd just let me tell them we're engaged. They'll welcome you with open arms, I promise."

The abrupt end of her dreams left Allison numb. She wanted to believe Gabe, but bitter experience had taught her otherwise. Gabe would never walk out on her like Bruce had, but he enjoyed a close relationship with his family. Could their love survive if she caused a rift with his parents? She honestly didn't know.

"How could anyone not love you?" he asked in a husky voice.

"You can tell them if you like," she answered tonelessly.

After looking at her expressionless face he sighed again. "I can tell I haven't convinced you of a thing. Okay, honey, I'll just have to keep digging."

"There aren't any more leads."

"Then I'll just have to turn up some. Let me think about it overnight."

"What are you two discussing so seriously?" Pinky asked. "You've had your heads together for half an hour."

"I've been telling Allison we were meant for each other." Gabe smiled.

"Don't take him seriously," Pinky advised her. "He's one of those guys you can catch, but you can't keep."

"Just what I need right now," Gabe muttered under his breath. "Are you ready to leave?" he asked Allison.

"You haven't had dinner yet," Pinky protested.

"We just stopped in for a drink," he answered.

As they were driving away, Gabe said to Allison, "Perhaps you wanted to stay. I should have asked you."

"No, I don't feel much like partying right now."

"That's what I thought. We'll find a nice, quiet restaurant instead."

"I'm really not hungry, but I'll have a cup of coffee with you while you have dinner."

"I have a better idea." He pulled into the curb in front of a small deli. "Wait here, I'll be right back."

He returned a short time later, carrying a large grocery bag.

"What did you buy?" Allison asked curiously. "If you have any thoughts about whipping up a snack in Armand's kitchen, forget it! He'd be terminally insulted."

"Especially if he knew we preferred a hero sandwich to paté à la maison."

Her spirts started to rise as they drove through the gates to his uncle's house. "I won't tell if you don't."

"I'm not allowed to tell *anything*," Gabe complained, but he put his arm around her shoulders and kissed her temple as they entered the house. "You can sit out by the pool while I make some sandwiches. I'll bring you a drink."

"No, I'd rather be with you."

"That's what I like to hear."

He kissed her lightly, then more purposefully as the flame that was always present between them ignited. When she turned to face him and put her arms around his waist, Gabe dropped the bag of groceries and took her in both arms.

Their bodies were molded together as they kissed and moved against each other in sheer delight. While his tongue probed deeply, he caressed her back down to the curved slope of her bottom.

Allison's hands wandered over him in the same way, tracing the width of his broad shoulders, the bunched muscles in his arms. She could never get over the wonder of his perfect physique. When she dug her fingers into his taut buttocks, Gabe uttered a hoarse cry and urged her against his hardened loins.

"There's never been anyone like you," he muttered. "I think about you night and day. Don't ever leave me, darling."

"Not if you really want me."

"Can you have any doubt? I couldn't live without you."

Swinging her into his arms, he carried her up the stairs to his bedroom. After setting her on her feet, he slid her zipper down and gently urged the dress off her shoulders. It slithered to the floor, leaving her in just a pair of brief panties. The night was warm, so she hadn't worn a bra or stockings.

Gabe drew in his breath audibly at the sight of her slender, nearly nude body. "God, you're beautiful," he said huskily. "You're almost too perfect to be real."

She gave a throaty laugh, feeling a heady sense of power over this magnificent man. "You should know how real I am." She pushed the jacket off his shoulders and loosened the knot in his tie.

"You seem different every time," he said, drawing her into his arms and sliding his lips over her bare shoulder.

"There haven't been that many times," she murmured.

"We're going to have a whole lifetime together, my love, and I'm going to know every inch of your exquisite body."

He began an inflaming exploration right then, lowering his head to string a line of scorching kisses from her breast to her navel. Allison anchored her fingers in his thick hair as his mouth continued its erotic path downward.

He removed her panties with tantalizing deliberation, pausing to kiss the smooth skin of her stomach. She quivered as his kisses grew more intimate, feeding her mounting passion.

Sinking to her knees, she flung herself into his arms. The impact caught Gabe off balance and he landed on his back, carrying her with him. Allison rained kisses over his face and neck, pressing her hips into his.

Gabe's arms tightened and he rolled over, taking her with him. His deep, sensuous kiss was a prelude of what was to come. After a few smoldering moments he released her.

"Don't leave me," she pleaded as he got to his feet.

"I couldn't if I wanted to," he answered tenderly.

Gabe threw off his clothes and returned to lift her into his arms and carry her to the bed. Without loosening his embrace, he positioned himself between her legs.

Allison raised her hips, inviting him into her depths. His entry was exquisitely satisfying. She clamped her arms and legs around him, rising to meet his thrusts as molten sensation flowed like a blazing stream through their bodies. The final eruption left them limp, but totally satisfied.

Much later, Gabe said softly, "Do you know how much I love you?"

"You just showed me." She smoothed his hair, gazing at him adoringly.

"Do you think you can stand a lifetime of this?"

"I'm counting on it." She smiled. Allison put aside her trepidation for the moment. No matter what the future held, nothing could take away what they had just shared.

They talked softly for a while, then Gabe swung his long legs out of bed.

"Do we have to leave already?" she asked wistfully.

"Not for hours. I just thought you might have worked up an appetite." He grinned, leaning down to kiss the tip of her nose. "Stay here. I'll make some sandwiches and bring them up to you."

"No, I'll come with you."

"Just can't let me out of your sight, can you?" he teased.

"Don't push your luck." She pretended to frown.

He cupped her chin in his palm and looked deeply into her eyes. "I don't know how I ever got this lucky, but you're mine now and I'll never let you go."

I hope not, Allison answered silently.

Gabe refused to let her help, so Allison sat on a kitchen stool and watched while he sliced a loaf of French bread in half horizontally. He piled cold meat and cheese on one half, and lettuce and tomatoes on the other. The finished product was tremendous.

"It looks delicious, but we can't eat all that," she remarked.

"Speak for yourself. I used up a lot of energy." He grinned.

"They just don't make men like they used to," Allison commented mischievously.

"Maybe not, but you're stuck with me. Till death do us part. So don't think I'll let you get away with changing your mind."

She was jolted back to reality. None of her problems had been solved. "What are we going to do now, Gabe?"

His laughing face sobered as he noted her dejected expression. "Can't you give it up, honey?"

"I guess I don't have any choice."

"All right." He sighed. "Let's figure out where to go from here."

"That's the whole problem. We're at a dead end."

"Not necessarily. We bombed out with Monica's boyfriends, but somebody must know who she was having an affair with. We just have to find out who that person is."

"Maybe she didn't tell a soul. Mary Louise said Monica was very secretive."

"It isn't normal for a teenage girl not to confide in *somebody*. Like a best friend, for instance."

"From all appearances, she didn't have any girlfriends. Except for Sandra Gresham. They were good friends for a while, but something happened and they broke up.''

''That sounds promising. I think we'll have a talk with Sandra tomorrow.''

Allison's face lit up with hope. ''Do you think that might lead somewhere?''

''It's a definite possibility.'' Gabe smoothed her hair lovingly. ''Now do you think I could have your full attention for the rest of the night?''

''You can have a lot more than that,'' she answered softly.

Chapter Ten

On the way back to Rosewood Manor that night, Allison's misgivings returned.

As they walked up the staircase she said, "If Sandra Gresham holds the only clue to Monica's past, I'm afraid we're in big trouble. You saw how strangely she acted around me. I doubt if she'd tell us anything even if she knew it."

"She was just out of sorts the night of the party," Gabe said reassuringly. "What could she have against you? She'd never seen you before."

"That's what's so puzzling. But if I'm right, how will we get her to talk to us?"

"Mary Louise can give us some pointers on how to handle Sandra. I'll speak to her in the morning." Gabe put his arms around Allison at her bedroom door. "You don't have to get up, I'll take care of it."

"No, I wouldn't be able to sleep anyway. Time is running out, and I'm getting really tense."

"I thought I relaxed you," he teased. "I guess I'll just have to spend the rest of the night taking your mind off the problem."

"I wish you could." She sighed.

"Are you doubting my ability?" he parted her lips for a sensuous kiss.

Allison allowed herself the luxury of relaxing in his arms for a long moment before drawing away reluctantly. "You'd better go to bed. We don't want to wake the family."

"Okay, angel, if you insist. But I won't accept any excuses after we get back to New York. I want to see your beautiful face on the pillow next to me every morning when I wake up."

"It's late, Gabe. We'll talk about it some other time."

"There's nothing to talk about. We're getting married." He tipped her chin up and kissed her briefly. "Get some sleep, darling, and stop looking for things to worry about."

Allison tried to shake off her apprehension as she got undressed. If only she had Gabe's confidence that their marriage would work. She didn't doubt his love, but could it survive the pressures that would be put on him?

The cold distaste directed at her by Bruce's parents was a memory that wouldn't go away. If it happened again she could live with it for Gabe's sake. He was worth putting up with almost anything. What she couldn't endure was to watch their relationship change as he was forced to make repeated excuses for her.

Allison's expression was bleak when she considered her alternative.

The atmosphere at breakfast the next morning wasn't as sunny as usual. Mary Louise and Sergei both seemed distracted and Allison was subdued.

Only Gabe was charged with energy as he explained their problem. "Sandra is just about our last hope. As far as I can tell, she's the only person Monica would have confided in. The difficulty is getting her to talk. She's not the most approachable person in the world."

"No, she's a difficult girl," Mary Louise agreed. "Sandra hasn't given her parents much pleasure. Not that Elinor has ever said a word to me, but I know they don't have a good relationship. It's hard to understand. Curtis and Elinor are both such charming people. Everybody loves being with them."

Gabe gently guided her back to the subject. "I might not get anywhere, but I'd like a chance to talk to Sandra. It has to be a casual meeting so she won't have her guard up automatically. I thought you could tell me what her interests are. If she plays golf or tennis, for instance, I could bump into her accidentally in the clubhouse and ask her to have a drink.''

''You needn't go through all that. Sandra is coming for tea this afternoon. The garden club is meeting here.''

''Fantastic! Mary Louise, you're a lifesaver.''

Allison frowned slightly. ''How can you make Sandra believe it's just a casual meeting? What would a man be doing at a ladies garden club meeting?''

''We have a few male attendees,'' Mary Louise said. ''Old Mr. Pennington is one of the charter members. He's hard-of-hearing now and he falls asleep if the reading of the minutes takes too long, but we don't wake him unless he snores.'' She smiled.

''I promise to be attentive and stay awake,'' Gabe said. ''I'll wait until—'' He paused as Florence approached.

''You have a long-distance telephone call, Mr. Rockford,'' the maid said.

He groaned. ''That must be Dad. I forgot to call him.''

''Give him my best,'' Mary Louise said. ''Your mother, too.''

Gabe's surmise was correct. His father's voice came over the line, slightly testy.

''I told you to take a short vacation, Gabriel, not an extended sabbatical. May I remind you that you still have a job here in New York?''

''I left a message saying I needed another week. Didn't you get it?''

''I received the message, not the meaning. Why haven't you phoned to give me a progress report? You *are* still working on the case, I presume.''

''I've been giving it my full attention,'' Gabe assured him.

''Then I don't understand why it's taking so long. You must have made up your mind by now. Either the girl is a fraud or she isn't.''

''There was never any fraud involved,'' Gabe said sharply. ''Allison always believed she was Monica's daughter.''

"And what do *you* think?"

"I don't believe there can be any doubt that Monica had a baby when she was eighteen. The evidence is pretty conclusive. Mary Louise said you checked the hospital records and found out Allison is telling the truth."

"We sent an investigator to Philadelphia to verify the allegation, which proved to be correct. That part isn't subject to argument, the girl's credibility is. You were supposed to ascertain that."

"You can drop the legalese, Dad. You're not arguing a case in court, and Allison isn't a suspected criminal."

Burton Rockford's eyebrows rose at his son's harsh tone of voice. "I wasn't accusing the young woman of anything," he said mildly. "I'm merely trying to find out what progress you've made in resolving the matter. Mary Louise is a friend as well as a client. I need to be sure her interests are being protected."

"You don't have to worry about that. Allison doesn't want a penny from her."

"Aren't you being a little naive? There are millions at stake here."

"I know it's hard to believe. You'd have to meet Allison to understand. She doesn't care about the money. All she wants is to find out who her parents were."

"And then what? If she succeeds in convincing Mary Louise that Monica was her mother, you think Allison will just leave it at that? Nice to have met you, let's have lunch sometime?" Burton's voice was derisive. "If she didn't already know what a grandchild would mean to Mary Louise, I'm sure she does now."

"You're as bad as Martin!" Gabe said heatedly. "You think everybody has some personal ax to grind. Okay, so maybe a lot of people are greedy, but that doesn't mean everyone is. I know Allison. She's the most honest, trustworthy person I've ever met."

After a long pause, Burton said, "Then you're telling me she really is Monica's daughter?"

"It certainly looks that way. The problem after all these years is getting absolute proof. The only way to do that is to find Allison's father. That's the reason it's taken me so long. I talked to two possibilities, but they didn't pan out. Now I'm going to talk to Monica's best friend, in the hope that Monica confided in her."

"And if she didn't?"

"Then I have to convince Allison that it doesn't matter."

"I don't understand."

"She had a bad experience with some bigoted people who rejected her because she's an orphan. I tried to tell her people like that aren't worth losing sleep over, but the poor kid is afraid it will happen again. She won't let me tell you—" Gabe stopped abruptly. "It was evidently a very traumatic experience. That's why she needs to find out about herself."

"I see," Burton said without inflection.

"You'd really like her. Mary Louise is crazy about her."

"Are you saying she believes Allison is her granddaughter?"

"She doesn't give a damn whether she is or not. Allison is everything she ever wished for in a grandchild."

"This is exactly the sort of thing I sent you there to prevent!" Burton exclaimed sharply. "The girl is undoubtedly clever. She's succeeded in charming both you and Mary Louise. I can understand Mary Louise's vulnerability, but not yours. I thought you were too mature to be taken in by a woman, no matter how beautiful and innocent appearing. That was evidently my mistake."

Gabe's anger rose to meet his father's. "You have no right to talk about Allison that way. The fact that she made something of herself with no help from anybody means nothing to you. All you can see is a nameless nobody looking for a handout. I thought you, of all people, would keep an open mind, but obviously I was wrong. She said you'd react like this, but I couldn't believe it. I still can't."

Burton took a deep breath. "I suggest we both calm down and discuss this reasonably. I get the impression that you're strongly attracted to her. Can you blame me for wondering if she's clouded your judgment?"

Gabe made an effort to rein in his temper. "I suppose it appears that way, but I haven't found a single indication that she's lying about her past, or her reason for coming here. I'm convinced that she isn't trying to exploit the Van Ruyders. If I can't prove she's Monica's daughter, Allison will bow out of their lives, even though Mary Louise would give her every inducement to stay. It's *because* of my feelings for Allison that I've done everything humanly possible to prove her story, one way or the other. I hope you believe me."

"I've never had any reason to doubt you, son," Burton answered more quietly. "I'm sorry if I seemed to judge Allison prematurely. She sounds like a very unusual young woman."

"That's not an unqualified vote of confidence," Gabe said slowly. "Are you bothered by her lack of background?"

"I can think of a lot of reasons for disapproval of someone, but that isn't one of them," Burton replied crisply. "When are you coming home? I can't justify this trip as work-related for much longer."

"You talked me into it." Gabe laughed. "Now you'll just have to live with the consequences."

Burton's face was impassive as he cradled the receiver. After a moment he picked it up again and tapped out a number.

"How would you like to go to Newport for a few days?" he asked when his wife answered.

"That might be nice," Lily Rockford said. "What date did you have in mind?"

"Tomorrow morning."

"You must be joking! I couldn't possibly get away that soon."

"Of course you can. How long does it take to throw a few clothes in a suitcase?"

"Men never understand all the things women have to take just for a weekend. But there's more involved than that. We have all sorts of commitments. The Willoughby's anniversary party is Sunday night, and we promised to show up at Midge Forsythe's gallery show on Saturday. I have a million other things to do besides."

"Are any of them as important as meeting your future daughter-in-law?"

"*What?*"

"I have reason to believe that Gabriel has finally met his match. I don't think we have anything to say about it, but I'd like to take a look at the young woman."

"When did this happen? What's her name? Do we know her?"

"I'll tell you all about it when I get home. In the meantime, start packing. Hebert and Jean are still in Europe, but we can stay at their house."

"Does Gabriel know we're coming?"

"No." Burton's smile was on the grim side. "I decided one surprise deserves another."

Gabe sat through the garden club meeting with more patience than Allison did. She fidgeted in her chair, wondering how they were going to get Sandra alone. The woman was avoiding her. Allison was sure it wasn't her imagination. Every time she approached, Sandra moved away.

After the meeting was over, the ladies broke up into little groups as they waited for tea to be served. Mary Louise moved among them graciously, pausing when she came to Sandra.

"Would you do me a favor, my dear?" she asked the younger woman.

"Anything at all." Like most people, Sandra was fond of Mary Louise.

"Will you take Allison into the garden and show her which roses we discussed today. I don't think she knows a Peace from a Tropicana." Mary Louise laughed merrily.

Sandra's smile vanished. "I'm not that knowledgeable myself. Get Crystal to do it."

"Nonsense, my dear. You're too modest."

"Mind if I tag along?" Gabe took Sandra's arm and steered her toward the door to the terrace. "I might learn something. The only thing I know about roses is that they're delivered in long white boxes."

Allison followed wordlessly as he led the way down a path away form the house. Sandra was equally silent, resentment evident in every line of her stiffly held body.

She stopped by a bush covered with clusters of sweetly scented pink blossoms. "This is one of the antique roses they were talking about. It's called Ballerina, although I know you couldn't care less."

"That's not true," Gabe protested. "I'll admit I'm no gardener. Unfortunately I have a black thumb. I've killed off so many houseplants there's a wanted poster of me in all the nurseries.''

"Then what are you doing at a garden club meeting?" Sandra demanded.

He smiled engagingly. "Nostalgia for the garden my mother used to have when we owned a house here. She was very involved in horticulture. I remember there was a rose festival every year. It was a big event," Gabe told Allison. "Lots of parties naturally, and even our very own rose queen." He turned back to Sandra. "Wasn't Monica elected queen one year?"

"She could have been. I don't remember."

"Really? I can recall every detail of those summers. I was just a kid then and I thought you teenagers were really neat. That's when I discovered it was all right for boys to like girls." Gabe laughed. "You and Monica were always surrounded by guys I admired, like Cokey Clay and Danny Wallace. Who were some of the others you ran around with?"

"That's ancient history," Sandra said curtly.

"It's fun to look back after all these years, though. I'll bet you two dated every boy in town."

"*She* did, anyway."

"She was really one of a kind, wasn't she? Did Monica tell you ahead of time about all those crazy escapades she cooked up?" He chuckled indulgently. "You were the only person who knew all her secrets."

"I don't know where you got the impression that Monica and I were close friends. We weren't. I hadn't spoken to her since we were seventeen."

"Why was that?"

Sandra's eyes smoldered with suppressed emotion. "It really isn't any of your business."

"I was just curious. You *were* good friends at one time—probably Monica's only girlfriend. What happened that was so terrible it broke up your friendship?" Gabe asked softly.

"I was fooled into believing we ever had one." Sandra's inner fury erupted. "She was the friend from hell! Monica didn't care who she hurt, as long as she got what she wanted. She was a monster! I didn't see it at first, and when I did it was too late."

"Teenagers can be cruel," he said gently. "But it isn't healthy to bury your resentment and let it fester over the years. Wouldn't you feel better if you talked about it?''

Sandra was breathing rapidly, almost oblivious to their presence as she relived the past. Then her eyes focused and she stared at Gabe with active dislike. "Leave me alone. I have nothing more to say to you."

When she turned to go back to the house, Allison blocked the path. She couldn't let her get away. Sandra obviously knew who Monica's lover was, and she'd been so close to revealing the information.

"Please don't go yet," Allison begged. "I don't want to probe any sore spots, but we need to find out some things about Monica."

"What makes you think I'm interested?"

Sandra tried to brush by her, but Allison held her ground. "Did you know Monica became pregnant when she was seventeen?" There was no time for subtlety.

Sandra laughed harshly. "She did *everything* when she was seventeen—and before."

"You did know, didn't you?" Gabe asked quietly.

"What difference does it make now? She's dead."

"I'm not asking out of idle curiosity. Anything you tell us will be kept in strictest confidence. I just want to know who fathered her child." Allison took a deep breath. "I think Monica was my mother."

"Big surprise! Am I supposed to gasp in amazement?" Sandra's mouth twisted sardonically. "I noticed the resemblance immediately."

"Then you must understand why it's important to me to find out who my father was."

"Pick any of a dozen men." Sandra shrugged contemptuously. "It could be any one of them."

Gabe stared at her with narrowed eyes. "If you really believed that, you wouldn't be so bitter after all these years. You know precisely who the man is. Why won't you tell Allison?"

"It's over and done with—or at least it should be. Why do you want to ruin his life? That's what Monica was good at." Sandra spat out the words. "She wasn't happy unless she was destroying somebody."

"I didn't come here to make trouble," Allison said earnestly.

"I promise not to contact him or let a word of this conversation go any farther. All I want to know is who I am. You can understand that, can't you?"

"If you're really sincere you'll go away and leave us alone."

"How can I convince you that I don't want anything but his name?" Allison looked helplessly at Gabe.

"At least tell him who Allison is," he suggested. "Let him make the decision about whether he wants her to know."

"If he had good sense, would he have gotten involved with Monica in the first place?" Sandra asked derisively.

"We don't intend to let the matter drop," Gabe warned. "It would stir up a lot less talk if you told us in confidence, instead of forcing us to question Monica's friends."

"You must have done that already," Sandra answered shrewdly, seeing through his bluff. "You've been snooping around here for two weeks. I can't stop your witch hunt, but I don't have to be part of it."

"Isn't there anything I can to do prove I'm not a threat?" Allison pleaded.

"You can leave and never come back." Sandra pushed roughly past her and almost ran up the path.

Allison's eyes were desolate as the other woman disappeared around a turn. "There goes my last hope."

Gabe tried to be consoling. "At least there's no doubt that you're Monica's daughter. Isn't that enough?"

"It only answers half the question. Now I'll always wonder who my father is. Although he wasn't any happier about me than my mother was," she commented ironically. "Why am I surprised at being considered unacceptable when my own parents didn't want anything to do with me?"

Gabe took both her hands in his. "You don't know that. Monica might have wanted very much to keep you, but I'm sure she wasn't given the choice. I knew Peter Van Ruyder. He was a very self-righteous man. You mustn't blame Monica, and certainly not yourself. Mary Louise is ready to welcome you into the family."

"I guess you're right," Allison said without conviction.

Gabe could tell it wasn't enough. "We aren't licked yet," he said with a confidence he didn't feel. "Sandra was never a promising source of information."

"She was the only one we had left."

"Not necessarily. I've been kicking around an idea. Somehow or other, we have to get invited over to her house tomorrow. Let's try to figure out how."

"Are you kidding? After what happened here, Sandra would have us arrested for trespassing!"

"She won't be at home. I'm sure Mary Louise can manage to lure her away if we ask her to. Just concentrate on wangling an invitation out of Pinky."

"What will we do when we get there?"

"Leave that to me. All you have to do is go along with anything I suggest." He took her in his arms and kissed her. "I haven't disappointed you so far, have I?"

"Never." Allison returned his kiss, feeling better in spite of herself.

That night at dinner, Gabe enlisted Mary Louise's help in carrying out his scheme.

She wrinkled her nose. "Two days of Sandra is a little much. Although I shouldn't talk that way, considering how friendly I am with her parents."

"Then make a date that includes her mother," Gabe suggested.

"I really want to help, but Sergei and I have a luncheon date. I've been looking forward to it." She smiled at the older man. "It's so seldom that he has a free day."

"Actually I have an appointment in the afternoon," Sergei said. "It would have been a short lunch. Why don't you go ahead and make plans with Sandra and Elinor?"

Mary Louise's smile faltered, but she tried to hide her disappointment under a joking manner. "All right, I suppose I can be patient for another day. But I warn you, I'll expect a very fancy lunch to make up for saddling me with Sandra again."

"I might have to give you a rain check. It's time I got back to work."

"I thought you intended to stay another week, at least!"

"It would have been nice, but all good things must come to an end." His smile was perfunctory.

"I hoped it wouldn't be so soon," she answered in a muted voice.

They were all a little subdued after that. When the evening ended, Gabe lagged behind for a private word with Mary Louise.

"Sergei doesn't really want to go," he said quietly.

"You aren't up on your psychology," she replied in a brittle tone. "Nobody does anything he doesn't really want to."

"Men have fragile egos. They have to feel needed."

"That's the whole problem. Sergei doesn't realize how badly I do need him."

"Have you ever thought of telling him?"

"I couldn't do that. It would put him in an awkward position. If he really loved me he'd tell me so. Evidently I want more from him than he does from me."

Gabe shook his head. "You two are unbelievable! You're both so cautious that you'll end up being alone and miserable. Take my advice and tell him what you just told me. Or better yet, say, listen pal, we aren't getting any younger so stop screwing up and let's get married."

Mary Louise laughed unwillingly. "Can't you just hear me saying something like that?"

"No, but I wish I could."

It was surprisingly easy to get an invitation to Pinky's house. Allison had prepared an involved story about dropping off something for Mary Louise. It wasn't very convincing and fortunately she didn't have to use it. Pinky invited them over without prompting.

"I'm so glad you called," she said. "Mother insists that I stay home today and wait for the pool man, so I have to waste the whole day here alone. Who knows when he'll show up? I'd love it if you and Gabe would come over and keep me company."

"We'd be glad to," Allison said. "I'd enjoy a nice, relaxing afternoon."

"Great! Come over anytime."

Just to double-check, Allison said, "It will be nice to see your mother again." She was fairly certain Sandra hadn't mentioned their meeting the previous day.

"She won't be here. That's why I got stuck. Mrs. Watkins,

our housekeeper, could just as easily tell the guy that the pump isn't working right, but Mother is sure she'll get busy and forget to watch for him. Isn't that the pits?''

"Well don't worry. We'll keep you occupied."

The Gresham home was a substantial house set in lovely grounds, much like Gabe's former home. Pinky took them through a center hall and out the back, where a swimming pool sparkled in the sunshine. Chaises and chairs padded with yellow-and-white striped cushions were grouped along the decking.

"Do you have your bathing suits on under your clothes?" she asked.

"No, we decided to be lazy today. We've been getting enough exercise." Gabe's remark was innocent enough, but Allison's cheeks warmed.

"Well, if you change your minds, I've got lots of spare bathing suits," Pinky said.

Whatever Gabe was planning, he didn't seem in any hurry to put it into operation. They lounged on chaises and drank lemonade, chatting idly about mutual friends and their jobs in the city.

Allison's nerves gradually tightened when he continued to make small talk. Did Gabe really have a plan, or had he just said that to make her feel better? If he didn't make a move soon, Sandra might catch them there. Allison's stomach knotted at the thought of the scene Sandra would make. She was really a little paranoid.

"When will your mother be back?" Allison asked when she could work it into the conversation.

"Not for hours. Mary Louise shanghaied her to work on one of her endless committees. She's the only one who can make Mother do something she doesn't want to do." Pinky grinned. "I must ask her how she does it."

"It's a knack," Gabe said. "Mary Louise has been coercing people in that genteel way of hers ever since I can remember—and I go back a long way."

"Come on, grandpa." Pinky laughed. "You're not that much older than I."

"You're a youngster," he scoffed. "You never knew what

Newport was like in the old days when Monica Van Ruyder and her crowd was getting into mischief.''

"I heard some of those stories. She was really outrageous."

"That's right, I forgot. She and your mother were really good buddies. You probably heard the stories firsthand."

"Not from her. I don't know what happened between them, but she goes ballistic whenever Monica's name is mentioned."

"Monica was quite a femme fatale, even at seventeen. Maybe she tried to steal your father away from her," Gabe suggested.

"It couldn't have been that. Mother didn't meet Dad until after she graduated from college."

Allison saw what Gabe was driving at. If Monica had set her sights on Ted Gresham, it might have accounted for Sandra's almost pathological hatred. That evidently wasn't the case, though.

"Well, it's too bad their friendship broke up," Gabe said. "They had a good group in those days. It seems funny now that I thought a bunch of teenagers were so cool." He smiled. "I wish I could see what guys like Cokey Pembroke and all the rest looked like back then."

"Mother has a lot of old snapshots. I could get them, but it wouldn't be much fun for Allison. She didn't know any of those people."

"I'd love to see the pictures," Allison said quickly. "I've met Cokey and Danny and a few of the others, and I've heard so much about Monica. I'd like to see what she looked like."

"Mary Louise must have shown you pictures of her," Pinky said.

"Only one. I'd like to see more."

"Okay, I'll go get them. It might take me a few minutes, but I think I know where they are."

When he and Allison were alone, Gabe said, "I had to take my time leading up to it. Was I sufficiently casual?"

"About what? I don't even know what you're trying to accomplish."

"I want to know who else was in the crowd Monica and Sandra ran with. I can't remember every one of them after all this time. I figured old snapshots might give us some new leads."

"Will you recognize them so many years later?"

"With any luck, Sandra wrote down their names."

Pinky returned with a bulky scrapbook. "There were more—Mother must have taken photos of every living thing in Newport. I thought this would provide enough of a trip down memory lane, though."

She placed the album on an umbrella table and they all pulled up chairs to look at it together. Sandra had been very methodical. Each snapshot was dated and the people identified, although sometimes only by their nicknames. She supplied other reminders, however, like "birthday party at Ashley's" or "Tommy's new car."

"Aren't these wild?" Pinky chuckled. "Look at those weird hairdos."

"Your children will be saying the same thing about you in thirty-some years," Gabe said.

"Where is Monica?" Allison asked, trying to conceal her intense interest.

"There she is." Pinky pointed at a snapshot of a beautiful young girl surrounded by gangling youths.

Gabe read off the names printed underneath. "Danny, Cokey, Mark—that must be Mark Levinson. I remember him vaguely. But who's the blond kid?"

Pinky peered at the printing. "It says 'Cowboy Bob.' Does that ring a bell?"

Gabe shook his head. "I can't recall anyone with that nickname, and his face isn't familiar."

"Maybe he was visiting somebody. Did anyone you know have relatives out West? He didn't get that label around here. This is fun." Pinky grinned. "Like playing detective."

"As long as we're sleuthing, we might as well be professional about it. Make a list of all the people we can't identify," Gabe told Allison. "We'll call them suspects."

Allison took a pocket notebook and a pencil out of her purse and wrote down Mark Levinson. Underneath she put Cowboy Bob.

Pinky glanced at the entries. "Mark shouldn't be on the list. Gabe recognized him."

"Oh, that's right. He was somebody I hadn't heard of before, so I got confused." Instead of erasing the top name, Allison put a faint line through it.

She started to get discouraged as the list of suspects grew.

How could they possibly question this many people? They'd have trouble just finding them all!

Pinky was having a great time. "This is my girlfriend Barbara's mother." She pointed to a plump teenager in white shorts that emphasized her generous hips. "She'd absolutely die if she saw this picture!"

They were all so engrossed that they didn't hear footsteps on the terrace. A moment later, Sandra was standing over them like an avenging fury.

"What do you two think you're doing here?" She was practically quivering with anger.

Pinky gave her a shocked look. "I invited them over."

"Go in the house!" Sandra ordered.

"You must be joking," Pinky said uncertainly.

"You heard me. Do as I say!" When Sandra noticed the scrapbook on the table her body tensed. "You have no right to come here and snoop through my private possessions," she told Gabe heatedly.

"*I* brought out the album, Mother. I didn't think you'd mind. We were talking about Newport in the old days, and we all thought it would be fun to see how you and your friends have changed."

Sandra turned on Gabe. "What did you expect to find out by prying into my personal life?"

"Mother, really! How can you—"

Sandra cut her daughter off in midsentence. "This doesn't concern you. Leave us alone this instant! I don't want to have to tell you again."

After opening her mouth to argue, Pinky thought better of it, realizing her mother was beyond reasoning with. "I'm sorry," she murmured to the others before going back into the house.

"I should call the police," Sandra rasped. "I will, too, if you ever come here to my house again. I won't be harassed this way!"

"I'm really sorry." Allison rose. "We never would have come if we'd known you'd feel this strongly."

"What did you expect me to do, roll out the welcome mat? I knew you were going to cause trouble from the minute I laid eyes on you. These past two weeks have been sheer hell!"

"I don't understand." Allison gazed at her in bewilderment. "What have I done?"

"Explain it to us, Sandra." Gabe was staring at her with narrowed eyes. "Why do you find Allison's search for her father so threatening?"

Belated caution made Sandra try for self-control. "It doesn't concern me personally, but nobody likes to see their friends get hurt. I'm simply outraged that she's being so selfish."

"What would you call the man who fathered her? I don't know why Allison would want to find him, but since she does, I'm going to track him down. With or without your help."

"You can't do that." Sandra's control slipped. "It wasn't his fault! Monica seduced *him!* It was just a game to her, another trophy."

"Is that what he told you?" Gabe asked softly.

"It's the truth. I knew what she was like. You didn't."

"So you've covered up for him all these years. Don't you think it's time he accepted his responsibility and met his daughter?"

Sandra's eyes took on a wild glitter. "He'd be just fool enough to do a stupid thing like that, but I won't permit it! Monica isn't going to reach out from the grave and destroy us all over again. Get out of my house and take that spawn of the devil with you!" Her voice rose hysterically.

Allison was thoroughly shaken. She trembled as she sat in the car next to Gabe.

"Take it easy, honey," he said gently. "I'm sorry things got so unpleasant, but at least we found out what we came for."

"We did?" She gazed at him uncertainly. "All we have is a long list of names from years ago. I don't think it was worth that awful scene we just went through. Sandra seemed actually unbalanced at the end."

"She was afraid we'd gotten too close to the truth."

"But we haven't!"

"She doesn't know that. Her apprehension has obviously been building for two weeks. Yesterday's conversation and our visit today finally blew the lid off."

"But why? It's so strange that the whole affair matters to her that much. The father of Monica's baby is evidently a friend, but does anyone get that worked up over somebody else's problems, even a very close friend's?''

"It doesn't seem likely, does it?" Gabe started the engine.

"Where are we going?"

"To the tennis club."

Allison stared at him in disbelief. "You want to play *tennis?*"

"No, I want to talk to a tennis player." He glanced over at her and smiled. "You can tear up that list of names you made."

Chapter Eleven

Gabe deflected all of Allison's questions on the drive to the tennis club. "Just be patient a little longer."

"Do you really know who my father is?"

"I think so. It's the only answer that makes any sense."

"Then why won't you tell me?"

"Because there's always the chance that I'm wrong. We'll find out together."

That was the most she could get out of him. Allison was plagued by conflicting emotions as she and Gabe entered the clubhouse. On one hand she was consumed by curiosity about her father, on the other was a strange reluctance to meet him.

Monica wasn't exactly the sort of mother anyone would choose. By all accounts she was selfish and heedless of other people's feelings. What if the man she was attracted to had the same traits? What kind of heritage was that? Allison was never more acutely aware of the old saying: you can choose your friends but not your relatives. Should she have left well enough alone? Well, it was too late now.

Gabe was glancing around the lounge, which was empty except for a group of women playing bridge in a corner. "Let's walk outside," he said.

It was late afternoon by then, and the tennis courts were deserted except for a pro giving a lesson. Two men had finished playing and were walking toward the locker room. One of them was Sandra's father, Curtis Mayhew. When Gabe called to him, the older man left his partner and came over to them.

"This is a nice surprise." He smiled at Allison. "Have you come to take me up on my offer of a guest card?"

"No, we just stopped by for a drink." Gabe was the one who answered.

"Capital idea. Would you like to go into the bar, or shall we sit outside on the terrace?"

"It's your call. Wherever will be more private."

After a moment's pause, Curtis said, "Let's go into the bar."

There were a few men playing liar's dice at the bar, and two couples sitting at a table close to them. Curtis led the way to a leather booth in the far corner of the room.

They made small talk until a waiter had taken their order, although Allison contributed very little to the conversation. She was totally confused and a bit disappointed. What could Curtis Mayhew know about Monica's affair? Did Gabe think Sandra might have confided in her father, of all people? It seemed highly unlikely. Even if she had, what reason was there to think he'd be any more cooperative than she?

Gabe waited until the waiter had served their drinks and left them alone. "We didn't just happen to drop by this afternoon," he said quietly.

"Were you thinking of joining? I'd be happy to sponsor you, but I must point out that it's a little late in the season." The older man seemed perfectly relaxed, but his eyes were like a poker player's, revealing no emotion.

"We came to talk to you about Monica."

"Mary Louise's daughter? Tragic about her death. Such a beautiful girl."

"There's no question of that, but you're one of the few people who have a good word to say about her."

"That's shameful! Monica might have been a trifle capricious at times, but the woman is dead. People should be more charitable."

"Your own daughter speaks very bitterly about her."

Curtis paused. "Yes, well, Sandra and Monica had a falling out a long time ago. I'm afraid my daughter doesn't have a very forgiving nature."

"What was the argument about?"

"Good God, man, how should I know? It was something that happened between two teenage girls over twenty-five years ago. A minor matter. How can you expect me to know what they quarreled over?"

"I don't mean to be rude, but I think you know very well. I believe you were the cause of it."

Allison made an inadvertent exclamation. Gabe couldn't suspect *Curtis!* He was old enough to have been Monica's father!

After the shock subsided she began to have second thoughts. Monica was always described as being very precocious. When Cokey and Danny said she was having an affair with somebody older, they inferred it was a college man. But suppose they both just assumed that?

Curtis didn't *act* guilty. He was looking at Gabe with incredulity. "I can't imagine what you're talking about. You think I took sides in a juvenile spat? That's utterly absurd!"

"A spat doesn't last a lifetime. Sandra found out you were having an affair with her best friend, didn't she?"

A fine sheen of perspiration broke out on Curtis's forehead, but he covered his uneasiness with indignation. "That's slanderous! I could sue you for an outrageous accusation like that. I will, too, if you breathe one word of this shocking allegation to anyone else."

"You don't have to worry about that. This isn't a shakedown. All I'm after is the truth. I know part of it, and I can guess the rest, except for a few details. How did Sandra find out about your affair?"

Curtis seemed about to repeat his denial, when suddenly his shoulders slumped. For the first time, he looked his age. Even his voice sounded old and tired. "Monica told her."

That took Gabe by surprise. "Why on earth would she do a thing like that?"

"Something happened between Monica and me. It was a...an accident, but she blamed me. In retaliation, she told Sandra about us. Quite understandably, it irreparably damaged my relationship with my daughter. She has never forgiven me for my... indiscretion.''

"Did your wife know about it, too?"

"No! Sandra never told her, thank God. Nobody knew except—" Curtis caught himself. "Nobody else knows, and I beg you not to rake up the sordid story now. I'm not asking for myself. I'm thinking of Elinor. She shouldn't have to pay for my transgressions."

"You don't have to worry, she won't hear about them from me. Or Allison," Gabe added when Curtis glanced at her. "Was Monica's pregnancy that accident you referred to?"

Curtis looked at him sharply. "How did you find out about that?"

Gabe didn't answer directly. "Her father discovered she was pregnant and took her to Philadelphia to have the baby. He was the other person you were alluding to. Was that why Monica was angry? Did she want to keep the baby?"

"Good Lord, no! She was merely furious that she'd gotten pregnant." Curtis stole an uncomfortable look at Allison. "Sometimes contraceptives don't work, but Monica was in no mood for excuses."

"Presumably you knew that could happen," Gabe said dryly.

"You can't blame me any more than I blame myself." Curtis sighed. "I've asked myself over and over again how I ever got involved with a teenage girl—the same age as my own daughter! You don't have to remind me."

"Monica was seventeen, and you were...?"

"Forty-two." His voice was barely audible.

He must have been very dashing, Allison thought. Curtis was still attractive to women. She could just imagine what a charmer he was in the prime of his manhood.

"I'd known Monica all her life," he continued. "She was just another one of the little girls running in and out of the house with Sandra. I never paid any attention to her."

"That couldn't have set well with Monica," Gabe observed. "She liked to be noticed."

"Maybe that's the way it started. One day Sandra had a group over for a swimming party. I was working in my den when Monica came in to use the telephone."

"Isn't there one out by the pool?"

"Yes, but I suppose it was too noisy out there. Or maybe she wanted privacy."

Gabe raised an eyebrow, obviously wondering how private the den was, with Curtis at his desk. He didn't interrupt, however.

"She was wearing a bikini, and for the first time I realized she was fully developed. Any man would appreciate a body like hers. I'll admit I enjoyed looking at her, but the thought of seducing her never entered my mind. She was like a lovely child in a woman's body. After she finished her phone call she came over and sat on my lap and put her arm around my neck. She called me Uncle Curtis and told me about some party she and Sandra were planning to give together."

"You didn't advise her that she was asking for trouble by sitting on a man's lap almost naked?"

"To tell the truth, I was ashamed of thinking of her as a woman. The way she climbed onto my lap was so trusting, not to mention the fact that she thought of me as her uncle. I was embarrassed enough at the effect she was having on me. I certainly wasn't going to bring up the facts of life."

"Didn't you worry about how it would look if someone came in and saw you like that?"

"It crossed my mind. As soon as I could get a word in, I told her I had work to do. I think she knew I was uncomfortable, because she laughed and put both arms around my neck and kissed me. I was alarmed, naturally. I stood up and said something stuffy like you should be ashamed of yourself, young lady. She merely said, 'Why? You aren't really my uncle.'"

"That sounds like Monica," Gabe murmured.

"I gave her a lecture and sent her back outside. It was an uncomfortable incident, but I thought that was the end of it. Then a couple of days later I went to get my car after playing tennis. Monica was sitting in it, waiting for me. I was really annoyed. When I asked her what she was doing there, she said she came to apologize. She said one of the boys had dared her to kiss me, and she hadn't realized what a dumb idea it was. She really seemed sincere, like a little girl who knows she's been bad and is sorry."

"She seems to have had that act down pat."

"I had no reason not to believe her. Even so, when she asked me to go for a walk with her, I said no at first. I'm not completely stupid, although you wouldn't know it from my behavior. She said I hadn't forgiven her, and what could she do to prove to me that it would never happen again? I didn't want to be unreasonable. I remembered the silly things kids do on a dare."

"So naturally you went for a walk with her," Gabe said sardonically.

"I didn't see any harm in it. We drove to the outskirts of town and walked through the fields. It was really quite pleasant. We talked about her school and she asked my advice on career choices. Monica picked wildflowers like any kid on a nature hike, and then we sat under a big tree while she twined them into a wreath." Curtis paused for so long that Gabe prompted him.

"And then what happened?"

"I honestly don't know. Monica was putting the wreath on my head and she lost her balance or something. Suddenly we were lying on the ground and she was in my arms. I kissed her. A man would have to be made out of stone not to. She was so alluring. I'd known a lot of women, but none as captivating as this innocent girl."

Gabe let out an inadvertent exclamation that he quickly stifled. Not fast enough, however.

The lines in Curtis's face deepened. "You don't have to tell me how loathsome I am. I've lived with it all these years."

"I didn't mean—never mind. Go on."

"She pulled off her T-shirt and she wasn't wearing a bra underneath. I wanted her—God how I wanted her!—but I still had a shred of decency left. I told her how wrong it would be for me to take her, but she said she wanted to become a woman in my arms."

With great self-control, Gabe forced himself to remain silent.

"It might have happened then and there, in spite of my rather dubious scruples. But a tour bus stopped by the side of the road and a load of tourists got out to look at the wildflowers. That gave me time to get a grip on myself." Curtis smiled cynically. "It turned out to be only a postponement. The next morning, Elinor received a telegram saying her mother was ill and wanted to see her and Sandra. They left immediately. I stayed behind to close up the house if it proved to be anything serious. We were concerned naturally, but Elinor's mother was a bit of a hypochondriac."

"Let me guess. Monica sent the telegram. It has her touch."

"I was asleep that night," Curtis continued woodenly. "I awoke to find her in bed with me, nude. Maybe you could have resisted her. I couldn't."

"So Monica did seduce you," Gabe mused.

Curtis was startled and chagrined at the implication. "I didn't mean to give you that impression. I accept full responsibility for our affair. I was a mature man. It was up to me to see that nothing developed between us, no matter how attracted I was to her. She was too immature to deal with her emotions."

But she wasn't, Allison thought, appalled at the cold-blooded purpose of that seventeen-year-old girl. Monica wasn't in love with Curtis. She'd merely wanted him, like she wanted a new car or a fur coat. The torment of guilt she left him with meant nothing to her. It was an emotion she'd never experienced personally.

"Monica was like a narcotic after that." Curtis sounded tired. "I knew what we were doing was bad for everybody. When I was away from her, I'd vow not to see her again. But every time she called I went running. And then it was over. Just like that. I didn't even know what had happened until she called me from Philadelphia in a rage."

"She didn't tell you she was pregnant?"

"Only over the phone."

"How did her father find out? Her condition couldn't have been apparent yet."

"She went to a clinic for a pregnancy test and they mailed the report to him. If you remember Peter, you can imagine his reaction. They must have had a terrible row. Monica wanted to have an abortion, but he wouldn't hear of it. He moved her in with his sister, whom Monica couldn't stand. I never met the woman, but if she was anything like Peter, the poor kid had a hard time of it."

"I don't imagine it was a picnic for Aunt Jane, either," Gabe remarked ironically.

"I couldn't marry Monica. It wouldn't have been in anybody's best interest. But I did offer to support the child. Both Peter and Monica refused. Neither of them wanted to have anything to do with it."

Allison had experienced rejection before, but never anything this crushing. She was aware of Gabe's compassionate gaze, but she couldn't look at him.

"Monica told me she was putting the child up for adoption. Telling Sandra about it wasn't enough for her. Monica's final revenge was refusing to tell me who the adoptive parents were." Curtis sighed. "I never got to know my daughter."

Gabe waited for Allison to make the revelation, but she was reluctant. The poor man had been through enough. All she had ever wanted was to know the truth, and now she did.

"Maybe it's just as well," she said quietly. "Sandra would have been furious if you'd had any contact with the child, no matter how discreet."

"My daughter is a very unhappy woman. For a long time I thought it was my fault, but I'm not sure I'm solely to blame. If she concentrated on making her own life more satisfying she wouldn't be so fixated on my one mistake, horrendous as it was."

"That's true," Gabe said. "You can't keep on punishing yourself for something you can't change. If Sandra persists in carrying on a vendetta, then she's the loser."

"She won't ever accept the situation," Allison said. "Sandra really hates me."

Curtis stared at her in surprise. "Why should she hate you?"

"Take a good look at Allison," Gabe said. "Who does she remind you of?"

As comprehension dawned, Curtis said, "You think *she's* Monica's daughter?"

"There isn't much doubt. Allison was born in Philadelphia at the same hospital on the same date that Monica had her baby. I'd say that's pretty conclusive, wouldn't you? She even looks like her."

"There's a superficial resemblance, but Allison isn't Monica's child. I know that for a fact."

Allison's first reaction was a sudden surge of relief. It was illogical after her insistence on knowing, but even anonymity was better than a mother like Monica.

"How can you be so sure?" Gabe asked. "You just said that Monica wouldn't tell you who the adoptive parents were."

"That's correct. I accepted the situation because I was in no position to argue about it, but I couldn't get the child out of my mind. Was it in a good home? Was it being cared for properly?

I've heard there's a waiting list of people wanting to adopt infants, but some of those couples might not be suitable. What if our baby was being neglected or abused? The worry wouldn't go away, so after a few years I hired a firm of private detectives to find her for me. It took a while, but they finally located her. She was adopted by a fine family who were able to give her everything. They named her Diane.''

"You're positive about this? You have absolute proof?" Allison had to be sure.

"There wasn't a shed of doubt," Curtis said.

"Did you tell her who you were?" Gabe asked.

"No, I didn't want to intrude on her life. I didn't have that right."

"You must have been curious, though. Did you ever see her?"

"Several times while she was growing up, although I never spoke to her. I had the same detective keep track of her and tell me what was going on in her life. She was very beautiful, the image of her mother." Curtis's eyes were sad.

"Was?" Gabe asked, sensing the story had an even unhappier ending.

"Unfortunately Diane inherited Monica's wild streak. At fifteen she was expelled from private school for drinking. The same year she was almost jailed for malicious mischief."

"History repeats itself," Gabe murmured.

"At sixteen she was killed drag racing with her boyfriend at ninety miles an hour."

After a shocked silence, Allison whispered, "I'm so sorry."

"I am, too—for everything," Curtis said heavily.

Gabe and Allison were both silent as they walked out of the tennis club. The story of lies and betrayal they'd just heard was sobering.

When they were in the car, Gabe looked at her with concern. "Are you all right?"

"I honestly don't know how I feel. I was so convinced that Monica was my mother. Finding out she wasn't, kind of leaves me in limbo."

"I know it's a disappointment, honey."

"That's the strange part. I'm sorry for everybody but myself.

I raised Mary Louise's hopes, almost drove Sandra over the edge and reopened old wounds for Curtis."

"It was an honest mistake. Mary Louise convinced herself because she wanted to, but you really believed you were Monica's daughter."

"You never did, though. Not truly. Why not?"

"Because you're such a thoroughly normal, warmhearted person," Gabe answered simply. "You couldn't have inherited any of Monica's genes."

Allison shivered slightly. "She destroyed everyone she touched."

"Thank your lucky stars she's out of your life—*our* lives. Let's talk about us. How soon can we get married?"

"I don't know, we'll have to talk about it," she answered vaguely.

"That's what I just said."

"I meant some other time. I can't even think straight at the moment."

"You're waffling and I'm not going to let you get away with it," Gabe said firmly.

"I just have a lot on my mind," Allison answered defensively. "It's unfeeling to think about ourselves when Mary Louise is due for such a disappointment. What am I going to say? I can't tell her all of the story. She's suffered enough because of Monica—Curtis, too. But she won't believe me unless I tell her how I know I'm not her granddaughter."

"You'll just have to clean it up, leave out the details about Monica climbing into Curtis's bed, things like that. She has to know about their affair, though."

"I suppose there isn't any other way."

Allison was relieved that Gabe had dropped the subject of marriage. After all, nothing had changed. She didn't want to argue about it right now, though. Her emotions were in too fragile a state.

Allison didn't realize they weren't going back to Rosewood Manor until Gabe drove through the gates of his uncle's house. He wasn't giving up on the argument. He'd just postponed it until the conditions were more favorable—for him. When they were alone and he held her close and searched out every hidden pleasure spot in her body, she would promise him anything.

"We don't have time for this, Gabe," she said quickly. "I can't put off telling Mary Louise."

He stopped the car in front of the house. "Relax, Angel, I didn't bring you here to make love." He was grinning as he opened the door and led her inside. "Did you ever think you'd hear me say that?"

She smiled in spite of her troubled state of mind. "I never had to be talked into anything."

He put his arms around her. "Of course, I could be persuaded."

When his mouth covered hers, Allison put up no resistance. Her love for Gabe was the one constant in her chaotic world. She clung to him almost desperately.

A man's voice startled them. "I presume this is Miss Riley?"

"Dad!" Gabe exclaimed. "What are *you* doing here?"

"Your mother and I decided to take a few days vacation."

"Mother is here, too? That's great!"

An older woman joined them in the entryway. She was attractive and poised, the product of an expensive finishing school and an exclusive college. The kind of person who would automatically expect her son to select a wife from the same rarefied atmosphere. Allison's heart sank.

Gabe went over to kiss his mother's cheek. "I'm so glad you're both here. I want you to meet Allison, the woman I'm going to marry."

"You promised you wouldn't tell!" Allison exclaimed.

"The agreement was, not until you met them. That's just been accomplished."

After politely acknowledging the introduction, Lily Rockford said, "Why don't we all go into the den and get acquainted?"

Allison sat stiffly on a couch next to Gabe, waiting for the inquisition to begin. His parents wouldn't be as crass as Bruce's had been, but that was cold comfort.

"This is quite a surprise," Lily began.

"Yes, we'd almost given up hope that Gabriel would ever get married," Burton agreed.

"*You* might have." His wife smiled. "I always knew that sooner or later some clever girl would make up his mind for him."

Allison tensed, even though she'd known this was coming.

Gabe's mother was planting the seed—ever so innocently—that Allison had tricked him into proposing.

"That wasn't the way it happened," Gabe said. "I had a devil of a time getting Allison to agree to marry me."

Lily gazed at her without expression. "You have some doubts about marrying my son?"

"Not doubts exactly," Allison answered carefully. "You might call them reservations."

"*I* call them nonsense!" Gabe said forcefully.

"You've known each other a very short time," Burton said. "Perhaps Allison is being more realistic than you."

"Time has nothing to do with it. I knew we were right for each other as soon as we met."

Burton's smile was faintly derisive. "The old love-at-first-sight defense."

"I'm serious, Dad! Maybe you've forgotten what it's like to love somebody so completely that you can't imagine a life without her. When you find someone like that, you know in an instant."

Burton's gaze went to his wife. "I haven't forgotten," he said softly. "After all these years, I still can't imagine being without your mother."

"That's very moving, my dear." Lily's eyes held his, full of shared affection.

"All right, now you know how I feel about Allison," Gabe said.

"We haven't heard from her," Burton commented. "Do you love Gabriel?"

"Very much," she replied in a small voice.

"Then I presume the matter is settled," he said.

Allison was tempted to let it go at that. But she couldn't. "Not if you object to our marriage."

"We don't have anything to say about it. You and my son have made your decision."

"Not really. There was one possible stumbling block, and I'm afraid we've run into it."

"You're imagining things," Gabe protested.

"Am I?" She gazed at him steadily. "I haven't noticed the open arms you were counting on."

"I get the impression that Lily and I are the problem," Burton said. "Why would that be?"

"Gabe values your opinion highly. The three of you have a very special relationship," Allison said wistfully. "I've never been that fortunate myself, so I know it's a blessing you don't give up lightly. I told Gabe I'd never come between him and his family."

"You must not love him very much," Lily observed.

Allison couldn't let her use that excuse. "You don't know what this is costing me! I'll never get over losing him. It's *because* I love him so much that I'm giving him up."

"Then all I can say is, you're a very foolish girl," Lily said calmly. "My opinion shouldn't matter, nor Burton's or anybody else's. The only important thing is whether you two believe you can be happy together."

"How can we be if I've alienated him from the people he cares deeply about? Gabe doesn't think it would affect his feelings, but I know he'd grow to resent me."

"For one thing, what makes you think Burton and I object to your marriage?"

"It's pretty obvious isn't it?" Allison's eyes were bleak. "I understand how you feel. You hoped he'd marry somebody more suitable. Your husband must have told you I grew up in an orphanage."

"Yes, Burton told me the story on the plane. He also said there's a possibility that you're Mary Louise's grandchild."

"I thought I might be, but I'm not. We found that out this afternoon."

Burton looked quickly at his son. "You have proof of this?"

"I got it from the horse's mouth, so to speak. I'll tell you all about it later. Right now I want to settle this thing with Allison, once and for all." Gabe turned her to face him. "I don't know if my parents approve. If they don't I'm sorry. I love them very much, but not enough to give you up—ever. I can't imagine them even asking such a thing. The only way I'll get out of your life is if you tell me you don't love me."

Allison's eyes filled with tears. "You know I can't do that."

"I think that's pretty conclusive," Lily said with satisfaction. "I'm sorry if you got the wrong impression, my dear," she told Allison. "Our concern had nothing to do with you, personally.

We were simply afraid that you were both confusing overwhelming attraction with something more lasting. You've more than convinced us that's not the case. Don't you agree, Burton?''

"Wholeheartedly," he answered with a warm smile. "Welcome to the family, Allison."

She found it hard to believe. "You don't mind that I don't know who my parents were?"

"Whoever they were, I'm sure they were a gorgeous couple," Lily answered. "You're very lovely. You and Gabriel should have beautiful children."

Gabe chuckled. "Aren't you being a little premature, Mother?"

"It never hurts to plant the idea," she answered complacently.

"Unfortunately I can't act on it." His eyes sparkled with deviltry. "You and Dad have seriously cramped my style. This was the only place Allison and I could be alone."

"Gabe!" Allison's cheeks felt fiery. "We came here a few times because I wanted to see where he spent the summers when he was growing up," she explained self-consciously. "It's a beautiful home."

"We enjoyed it, although it's nothing like that palace Mary Louise lives in. Rosewood Manor is magnificent, but I must admit I don't envy her the upkeep."

Allison was reminded of the unhappy task ahead of her. "We really have to go talk to her," she told Gabe. "I'm dreading the prospect, though. She was so sure I was Monica's daughter. It's going to be quite a blow to find out it was wishful thinking after all."

"Will it help if we come along?" Lily asked.

"You might be able to lend some support," Gabe said.

"I'll phone and tell her we're on our way."

"I'll look forward to seeing you, Lily. And Burton, too, of course," Mary Louise added, concluding her conversation. She turned with a happy smile as Sergei entered the den. The smile faded when she noticed the suitcase he was carrying. "Are you going somewhere?"

"I told you I had to go back to work."

"I didn't think you meant immediately."

"It won't get any easier." He smiled, as if it were a joke.

"Couldn't you at least stay for the weekend? Gabriel's parents are in town. They'll be over shortly."

"I can spare a few minutes to say hello, but that's all. My plane leaves in an hour."

"We both know you don't have to go," she said quietly. "Why are you really leaving, Sergei?"

"It isn't like you to provoke a confrontation." His voice was gently teasing.

"Maybe that's been my trouble. I'm always so ladylike that I never say what's actually on my mind. And I never force anyone else to speak frankly, either. Just once I'd like to break all the rules of etiquette and be incredibly direct."

"I doubt if you could do it." He smiled. "You can't change the habits of a lifetime."

"I didn't think so, either, but I've suddenly realized that time is running out."

"I suppose it had to eventually," he said heavily.

She gazed at him impassively. "Are you in love with me, Sergei?"

For a moment he was too surprised to speak. "That's really laying it on the line," he said finally.

"You haven't answered my question."

"What difference does it make? It doesn't change anything." He thrust his hands into his pockets and paced the floor. "We have no future together."

"Why not? When two people love each other, it usually makes a difference in their lives."

"Are you saying—" He broke off to stare at her, afraid of misinterpreting her meaning.

"If you need it spelled out for you, I love you very much."

Sergei's eyes lit with dawning joy. "Mary Louise, my dearest, I don't know what to say."

"Perhaps I can help you." She smiled mischievously. "Sergei, my love, will you please stop screwing up and ask me to marry you?"

Mary Louise and the Rockfords were friends of long- standing. They all greeted each other fondly. For a short while the conversation was about mutual acquaintances and reminiscences of the last time they'd seen each other. Allison sat silently, reluctant to spoil their happy reunion.

Gabe knew how hard it was for her, so finally he squeezed her hand and said, "Mary Louise, we have something to tell you."

"You're getting married!" she exclaimed happily. "I *told* Sergei that things always work out when you're in love. Aren't you thrilled, Lily?"

"Well, yes, of course."

Mary Louise misunderstood her friend's suddenly sober expression. "If you're concerned over their whirlwind affair, don't be. Allison is a darling girl. You'll find that out when you get to know her."

"That's no problem," Gabe said. "What I want to—"

"I'd love to hold the wedding here. We can have the reception in the garden, and you can wear my wedding gown," Mary Louise told Allison excitedly. "If you want to, that is. Monica wasn't interested in tradition, but I've saved it all these years, just in case." Her voice had a wistful note.

Allison was close to tears. "I wish things had worked out that way. It would have been a dream come true."

"Allison is trying to tell you that she isn't your granddaughter," Gabe said gently. He related a highly edited version of Monica's affair with Curtis.

Mary Louise was surprised and troubled by the story. The haunting sadness in her face at its tragic conclusion broke Allison's heart.

She put her arms around the older woman. "I'm so sorry. If I'd never come here you'd have been spared all this pain. Can you ever forgive me?"

"There's nothing to forgive. You've given me more happiness in two weeks than Monica gave me in a lifetime," Mary Louise said quietly. "When I dreamed of having a granddaughter, she was someone exactly like you."

"It can still happen. Maybe someday Martin and Laura will have a child, and you'll get your wish."

"That would be nice. I hope they do, but I've already gotten my wish. I have a grandchild to love and cherish. Our relationship is based on mutual caring and respect. That's a lot more important than heredity. In every way that counts, you are my family.''

All the women were misty-eyed, and the men had lumps in their throats.

''Well, now that that's settled, how about telling them *our* news,'' Sergei suggested.

''Sergei has asked me to marry him—after I insisted on it.'' Mary Louise laughed like a young girl.

''You didn't!'' Gabe exclaimed. ''I wouldn't have believed it.''

''Not only that, I used your exact words,'' she said proudly.

Congratulations were exchanged all around, and the subject of weddings was discussed. Mary Louise was as excited about the young couple's as she was about her own.

After a while, Gabe said, ''Allison and I have something to talk about. We're going out for a little walk.''

''Why don't you go over to Uncle Herbert's? We'll be visiting here for an hour or so,'' Burton said casually.

Gabe grinned. ''It really pays to have an understanding father.''

Allison felt a twinge of apprehension. Gabe's expression had been serious when he said they had to talk. What new problem had arisen? Whatever it was, he wouldn't discuss it until they reached his uncle's house. By then, his refusal had set off all kinds of alarms in Allison's head.

Gabe led the way into the den. ''Can I fix you a drink?''

She stood in the middle of the room, regarding him warily. ''Am I going to need one?''

He gave her a puzzled look. ''I don't understand.''

''When everyone was discussing our wedding, you didn't join in. Are you feeling pressured now that it's official? Do you want to wait a few months until we get to know each other better? You can be honest with me.''

''I always have been.'' He came over to take her into his arms. ''How can you possibly doubt my commitment? If it were possible, I'd like to get married tonight. That's the only kind of pressure I feel.''

Allison flung her arms around his neck. ''Oh, Gabe darling, I love you so!''

His kiss was deeply reassuring. They clung to each other murmuring words of endearment. In the beginning it was an innocent affirmation of their love, but the sexual attraction that was always present between them became insistent.

Gabe's caresses grew more sensual, his need more evident. Allison moved against him in mounting anticipation. When he whispered something in her ear she smiled seductively and tugged his shirt out of his slacks.

They walked up the stairs slowly, undressing each other as they went. By the time they reached Gabe's room, they were both completely nude.

As they stood by the bed he cupped her breasts in his palms and kissed each rosy peak. "My beautiful bride," he said in a husky voice. "What did I ever do to deserve you?"

"I'm the lucky one." She traced the lean triangle of his torso down to his taut stomach.

When she continued on, he tensed and drew in his breath sharply. "Not yet, sweetheart. I want to make this special for you."

"You always do." She clasped him around the waist and carried him with her as she fell backward on the bed.

Gabe was powerless to resist when her legs circled his hips invitingly. He plunged deeply, joining their bodies. They were welded into one person, sharing the molten excitement that zigzagged from one to the other.

Allison welcomed his driving masculinity. She arched her body to return his thrusts as the throbbing ecstasy mounted to unbelievable heights. They reached the pinnacle together in a fiery burst of sensation that reverberated like thunder inside of them. The storm subsided into a satisfying glow of pleasure that left both utterly contented.

Gabe stroked her hair lovingly. "That was a lot more gratifying than what I planned."

"You expect me to believe you had something else in mind?" she teased.

"Actually I did. I wanted to have a private talk with you." He levered himself up on one elbow so he could watch her reaction. "Everything turned out pretty well today—with one exception."

"What do you mean? It's been a fairy-tale day! Your parents

are happy for us, Mary Louise and Sergei are going to get married. What more could we possibly ask?''

''You still don't know who your parents are,'' he answered quietly.

A look of surprise crossed her face. ''I didn't even think of that!''

''Does that mean it won't bother you anymore?''

''I guess I'll always wonder about them,'' she said slowly.

''That's what I was afraid of.'' Gabe suppressed a sigh. ''Okay, honey, it won't be easy, but this time we'll leave it to the professionals. I'll hire a top-notch private detective and let him take it from here. If you'll just be patient, we'll find your parents sooner or later.''

''You don't have to go to all that trouble. It doesn't matter any longer.''

He gave her a puzzled look. ''You just said you'd continue to wonder.''

''That's different from needing to know. I suppose it sounds strange after my insistence on ferreting out the truth, but these past two weeks have changed my whole outlook. I'd like to leave things as they are.''

''Because you're afraid of what you might find out? It's understandable. The possibility of having someone like Monica for a mother would scare anybody off.''

''I'm sure my real mother wasn't anything like her. I have a feeling she gave me up out of love, hoping I'd have a better life than she could provide. That's what really matters, not bringing up memories that might be painful for her. It took me a while to realize what an unselfish gift she gave me. I never would have found you, otherwise.''

''My beautiful bride.'' Gabe held her so tightly she could feel his heart beating against hers. ''Whoever your parents were, they must have been wonderful people to have produced a jewel like you.''

Allison managed a watery smile. ''The best part of all this will be having a name that really belongs to me.''

''The best part?'' Tiny flames lit his gray eyes as he raised his head to gaze at her.

"Unless you can think of something that will make me feel even better." She smiled enchantingly as she lifted her face to his.

* * * * *

HEROES
AGAINST ALL ODDS

HARLEQUIN®

Silhouette®

Please address questions and book requests to: Harlequin Reader Service U.S.: 3010 Walden Ave.,
P.O. Box 1325, Buffalo, NY 14269 CAN.: P.O. Box 609, Fort Erie, Ont. L2A 5X3

PAHGEN

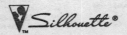

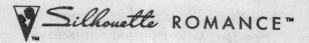

♥ *Silhouette* ROMANCE™

What's a single dad to do when he needs a wife by next Thursday?

Who's a confirmed bachelor to call when he finds a baby on his doorstep?

How does a plain Jane in love with her gorgeous boss get him to notice her?

From classic love stories to romantic comedies to emotional heart tuggers, **Silhouette Romance** offers six irresistible novels every month by some of your favorite authors!

Come experience compelling stories by beloved bestsellers **Diana Palmer, Stella Bagwell, Sandra Steffen, Susan Meier** and **Marie Ferrarella,** to name just a few—and more authors sure to become favorites as well!!

Silhouette Romance — always emotional, always enjoyable, always about love!

SRGEN99R